continued . . .

P9-CEI-776

Laird of the Wind

"A lavishly crafted love story that brilliantly combines history and romance . . . mysticism, passion, beauty, treachery, intrigue, and unforgettable characters."
—*Romantic Times*

"King spins a complex, mesmerizing story . . . lyrical, compelling, exquisitely vivid."   —*Library Journal*

"[*Laird of the Wind*] is a treasure."   —*Bell, Book & Candle*

Lady Miracle

"Masterful plotting, compelling love story—and more. . . . Extraordinary . . . mythically lovely . . . brilliant storytelling."   —*Publishers Weekly* (starred review)

"King is a master storyteller . . . mythical and exciting . . . excellent."   —*Romantic Times*

"*Lady Miracle* is the latest treasure from a writer whose star is in ascendance. . . . Marvelous and superb. . . . Truly a treat, like savoring fine Belgian chocolate, reading her work is almost sinfully delicious." —*Painted Rock Reviews*

The Raven's Moon

"A marvelous Scottish tale . . . absolutely wonderful characters, breakneck pacing, and a great setting. A real page-turner. I couldn't put it down."   —Patricia Potter

"King keeps the tension high. Nonstop outlaw raids, bone-chilling storms, bonds of kinship, feuds, spies, betrayals . . . all lead inexorably to an explosive resolution."   —*Publishers Weekly*

"A wonderfully dark and delectable read. Susan King evokes the Lowlands as few writers have—with all the passion, intrigue, mystery, and beauty of the land—and tells a unique, well-crafted romance."   —*Romantic Times*

The Angel Knight

"Magnificent . . . richly textured with passion and a touch of magic." —Mary Jo Putney

"Susan King, a visual writer extraordinaire, has blended a mystical and historical tale so precise that the reader will be drawn in and won't ever want to leave."
—*Romantic Times*

"Susan King has written a romance of tremendous beauty and heart. Her books will stand the test of time."
—*Affaire de Coeur*

The Raven's Wish

"Powerful, magical, and delightful . . . will keep readers on the edge of their seats." —*Romantic Times*

"Susan King [has] the heart of a romantic, the deft touch of a poet, and a historian's eye for detail." —Rexanne Becnel

The Black Thorne's Rose

"Magnificent." —Virginia Henley

"A glorious medieval romance from an exciting talent."
—*Romantic Times*

"Excellent . . . filled with mythical legends and deep-rooted superstitions that add mystery and mayhem to an extremely powerful story." —*Rendezvous*

"Fantastic. . . . A medieval tapestry that will enchant the reader." —*Affaire de Coeur*

ALSO BY SUSAN KING

The Swan Maiden

The Stone Maiden

The Heather Moon

Laird of the Wind

Lady Miracle

The Raven's Moon

The Angel Knight

The Raven's Wish

The Black Thorne's Rose

"The Snow Rose" in *A Stockingful of Joy*

The
Sword Maiden

Susan King

A SIGNET BOOK

SIGNET
Published by New American Library, a division of
Penguin Putnam Inc., 375 Hudson Street,
New York, New York 10014, U.S.A.
Penguin Books Ltd, 27 Wrights Lane,
London W8 5TZ, England
Penguin Books Australia Ltd,
Ringwood, Victoria, Australia
Penguin Books Canada Ltd, 10 Alcorn Avenue,
Toronto, Ontario, Canada M4V 3B2
Penguin Books (N.Z.) Ltd, 182–190 Wairau Road,
Auckland 10, New Zealand

Penguin Books Ltd, Registered Offices:
Harmondsworth, Middlesex, England

First published by Signet, an imprint of New American Library,
a division of Penguin Putnam Inc.

First Printing, October 2001
10 9 8 7 6 5 4 3 2 1

PUBLISHER'S NOTE
This is a work of fiction. Names, characters, places, and incidents either are the
product of the author's imagination or are used fictitiously, and any resemblance to
actual persons, living or dead, business establishments, events, or locales is entirely
coincidental.

For Jeremy, the warrior

Acknowledgments

I wish to thank Rob Miller, a bladesmith on the Isle of Skye, for insights and information regarding medieval and specifically Scottish smithing; the Mid-Atlantic Association for Historical Swordsmanship for information, advice, drills, and for letting me whack away with a wooden sword myself; and Howard and Amy Waddell of Albion Armorers for sharing their knowledge of swords and showing me some beautiful examples of medieval weaponry.

And special thanks to Coleman and Laurienzo Builders, Inc., for the inspirational sound of hammering while I wrote my smithing story.

With every book, some more than others, I am indebted to several wonderful writers and friends for inspiration, support, and much patience with the process. Someday I hope to return their kindness. For now, I can only say thank you from my heart.

I'll grow into your arms two
   Like iron in strong fire;
But hold me fast, let me not go
   I am your heart's desire.
                    —*Tam Lin*

Prologue

"Eisg, o eisg!" ("Listen, oh listen!")
—War cry of the MacArthurs

Argyll, Scotland
Summer, 1418

"Be still and silent, and you will hear a tale of long ago, in the time of the mists, when a prince lived beside our great loch," Alpin the ferryman said. He leaned forward and directed his rich, rumbling voice to the children gathered at his feet inside his cozy stone house.

Eva MacArthur sat fidgeting beside her cousin Margaret, who never fidgeted, and looked up at the ferryman. He was solidly muscled, with a face craggy and kind all at once. Alpin MacDewar, her mother's old cousin, was not a story-teller by trade, but the children—Eva and her brothers, their cousins and friends—sometimes coaxed him to tell tales on rainy afternoons.

Alpin had been a fierce warrior long ago, and Eva wanted to hear a tale of those adventures. She had heard the story of Innisfarna, her island, countless times, and she was not in the mood to hear it again. The legend reminded her painfully of her beloved mother, who had bequeathed the isle and its castle to Eva with her death but a year past.

"This prince was the youngest of the king's sons, a fine warrior skilled in arms, but desirous of peace," Alpin continued.

Eva sighed and rested her chin on her upraised knees.

The story of the prince, the faery, and the sword it was, then; she would be rude to protest, so she closed her eyes to listen to the deep thunder of the ferryman's voice.

"His people had long warred with the dark faeries who lived in the hills and the water, those creatures of power, magic, and beauty who were as tall as and stronger than most humans. The prince wanted an end to the troubles. Peace and plenty would never come to the people, it was said, until a bargain was struck with the faeries. But no one seemed to know what sort of bargain could be made.

"So the prince set out to seek an answer to the troubles. He was strong and handsome, and courteous to everyone he met, but when he asked how to end the warring, they only shrugged, one after another."

Eva opened her eyes and gazed around the circle, past Margaret's cool blond perfection, past Eva's brothers' brown and glossy heads—Simon with a twig still in his hair from a morning wrestle, Donal more dignified as the MacArthur chief's heir, until he stuck out his tongue when he saw his sister.

She ignored him and gazed at the boy beside him. Lachlann MacKerron, the blacksmith's foster son—adopted as an infant when his own parents had died somehow—was older than her brothers. He was lanky and black-haired, his muscles as taut as a man's from working in the smithy, though his voice had scarcely deepened and his cheeks were not yet bearded.

Whenever she heard the tale of her isle, Eva imagined Lachlann as the prince. She knew that a smith's lad was no king's son, but Lachlann was handsome, kind, quiet, and strong. Eva could not imagine her brothers as princes, or any of her male cousins, who were scruffy and annoying.

Simon poked Eva to remind her to listen, for she had leaned over to look at the smith's son. Lachlann flashed a stern blue glance at her, a reprimand more effective than her brother's jab. She subsided and looked intently at Alpin.

"One day the prince encountered an old woman at a well, and carried heavy buckets of water home for her. In return for his kindness, she answered his question.

" 'Ah, you must seek the princess of Bright Island, Aeife the Radiant One, the fiercest woman warrior of the warlike dark faeries,' the old woman told him. 'You must steal the three secrets of her power: her silver bowl, the golden ring upon her finger, and *Claidheamh Soluis,* the Sword of Light. That blade is the key to end the troubles. If you hold it, she will ask you for a bargain.'

" 'How do I find Aeife the Radiant One?' asked the prince.

" 'Follow the hawk for a day. When you come to a river, follow the salmon for two days, and when you come to a mountain, climb it for three days. Then look east, west, north, and south, and you will see Bright Island.'

" 'That sounds simple enough,' said the prince, although he was not so certain.

" 'The Radiant One sleeps in the daytime, and only then can you steal from her the sword, the bowl, and the ring. If you wake her,' the old woman warned, 'you must do battle with her. She will defeat you, and then all will be worse for your people.'

"The prince thanked the woman and went on his way. He followed the hawk and swam with the salmon and climbed the mountain. In the loch below, an island appeared that had not been there before.

"He rowed over the water and set foot on the isle in a mist so thick he wondered why the place was called Bright Island. Then he saw a light glowing like a thousand candles, and he went toward it."

Eva shifted again, unable to sit long without doing something. She had a bold and fiery nature, lacking Margaret's calmness. Eva's father, the chief of the MacArthurs, said that someday he must find a strong man, a laird or a chief's son, to wed his only daughter and benefit their clan. But until she was a woman grown, her boldness, and her father's distraction with his grief after her mother's death, gave her the freedom to run with the boys in their games, as she preferred.

She itched for that now, and she never liked hearing the end of the story. Scuttling backward on hands and knees, she neared the door. Alpin glanced at her, and she sat to listen again.

"The prince entered an empty, silent castle and followed the strange light," Alpin continued. "He went from room to room—hundreds of them—seeking the sleeping princess. He knew he must find her before she woke to do battle with him. He opened the last door, and saw her asleep on a bed draped in gossamer.

"The Sword of Light lay upon her long, slim body, clasped in her hands. The golden ring circled one of her fingers, and the silver bowl sat upon a table. The sword gave off such a bright light that the room was as clear as a sunlit meadow, but the princess slept deeply.

"He approached and took the silver bowl from the table, slipping it into his pocket. Then he slid the golden ring free and put it upon his smallest finger. He touched the Sword of Light and stopped—for he had gazed upon Aeife's face.

"She was the most beautiful girl he had ever seen, with hair like shining black silk and skin like cream. His heart stirred in his breast like a wild thing. He knew that if she woke, he could never lift his own sword against this girl.

"Her eyelids fluttered, revealing eyes like silver clouds, and her hands stirred. The prince remembered that if she woke, she would best him in battle. He could not believe that such a slender, lovely creature could defeat him. And he had lost his heart to her already, gone down and down like a stone in a loch.

"Quickly, he bent down and kissed her full on the mouth, a taste like honey and berries. That kiss was the first the prince ever gave, and the first the princess ever took, and it contained the purest magic of the truest love. Aeife returned the kiss, and the prince was lost further, and he stayed with her until morning came again."

Eva closed her eyes as Alpin described that kiss. She was glad she sat near the door, where her brothers and cousins could not see that the love between Aeife and her prince had melted Eva's heart, as it did each time. She looked at Lachlann the blacksmith's lad once more, and wondered if someday he would kiss a girl—perhaps even Eva herself—with such tenderness.

He glanced at her, that keen blue flash again. She scowled.

"The kissing woke Aeife the Radiant One, of course," Alpin said. Eva's brothers snickered. "The Sword of Light lay between her and a handsome young man. He had stolen from her the silver bowl that filled with porridge whenever it was tapped, and a golden ring through which one could see the future. But he had not yet taken *Claidheamh Soluis,* the Sword of Light. Now she must do battle with him, for her people, the warring dark faeries, would expect it of her.

"But she looked upon his sleeping face and remembered his gentleness. And her heart, which had been enchanted and filled with thoughts of war against the humans, stirred within her like a butterfly set free. She rose from the bed and took up the sword, and unwillingly lifted it above her head, knowing what she must do.

"The prince stood to face her. 'I will not do battle with you,' he said. 'Give me the Sword of Light to end this feud.' He placed his hand upon the blade as she held the hilt.

" 'Let go of the Sword of Light so I may protect my people's rights,' Aeife said. They faced one another, human and faery, lovers new made from enemies of old, until the moon sank and the sun rose three times.

"At last they both grew weary, and their knees began to fail, and they caught each other as the other one fell. The Sword of Light was pressed between them. Then the prince took up the sword and flung it from the castle window into the water of the loch below, where it went down and down like a lantern.

"Both of them knew that a blade tossed into a body of water marked a truce between warring clans, and both of them pledged their hearts to peace, then and now. 'Forever,' Aeife said, 'the Sword of Light will guard the border between the earthly and the faery realms, for beneath this island lies the threshold. But you must fulfill a bargain. You must stay with me always on this isle.'

"The prince agreed, and took Aeife the Radiant One into his arms and kissed her. Together they shared the bowl that gave food, and the ring that showed the future, and they lived in joy on Bright Island.

"And when enemies—humans who craved the power Aeife held as her own—came to take the isle from Aeife's keeping, she faced them valiantly with a shining sword of faery make, with her husband at her side. The island and its treasure were protected.

"The Sword of Light still lies at the bottom of the loch, sheathed by the water," Alpin continued.

Eva reached up to open the latch. She did not want to hear what came next.

"Peace and plenty reigned between the humans and the faeries. In time, the daughter of Aeife and her prince took up the safekeeping of the isle. And every first daughter descended from Aeife guards the isle and the special sword in the waters of the loch. Enemies should always beware the power of this place, for they cannot triumph here."

Alpin looked toward Eva. "Our own Eva guards it now

that her mother, bless her soul, has passed it on to her. If ever there is war or strife on the isle, Aeife's descended daughter must take up a sword in her own hand and use it to defend her home and her people."

Eva cracked open the door and bolted.

Chapter 1

Argyll, Scotland
Spring, 1428

Wild as blackberries she was, sweet and dark and un-
ruly, and she would never be his. Lachlann MacKerron knew it, had always known it. Yet he paused in his work
and leaned in the doorway of the smithy to watch her. He allowed himself that much.

Eva MacArthur, daughter of the clan chief, stood in the
yard talking quietly with Lachlann's foster mother, holding
a basket of cheese and oatcakes as an offering of comfort for
the new widow. Ever since his foster father's death, many
neighbors had made kind gestures, but only Eva had come
to visit every week.

Inside the smithy, a piece of steel heated in the forge, but
it could be left for a few moments. Lachlann lingered in the
doorway. Sunshine gave Eva's dark hair a warm sheen, and
he knew without looking that her eyes were the gray-green
of a stormy sky. He tipped his head to admire the lean line
of her body; she was not tall, though made with grace and
strength.

She had outrun him often in childhood, when they had
played together in the hills with her brothers and MacArthur
cousins. He did not doubt she could outrun him still, had she
wanted. In the past few years womanhood had tempered her

natural penchant for boldness, and he liked that softening well upon her. She would make a fine wife for a man—but she was not for him.

The only daughter of a chief would never be matched with a smith's foster son, even if the young smith's true birth name and birthright were grander by far than anyone suspected. The secrets that Lachlann had learned as his foster father lay dying had changed him forever. His past, his identity, his future had altered in the past weeks. Lately he had struggled to accept the burden of his knowledge.

Shaking his head, he stirred himself from his thoughts to watch Eva as she spoke with his foster mother. Changes would come into Eva's life, too. He had heard that her father, the chief of the MacArthurs, wanted to betroth his daughter soon and would consider only men of influence and power, such as chieftains and the sons of clan chiefs.

News and gossip spread quickly at the smithy, and Lachlann did not usually listen to it—but he gave discreet attention to the discussion of Eva's marriage. His customers said her father most preferred her to wed a Campbell, especially one who was an advisor to the king himself, though a man far older than Eva. Lachlann knew that he should be happy for her, but he was not. He had reason to dislike that particular Campbell.

Eva turned and smiled at him then, and it seemed as if a sunbeam came through a cloud. Grief and anguish had tormented him for weeks, but he felt himself brighten in the bask of that smile. Returning a brisk, somber nod, he wiped his hands on the leather apron that covered his belted plaid.

He was aware that he filled the space of the doorway awkwardly, too tall, too broad in the shoulders, his head bowed beneath the lintel. Suddenly he felt large and clumsy and crudely made, with her clear-eyed gaze upon him. His dark hair sifted over his eyes, and he shoved it back, his long fingers grimed with ash and the handling of iron.

Eva embraced his foster mother and took her leave, and Lachlann turned away. He entered the dark haven of the smithy, where the fire glowed red and much work awaited him.

Soon he would leave Balnagovan and Loch Fhionn in Argyll. When his path and Eva's crossed again, years from now, she would not come to love him as he loved her. Surely, he thought, she would despise him for what he must do.

But he could not turn away from the obligation of vengeance that rested with him now—even if the man he now regarded as his enemy, a man he had heard little about until recently, was to become Eva's Campbell husband.

Lachlann turned toward the forge, and soon Eva peered inside the smithy door. A sunlit rectangle spilled through the doorway, and her shadow touched his feet. He stepped back.

"God's greeting to you, Lachlann MacKerron." Her voice was as mellow as honey.

"And to you, Eva MacArthur." His words thrummed inside the dim, stone-walled smithy. "I thank you for visiting my foster mother so often. She values your kindness."

Eva smiled ruefully. "We all care about her, and miss your foster father. Finlay MacKerron was a good man. My father laments losing an armorer of his merit, but he says that you will be as good, if not better, one day. He admires the blades you have made for him."

"Give him my thanks." The late sun made a fiery halo around her head; the glow suited her, he thought.

"I hear you will be leaving Scotland soon. My MacArthur cousins say that you will go with them to join the king's army, perhaps even sail to France to fight the English there."

He nodded. "Scotsmen can earn land grants and knighthoods by doing so."

"But they must endure a brutal war, one that is not their own, to earn such honors."

"It is the price some must pay to earn privilege. And I owe three years' military service, since we rent Balnagovan from Innisfarna. From you," he added softly.

She nodded. "Can you fulfill the service another way? I thought you might stay now that your foster mother is widowed."

"I do not have much choice in how I fulfill the knight service. That is determined by the crown. Muime's sister will come here to stay for a while, and may bring her daughter and grandchildren. I am not needed among so many."

"Will you be gone long?"

He shrugged. "Who can say? Your father can use the smith in Glen Brae, across the loch, for whatever tasks are needed."

"Until you return." She stepped inside the smithy and walked toward him, her shadow long upon the floor. Lachlann stepped back a little.

"I might come back," he said cautiously.

"You will." Nearing the forge, she paused beside him and looked up. Golden light flowed over the gentle contours of her face, enhancing the creamy flush in her cheek, the dusky sparkle in her eyes. Her smile was teasing, winsome. He watched her silently, filled with a sudden, hot hunger.

"How could you stay away from this lovely glen, with its loch and its legends?" she asked.

He frowned, aware that when he returned, his grim mission would destroy her life, if she had wed Colin Campbell by then. Hoping she would not sense that intent in him, he glanced away.

"How indeed?" He picked up a leather gauntlet, drawing it slowly over his hand. "I have work to do now. Tell your father that I will finish the pieces that Finlay left undone at his death, weapons and armor that your father commissioned from our smithy. They will be done by Beltane, a few days before I leave, and I will bring them over to Innisfarna.

If he would pay what is owed for the work to my foster mother, I would appreciate it."

"I will tell him. But you will need to labor as hard as two men to finish the pieces alone in so short a time."

"I do not mind." He found deep satisfaction in the solitary nature of his craft, and could work for endless hours unaided but for specific tasks.

"Are those the weapons?" she asked, looking past him toward the pile of steel that glittered in the low light.

"Some of them," he answered. He stepped toward her and reached above her head to grasp the horn handle of the great bellows, its huge leather casing braced behind the stone structure of the forge. Pausing, his arm lifted, he looked down at her. He could not pull the handle without asking her to move, yet he did not want her to leave.

"Well, then." She glanced up his long, bare, muscled arm to his poised hand. "I suppose I must go."

"Congratulations to you," he said stiffly. "I hear you will be married soon."

She shrugged, her cheeks coloring a delicate rose gold in the forge light. "So my father insists. He says he has allowed me much freedom, but now he will make the decision in the matter of my marriage. It is for the good of Clan Arthur."

He lifted a brow. "And how does that sit with you, my friend? You like your independence well and never let others tell you what to do." He smiled a little, with faint humor.

"I . . . understand my duties as the daughter of the chief of the MacArthurs." The blush deepened. "I love my father and my kinsmen. And our clan faces trying times now, with the king not so pleased with the Highland chiefs. If my marriage will bring my clan favor . . . I must do what I can to help."

"Ah," he said noncommittally, still gripping the bellows handle just above and beside her head.

"I am keeping you from your work. Farewell, Lachlann.

I hope to see you again before you leave. If not. . ." Her gaze was steady upon his. "Then I wish you blessings on your journey."

"Blessings," he murmured in return, "Eva."

She watched him, seemed to melt toward him slightly. In her uplifted gaze, he saw trust, and beautiful, clear sincerity. The air between them pulsed and swirled with the invisible heat of the forge. He felt himself incline toward her, as if drawn to her, as if he could not stop the progress.

Never again would he stand alone with her like this, he thought. Never again would there be this peace and accord between them. He knew he must stop loving her, but it still existed, untapped and deep, within him.

Just once, he wanted to savor its purity.

He leaned down, blood surging, his grip tight on the bellows handle, and touched his lips to hers.

Her mouth was pliant, warm, and as soft as he had known it would be. He sighed, and she did too, leaning into him and resting her hand upon his chest.

The kiss scarcely ended before it was somehow renewed, tentative but exquisite. What spun through him had force enough to buckle his knees. He stood strong despite it, stood still, hand lifted, heart thundering. Honeyed fire, brilliant and sweet, poured through him. With his free hand, he took her by the waist and drew her closer to kiss her again. She uttered a quiet little cry, joyful and astonished.

Water to flame, that sound. She trusted him, and one day he might destroy her life. This instant of joy would become a bitter memory for both of them. He released her.

"Farewell, Eva my friend," he murmured, "now and in your future." He knew he should apologize, but he could not regret such a simple, stirring kiss. It would never happen again, and he was sure they both knew it. Her eyes sparkled, her breath was quick, her mouth curved; he knew she did not mind the kiss.

"Was that . . . a token of friendship?" she asked.

"If you like," he murmured. He smiled at her with deliberate casualness. If he had dared to reveal what he truly felt, his whole soul would be laid open to her. He was not prepared for that, now or ever. "Thank you for a sweet token."

She nodded, gulped, and her glance followed his raised arm. "You must finish your work." She stepped back.

He pulled the handle down at last, and a long, low sigh of air fed into the fire in the forge bed. The flames grew, flickering like hot gold. When Lachlann looked up, Eva stood in the doorway. Using the tongs, he lifted the length of steel from the fiery bed of charcoal. The metal glowed pale yellow.

She lingered, then left. He did not glance up, but knew she was gone. Felt it, somehow. As he turned his attention to the work, his hands, always steady and strong, trembled a bit.

Hot new steel gleamed as he tipped the raw blade into the fire and watched yellow flow into a deep brown. The dirk would be strong and true when it was done, as fine as any weapon made in this smithy when his foster father was alive.

Once again he would work late into the night, he thought. The subtle, beautiful color changes that told the state of the metal were brightest in the darkness, and he still had much to do now that he worked alone. He had become a master smith while still a lanky youth; he could handle the commissions easily. But he missed Finlay's wry wit, generous guidance, and companionship, both in the smithy and at home.

He glanced at the pile of weapons in the corner, work already paid for in part; some of those pieces showed Finlay's skilled hand, and the sight tugged at him. Weaponsmithing had provided strong medicine for grief in the last weeks. Heating iron into steel, hammering it, shaping and cooling it, Lachlann could forget, for a while, all but the work itself.

Now he had something else to forget, for his heated blood still pounded. Yet he knew that he would never give up the tender memory of kissing Eva.

Once, when life had been peaceful and the future a reliable thing, he had planned to craft fine swords in his own forge one day—he even dared to dream of a fine wife, a chief's daughter. But Finlay had grown ill unexpectedly, and told Lachlann more than a peaceful man needed to know about revenge.

He had also learned, in Finlay's failing words, the most carefully guarded secret of the MacKerrons, passed from one generation to another: the method of forging a faery blade.

The shock of that day still resounded in him. Like a bloom of iron newly fetched from the fire, he had been heated and reshaped.

As he held the length of steel in the fiery charcoal, he watched brown burst into purple. That clue told him the fire had peaked. He pulled out the blade and plunged it into a trough of warm brine. The metal sizzled and the salty quench bubbled as the brittle steel was tempered. He felt a little in need of tempering himself.

He frowned as he worked, and sighed, bitter and slow. To Eva, he was a childhood friend, the smith's lad who shod her pony and repaired her father's weapons. But if the blacksmith's lad killed Eva's husband, as he might well do one day, she would regard him as the one who had destroyed her happiness.

A poor choice indeed for a man's future.

He plunged the hot blade into the fire and sprinkled white sand over it, gathered under a new moon, to add brilliance to the steel surface. The sand particles sparked and flew about like a rain of stars.

Another secret of his craft: the gathering of the sand. His foster father had taught him to protect his knowledge—but the newest secrets in his cache had to do with the smith, not the smithing.

Soon the weapons would be finished and he would be gone. Yet before he returned to Scotland, he must harden his heart.

Chapter 2

"Come with us, Eva," Margaret coaxed. "It is Beltane night, and so we are free to roam the hills and do what we will until dawn. Do not go home so soon. Come with us to the faery hill to roll bannock cakes down the slope—if the burned side or the plain side comes up, we will know if we will marry soon or not!" She tipped her golden head, pale and graceful in the dim light of the moonless evening, and smiled.

Eva glanced past her cousin toward the group, including her two brothers, who waited beneath some trees at the edge of the lochside beach. She shook her head and looked out at the water.

"I am not in a very festive mood," she said. "What good can rolling a bannock do me? My father has decided to promise me to Green Colin Campbell soon. Go on, Margaret, they are waiting. I will call for Alpin to ferry me back over to Innisfarna."

Margaret sighed. "Well, if that is what you want. Besides, you already know who will wed you. I wish I knew my own true love. Perhaps I will learn it tonight—on Beltane, I might even hear it in the faery winds." She smiled again, prettily.

"Colin Campbell is hardly my true love. He just wants my island," Eva muttered. She glanced toward Innisfarna, where light twinkled in the island castle in the center of the loch. "But my father insists his influence will benefit our clan."

"If it were me, I would marry Green Colin. He has the

king's favor, and likes you well. He even gave you a puppy from one of his castle litters. Marriage with him will not be unpleasant—he is rather handsome."

Eva smiled, thinking of Grainne, the tiny gray terrier that Colin had given her the last time he visited Innisfarna. But the thought of the surly, authoritative man who had handed her the puppy made her frown. "Then you marry Green Colin," she muttered, "and I will keep the pup, for her temperament is better than his. Go on, Margaret, they are waving to you. Angus the carpenter's son is with them. I think he likes you well."

"Angus is always the jester," Margaret said dismissively. "Oh—who are your brothers talking to? The blacksmith's lad!" she whispered. "I did hope Lachlann would come out tonight!"

Eva felt her heart leap as she glanced again at the group beneath the trees. She saw that Lachlann, taller than the rest, had joined them. Beside him, she saw the pale form of his white deerhound, a leggy pup.

"Perhaps I can convince Lachlann to walk out with me on the moors later," Margaret said. "Eva, do you think he likes me a bit? I think he is the most beautiful man in Argyll," she confided in a quick whisper, then giggled.

"Soon he will be the most beautiful man in France," Eva said wryly. "He is leaving with my cousins in two days."

"How could you understand? He is like a brother to you!"

"Indeed," Eva murmured, understanding better than Margaret suspected. His kiss the other day, though meant as a token of friendship, had stunned her to her core. She had always regarded him as a cherished friend, but the astonishing burst of passion she had felt for him, and from him, had opened a door—and she did not know what lay on the other side of it.

"I am sure Lachlann likes you," she assured Margaret. "How could he not? You are charming and lovely."

"Well, with a widowed mother, I must find myself a husband. I have little dowry to bring to a marriage, though my five brothers might be able to help a man at his tasks."

"Might help," Eva said, chuckling. "Between pranks. Go on, now. You never know what sort of good fortune you might have on a night like this. Good night to you." She gave Margaret a breezy hug and walked away, her feet in leather brogues digging slightly into the soft sand. Margaret hastened toward the others, and Eva heard them chatting near the trees. She glanced back once when she heard the deep, familiar rumble of Lachlann's laughter. But he seemed engaged in conversation with Margaret and did not look toward Eva.

Cold and willful, the wind pushed at her as she stood near the water's edge. Under a dark new moon, only starshine reflected in the sifting sand and the loch's surface. Glancing around, she saw torchlight starring the hillsides, and she heard singing and laughter faintly on the wind. She sighed.

On Beltane, unmarried young people walked about in groups or as couples to celebrate the coming of spring. No one wanted to walk out with her, or discover with her the joy of true love, as Margaret hoped to find for herself. Eva's betrothal to a man of her father's choosing was inevitable, and it weighed upon her mind.

Wavelets lapped at her feet, and the dark water sparkled. Far out on the loch, Innisfarna's lights gleamed. Her island had passed from mother to daughter in a direct line for generations, roots tracing to an ancient clan, and further back, it was said, to the faeries. Eva had been ten years old when her mother's death left the island to her daughter, as tradition demanded.

The isle, the castle, and the ancient treasure—*Claidheamh Soluis,* the Sword of Light said to lie beneath the island—were in her safekeeping now. The legendary sword guarded the border between the earthly and the faery realms;

that magical threshold must remain in the protection of Innisfarna's lady, or disaster would befall Scotland. Eva shivered at the thought.

She faced into the wind, her plaid shawl billowing and her dark, braided hair nearly unraveling, and cupped her hands to call out. Alpin MacDewar, her late mother's cousin and her father's old comrade-in-arms, would fetch her soon. More like an uncle to her than a servant, Alpin had guided the crossing boat for as long as Eva could remember.

Although her father held his own properties as chief of the clan, Eva preferred her mother's island. She loved its tall stone castle and its alder trees, surrounded by loch and legends, and the kin and friends who lived in the glen.

At Innisfarna, she felt balanced and safe. She could never live elsewhere, nor could she allow anyone to take it from her.

The loch rushed and the wind sighed, creating a soft, urgent harmony that seemed to speak to her. *Eisg, o eisg,* it said; *listen, oh listen.* Chills ran along her arms, for that phrase was the war cry of the MacArthurs. For a moment she sensed a formless, ancient knowingness all around her, as if the sky were about to open like curtains to reveal something timeless and powerful. She waited, utterly still.

Eisg, o eisg, wind and water said again. *Lachh . . . lannn.*

She heard the name clearly, and her very soul seemed to turn like a fish inside her. *Lachlannnn . . .*

She shook her head. Yearning conjured that name, born of her desperate wish for something wonderful, something other than the marriage her father planned for her. Or could the wind have named her true love, as Margaret said? She wanted to laugh.

She wanted to cry.

Hearing more chatter behind her, she turned. The others were leaving the beach at last. And Lachlann was walking over the sand toward her, alone. Her heart quickened.

*   *   *

He had come to the lochside beach to gather white sand in the darkness of a new moon for the working of steel; he had hoped for peace and privacy, even on Beltane night. But when he saw Eva there, his desire for solitude vanished as if it had never been.

Glad that his friends had decided, finally, to depart, Lachlann approached Eva, carrying the bucket that was half full of sand and whistling softly for his dog, Solas.

The dog ignored him, as she usually did, nosing along the beach, head down, tail wagging. He called again. Solas turned to look at him, then bounded away with undisguised delight.

Sighing, he followed in the crazy wake of the white dog, laughing when he should have scolded her. He found a stick and tossed it up the beach for her to chase. She was fast and clever, but a willful pup yet. Despite strength and heart, she would never be a well-trained hound, for her master was leaving her. Solas would become his foster mother's hearth hound instead; Lachlann was glad that Mairi MacKerron would have a loyal guardian and companion.

Ahead, Eva faced the dark, misted loch, water frothing about her toes. She turned to glance at him, then turned back. Noticing her cool response, Lachlann slowed, suddenly wondering what to say, what to do. He had not forgotten their surprising, exquisite leavetaking in his smithy.

Walking on, he felt drawn toward her, as he always had been. In boyhood, he had spent long hours in the smithy, but whenever he played, Simon and Donal MacArthur were among his closest friends. Their spirited, demanding sister was often with them, and Lachlann had come to know Eva well as they ran over the hills, climbing, competing, and getting into mischief.

He smiled, remembering how he and her brothers had lost one footrace after another to Eva. But though she was swift and determined, eventually Lachlann's legs grew so long that not even Eva could outrun him.

One day he had realized, simply and wholly, that he loved her. He was not certain how or why it had happened, but he was aware of its strength. He had always been fond of her, had always given her his loyalty, respect, and protection. Then she bloomed into a stunning young woman, strong and willful, tender and unpredictable. And his heart had dropped through him like an apple tumbling from a tree.

Solas whipped past him, and he whistled again, lengthening his stride over the sands. Eva turned as the dog sped by her.

"It is a good thing that dog is white," she said. "You will never catch her in the darkness, otherwise."

"No doubt you, Eva my friend, could run fast enough to catch her no matter what." He grinned and stopped beside her.

"No doubt." She smiled up at him. "I thought you would walk out with the others." Her gaze seemed wide and luminous in the starlight.

"Beltane is not for me. I came here to collect sand for the steel. Did you call for Alpin?"

"I did, but I do not think he heard me over the wind."

"He is probably asleep in his little cottage on the isle. You will have to use the ram's horn that hangs on a tree on the other beach. I can walk you there if you like."

She watched him, and he wondered what she thought, if she guessed his feelings. Fool, he told himself; he should have gone on his way. Only distance would slow the drumming of his heart and cool his blood again.

"I do not want to keep you," she said.

"Keep me," he said generously, then regretted such a flippant, suggestive remark. "I am in no hurry," he amended, and began to stroll beside her.

"The water is so black tonight," she mused. "The fog sits

like faery wings upon it. I was thinking about the legend, and the Sword of Light that lies so deep in the water."

"Ah. Aeife's tale." He smiled. "That was always one of my favorite tales. When I was a boy, I thought the loss of that sword in the water was a great tragedy. Faery blades are hard to come by," he added wryly.

Eva laughed. "Well, you do know how much work is involved in making a sword. It was customary in those days to throw a sword into a body of water to mark the end of a feud. There is a tradition that MacKerrons once crafted faery blades, I think."

He shrugged. "Long ago, a MacKerron boy was stolen by faeries. His father searched for him for years. When he finally found the boy, he was working at a faery forge, making magical blades. They went home, and the son made a good living as a weaponsmith," he finished lightly.

"If you knew his secret, you could make an excellent living too. Then you would not have to go to France to earn a knighthood."

He glanced at the loch rather than at her, for those storm-green eyes often saw too deeply into him. "But I will go."

She paused, and he stood beside her. "They say the Sword of Light must never be disturbed in its place of peace." She gazed at the dark water. "Do you know what will happen if Innisfarna is lost from the keeping of a woman of Aeife's line?"

"Some kind of a disaster, I think."

"Devastation in the Highlands," she said bluntly. "And destruction of the Highland ways. Only the woman who holds Innisfarna can avert it."

He lifted a brow, looked at her. "Do you believe that?"

She shrugged. "It is a powerful legend, and I am not certain what I believe. But I know I must keep Innisfarna safe however I can, and give it to my daughter one day. If I have only sons, it will go to my granddaughter."

"Someday you will have a daughter as lovely as you . . . as the princess Aeife is said to have been," he said, catching himself.

He shifted the bucket to his other hand.

"I hope I have a daughter someday. Lachlann, why do you gather sand in such darkness, instead of during the day?"

"White sand is excellent for hardening steel, and it is best collected under a new moon. It is a perfect time for beginnings." Yet all he had known in his life was ending in one way or another.

"Will you make another sword with that sand?"

"Just one. I must finish my own blade before I leave for France in two days."

Her face as she looked at him was a gentle shadow. "When will you be back?"

"I do not know," he answered flatly. He glanced at the loch. "The mist is thickening. Alpin MacDewar will never see you here."

"And his hearing is not so good now."

"Or so he pretends, when it suits him."

She laughed. "You know Alpin well."

"He is not a biddable man, but we share an interest in good weapons. He was once a gifted swordsman, and knows much. He taught your brothers and me how to handle swords."

"Be careful. You might lose your privileges when you leave. You will have to woo his favor when you return." She chuckled.

He walked beside her in silence, carrying the bucket.

Solas scampered toward Eva, bumping into her, and the silver brooch flew out of her shawl. Eva caught it up again.

"Oh!" she cried. "The clasp is broken."

"Let me see." He wiggled it carefully, then turned to pin it into the wool, his hand brushing her upper chest. Even through the layers of wool and linen, she felt warm, firm, and delectable. His body tightened, surged. He drew his hand away.

"Bring it to the smithy and I can repair it more fully."

"Ah, is the blacksmith a silversmith too?"

"The metal needs reheating and twisting. I can do that."

"It is a shame to take such skill to France." Her gaze searched his, her eyes as silvery as the brooch. "We need a good smith here at Balnagovan."

"Do you?" he murmured. He meant her, alone. She nodded, her head tilted back as he leaned closer. His heart slammed, his mouth went dry. He wanted desperately to touch her, to kiss her again. Silence wreathed them like the fog rolling on the loch.

"I . . . I should be going," she finally murmured. "But this is my last Beltane. Next year, I will be . . . a wife."

Next year, he might still be in France—if he lived. Then he would return home to make Eva a widow. He sucked in a breath at that ugly thought, so out of place here, with her.

"We should bid good night," he said. "It is late."

She smiled. "No token of farewell?" she asked softly, coy and yet innocent all at once.

He huffed, part relieved laugh, part sigh. "I gave you one the other day, and I should have apologized for it. Do you want another?" His heart pounded, though he tried to speak lightly.

Her eyes were wide as she nodded. "Oh . . . very much."

In that instant, a power engulfed him, and he gave in to it, pulling Eva toward him swiftly. Her lips softened beneath his, and his hands fit the supple curves of her waist. She circled her arms around his neck, all warm grace and willingness.

Caressing the arch of her back, he scarcely believed that he held her again. Her mouth fit beautifully to his, her body curved in complement. Desire built a storm within him, despite the inner voice that cautioned him to think, to slow down—

Stop. He forced himself to pull back. "Eva—"

But her lips were hungry beneath his, her hands heated where she touched his chest through his linen shirt and belted plaid. Drunk with an irresistible blood fire, he kissed her urgently, then once again forced himself to pull away. Leaning brow to brow, he held her waist and tried to catch his breath. "Eva—"

"Hush, you," she whispered. "Do not speak. Do not end the dream." She touched her nose to his, inviting another kiss.

He resisted it like a salmon going against the river. "What dream?"

"Mine," she whispered. "Lachlann—" His name was a breath upon her lips. "I wonder . . . what love is like. I think I may never know, unless you show me tonight."

Had she knocked him over with the flat of a blade, he could not have felt more stunned. Brushing her hair back, he cupped her face. "One day soon you will know," he said, although the implication—her husband—wrenched at him.

"Listen to me, oh, listen." That breathless phrase was familiar, but his fogged mind could not grasp it. "This may be foolish of me, but . . . tonight is Beltane, when we celebrate our life, our youth. Loving is all that matters on Beltane."

"Eva," he cautioned. She had always had a hot spark of boldness, and a curious nature. He sensed no wantonness in her, only sincerity, and a need that matched his own. "Soon you will be wed," he said. He felt her trembling in his arms.

"I am not yet pledged, and I still make my own decisions." Her fingers flexed, buried in his shirt. "And if I were free to choose a man to pledge with me, I would take you."

Oh, God. His heart nearly burst from him. He pulled her to him, slid his fingers over her head. Her dark plait loosened and her hair spilled free, thick and cool and rich. Kissing her, deepening it, he let his tongue find hers, seeking, giving. Her delight and eagerness inflamed him further.

Cradling her face in his hands, he could scarcely think past the thick throb of his body, the luxuriousness of her. Yet he forced himself to draw back a little. "Unless we stop now, I will be needing your forgiveness."

"I would forgive you anything." Her lips caressed his. "Do you think me foolish for this?"

"Not at all." Was he foolish to think of her as part of him, blood, bone, and soul? She lifted on her toes, melding to him as if she were made for him alone, her breasts soft against his chest, her willingness delicious, unexpected, intoxicating. The thundery demand within his body urged him to let go his caution and pursue this alluring secret with her.

He kissed her again, feeling his lonely yearning for her ease a little; yet his craving increased, driving him onward.

Then his thoughts cleared like sunlight melting fog. He set her firmly away from him. "This is beyond a mere token. You will know loving soon enough, but not here, not like this."

Her breath came as fast as his, and her hands circled his wrists where he held her shoulders. "Better you than—"

"My friend, not like this." His voice was ragged.

"Lachlann," she said, "do you not want to pledge with me?"

"Eva," he said, a sudden suspicion growing. "Would you use this to avoid the marriage your father wants for you?"

She shook her head. "I had not thought of that."

He believed her, but his body sobered, and his guard fell into place. He lifted his hands from her. "And what would your father do?" he asked bitterly. "A smith's lad touching his daughter—he would be after me for murder and seal you up for safekeeping. Go home, Eva."

"I did not mean to anger you. I only wanted—I hoped—"

"You hoped I was so good a friend? I will be an even better friend, and tell you to go home. Your brothers, your father, and your *friend*"—he thumped his breastbone savagely—"do not want you disgraced."

She nodded miserably. "I know."

"This is only Beltane foolishness, Eva. It is in the air. Girls rolling bannocks to determine their lovers, and wishing to be courted—I would not want you hurt by it."

She began to gulp as if she might sob. "But—"

"Hush." He touched a finger to her luscious mouth, still warm from kissing, and brushed a silky curl from her cheek. "Listen to me. Of course I want you. I am a man, and you are lovely. But we will not do this, hey?" he said gently.

"Tell me . . . do you want to pledge with me?"

"Of course. Who could resist you?" he asked, heart slamming. "Now be off with you. I swear if I touch you again, I could not stop so quickly. And you deserve better than a blacksmith's fostered lad, fine as you are," he murmured.

He had never wanted anything so fiercely as he wanted her now. Yet he fought to resist what she offered him with such seductive innocence. He did not want her out of some headstrong passion. He wanted her wholly, utterly, two equal loves shining like twin stars. If he thought there was some chance of that, he could go away with hope in his heart, and wait forever.

He would not hurt her, in heart or in flesh, with hasty, hungry, ill-timed loving. What filled him was too powerful to let out all at once. He must tame it—smother it, if need be.

Her gaze was vulnerable, needy somehow. "Can a kiss be a pledge?" she asked. "Is a token like that not binding?"

He smiled ruefully. "Sometimes. And sometimes it is Beltane fever. And sometimes it is a convenience to prevent another betrothal." He cocked a brow at her.

"That is not what I intended," she said haughtily.

"Eva, we can pledge if you still want it when I return

from France, and if your father agrees," he answered with a calm he did not feel. "If you are not wed by then."

"Oh," she said. "Oh." She looked down again, and he knew she felt rejected. He sighed and let her think it, for that was safest for both of them. But in his heart he had made a pledge to her long ago. He reached out, began to speak.

The blare of a ram's horn split the silence between them. "Someone is on the other beach, summoning Alpin," he said, looking that way. Eva's name echoed out.

"Simon and Donal. I must go." She leaned forward and kissed his cheek. "My fine friend," she whispered.

Friend, he thought. She did not suspect. He would keep his heart guarded, as he must for now, and he would see where her own heart lay when he returned. If she still waited for him, and truly desired him, it would be heaven's own grace in his life.

"Go on, then," he told her. She hastened ahead, beckoning to him. Loathe to see her leave so soon, he followed her.

As the horn sounded again, Eva turned to Lachlann. "If they see us together, will they think—"

"Not those two," he assured her wryly.

She hesitated, her heart still tumbling within her. "Lachlann, I . . . I am sorry to bother you with my silliness."

"Do not fret over it." He said no more than that, though she waited. Her heart sank like a stone.

She whirled and hurried ahead, feeling her cheeks heat with embarrassment—and with a yearning that would not lessen. She had hoped for more than friendship from him, but that was all he would offer her. She would not plague him for more. Crossing the stand of trees that divided the two beaches, she did not look back, though she knew Lachlann followed her.

Simon turned to see her, while Donal replaced the ram's horn on a tree limb. Her brothers loped toward her with lean animal grace, their long legs, dark heads, and wrapped plaids much alike in the darkness.

"There you are!" Simon spoke impatiently, but she heard his concern. "You were not where we left you, and we saw Alpin's boat coming over the water."

"I went for a walk," Eva said.

"I am glad you are with her, Lachlann," Donal said. "She is safe with you. On Beltane, unmarried girls should take care, or find themselves having to wed quickly." He grinned.

"The man who wants to wed me is not here, is he," Eva said irritably. She would not look at Lachlann, though she felt his gaze steady and sober on her.

Hearing splashes, she looked toward the loch. A yellow spark floated over the dark water, and a boat emerged, with a lantern hanging from a pole. The golden haze expanded as Alpin rowed to the shore. "Is it you, young MacArthurs?" he called.

"It is," Donal replied. "Eva and Lachlann are with us."

They walked close to the water's frothy hem. Alpin beached the prow, his broad shoulders and the wild white halo of his hair silhouetted in the light. "Into the boat with you," he said, waving. "Hurry, for it is late and I am an old man." He helped Eva over the side, and she sat on one of the cross benches. While her brothers boarded the low craft, Alpin peered at Lachlann.

"Blacksmith's lad, I will not ferry you this time of night!"

"I only came to say farewell to the MacArthurs, and to you, Alpin MacDewar."

"Ah. Luck to you in France, lad. We will pray for your safety. Now go home—foolish to be out on so dark a night." Shaking his head, Alpin sat, and the boat rocked.

"Farewell to all," Lachlann said. "Eva," he added quietly.

"God speed you well," she murmured, glancing at him. She could not look away. The lantern light poured like bronze over his black hair and wide shoulders. The need to be in his arms again was so strong it tugged at her like a wild thing.

Alpin picked up the oars. "Did you stay with your brothers and cousins, as you were told to do this night?" he asked her. "Or did you wander and get into mischief, as is your wont?"

She frowned under his stern, affectionate gaze.

"Eva was with Lachlann," Simon answered. "She was safe."

"*Ach,* and is that safe on Beltane?" the old man muttered.

"Alpin," Eva scolded.

"Lachlann loves Eva like a sister," Simon said.

"Is it so?" Alpin growled.

"How else would it be?" Lachlann asked.

"Give us a shove, blacksmith," Alpin said. "Do not stand there looking like a sheep."

Lachlann pushed at the prow, and the boat floated backward. Alpin pulled on the oars and moved the craft into the darkness and the mist. Within moments Eva could hardly see the shore, though she saw the pale blur of Lachlann's shirt where he stood in the shallows a long while.

Her body still thrummed, her breath was still quick. A few moments of passion had become a little thread of fire in the weaving of her heart.

The oars dipped, and the boat pulled onward. The world shrank, in that inky darkness, to the pool of light cast by the lantern. Alpin rowed, and her brothers were silent as the water rocked them toward home.

Once again Eva looked over her shoulder. This time she saw only blackness. Lachlann was gone.

Chapter 3

"Wine." Colin beckoned, seated in Iain MacArthur's customary chair beside the hearth in Innisfarna's solar. Holding a bowl of hot stew, he spooned it steadily into his mouth.

Eva refilled a goblet and handed it to him. Waiting while Colin drank with gusto, she wondered again what brought him here. Upon his arrival, she had informed him that Iain MacArthur had left weeks earlier with Donal for Inverness, where King James had called a meeting of the Highland chiefs.

Colin seemed to know that, and as yet had said nothing of his errand at Innisfarna. Eva had offered food and drink first out of courtesy, and waited with as much patience as she could muster.

She studied him as he ate. He was a fair and ruddy man, large-boned and thick-bellied, blond even in his fifth decade. He dressed like a Lowlander, in a knee-length tunic, hose, and leather boots, and his cloak was cut from a Highland plaid in red and green. On his shoulder, a wide pewter circlet set with a green stone gleamed like a cat's eye.

Green Colin, most called him, and Eva wondered if it was because of the brooch he always wore. Had she felt more comfortable in his gruff presence, she might have asked.

For months, she had stayed insulated but embattled at Innisfarna while stubbornly resisting her father's wish that she marry Colin. Though she had managed to keep her freedom so far, she knew her father was not ready to give up—nor, she thought, was she.

Although she had never told anyone of her hope that Lachlann MacKerron would return to pledge with her, as he had hinted might happen, she kept that bright dream close in her heart. Colin's arrival did not bode well for her secret cause, and she knew it.

Beside her, the little terrier Colin had given her barked and pulled at the hem of her dress. Eva lifted the dog to pet her. "Hush, Grainne!"

"Perhaps she smells a rat," Colin said. "Her breed is good at catching rodents, and they go after foxes too, right into their dens. She will be useful if you do not spoil her into a lap dog," he added, scowling.

"She is young yet," Eva said. Grainne licked Eva's chin as she spoke, and she giggled, turning her head. "I thank you again for the gift of her. She is delightful."

"The pup was my son's idea for you," he mumbled as he ate.

"How kind of him," she said, smiling, and looking at him with new interest. "You have never mentioned a son before. Is he young yet?"

"If you long to be a mother, I can oblige you with better sons than that one," he growled. Eva blinked at such coldness. He waggled his fingers. "He is too old for mothering, and he is an odd boy. I will send him out to be a page, but he lacks the wherewithal to become a knight."

She felt immediate sympathy for a son so harshly criticized by his father. "I am sure he is a worthy young man, and I look forward to meeting him. What is his name?"

"Ninian. His mother died bearing him, and a good thing she never saw him. He is an oaf and an idiot."

Unsure how to respond to that, Eva cuddled the dog

closer. Grainne yelped then, as the solar door opened. Eva looked up to see her brother enter.

"Simon!" She set Grainne on the rush-covered floor, and her brother crouched to greet the pup with a friendly pat. He stood, remaining by the door while Grainne scurried away.

Sunlight sheened his dark, braided hair, and brightened the reds in his belted plaid. With lanky grace, he leaned against the doorjamb and crossed his arms. A frown settled on his dark brow and marred the pleasant balance of his features. His blue-green eyes narrowed.

"Colin Campbell," he said, lifting his chin as if inviting a fist on it. "My father and brother are in Inverness with the king. No doubt my sister told you so."

"I knew that already. I rode a long way today, boy, and I am damned hungry. Your ferryman looked as if he would rather stick a dirk in me than row me anywhere, and I had to stable my horse on the mainland. You need a bridge and more boats, and a ferryman who knows his place."

"Old Alpin suits us. And we have neither coin nor stone to build a bridge from the mainland to here," Simon said.

"Nor the desire to do so," Eva added. "We have always stabled our horses on the mainland in the care of the smith, though he . . . our smith has gone to France to fight there." Her cheeks heated as she thought of Lachlann, gone months now with Margaret's two older brothers. "Until he returns, we go there each day to care for our animals."

"Return? Your smith may well be dead," Colin said bluntly. "Have you heard nothing of the French war lately? Many Scots have died in their battles, along with thousands of Frenchmen. Their fight against the English is a devastating failure."

"*Ach Dhia,*" Eva said, flattening her palm upon her breastbone. She glanced at Simon, who frowned deeply. "I—we had not heard. There have been no messages since they left."

"Then figure your smith dead with the rest," Colin said. "I hear that the French are so desperate now that they have put their faith in a young peasant girl. She now heads their royal army! Can you imagine!"

"Girl?" Eva scarcely listened, her heart pounding. No one had received word from Lachlann or her cousins, but she could not imagine him gone. She would not. She would always imagine him strong and willing to return to her, until he did. She lifted her chin. "A girl? How can that be?"

"Jehanne la Pucelle, they call her—Jehanne the Maid. She came to the dauphin and said God told her to save France." Colin laughed abruptly. "The dauphin gave her armor and set her at the head of his army. No wonder the French need help."

"It does not seem odd to me," Eva said. "Our own legend says the warrior princess Aeife guarded the Sword of Light, and her female descendants have the obligation to defend the isle."

"Well, you will never need to do such a ridiculous thing. I will ensure Innisfarna's safety." Colin set his empty bowl aside. "Simon, why did you not go with your father and brother?"

"I stayed here to protect my sister from wolves," Simon answered, staring at him.

"Oh, do they swim?" Colin asked, and chuckled at his wit.

"Some take boats," Simon drawled.

"Perhaps Colin has some news of the king's parliament in Inverness," Eva said, hoping to dispel the building tension.

"That is not a parliament," Simon said. "It is a trap. I hear King James is jealous of the power of his Highland chiefs. Ever since his return from those years of custody with the English, I hear he wants to center the Scottish government around himself, like an English king."

"You hear wrong," Colin replied calmly, sipping his wine.

"The rumor is that the king will punish those who will not bow to his game. But we are not biddable like the English, or even the Lowlanders. If the king takes rights from our Highland chiefs, we will rebel. I will be with them. Make sure you report that to the king. I hear you are deep in his pocket."

"I serve my king," Colin growled. "That is what you hear."

"Simon, please," Eva said, disquieted by her brother's hostility. Simon had an affable nature except when righteous matters stirred him, and he greatly disliked Colin, arguing with their father against Eva's possible marriage with the man.

Colin Campbell was of an age with their father, and held Strathlan Castle at the far distant end of Loch Fhionn, more than thirty miles away. As a powerful Campbell laird and a king's advisor, he had considerable influence, and a marriage alliance would promote and protect Clan Arthur. That point, of all her father's reasons, was hardest to argue against.

"I have news," Colin said. "First, the king has appointed me to France as an ambassador."

"Are you going to France, then?" Eva asked, surprised.

"When do you leave?" Simon asked quickly.

"Soon. We have an old alliance with France, and they need more troops and assistance. The post is an honor, of course. The Campbells have long been indispensable to the Stewart kings of Scotland." He smiled at Eva. "I would take Eva with me as my wife. Your father and I discussed the possibility weeks ago."

Eva bristled. "I prefer to stay at Innisfarna. I will not leave my home."

"Of course," Colin murmured. "Women should stay by their hearths." He held out his goblet for more wine.

Eva took the cup again, filled it, handed it back. She dashed some into another goblet for herself out of sheer nervousness, sipping to mask her distress. French claret was sweet and heady, and she did not care for it. Nor did she care to think about living in France—or anywhere—with Colin.

But Lachlann was in France, too. Eva took another hasty sip, but the wine's burn could not diminish memories of wild, passionate kisses, tender and secret under the dark of the moon—

She gulped more wine, and coughed.

"Six thousand Scots have gone over there in the last few years," Colin was telling Simon. "Some of them gain wealth and titles in France."

"If they live," Simon said harshly. Eva caught her breath.

"Take your chances and go there too. Give up that plaid for a suit of good steel. It would make a man of you."

"I am a man," Simon growled. "A Highland man."

"Simon and Donal are the chief's sons, and so are needed here in Argyll to help our father," Eva said.

"I discussed Innisfarna with the king before he rode to Inverness. He approves of installing a garrison here to ensure military presence. They will arrive later this week."

"A garrison?" Eva asked indignantly. "We do not want it."

"We need no added protection here," Simon said.

"Innisfarna has a strong location, yet it is overseen by a female, with one kinsman, a few servants, and no troops. I am appalled that your father never properly manned this place."

"Innisfarna is not a military fortress," Eva said. "It is neutral in any dispute the crown may have."

"Our father keeps other properties manned," Simon added.

"This isle is part of a triangle of fortresses that can protect the Highlands. It must be fortified."

"For your purposes," Eva said. "Not ours."

"I wish only to protect you in your father's . . . absence," he said. Something in his expression sent a chill down her spine.

"She has no need of it," Simon said, stepping forward.

"You," Colin said, waving impatiently. "Out. I have heard enough of your insolence. I wish to speak to your sister alone."

Eva hastened toward Simon, nearly tripping on Grainne, who scurried underfoot. She scooped up the little dog. "Take her outside," she pleaded, thrusting the terrier into his hands.

"You will not marry that man if I can help it," Simon hissed. "No matter the good to the clan. Eva, I must ride out to Inverness immediately, to warn our father that Colin intends to take Innisfarna." He stepped into the corridor. "But I do not want to leave you here with him."

"I can take care of myself. Please give my love to our father and Donal," she added.

"Take care, Eva," he said, and walked away, cradling the pup in his arms. Eva closed the door and crossed the room.

Colin handed her his goblet wordlessly. Seeing the flush in his cheeks and the glint in his blue eyes, she set the cup down. "That claret is new and strong," she said. "I will prepare you some watered, spiced wine. It will aid your digestion better than this." She capped the jug.

"You will make a good wife. I feared that you might have too much of your brother's wildness—raised too loosely, you were. Though I like some spirit in a woman," he purred.

Another chill went through her. She did not like being alone with Colin, who sometimes looked at her with a salacious glint in his eye. After the ecstasy of Lachlann's kisses, the mere thought of Colin's kiss was repulsive.

He moved toward her, stumbling, and she realized that the drink had soaked into his blood. She stepped away.

"I apologize for Simon's rudeness," she said. "But I share his concerns." A sense of dread swept through her, heavy and dark. "Something frightens me about this meeting at Inverness. Can we not send a message to summon my kinsmen back home?"

He frowned and came closer. "That is impossible now. I thought you might be anxious, so I came here to offer you my comfort." He smiled. "When I am laird of Innisfarna, I can offer more than that. I know you mince about saying you will not wed me, but I also know it is just your fiery spirit. I once told your father that I can be patient." He reached out to pat her arm.

She stepped back. "This island can be held only by me, and you know it. My father honored our ancient agreement with the faeries when he married my mother. No doubt he told you that."

"Faeries!" Colin looked sour. "The faery women of Innisfarna have led their men by the noses. I am not so weak."

Anger surged in her. "If you cannot respect our legend, that is one more reason this place should never belong to you!"

"Rule your temper. Passion in women belongs only in the bedchamber." He touched her arm, then drew her toward him with unyielding strength. "By God, you are a lovely creature. Dark, delicate, fiery. I hear there is faery blood in you. And I like it well," he breathed, leaning toward her. "Our sons will have a touch of it, and be fine young men."

"You assume too much," she said.

"With reason, as you shall see," he answered. "I came here to speak privately to you, but you may need some reassurance before we can proceed with the news I bring."

"What—" she began to ask, but he moved closer, taking her face in his hand. She turned her head away, but he slid his lips over her mouth, pulling her against him with his other hand. His mouth was wine-sour and clumsy.

"Stop." She struggled, but he tightened his hold.

"Easy, now." He kissed her again.

"Let me go!" Eva pushed at his chest, but his kiss and his hands grew rougher, despite her struggling. Then her lifted knee connected with the soft sac under his firmed groin.

He grunted and let go, cursing while he clutched himself. "Your father deceived me! He said you were obedient and quiet. You are a she-wolf, and a frigid one, too. I was showing you my affection! What did you think? Rape?"

"You touched me with a forceful hand," she said, though she felt some remorse; he looked pathetic now, and no threat.

"Saints save me from ignorant virgins!" He straightened. "That is how loving begins between a man and a woman!"

I am not ignorant about loving, she wanted to snap at him. "That is not the way to woo a woman."

"I wooed my first bride before you were born," he grumbled. "My current leman does not object to bedsport. Why should you?"

"Go to your mistress if you want games like that."

"I suppose you want hand kissing and poetry," he groused.

I want gentle passion in my bed, she thought. *Tender hands upon me, and deep kisses in the dark—from a man who is not here and may never return.* She lifted her chin. "All I want from you is the news you came to deliver."

"Very well. I will not spare you, since you are determined to be a she-wolf." He rubbed his belly as if it still ached. "The truth is this—matters have gone poorly at Inverness."

Her blood went cold. "What do you mean? You assured me—"

"I assumed you would need assurance and comfort. But

any woman who can knee a man in his stones can take hard news."

Her heart slammed. "Has something happened to my kinsmen?"

"The king has taught the Highland chiefs a lesson they will not soon forget. Iain and Donal have been arrested and accused, along with more than forty Highland chiefs, of treason."

"What?" Eva stared, stunned. "They have not committed treason!" Her hand found the carved back of the chair and she grasped the solid wood with shaking fingers.

"The Highland chiefs resisted the king's bid for a centralized Scotland, which would unite and benefit all of us. Many of the clan chiefs are unpredictable and ungovernable, and pose a danger to his plan. He must take a forceful position."

"Where are my father and Donal now?" Her breath came fast.

"They were in Inverness, but Donal was among those moved to Edinburgh. And twenty chiefs, including your father," he added grimly, "were sentenced to execution. I had a letter yesterday that reported most of those gone by now."

Inwardly reeling, Eva stared at him. "Gone?"

"Iain is dead, Eva." His voice softened, and he reached for her. She twisted away. "He was in the first group to be executed at Inverness a few days ago. The word is just getting out. The king acted swiftly and secretly in this matter."

"Why did you wait until Simon left to tell me this?" she demanded. "He took the only boat to shore, and is riding hard to Inverness by now. Why did you wait?" Her limbs shook, her heart pounded. Suddenly she could barely think, scarcely breathe.

"Simon is a hothead, and there is no reasoning with his sort. I decided to tell you first. He will discover in Inverness that he is outlawed and his father gone. When he returns—

if he is not arrested—the garrison will be here to control him if he tries to rebel. I assume he will."

"Outlawed?" she asked. Moments ago, she thought she would fall to her knees with the shock of the news, but now a strange, cold calm filled her, clarified her thoughts, kept her feet firm on the floor. "What do you mean?"

"There is more news," he said. "Are you strong enough?"

She nodded, feeling numb. "Tell me."

"Clan Arthur is summarily dispossessed, with all lands and rights forfeited to the king."

Blood rushed in her ears. She gripped the chair's rim. "Why?" she gasped.

"The king has his reasons. Eva, you look pale," Colin murmured. He turned away, poured a cup of wine, offered it to her. She shook her head. "Listen to me. If you and I were already wed, I could have helped your father. You made a mistake, avoiding my suit, but it is not too late to save your kinsmen."

"Ach Dhia," she moaned, feeling his reproach like another deep stab. "How could I have known?"

"I have some influence with the king. I cannot help your father now—would God that I could—but I can request a pardon for Donal, and the return of the rights. I am among the few who can whisper in the king's ear. But if I give you my promise, I must have yours in return."

"My promise of marriage," she said woodenly.

"That," he said, "and Innisfarna, without condition."

She stared at him. "I cannot do that," she whispered.

"Eva," he said sternly. "Your father died because of your stubbornness. Do not let your brother Donal die too."

"Dear God, how can you say that to me?" She drew a breath. "And you know I cannot give Innisfarna to you. The legend—"

"I know the legend, and it does not frighten me," he said curtly. "Marry me and give me this island, and you will save

Donal, and Simon, and the rest of your kinsmen. They are all outlaws now, and I alone can help them."

"Oh—please—give me time to think!" A sob filled her throat and she swallowed with effort.

"Are you so coldhearted as to refuse to help them, just to keep one small island castle to yourself?" he murmured.

"It is not that—it is—" But she hesitated, unable to tell him that she had waited, hoped, for Lachlann to return. In the midst of the storm that surrounded her now, that hope was gone with so much else, suddenly a remote, impossible dream. Colin had said she might never see Lachlann again.

"You are greatly distressed. I may have been too harsh with you. Women are fragile creatures. Come here," he said, taking her wrist and pulling her toward him. He kissed her hand, kissed her brow, moist, lingering contacts that made her flinch.

"Leave me be." She tried to turn away.

He trapped her with heavy hands on her shoulders. "I must go to France soon, but first I want your betrothal promise before a priest. If you will not agree, I assure you that Donal will die the same death as your father. An awful death."

"Stop," she moaned. "Please stop. Give me time—"

"And I will make sure," he went on, "that Simon is caught like a wolf and stripped of his skin. The garrison that will come here will be under my orders even while I am gone. Simon will not escape this fate, nor any of your outlawed kinsmen."

"You cannot do this—"

"Can I not?" He kissed her softly on the cheek. "There, our first pledge is made. Remember our agreement. Be my wife, give me this isle to safeguard for you, and your kinsmen will be snug and safe as bugs in the woodwork."

She gasped, then nodded without looking at him. "I will marry you," she said. "But you can never have this island!"

"Eva, you can save them all with this bargain. Or you can ensure that their Highland hearts are roasted and served on the king's charger. It is your choice." He smiled down at her, and she stepped back with a muffled sob.

"I warn you to say nothing of our agreement to anyone. No one but you and I understand the importance of this, eh? Good," he said, when she was silent. "I will summon a priest to bind the betrothal tomorrow. While I am in France, you will be safe here in my absence, with the garrison." He paused. "I trust you have women to aid you, for you are pale and trembling."

She locked her hands, lifted her head. "I have no women, and no need of any. I am fine. Leave me be."

"Until later, then." He went to the door.

Eva stood stone calm, as if she had been emptied of emotion. Slowly she sank into the chair by the hearth and stared into the fire, aware that her world, her hopes, her most cherished dreams had crumbled away.

Chapter 4

Aussy je croy, en bonne foy,
Que les anges l'accompaignassent
(So I believe, in good faith,
That angels accompanied her)
—Martin le Franc, *Champion des dames,* 1440

Perth, Scotland
September 1431

"**S**o there you are, MacKerron."

Lachlann looked up. Alexander Beaton stood over him, wrapped in a cloak. The brisk evening air clung to its folds, refreshing in the close atmosphere of the crowded tavern.

"Aleck," Lachlann said, masking his surprise with a casual glance, which triggered, in his left and injured field of vision, the flashes of light and shadow he could neither control nor predict. "Just over from France?"

"Aye, and headed home. But I came here to Perth to find you before I go north to Kintail. How long have you been here in Perth?" Aleck peered at him. "You look terrible."

"Trust a physician to be blunt. Sit down." Lachlann gestured toward the bench opposite him. Aleck sat, his back to the busy inn. Lachlann preferred his own back to the wall. "I have been here much of the summer," Lachlann said. "I did not see you after . . . Jehanne was imprisoned in Rouen." He said it mildly, though he felt the weight of the words.

"I rode with the campaigns in northern France longer than I expected. I thought you would stay in that monastery hospital for months to recover from your injuries."

"A Scotsman heals better in Scotland," Lachlann said.

"The duke of Argyll ordered me sent home with some other Scots, but I went to Rouen first."

"Did you see Jehanne? The angel herself? Pray God, I hope you had that chance."

Lachlann frowned, gazed at his cup. "I did. And I sent a message to you to say that I would take a ship out of Nantes in April."

"I never got it. France is in such upheaval now that 'tisna surprising the message was lost. But I am glad to find you here, and hearty."

"Hearty enough," Lachlann muttered, and sipped from his cup.

"My ship docked in Leith a few days ago. A sergeant at the king's castle here in Perth told me you could be found at this place every evening." Aleck glanced around. "I thought you would have gone home to Argyll to start your blade-smithing forge. You spoke often of doing so."

"I did not count on an injured eye—'tis hardly an advantage for a bladesmith. Once my knight service was fulfilled, I decided to stay here and work at the castle smithy—shoeing horses, repairing weapons and armor, making nails. I can do ironwork well enough." He shrugged. "Summon the serving girl if you want food or drink. Meggott is her name. She likes coin and courtesy well." He beckoned to the girl.

Although the small inn was not the most popular in Perth, Lachlann was a frequent customer. The place was clean, and the innkeeper was honest enough. And Meggott was especially generous with Lachlann; she often invited him up to her room after the tavern closed at night.

Meggott came toward them, her wide hips and creamy shoulders swaying. Lachlann inclined his head to show his interest. His body, familiar with her warm curves and warmer recesses, craved her out of habit. He had spent hours in her passionate, eager company, but he had kept his heart distant.

And new ale dimmed life nicely, he had learned, though he never drank to idiocy. He had a dulling of the vision in one eye; a little dulling of the memory to go with it was welcome.

Aleck asked for ale and food, and Lachlann lifted his own cup, using a smith's penchant for gestures over words. Meggott smiled coyly and poured ale for both men, tipping the frosted belly of the jug against her full breasts. Her dark hair slid over her shoulder, and her body swayed, posing a question for Lachlann, offering an invitation.

He answered with a meaningful lift of his brow. Tonight he might seek oblivion again. Her ebony hair brushed his shoulder, and he remembered another dark-haired girl, not coy and round, but lean, bold, and graceful, with kisses like sweet fire.

He knew why he went to Meggott's bed, and he did not like himself for it. Eva haunted his dreams—eyes like the heart of a storm, and kisses he could not forget. God knew he had tried.

Ever since he had learned what had happened to Eva and her kin, he had felt conflicted. Haunted. Upon his arrival in Perth, he soon heard about the king's betrayal of the Highland chiefs at Inverness three years earlier. Iain MacArthur was dead, his clan disbanded and forfeited. The shock had struck Lachlann like a blow; he had listened, stunned, to the reports of outlaws in the hills above Loch Fhionn, led by Simon MacArthur, who now rebelled against the crown.

He was sure that his foster mother was safe, for she had no blood ties to the MacArthurs. Months earlier, he had sent her a message telling her of his arrival, and to say that he would remain in Perth for a while to do smithing work for the king.

In truth, he remained because he had heard another rumor: the daughter of the deceased MacArthur chief had betrothed to a Campbell chieftain, a royal ambassador who had been in France. Colin Campbell's name was bitterly familiar to Lachlann, and while in France he had heard that the man had come to the French court. He assumed that the marriage would be made by now.

That, more than any other reason, kept him in Perth. He took a swift drink, smacked the cup down again. His head spun. *Good,* he thought.

"Potent stuff," Aleck commented, after sipping the ale.

"Besides cleanliness and the ever-willing Meggott, this fine brew brings me back to this inn," Lachlann drawled.

Meggott brought Aleck stewed meat and onions on a bread trencher. Lachlann wiggled the cup he held, and she filled it. She was all blush and bosom, but he did not love her—could not. Though he willingly played lusty games with her, their lovemaking felt hollow to him.

Passion and emotion were limited now to the kick of the ale, the lush thunder of the girl at night, the hot red glow of the iron he worked each day. Small surface thrills, allowing him to ignore the ache within: Eva had not waited, and his heart felt sundered.

Aleck was staring at him. Lachlann began to drink, but he did not want it. He was not sure what he wanted. He pushed the cup away. "You didna come from France only to find me," he said.

Aleck ate a little, paused to answer. "My knight service is fulfilled, as is yours." He wiped his mouth on his sleeve. "How is it you left the king's guard for town smithing?"

Lachlann waggled his fingers. "My news isna so interesting. Tell me yours."

"When do you mean to return to Argyll?"

"I may not go back at all." Lachlann smoothed his fingers over a spill on the table. "Nor will I enlist in the king's army again. I am tired of hacking at strangers."

Aleck pushed his soggy trencher away. "I, too. That French war was the most brutal a man could ever witness."

"Brutal for women as well," Lachlann said with a sharp glance.

"God rest her soul," Aleck murmured. "But I find some peace in knowing that we were loyal friends to that extraordinary girl. Surely you feel that, too."

" 'Twas a rare privilege to ride as one of the Scots guards to Jehanne the Maid," Lachlann said. "But if I had my way, she would still be alive to harry the Goddams—the English." He huffed a sad laugh, remembering her feisty name for the enemy, and remembering her remarkable spirit and devotion to her cause.

"She had complete faith in her voices, even to the end. Her saints promised her salvation, but she thought it would be . . . of an earthly nature." Aleck sighed heavily. "So you were able to see her in Rouen?"

"Briefly, during the trials. I was allowed into her cell with some others. She was . . . forlorn. Half-starved, filthy. And still spitting fire, still stubborn, still devoted to her voices and to her mission. Some said her faith flagged toward the end, but I did not see that in her. We had some private words." He sighed, shook his head. "Jehannette is gone. Dear God." He rubbed weary fingers over his face.

"I was able to see her a few times myself. And I smuggled a priest into her cell to pray with her and shrive her in secret." Aleck frowned. "Her captors would not even allow her to be confessed."

Lachlann nodded. "I am sure what you did meant a great deal to her."

"You left France before the trial ended? Before . . . ?"

"I was on my way to Nantes when I heard the trials were concluded. I rode back, but I reached the city . . . too damned late." The ale had not done its work; he could still remember, all too clearly. He thought his voice might break. "It was over for her by the time I arrived, several days later."

"We were not meant to witness that, or God would have

placed us in that market square," Aleck said. "I am sure of it. Nothing her friends could have done would have saved her. What happened was God's will. It brings me some peace to know that she has found peace at last, and is with her angels."

Lachlann closed his eyes, stroked his fingers slowly over the lids. Lights flashed in his left eye, and his head whirled like a top, full of awful images and sounds. He had not witnessed her death, but he had heard many accounts of that day in Rouen. Too many.

"Are your injuries healing well?" Aleck asked, watching him with a narrowed, concerned gaze.

"Damned inconvenient to know a Scots knight who is also a physician," Lachlann grumbled. "The man asks too many questions." Aleck chuckled a little, and lifted his cup to drink, but Lachlann knew he waited for an answer to his medical query. "I am well enough, though I canna see properly in the left eye, as you know. But then, some of that may be new ale." He gave a careless shrug.

"Your vision will never again be perfect, as I told you, and the sight in the left eye will diminish, but the right one is fine. There simply is no cure when a heavy blow to the head damages the sight. You are lucky to have survived, and fortunate to have your sight. But eye injuries can heal remarkably well. If you wish me to examine you again, I will. Perhaps there is some improvement."

"Very little. What news do you have?" Lachlann demanded. "I canna linger here. The wench expects me in her room later. And you and I are done, I think, with our reminiscing." He said it harshly. "I dinna like to discuss my injury or my losses. 'Tis why I sit here in this damned tavern night after night—so I willna have to think about such things."

"The hell," Aleck ground out. "What has happened to you? One of Jehanne's most trusted guards, one of her best swordsmen, one of the finest men I ever knew . . . drinking, wenching, and acting as if he doesna give a damn about life. But I know that man cares deeply."

"Ah, her trusted guards. We kept her safe," Lachlann drawled. "She was taken at Compiègne under our very noses."

"The gates were shut so fast, we couldna get to her before the Burgundians took her. None of her guard could help her. 'Twas a trap, and you know it. You were nearly killed defending her. I thought you would die from the injuries you took."

"We all risked our lives trying to keep her safe. For what purpose? She was safely tried, safely imprisoned, safely murdered. Martyred, many say."

"*En nom de Dieu,*" Aleck hissed. Lachlann remembered it as Jehanne's most favored oath. "Do you think you are the only one to suffer grief over what happened?"

"Nay," he said, and emitted a heavy sigh. His friend's words were like a cold rinse. "Nay. I dinna think so. And I realize there was naught else we could have done." He turned the cup in his hand. "Naught."

"Then what grieves you so sore, man?"

Lachlann paused. "Another matter," he finally said. "Something I learned about when I came back to Scotland."

"News from home? The loss of a loved one, perhaps?"

"In a way," Lachlann said carefully. "The loss of . . . the dream that kept me sane while I was in France. Kept me hoping." He shrugged. "No matter. I will survive that, too."

Aleck scowled. "Well, whatever it is, you look awful— worse than when you were injured, somehow. Weary, beaten about the edges, surly as an old wolf in a cage. I have never known you to drink so much, or to talk so bitterly."

Lachlann raised the empty cup and saluted him.

"You will make yourself sick. Your cheeks are bloated, and your face is pale and shadowed. Hell, Lachlann. Town life suits you ill, and too much choler and melancholy will undermine a man's health. You have too strong a fiber to let drink and anger take you down."

Lachlann scratched his whiskered chin. He could not remember the last time he had bought a shave, a bath, a hair trimming. Earlier in the day, he had seen his reflection in the dousing trough in the smithy. He looked like a wild man, his black hair and beard scruffy, his eyelids swollen. That view into the water had startled him. He had questioned himself, just as Aleck questioned him now.

He spread his hands, long, well defined, and sinewy, the fingertips and nails grimed with iron and soot, though he had scrubbed them earlier. Sometimes he felt as if the blackness had seeped through his skin into his soul.

"My advice, as your physician, is to water your ale, disdain beef and suet, and dine on vegetables and fish for a few weeks. And get more sleep, for God's sake. You look . . . haunted."

"I am," Lachlann growled.

"Do you need treatment for the eye, or the wounds and stitchings in your abdomen? You were fevered a long while, and that sort of illness and injury can weaken a man permanently. I can order packets of herbs from an apothecary. A few pinches added to wine every evening will help to heal and strengthen your spirit and your manhood, if you need it."

"I am hearty enough. And Meggott can attest to the quality of my manhood. I am content. Leave me be."

"You give up a chance to start your own weapons forge as you once dreamed, in favor of shoeing horses in a town smithy, drinking alone in taverns, and wenching. That is content?"

Lachlann fixed him with a stare. "Dispense your message, and give me no more advice."

Aleck leaned forward. "I came here to ask you something. The sword, man. Jehanne's sword. Do you still have it?"

"Did you think I would lose it?" Lachlann growled. "She is dead, and her sword, once said to be magical and invincible, is broken. She admitted that at her trial when her judges asked what she had done with the sword Saint Catherine gave her. What does it matter where it is now?"

"Jehanne told them it had broken, but she refused to say where it was, or that she had given it to you. Does anyone else know you have it?"

Lachlann frowned thoughtfully. "After it broke at Lagny, Jehanne asked me to fix it. I told her it could not be done, at least not in the field over a fire, as I had repaired other weapons. She told me to keep it safe. I still have it."

"Her persecutors fear the power of anything associated with her. A man could raise an army of zealots with that sword to stir them up."

Something burst within him like a fireball. He slammed his fist on the table, and the cups wobbled. Aleck did not flinch. "She is gone," Lachlann growled. "They burned her for a heretic, though she was only a brave, foolhardy young girl. Her cause is gone with her! And I am done with fighting."

"I know. I am too."

"Aleck, I dinna even know what to do with the thing," Lachlann snarled. "That sad bit of steel. I canna even repair it well, with my eyesight as it is." He blew out a breath. He wanted a fresh drink, a new topic of conversation. His heart curled within him like a cinder. "Go. Leave me alone."

"I ought to. You have become a foul-tempered beast. But I had to know if you still have the sword. Keep it, just as she wanted you to do. Protect it, for it is all that remains of her. And get away from this place. Take the sword into hiding."

Lachlann slid him a dark glance. "I thank you for your concern, physician, and I will see to the payment for your meal. Luck to you on your journey."

"Shall I wish you luck on a journey, then? I hoped to convince you to go back to Argyll."

"To rebellion and strife?" Lachlann asked curtly. "Surely you heard about the execution of the chiefs, and the forfeitures and outlawing of so many Highland men."

"I heard. There is much talk of it everywhere I go. They say the king will send troops to Loch Fhionn to stamp out the small rebellion there. Do you know the men who are involved in the raids and skirmishes near your own home?"

"I do, if the reports I have heard are correct," Lachlann murmured. He looked into his cup. Still empty. "They say Simon MacArthur, brother to an imprisoned young chief, leads men in the hills above Loch Fhionn. I know both men, and likely I know Simon's rebels. There were MacArthurs with us in France, if you recall, who sailed home before I did."

"More reason for your bitterness, then," Aleck observed shrewdly. "Your friends face real difficulties. If they move beyond local attacks, they invite trouble from the crown."

"The king invited the trouble," Lachlann snapped, "when he executed twenty Highland chiefs at Inverness. I knew one of those men well. He did not deserve that fate."

"The MacArthurs are not the only pocket of rebellion in the Highlands now, as a consequence. We left France's war to return to a Highland war, courtesy of our king." Aleck watched Lachlann. "You may be able to help them if you go back."

"I dinna care to embroil myself in a rebellion." Lachlann drew circles in a spill of ale. "I hear the MacArthur's daughter has married a Campbell. That alliance will help them better than anything I could do. There is no point in my returning."

"You must protect Jehanne's sword, and you must think of your own well-being. A remote location is best for both matters. Start up your forge, as you always meant to do—

and warn your friends. Tell them the king intends to destroy
them if they continue their small rebellion."

Lachlann pushed his fingers through his hair, thinking. "I
suppose I could tell them what I have heard."

"More than that, you could go to the king and offer to
take a message to the rebels. You know the men and the
area."

Lachlann narrowed his eyes, studying the empty cup. He
felt a new stirring of purpose. In the past year he had lost
part of his vision, most of his hope, all of his dreams. For too
long he had felt flat, as dark and cold as the iron he worked.

At last he had a reason to return home, to his forge, to the
place where he had grown to manhood. And he had a dou-
ble quest now, if he wanted it: to hide and protect Jehanne's
sword and to bring warning, perhaps even help, to the
MacArthurs.

But he would have to see Eva again, and he would feel
obligated to pursue vengeance against her Campbell husband.

Poor vision had ruined his ability to repair Jehanne's
sword, and three grim years of war had made his need for revenge, once so hot, grow cool. But his feelings for Eva still
simmered. He had tried to stop loving her, but he could no
more do that than cease to breathe. He sat silently, brooding
in his thoughts, while Aleck waited.

Finally Aleck stood. "Well, you are a stubborn sod, so do
what you will. I have said what I had to say, and I must go.
A ship departs for Aberdeen at dawn tomorrow, and I have
passage on it." He tossed a silver coin on the table.

"Wait," Lachlann said. Aleck turned. The dark swirl of
his cloak made the sparks fly again in Lachlann's field of
sight. "I will walk out with you. I, too, am going home." He
turned his cup upside down on the table, a final gesture of
his decision. "In the morning I will apply to the king for an
audience." He rose to his feet.

Meggott came toward them and took Aleck's coin, dropping it down her bodice. She nestled up to Lachlann as he reached for his own cloak, but he eased her firmly away.

She pouted. "Where are you going?"

He touched her cheek, did his best to smile. "Home. I wish you well." He kissed her like a fond brother. She stared at him, then nodded slowly.

"I knew it would come. You carry your home like a fire in your heart, and so you were bound to go back. Luck to you, then." She turned away with a stiff smile.

He watched her, struck by the truth in her words. Home was indeed a fire in his heart—and home was Eva, for good or ill.

He had to return, no matter what would come of it.

He stepped out into the cold snap of the evening.

Chapter 5

Mist swirled over the water, and the dawn quiet seemed like a blessing. As Eva waited for Alpin on the lochside beach below the smithy property, she shivered in the early chill. Wrapping her arms around herself, she remembered, as she too often did, Lachlann's warm, strong embrace. That long-ago night seemed like a cherished dream that would never come true.

Through the fog, she could see the isle of Innisfarna, with its grove of trees and its massive castle at opposite ends. She had not set foot inside Innisfarna Castle for a long while, and she missed her home so much that it hurt.

Through Mairi MacKerron's generous hospitality, Eva lived in the smith's house now. At night she slept in Lachlann's own bed, curled on his heather-stuffed mattress. Her dreams—poignant sequences of yearning, passion, and gentleness—were filled with him.

Although Eva had cooperated with the garrison that had taken over the castle, remaining in her own home had proved difficult. Acting as chatelaine, she had supervised new and unfamiliar servants to oversee the demands of a huge household, while struggling with her dislike of the situation.

Late one night, after soldiers had knocked and pleaded and snickered at her bedchamber door—not for the first time, despite the garrison leader's sincere attempt to keep her safe—she had packed her belongings, tucked Grainne into a basket, and asked Alpin to take her over the water to seek sanctuary with Mairi MacKerron.

Now her visits to the island were clandestine. Often she met Alpin before dawn; concerned for her safety, he had offered to teach her how to defend herself, and a few instructions had developed into regular lessons in swordplay. Eva looked forward lately to the practice sessions, welcoming the challenges and finding enjoyment and relief from tedium and frustration.

Most mornings, soldiers crossed the loch in two or three boats to tend the horses in the stable and to ride out on patrols to look for rebels—including her brother Simon and their kinsmen. Only Eva and Alpin knew where the MacArthur rebels hid in the hills above the loch, and both of them had been sworn to secrecy.

Hearing the splash of oars, she soon saw the boat glide through the fog. Alpin stilled the craft on the beach so that Eva could climb inside, and then he rowed back toward the island.

"Today," Alpin murmured, "we will work on high strokes. Stay down until we reach the far side of the island so that you will not be seen." Complying, she drew her plaid over her dark, braided hair. For the swording lessons, she usually wore an old belted plaid and shirt borrowed from Mairi's storage chest; she enjoyed the freedom, comfort, and disguise offered by the male garments.

Rounding the island, Alpin drew the boat into a cove fringed by alder and pine trees. Eva leaped out while Alpin secured the rope, and both walked into the cover of the trees. When he handed her a wooden practice sword, taking one into his own hands, she adopted a ready stance and waited for the first strike. She countered it with confidence, earning his murmured praise.

Their practice was demanding as usual, leaving her

breathing hard and wiping her misted brow. Soon the sun crested the hills and began to burn off the fog, and she knew the soldiers would venture out of the castle, as was their established habit. Eva followed Alpin to his little house on the banks of the loch below the castle to accept a cup of cool, watered ale and some breakfast.

"I cannot stay long today," she told him. "Margaret and her husband, Angus, have a new child, and I promised to help them this week. Their little girl just turned two, and she does not much like her new brother." She smiled.

He nodded. "I will take you over the water," he said. "But first I want to talk to you. Come into the garden." He opened the door.

Eva walked with him around the house, where rose-bushes grew on the grassy shore that sloped toward the loch. She moved toward the lush, lovely tangle of vines and blooms, inhaling the soft fragrances.

The rose garden had belonged to Alpin's wife, who had died a few years earlier. Alpin claimed he had no time to dig up the rosebushes to plant onions and carrots, as he said ought to be done; he complained that he was too busy ferrying soldiers across the loch and could not learn flower gardening.

Yet the roses grew profusely, and Eva suspected Alpin encouraged them. She loved the haven provided by the rose garden, with its graceful shapes, heavenly fragrance, and delicate hues reflected in the calm loch.

"Look at this one," Alpin said, pulling a fat rose toward her. "It opened yesterday."

The large, soft flower filled her palm, colored pale salmon pink. "Alpin, it is beautiful! I have never seen a rose like it! And so late in the season—will there be more like it?" She leaned forward to sniff it.

"How do I know? They grow, and I cut them back, and they grow some more. They are a nuisance." But his gaze when he looked around him was serene.

She smiled. "What did you want to tell me?"

"I heard the soldiers say that Green Colin will soon return from France. They say he intends to petition the king for full ownership of this island. Eva, we must prevent him from taking Innisfarna—even if we cannot prevent him from marrying you."

She felt her heart tumble with dread, and she inhaled the scent of the flower again, as if its sweetness were a remedy. "We are legally betrothed, and that is near as binding as a marriage. I refuse to give up the island, and I told Colin so before he left. If I must appeal to the king myself to retain it, I will. My claim is a hereditary right, with no tie to the MacArthurs. I hope the king will respect such an ancient tradition."

"Not everyone is as honorable as you are, Eva, and we already know how dishonorable our king can be. This isle must remain in your keeping, or there may be dire consequences for all of Scotland, according to the legend. Now that you are no longer living on the isle yourself, your claim is weakened."

She frowned. "I am doing what I think best. Colin sent me a letter last year saying that he had requested the return of my clan's rights and my brother's pardon. He is keeping his promise to me. The pardon may even be accomplished by now." She tried to smile. "We will find out soon."

"Bah. Green Colin serves himself, not you and your clan! You have heard little from him in all this time. Both Simon and I want you to break that betrothal and let the rebels take their chances. Do not sacrifice your happiness."

She shook her head. "I gave my promise in exchange for his help," she murmured. "I will honor it." She had never told anyone about Colin's threat to have Donal killed and Simon hunted down if she did not go through with the marriage. Aware of the risks that her marriage might hold, she still hoped to keep her kinsmen safe. She did not look at Alpin as she fingered the rose petals.

"Tcha," he said. "Stubborn girl. You do not want this. Where is the bold Eva I once knew, eh? What does she want?"

"I want what is best for my clan, and Innisfarna. What more could I want?" Once there had been more, but now her true desires emerged only in dreams, where she shared her misty, lovely island home with a dark-haired man who ruled fire and made iron yield to his will, and whose deep, tender embraces made her yearn for far more than dreams. She sighed.

"There is something you can do," Alpin said. "You were named for the valiant and beautiful Aeife, who defended this island long ago. Do what she did. Fight for Innisfarna. I have been training you for it," he added, giving her an odd glance.

Eva stared at him. "Fight? You taught me how to use a weapon to defend myself, but I am no warrior!"

"Listen to me." He pointed to the loch. "The Sword of Light lies in those waters, guarding the doorway to the faery world. Only you and I truly understand its importance. This isle must never leave the safekeeping of Aeife's female line. Look what has happened since the peace of this place was disturbed. Garrisoning, forfeiture—and the loss of twenty Highland chiefs, including your father."

"Alpin, that is not the legend come to bear!"

"Is it not? Legends are powerful mysteries. If Innisfarna is threatened, the Sword of Light is not safe, and neither is Scotland. You must fight, as Aeife did," he urged. "I saw this coming, and so I have prepared you."

She stared at him. "Why did you not tell me this earlier?"

"You would have refused. For all your boldness, you never liked to fight with the boys, nor did you like to hear about that part of your island's legend. But now that you have the skills, we will find the warrior in you," he confided, grinning.

"Alpin, it is just a tale! You cannot expect me—"

"What are legends but pure truths? This one teaches courage and righteousness. We must heed it, or lose all."

"I cannot go against a garrison. I have no army, no weapons—and no desire to fight!"

"Look at this." Alpin pulled the fat pink bloom forward again. "Tell me the secret of the rose."

"The secret?" She frowned, confused.

"It is beautiful. Take it. Go on."

She reached out, wincing as the thorns stung her thumb. She let go, sucking on the wound, watching Alpin.

He nodded. "The rose defends itself, and you will do the same. You are a strong and nimble girl, with a bold heart. Put that to use. You have much potential, and some skill already. And of course you have an excellent tutor." He winked.

She stared at him. "You sly old warrior."

"I am that, Aeife," he said, using the old, breathy pronunciation of her name: *Eh-fah.*

She regarded him thoughtfully, remembering the stories she had heard of his prowess as a warrior before her birth, before he had become their ferryman. He had instructed her brothers and other boys, including Lachlann, in swordplay, and now she understood the extent of his willingness to teach her. "I will not act out this legend for you," she said firmly.

"We will discuss this later," he said. He plucked two fat pink roses from another bush as he spoke. The thorns did not seem to bother him. "For now, you have enough to think about. Here, take these to Mairi MacKerron. She will like them, even if they come from the old ferryman."

He led her the short way to his boat, and Eva sat clutching the flowers while he rowed her across the dawn-bright water. Her thoughts tumbled and sparked, but she stayed silent, finally stepping out of the boat onto the white beach.

"We will continue to practice on Innisfarna's soil," Alpin told her. "The isle gives you strength and will. Come to the loch at dawn tomorrow, and I will show you how to use a longsword. It is time you fought with steel, not wood."

She regarded him in silence, unsure of her feelings.

"Girl," Alpin said, "you do not feel the urge to fight now, but you will. When Colin tries to take your isle, it will spark in you like fire. I know you, Aeife. You will not hold back your courage when that day comes. You will do what must be done. And I intend to prepare you for it." He pulled at the oars and moved out into the loch.

As she walked up the long bank toward the smith's house, she knew that Alpin was right. She must defend Innisfarna somehow, and so it was fitting that she learn to be a warrior like the valiant and proud Aeife. Though she lacked faery magic and a warrior's heart, someday she might have to fulfill a legend.

And she must find some way to see it through.

Chapter 6

The night sky sparkled under a full moon, and a crisp, cool wind lifted his cloak as he rode home. Through the trees, he saw the glittering dark surface of a loch and recognized the surroundings: Loch Fhionn, at last.

He guided his sturdy garron along a well-worn, well-remembered path. The animal, purchased in Perth, was a capable horse for the westward journey into Argyll. After a full day's ride, Lachlann was deeply tired, but glad to be out in the hills again, after months of living in town.

He had spent the past week pacing in the king's castle, waiting for a royal audience and the official message that he was to carry to the MacArthurs. Bearing the king's letter and forewarned of possible danger in the area from rebels, he wore his steel cuirass—breastplate and backpiece—and carried weapons ready for use. He watched the hills and forest carefully as he rode.

Following the loch's banks, he headed toward the tiny village of Balnagovan, which consisted of a hillside chapel and a few farms. The lands here had been inhabited by MacArthurs, but the clan's proscription would have evicted and exiled most, if not all, of them. He was not surprised to see deserted homes with boarded windows and empty byres.

Further down the length of the loch, he could see the familiar shape of Innisfarna, isle and stout castle rising upward, dark against dark. Light twinkled in the windows, and he wondered if Eva was there now, with her Campbell husband. His heart seemed to turn at the thought.

Soon he approached the smith's house and the smithy. His property was called Balnagovan as well—"village of the smith" in Gaelic. The smithy itself, with its nearby stable, perched on a hill above the loch. Across a wide meadow was the house. Home at last, Lachlann thought with enormous relief, and nudged the horse forward.

The drystone building, long and low with a thatched roof, presented two shuttered windows flanking a stout oak door. A stone-and-wattle byre protruded at the back beside a privy and a large garden. Though all was dark, pale smoke drifted from the central chimney. Lachlann heard a hound begin to bark inside the house.

Solas, he thought, smiling. His foster mother, Mairi MacKerron—Muime, as he always thought of her—would no doubt be awakened by the alarm, and alert to a stranger's arrival.

Dismounting, he tethered his horse, who whickered softly. Faint snorts answered from the stable across the meadow. The horses kept there must belong to those inhabiting Innisfarna. Sooner or later, then, he would see Eva— and her Campbell husband. His gut constricted at the thought.

The barking grew louder, joined by the yapping of a smaller dog. Muime must have acquired another mutt in his absence, Lachlann thought. He knocked on the door and called out.

Both dogs erupted in a frenzy, and a woman's voice, barely audible over the noise, hushed them.

"Mairi MacKerron," he said, "I am home!" He raised his voice, hoping she could hear what he said over the barking.

"Go away," came a muffled reply.

"I am come home," he said. "Let me in." He grabbed the iron latch and pulled, expecting it to open easily.

It stuck. He tugged. The iron must have rusted, lacking a smith to keep it oiled. In the moonlight, he noticed new rivets, marking additional locks on the inside of the door; the door was bolted and barred, though it never had been before.

"Go away," the woman said again.

Puzzled, he knocked again. "Who is that?"

He heard a heavy thump and a creak, as if a dog leaped against the door. Anguished yowls nearly drowned his voice. "Woman, open this door!" He had to shout to be heard.

"Go away, you! Solas, get down! Grainne, you too! Leave us be, sir—the dogs are in a temper! And I have a blade, and I know how to use it!"

"Blade! Jesu," he muttered. "I live here," he yelled, placing his mouth near a seam in the oak planks, raising his voice to a boom. "Open the door! It is Lachlann!"

A pause followed, as if both woman and dogs were stunned into silence. "Lachlann MacKerron?" Now he heard her clearly: a young woman, her voice mellow as honey, blessedly familiar.

His heart slammed, and he leaned hands and brow against the door in both gratitude and dread. "Eva?" he asked. "Eva MacArthur?"

Eva flattened her palms against the door, heart pounding. "Lachlann!"

"Eva, let me in." The deep timbre of his voice, not heard in more than three years, sent thrills along her spine.

Solas leaped at the door. Grainne leaped too, yapping furiously, rising on her hind legs. Eva pushed Grainne out of the way as she fumbled at the locks.

"*Ach Dhia,* Solas, you knew!" Eva murmured. "You knew Lachlann was at the door, when I thought the man was another soldier from Innisfarna, come drunk in the middle of the night!"

She slid free the wooden beam from the iron bars that held it, and pulled at the other fastening, an iron hasp and chain. The eye of the little bar fitted over a protruding iron staple, now jammed together. She tugged but could not loosen them.

Lachlann knocked again. "Eva!"

"The latch is stuck," she answered, pulling futilely. "It sometimes does this." Solas set up a heartbreaking howl, as did Grainne. "Oh, hush, Grainne. You too, Solas," Eva said, distracted by her struggle with the latch. Pulling on the center ring handle, she opened the door as wide as she could—a few inches at most—and peered out.

Moonlight haloed Lachlann's head and shoulders and glinted on the shoulders of his polished steel cuirass. His face was shadowed, and he seemed even taller and larger than she remembered. She gaped up at him.

"The bar may be rusted," he said. "Where did these bolts come from? Finlay and I never put them on this door."

"The blacksmith from Glen Brae installed them." She yanked again to free the snug bite of the metal, but failed. Lachlann stood so close she could scarcely think. "How is it you are here?" she asked, flustered.

"I live here," he answered. "Why are you here? And where is Mairi?" Solas poked her nose through the door crack, and Lachlann reached down to pat her head. "Ho, Solas, silly girl. It is good to see you again, too," he murmured.

Eva gasped in frustration. "It will not come loose!"

"Let me." Lachlann slipped his hand upward to find the iron fittings. His fingers touched hers, a warm, delicious shock of contact, and flexed, strong and swift, on the hasp. Eva pulled the door open, and Lachlann ducked his head under the lintel to enter the house.

In the ruby glow of the peat fire, he loomed beside her like a faery king, all gleam and shadow, vibrant, sultry, compelling. Stunned by his arrival, she was further astonished by his wild, dark, hard beauty, which seemed more intense than she remembered. He emanated a simmering masculinity that dreams and memories could never match.

Summoning her wits, she fetched a candle from a shelf and lit it from the peat embers. Shielding the golden halo, she turned. He was still there, and this was no dream.

Solas leaped at him, and he laughed, rubbing her shoulders with affection. Then he took her head in his hands to speak softly to her. Grainne watched, head cocked, tail wagging.

Eva smiled. "Solas remembers you well."

"She does." He glanced up. "Do you?"

She faltered, shrugged. "I do," she murmured. "Welcome home." She said it calmly, as if her heart did not race, as if her knees and hands did not quiver.

He leaned down to pet the terrier. "I see Mairi found herself another dog. Who is this little one?"

"She is mine. I call her Grainne."

"*Cràineag*, more like," he said wryly.

"She does not look like a hedgehog!" Eva said indignantly.

"Small and round and brownish gray, with fur standing out like spikes—she surely does. Ho, little *cràineag*," he said. Grainne licked his hand liberally.

"Grainne," Eva said, enunciating the name: Grahn-ya. "Colin gave her to me."

Lachlann's smile disappeared. He turned, looking around the house. Strolling toward the fireplace, he peered into the tiny room tucked behind the stone wall of the hearth, the private bedchamber that Mairi used as wife and widow. Solas and Grainne trotted with him.

"Where is Mairi?" he asked, as he turned and strolled to the other end of the house. The far wall contained his bed, snug in a niche cut into the thick stone. The curtain was pulled back, exposing the bedclothes, draped askew.

"Were you sleeping there?" he asked.

"I was." Standing barefoot, she folded her arms over her chest, aware that she wore only a thin linen chemise. Her hair, long and loose, hung over her breasts. "Mairi is staying with her niece Katrine and her family in Glen Brae."

"I expected to find her sister living here." Lachlann fixed her with a steady, grim look. He seemed shadowed and weary suddenly, his beard recently shaven, his hair untrimmed, his eyelids drooping. But his eyes sparked with the vibrant blue that she remembered well.

"Her sister was here for several months," she told him. "Recently Mairi went to Glen Brae to help her niece, who had a difficult confinement. She will be gone a while, for the niece was delivered of a daughter and has three young ones already. Lachlann, please sit. Let me fetch you some food."

He frowned. "I will go to Glen Brae. Did Muime get the message I sent?"

"We had no word. Mairi traveled northward to see her other niece, whose children had a coughing sickness. Alpin will know when she returns, for he often goes to that side of the loch."

He looked at her thoughtfully. "Why are you here tonight? Did Alpin refuse to ferry you across the loch?"

"He ferries me whenever I like. I live here now."

He shoved a hand through his hair. "I do not understand."

"Explanations can wait until you have eaten and rested."

"First I must tend to my mount." He turned to the door.

"Let me show you to the stable—"

"I know the way to my own stable," he replied brusquely. He skimmed his gaze down her body. "Besides, you are not dressed, and the wind is cold tonight."

She blushed. "Turn away, then." He did, walking over to the door to examine the locks, his back toward her. She went to the curtained bed and snatched up her brown serge gown from a peg on the wall. Tugging it over her chemise, she left the side lacings undone and turned back to the room, and Lachlann, again.

He manipulated the locks, his hands strong and confident. The last time she had seen him, she had shared deep kisses with him, and she had made a bold advance that he had sensibly refused. Since then, dreams of him had brought her yearning and delight. Cheeks blazing, she wondered what, if anything, he recalled about her.

"Rusted and ill made," he pronounced, jiggling the hasp. "Locks, bars, windows fitted with iron—" He gestured toward the shutters. "This place is like a fortress."

"Life is not so peaceful at Balnagovan as it once was."

His frown lingered. "I hear the MacArthurs are rebelling."

"It is not MacArthurs who bother me."

"Do your kinsmen hide here, and defend from here? Is that the reason for the barricading? Where are Simon and the rest?"

"I cannot answer those questions," she said, instantly wary.

"Why not? I have been a friend to them all my life."

"But you return an armored knight, no doubt with weapons. That speaks of a king's man intent on finding outlaws, not a smith returning home to work. My kinsmen and I have learned caution in the years you have been gone."

"So I see." He narrowed his eyes.

Aware that her words still stung the air, she sighed. "I am sorry. You deserve a better welcome than that."

"*Ach,* a fine homecoming," he drawled. "Hearthfire and cozy home, and a lovely woman with a willful tongue. Some men might be content with that."

"Not you," she said crisply.

He grinned, wry and apologetic. "It is good to speak the Gaelic again, after years of French and English. You look fine, Eva." His gaze slipped down her body as if he saw all of her, clothed and naked, down to sin and soul. "More . . . womanly." He cocked a brow, and she felt a blush rise into her cheeks.

"You look older. Tired," she ventured.

"I rode a long way since this morning."

"Not that." She tilted her head. "You are more mature, and stronger. There is . . . a weariness of spirit in you, some-how."

She did not say the rest of her thoughts—that he looked powerful but somber, as if some darkness in his soul shad-owed him and made him simmer. A new scar cut through the black bearding of his jaw, and smudgy circles and fine lines wreathed his eyes. The sky blue clarity of his eyes had grown hard and piercing.

She wanted to ask what troubled him, and how three years and more had changed him so much. She wanted to know what brought him here in the middle of the night. But she held her silence.

And she knew that he would not have answered had she asked, for the look in his eyes shuttered his thoughts and his past.

Chapter 7

When Lachlann opened the door and waited for Eva to pass through, she grabbed up her plaid shawl and went outside with him. Solas bounded out and away, disappearing like a wraith, while Grainne stayed in the house. Lachlann walked the garron over the meadow to the stable, Eva strolling beside him.

"How is it you came home so sudden in the night? Are you well? Your face is scarred—you were wounded in the war."

"I am fine, Eva," he murmured.

"Are you a knight now?"

"I am."

"When did you leave France?"

"A few months ago."

Despite his terseness, she plunged onward. "A knight and a landholder? How did you fare in France? Have you been in Scotland long?" She knew she chattered, and could not help it. Still stunned by his arrival, she suddenly craved the reassurance of their old friendship, if it could be reclaimed.

"Ho," he said, half laughing. "I was never as fast at answering your questions as you were at asking them. I am well enough. I came back alive." He walked beside her without looking her way. "I am a knight, but not a landholder yet. France was . . . a harsh place. I returned to Scotland last summer and stayed in Perth."

"My cousins Parlan and William came back last winter, and told me about their sojourn in France. They said the war was difficult for everyone—French, Scots, English."

"It was. Why are you here instead of Innisfarna? And where is . . ." He paused. "Where is your husband?"

She halted in the stable yard. "I cannot stay at Innisfarna just now. And Colin is not my husband—yet," she said bluntly. "We . . . we are betrothed now. He has been in France also."

"Ah," he murmured, looking away from her. "When is the wedding?"

She hesitated, wishing she did not have to answer, but he turned to look at her. "Whenever he returns to Argyll."

"Ah," he said again, nodding slowly.

"Colin is an ambassador to France. Did you see him there? My cousins said you were a guard in the French court."

"I never saw him, but there are thousands of Scots in France these days. I was at court only a short while. After that I rode with . . . a special company. If you are not at Innisfarna, who is? There are horses in the stable," he remarked abruptly. "Whose are they?"

"The king installed a garrison there, and I refuse to stay at the castle, one woman among so many men. The soldiers came here just before my father—" Her voice wavered.

"I heard." His voice gentled. "I am sorry, Eva."

She drew a shaky breath. "There is food and water stored in the stable. Bring your horse this way."

He led the garron inside and Eva followed. While he found an empty stall, she went down the aisle and lifted one of the large buckets of water placed there. Lachlann came toward her.

"Let me take that," he said. "It is heavy for you."

"It is no trouble," she said, but he took the bucket. "I am accustomed to hard work. Since I have been here, I have been not only fetching water but hoeing the garden, tending livestock, cooking and brewing, weaving baskets and mats, even cutting peat."

He carried the bucket into the stall and emptied it into a low trough for the horse to drink. "I expected to find you the spoiled wife of a wealthy man, not doing the work of a farmer's wife."

She bristled. "Spoiled? You know me better than that!"

"Do I?" he murmured. His gaze met hers, held it. Then he turned away to remove the horse's saddle.

Her cheeks heated again. "I will go back to the house and prepare you something to eat," she said stiffly. "Tomorrow I will find another place to stay."

He set the saddle down. "Why would you do that?"

"We can hardly stay here together!"

"I will not toss you out. It is your house, after all." He began to brush the horse's back. "I will sleep in the smithy after I clean it up tomorrow. And I may not stay at Balnagovan for long."

Disappointment plummeted through her. Hoping to hear more of his plans, she waited, but he silently tended to the horse. She studied his gleaming armor, the good leather harnesses for the horse, the carved and padded wooden saddle, the scabbarded sword and other weapons.

"That is fine gear for a Highlander," she said. "My cousins said you did well in France. They said you rode with the Maid who tried to save her country. We heard of her even here," she added, letting her curiosity show, hoping to learn more.

"I rode as one of her Scots guard. There were seven of us assigned to watch her back."

"Did you earn accolades and rewards for your deeds there?"

He slid her a glare and said nothing, bending to lift one of the horse's back feet to examine the hoof. His hands were knowing, his voice quiet as he murmured to the animal. Eva watched, her thoughts tumbling, but one question burned within her.

"Do you have a wife?" Her heart thumped hard.

"I do not." He did not look up.

His reticence frustrated her. "Why did you come back here so sudden and covert, armed like a king's man?"

He straightened. "You were ever a curious girl, with a nimble tongue for talking. I see it has not changed much."

"Not much," she said testily. "And you were ever given to secrets. I see that has not changed either."

"No secrets worth digging out. I simply came home."

"I think you intend to do more than smithing." She folded her arms expectantly.

"I have a letter for Simon," he said as he settled a blanket over the horse's back. "From the king himself."

She gasped. "Did you come to arrest him? You will not find him easily."

"I am a messenger," he murmured. "Only that." He glanced up. "Eva, it is late. Tomorrow you can tell me where to find your brother. For now, all I want is a bed. Just for tonight, I would like to sleep in the house."

Her heart bounded again, but she looked at him calmly. "Mairi's bed will do for you."

"Of course," he said. "Did you think I meant with you?"

She sucked in a breath sharply. Yearning, loneliness, disappointment swamped her. He was not the tender, loving man who haunted her dreams; he was cool, snappish, reserved, nearly a stranger. She had no reason to expect anything different from him, after so long.

She whirled and fled the stable.

Lachlann greeted the eager, panting dogs on his return to the house, and glanced at Eva, who was stirring the kettle over the hearth. Her cheeks were bright. He wondered if that was the fire, or if his arrival had set her world askew. Perhaps only his own world seemed tilted awry.

He began to divest his cuirass, unbuckling the leather straps at his waist, reaching up to unfasten the straps at his shoulders. Eva came toward him.

"Let me help," she said. Accepting wordlessly, he leaned down. Her hand brushed his neck, and her breath swept his cheek. When the back and breast pieces were separated, he laid them aside and unlaced his quilted jacket, joined to mail sleeves and collar. Eva lifted the heavy garment and laid it on a stool.

Lachlann stood shirtless in trews of dark wool, and the worn boots that had taken him every step of the way through France and home again. He felt the gentle slide of Eva's gaze as she studied his chest and abdomen, thickly dusted with black hair, and his shoulder and sides, creased with new scars.

"Oh, Lachlann," she murmured in sympathy. She touched the long pink crescent that marred his left side, above the drawstring waist of his trews. The memory of that injury—taken when Jehanne had been captured at Compiègne—was more raw than the healed cut itself. Her fingers conveyed compassion, and his heart turned within him. "This was a serious wound," she said.

"It was nothing," he said tersely. "Done with."

She handed him a shirt and a folded plaid, which he recognized as his own. He had not dressed like a Highland man since leaving for France. He pulled the shirt over his head, and Eva straightened the shoulders for him.

"You are a fine page," he said. "The shirt will do for now. I will wear the plaid tomorrow." He went to the table and sat. Eva set a bowl of steaming porridge before him and poured ale into a wooden cup. How strange and ironic, he thought, that Eva instead of his foster mother filled the familiar old cup for him.

He tasted the oats. "Excellent. Hot, salty, and sweet, and nicely thick. You have learned to cook." He smiled at her.

"I always could," she said stiffly. "You just never knew."

"I was teasing. It is good to eat Highland oats again. They cannot be had in France, and even in Perth they are not as good as in the Highlands. I am grateful for the meal, and I apologize for dragging you from your bed in the dark of night."

She blushed, a rosy glow. His tone had been too intimate, he thought. He wanted to stay reserved and distant, but talking with her felt natural, as satisfying as water for thirst. He had known her nearly all his life—had seen her take her first toddling steps, while he and her brothers cheered—and he was deeply glad to see her again.

And he knew for certain now that he had never stopped loving her, though he had tried. Scowling a little, he turned back to his meal, but kept glancing at her while she attended some chore at the hearth.

She had always been a lovely creature: whimsical, graceful, yet tough too. Time had clarified her into a beauty, though more somber than he remembered. Her mouth and small nose were still mischievous, her lips more sensual. The stubborn line of her jaw echoed her straight, dark brows, above winsome gray-green eyes. Alluring but innocent, he thought, a face that made a man want to look again, want to remember, want to linger.

She smiled, quick and shy. He looked away.

A moment later, he tasted the drink tentatively, unwilling to risk an ale haze. But it was the stuff he had tasted all his life, which had never made him drunk. "Fine ale," he approved. "Light and a little sweet. Did you brew it yourself?"

"I did. Mairi taught me. Is it sweeter than you like?" She sat across from him.

"It is good. French ale is strong and lusty and bitter, and the stuff in Perth is so strong that one full goblet can strip a man's stomach and spin his head. Nothing as delicate as this."

"It is the heather. Mairi showed me how to gather the best heather bells to add to the barley malt, with some honey."

He nodded, finished the oats, and glanced around the house. The stone walls needed a coat of limewash, and the earthen floor was covered with woven reed mats, newly made. The thatch roof smelled clean and grassy, as if it had been freshened recently. Rafters of smoke-darkened wood were hung with cooking utensils and storage baskets. Many of the baskets looked new as well.

At one end of the room, the stone hearth, which served as a partition and had always been his foster mother's pride, was swept clean. The glowing peats gave off a sweetish, musty odor, and smoke tunneled efficiently into a good drawing chimney. He and Finlay had built the fireplace together years ago, replacing the earlier hearth, a circle of stones.

He glanced at the familiar furnishings and looked again at the snug bed in the far wall, made cozy with a fur robe. His mind conjured Eva sleeping there. He glanced away. "You keep the house well," he said. "It is just as I remember it."

She shrugged. "Better to be busy than lonely."

"Lonely?" He narrowed his eyes.

"It is so quiet here now. I take care of the house and the animals, and I see Alpin often, though I do not go to the castle anymore. Sometimes I see Simon, or Mairi, or the priest—Father Alasdair is at the chapel only a day or two a month now; he serves four parishes since ours is so small. I see Margaret too, though her children keep her busy. There was always so much to do here . . . before so much changed."

"Lives change, Eva," he murmured. "We have changed. Tell me about Margaret. She is married?"

"She married Angus Lamont, the carpenter. They have two little ones now."

He smiled. "I am glad for all of them."

"You will see them soon, no doubt. They live not far from here. Otherwise, there are few left in this glen. Many MacArthurs settled here when my father married my mother, but they are gone now—thanks to the king." Her voice caught.

He felt a swift pull like a taut thread between them, and he wanted to comfort her. But she stood and turned toward the fire. "I heard what happened, and I am sorry, Eva. Iain MacArthur deserved better."

She nodded. "I was sad, and angry at first. Now I think I am resigned to it." In profile he could see that her eyes were glossy with tears, but her chin was set stubbornly.

He approached her. "I lost Finlay not long before I left here. Grief has an edge that dulls with time," he said quietly.

"My father's death was unjust, and my kinsmen have suffered, too. The edge of my grief is very sharp."

"Eva, I am sorry I was not here for you . . . for all of you."

She sucked in a breath. "My brother Donal is still imprisoned. Our only hope now is that Colin will secure his release and the clan's pardon. Colin promised he would try."

Her anticipation of her betrothed's help felt like a dousing of icy water. Lachlann reminded himself that Eva did not need him—nor did he need her. "I am sure all of this will sort itself out in time. I wish you well of it," he said.

She nodded. "I . . . we thought you were dead," she said abruptly. "My cousins said you rode with the French girl who led the army over there, but they did not know what became of you when she was captured and tried. She was burned, we heard. Yet another horrible and unjust death."

Concern and compassion softened her gaze, but he looked away. He did not want to discuss that part of his life. "I would have sent word again had I known you and Muime thought me dead."

"I wanted to send word to you, but did not know how. I

wanted to tell you about my . . . father—" She gasped suddenly, and covered her mouth to suppress a sob.

He touched her shoulder. "I am sorry," he whispered, bowing his head toward hers, aware that her hair smelled like heather flowers. He felt swamped by the urge to hold her. Even more, he wanted to kiss her, though that was not in keeping with the moment or with her grief.

She sighed, looked up at him. "I am glad you came back safely, Lachlann. And I still remember our . . . leavetaking."

He had not forgotten either, and he already struggled against the natural allure she held for him. He shook his head and smiled a little, as if in dismissal.

"Do you mean Beltane night?" he asked. "We were younger then. Though I certainly was old enough to know better." He tried to make light of it, though he disliked doing so, with her gaze so wide and trusting upon him. "And here you are about to be wed. Best forgotten, my friend. It is late, and I am tired. Good night to you."

Brusque and harsh, he knew, but he did not want her to fear being alone with him. He feared that enough himself.

She stared up at him, and the glimmer in her eyes confirmed that he had hurt her. Grief and strain had made her more vulnerable, though she was still the bold girl he remembered. Turning, she crossed the room, climbed into the bed niche, and yanked the curtains shut.

Perturbed with himself, he went into Mairi's little chamber and kicked off his boots. He fell into the springy comfort of the heather-filled mattress, which released its faint, sweet scent. Sleep came swiftly, despite his awareness that Eva lay not far away, in his own bed.

Tomorrow, he thought, as he succumbed, he would move his belongings into the smithy.

Chapter 8

Before dawn, Eva woke, blurred with sleep and still wrapped in the wonder of a dream in which she had lingered in Lachlann's arms. She sat up, skimming a hand through her tousled hair, and remembered that he was home at last, and here in the house. Blushing at her dream, she slipped out of bed and dressed quickly in the shirt, woolen trews, and plaid that she wore for sword practice. She tiptoed past the sleeping dogs, who did not stir beyond the flip of a tail; they were used to her early risings.

She peered around the partition of the fireplace to see Lachlann through the shadows. He slept deeply, his faint snores and his long, solid form beneath the coverlet somehow reassuring. She gazed at him for a long moment, then turned in haste, realizing that Alpin would be waiting.

Tucking an oatcake into her bundle, she left extra cakes for Lachlann, covered and placed where the dogs could not get them. Then she opened the door quietly, struggling a little with the hasp bar, and stepped out into the cool, crisp air.

Scattering feed to the chickens and the goats, she took a few minutes to milk the cow, and then led the animal to the meadow; her chores must be tended to now, for she would be out most of the day. After meeting Alpin, she intended to walk up into the hills and find Simon to tell him about the smith's return.

She ran down the long bank to the loch, and found Alpin

already waiting. In silence, she climbed into the boat and drew part of the plaid up to hide her head and shoulders. Although she was bursting inside with her news, she waited while he had rowed them to the hidden side of the island and walked with her into the shelter of the trees before she spoke quietly.

"Last night Lachlann MacKerron arrived at Balnagovan."

"The smith's lad?" Alpin grinned. "So he survived the French war. Good! We need a skilled smith here once again." He stood beside her, not much taller than she but solid as oak, his white hair somewhat wild, his blue eyes vivid, creased with age and sun, and narrowed in curiosity.

"He intends to stay for a short while only. He offered to live in the smithy so I could stay in the house."

"Ah. That one always cared about you." He winked at her.

"He tolerated me, that is all. He is a knight and a king's man now."

"I want to hear about his adventures in France. Your cousins said he rode with that remarkable peasant girl. Sent by God, they say she was. The French called her a savior—and the English called her a witch and burned her. A pity," he muttered, shaking his head. "From what I have heard, she was surely a bold girl with a good heart, to sacrifice so much for her people."

Eva sighed, nodding. She looked at the castle, watchful for activity. The dawn sky brightened, and she could not stay long.

"Lachlann will have stories to tell!" Alpin went on.

"He seems reluctant to talk about France, or much else. I am not certain why he came back. I think he hides something."

"That lad always kept to himself. But he is a good smith, and we need one. And Mairi MacKerron will be pleased."

"He wants to see her when she returns from Glen Brae."

"Tell him I will take him over the loch as soon as Mairi MacKerron is back." He paused, peering into the trees. Eva heard a rustling sound, and a thump or two, and she looked around. For a moment she was sure she saw a flash of gold and a small, faerylike visage that quickly disappeared. She blinked.

"Someone is there!" she whispered. "I saw a face!"

"Hmm . . . no one. You may have seen an otter." Alpin shrugged. "Eva, I have news too. A messenger came to Innisfarna since I saw you last. He came to the far side of the loch and called out for the ferryman—he might have stood there all day if I had not looked in that direction!" Alpin chuckled. "When he sat with the king's men, I stayed close to listen. I even served their dinner. And you know I am no servant." He sniffed.

"I know," Eva said. "Did he bring a message from the king?"

He frowned. "From Green Colin. He is in Edinburgh now."

Her heart plummeted. "So he has finally returned."

"He is not free to come here yet, but says he will soon."

"Do you know if he sent word about Donal, or my clan's appeal for pardon?"

"Nothing was mentioned of that in his message to Robson, though he inquired after you—the safety and well-being of his beloved bride, he wrote."

Dread filled her. "If Robson sent word to Colin, I hope he told him that I left Innisfarna. Was there anything else?"

"Apparently the Campbells in Argyll complained to King James about raids and stolen cattle at the hands of the outlawed MacArthurs." Alpin lifted a brow meaningfully.

"Surely Colin knows my kinsmen are responsible."

"If not, he will know quick enough. The messenger said the king will send a man to deliver a warning to the renegades, and troops will be sent to quell them with fire and sword."

Eva gasped. Fire and sword—the brutal persecution of a clan by royal troops in order to stamp out disobedience— was rare and unforgiving punishment. "Lachlann said he has a message for Simon from the king."

"Then he is the one who was sent." Alpin rubbed his chin. "When Colin arrives, you will be wed quick . . . unless you change your mind, as some think you should do," he added pointedly.

Eva looked away. Ever since the forfeiture, her kinsmen, including Alpin and Simon, had objected to her betrothal. But she had never told them of Colin's cruel threat toward her brothers. "I cannot change my mind," she said. "I am caught."

Alpin frowned, watching her, but she would not elaborate. Now Lachlann's arrival brought out another thread in the weave, one that was already in the design, discrete and strong. For years she had yearned for him, wondering if he would survive the war and return to her. Now he was back, but instead of seeing her dreams come true, she was trapped by her promise to Colin.

"So Lachlann refused to tell you what he came here to do," Alpin said. "Might he lead the king's troops against our lads?"

"I do not know." She shook her head, confused, unwilling to believe that the smith's son who had grown up among her kinfolk could betray them. Yet he was not the same man she had known before. Secrets lurked in his eyes.

"Eva," Alpin said. "The messenger said the king may forfeit your right to Innisfarna, and grant it to a man who will champion his interests in the Highlands."

"You mean a man who will support central government in Scotland," she said bitterly.

"I mean Colin," Alpin said. "He will fawn for the king's favor in this matter and arrive here with the deed to the isle in his pocket. We cannot let him take this place from you."

"I agree. At least I have a choice in that matter."

"You do, and I am training you for it."

"Then we should get to it." She walked over to a tree where Alpin had left the two wooden swords they normally used.

Eva lifted her weapon, its polished oak blade gleaming in the early light. She faced Alpin, who held a matching carved, wooden practice weapon. Having advanced to the use of steel, she still preferred the wooden wasters, as they were called, for practice. Alpin had wrapped the blades with cloth to muffle the clacking sounds and keep their practices secret.

Adopting a basic stance, she placed her right foot—her sword foot—ahead, balancing her weight between her forward and back feet, knees slightly bent. She raised the sword and waited.

Alpin lifted his sword and brought it down in a rapid, controlled movement, which Eva expected. She swung to counter the strike. The wooden blades knocked together, and she felt the jar in her bones. Swinging again, she lunged diagonally forward and out of the path of his answering stroke, so that he missed.

As she moved, she raised the hilt and let the wooden shaft angle downward, hanging behind her shoulder to defend her back. She resumed the guarding position and waited for Alpin's next overhead strike, then repeated the moves like a dance. She defended while he attacked; then they switched roles. All the while, she stayed alert, quick, and watchful while she and Alpin circled within the alder grove.

The short, intense practice left her heart pumping hard and her body taut and alert. When it ended, Eva followed

Alpin back to the beach and stepped into the boat. Dawn poured rose and lavender over the water as he rowed back to the mainland.

Behind them, Innisfarna, isle and stone, glowed in the lovely light. Aeife's legend demanded that Eva fight for the isle. Now that she had some skill with a sword, she felt better prepared to demand her rights at sword point, if need be.

The prospect frightened her, although she would never have admitted it to Alpin. He expected her to rise to the impossible example of Aeife the Radiant One.

But she had no illusions about herself. She was no faery-bright, enchanted warrior princess. She was an ordinary girl who had some skill with a sword, temper enough to fake bravado, and no stomach at all for hurting anyone.

She sighed, watching the calm, glassy water, and wondered if Aeife and her prince had been real, in ages past—or if Eva defended only a tale, as lovely and empty as the mist.

Pausing on the sunlit doorstep of the smithy, Lachlann inhaled the crisp air. He glanced toward the loch, shining beneath hills carpeted in autumn golds. A night's rest had improved his eyesight somewhat—but then the sun flashed on the water, and the sparkles appeared again in his vision.

A breeze fluttered his hair and the hem of his belted plaid. He shaded his eyes with his hand to gaze over the meadow and the hills, and wondered where Eva was. Waking late, he had found himself alone but for the dogs, and he had felt disappointed. Loneliness for her—that same longing he had resisted for years—tainted the pleasure of his first morning at home.

Turning, he entered the smithy. The shadowed interior was as he remembered it, and he inhaled the familiar odors of iron, charcoal, and stone. His footsteps echoed on the slate floor.

The forge sat in the shadows to one side of the room like

a dormant beast, bleak and empty. He touched the cool stone, then stepped toward the huge bellows behind the chimney. His fingers left a trail in the dust and ash on the leather casing.

The anvil, shaped of cast iron with a flat top and two beaked ends protruding like horns, stood a few feet away from the forge, anchored to a stout upright log. Tools—tongs, hammers, chisels, swages, pokers, shovels, and points—hung on racks on the walls and the forge. Others were stored in a wooden chest on a table. Inside another chest were small, essential items: nails and rivets, vials of oil for polishing, scraps of leather for wrapping hilts and making sheaths.

A wooden tub stood near the door, stacked beside empty buckets. Leather gloves and aprons hung on pegs, and other implements were scattered on the table. Dust and soot lay thick upon most surfaces. Beneath a canvas beside the narrow back door of the smithy, a store of iron—broken pieces as well as rods and ingots—required sorting and cleaning before he could determine what materials were available for forging.

He sighed, aware that much needed to be done before any smithing work could begin.

He fetched the pack that he had left on the doorstep and brought it inside, closing the door. Rummaging among his few items of clothing and possessions, he withdrew a wrapped object and laid it on the anvil face. Carefully he unknotted the twine ties and peeled away the layered cloth.

Two halves of a broken sword shone bright in the dimness. He traced his fingers over the brass pommel and leather hilt, and touched the second piece, the separate remnant of the blade. The first time he had seen this weapon, it had gleamed like molten gold reflecting a sunset sky in France. A girl who shone with courage had gripped the hilt.

Its design was simple but elegant, a single-handed hilt

with a brass disc pommel and a sloping crossbar. The blade, cracked in half, was tapered, its fuller engraved with five fleurs-de-lis filled with gold. He took the worn leather hilt and turned the sword point upright.

The gold engravings glittered. Even broken, it was a fair sword, he thought, and he felt privileged to have the safe-guarding of it. Light caught the steel, set it afire in his hands. Brilliance rayed outward like diamond strands as he turned the blade.

Magical swords and warrior maidens, he mused. Strangely, they seemed to be a repeating motif in his life. Sighing sadly, he wrapped the blade in its cloth again.

Jehanne had once told him to keep the sword because one day he would know what to do with it. But he did not know, and neither heart nor reason told him.

He did not think he could fix the break. Regardless of his flawed eyesight, he could not touch fire to the marred beauty of this particular blade.

He tucked the cloth bundle high on a ledge and walked away.

Chapter 9

"We must find out what Lachlann intends to do now that he has returned," Simon said, frowning thoughtfully. Eva sat beside him, having already explained what she knew, while her brother and kinsmen listened in grim silence.

A few of the fourteen men in Simon's band of rebels had gathered in a clearing on a wooded slope in the wild hills above Loch Fhionn. The view through the autumn leaves revealed the loch at the foot of broad mountains. Far out, Innisfarna and its castle seemed to float upon the water like a jewel.

"He must be the king's messenger," Simon mused, frowning.

"We cannot trust him, if so." Iain Og spoke; he was the oldest of the MacArthurs—despite his nickname, Og, "the younger"—who followed Simon. Iain was a huge man, tall and wide, though Eva noted that his bulk had lessened in the years with the rebels. He stood apart from the rest, his arms folded, brow creased beneath a shock of graying hair.

"You do not know the man, Iain Og," her cousin Parlan said. Margaret's eldest brother, like his younger brothers, was brown-haired and lean; with his siblings, he shared finely made features that suited their blond sister better than five young men. "Lachlann was trustworthy before. Why would he change?"

"Eva says he seems different now," Simon reminded them.

"We must be careful not to trust him too quickly."

"All of us are changed," Micheil, another of Margaret's brothers, said. He had grown into a tall and quiet-spoken young man. "Some of us went to France, like Lachlann and Parlan and William, in good faith to fight a war that was not ours. The rest of us stayed here—Simon and Andra, Fergus and I, and the others—to be betrayed by our own king. Our lands are lost, our old chief gone and our young chief in prison, our good name taken from us. How could any of us be the same?"

Eva nodded in sympathy. With their lives torn asunder, her kinsmen had sent their families to safety, then banded together, hiding in the hills to fight those who had taken over their lands by king's grant. They would not give up those lands easily, nor would they accept the wrongful forfeiture of them.

"The MacKerron smith is not one of the MacArthur dispossessed," Iain Og pointed out. "He has no allegiance to us. He is a king's man from Perth—even if he grew up a lad in Balnagovan."

"His family have been smiths near Loch Fhionn for generations," Fergus said. "We were all children together."

"And we were with him in France," Parlan said, nodding to William, his twin; they were similar though not identical. "I will trust him, no matter his message." William nodded.

"And I," Andra echoed. The youngest of the renegade MacArthurs at nearly sixteen, with light brown hair and a slender build, he had turned a youthful taste for mischief into a talent for clever spying whenever the king's men rode out on patrol.

Simon ran his thumb along his whiskered chin. His dark hair gleamed in the sunlight. "Eva, what do you think? Is Lachlann for us or against us?"

"Ask him yourself," she said stubbornly.

"No matter what his message, or his intent, nothing can keep us from our business," Simon told the others. "We will win back our rights, and protest the wrong that was done to our people." His kinsmen nodded grim acknowledgment of their shared purpose.

"Raids in the night will not do that," Eva said.

"You seem to think Colin will solve all our troubles," Simon said.

"And you believe attacks will gain back our rights and save Donal," she returned bitterly. The dispute was old between them.

"Green Colin will not do it," Simon snapped. "You set great store by his promises, yet we see no result."

"Donal is still alive," she pointed out. She looked away, sighing. She and Simon argued so often lately that she felt as if she faced a man of stone with a stranger's face rather than the easygoing brother she once had known.

"Perhaps Colin truly loves the girl and means well," Micheil suggested. "Who could resist our Eva?" He winked at his cousin.

"Bah," Simon growled. "Colin loves her island. He kept her dowry lands, too, after the forfeiture, and put his kin there in place of the dispossessed MacArthurs."

"A shame those lands have been so short of cattle and sheep lately," Fergus drawled. "Raiders are a persistent problem, I hear. Or is it that livestock wander in their sleep?" Andra laughed, and Fergus grinned. "We will get rich if we continue to take such fine fat cattle to the Lowland markets."

Eva frowned, well aware of their activities after dark. "I beg you to be cautious. Stealing from Colin's kin will not help our clan's cause."

"And we beg you again to reconsider the marriage," Simon answered. "There are other ways to win back our lands."

"Why do you think I bruise myself learning swordplay? I have my own rights to consider," she said. "You will not fight for Innisfarna, and I understand that. It is not part of your inheritance, but came to me through my mother, and you have other concerns. Innisfarna is my trouble, and I must solve it."

"Alpin wants to turn you into a warrior maiden to solve it. That is as foolish as waiting for Colin," Simon muttered.

"Foolish? Have you seen the girl fight? She is not bad," Micheil said. "Colin will run for cover when he comes home."

"He will not, because Eva hates to fight," Simon said. "I do not think she will do it when the time comes."

Though she scowled at him, she knew there was truth in what he said. She enjoyed the grace and the power of wielding the sword, but she could not bear to hurt anyone, nor did she want to risk being hurt herself.

"And there is the Sword of Light to consider," Fergus said. "It must be protected, or all Scotland will fail."

"You should be listening to stories at your mother's knee, young one—and not wasting our time with fantasies," Iain Og muttered. "Eva, if you draw a sword on your new husband, make sure you use it on him," he added. "That will end the trouble."

"She would not slice an apple with that thing, for fear of harming the apple," Simon said.

"You cannot just wave it about and scare Green Colin off your isle," Parlan told her. "We have seen war, girl. It is not so easy to win back lands lost to the enemy. Be careful."

"I mean to show Colin that I will not give up my privilege as guardian of Innisfarna," Eva answered. "I alone have the right to the isle. I will marry him if I must, but I will not let him have my isle."

"Do not sacrifice yourself for us. We can sacrifice ourselves on our own, if we have to," Simon said sarcastically.

"Oh, Simon, please, let there be peace between us again," she said wearily. He looked away, sighed, and did not answer.

"If you two are finished squabbling," Parlan said sternly, "we have more immediate problems. Our best hope is rebellion."

"A fine and brave word," Eva answered. "And meaningless if it takes your lives and leaves your clan with nothing gained and Donal dead too! There are but fourteen of you, with too few weapons or armor!"

"Fifteen, if we can trust the smith," Parlan said.

"Sixteen, with Eva," Fergus said. "Seventeen, with Alpin."

"Seventeen is still just a handful," Eva pointed out.

"There have been insurrections all over the Highlands since the arrests at Inverness," Simon reminded her. "Each small rebellion is a pocket of fire. If those flames come together, they will make a great blaze."

"We have something we did not have before," Fergus said. He smiled.

"A master weaponsmith!" Andra said, grinning.

Simon whistled low. "True! That could make the difference for us. Lachlann has the knack of making good weapons."

"Does he have the knack to turn away the king's forces, and change the king's mind?" Eva asked. "That is what you need."

"We could take Innisfarna and make it our stronghold," William suggested.

Simon nodded. "I have been thinking that very thing."

She shook her head. "The legend says—"

"Hang the legend," Iain Og said irritably. "Women's tales. A faery princess and her magical sword! Hah! I say we arm ourselves and take Innisfarna. That solves Eva's trouble."

"Listen to me," she pleaded. "I will show my sword and show Colin that I am not afraid of him—and prove to him that the legend has power."

Iain Og snorted in disdain. William shook his head. "Dreams, cousin," he said. "There is only one way to use a sword if you want results."

"Eva, what we are doing may come to real war some-day," Simon said earnestly. "Real battles. We need that swordsmith. Find out which way his loyalties lie. You are a woman, and he is a man. Use that to gain his help for us."

She lifted her chin. "I will not use wiles."

"Knowing him, I would guess that he would not mind if you did," Simon murmured.

Parlan grinned. "If Eva would wed the blacksmith instead of Colin, we would have the smith's loyalty for certain—and his skills!"

"Oh, I like that," Iain Og said in his booming voice.

"Interesting," Simon mused, watching his sister.

"Ridiculous," Eva muttered, though her heart pounded. "That would gain you nothing! He has no influence to help Donal!"

"At the very least, it would gain you a better man than Colin," Parlan told her, while his twin brother nodded.

Simon huffed impatiently. "Marry the blacksmith or bed him, make his dinner or mend his plaid. Whatever you do, find out what he intends, and where his loyalties lie, quick as you can."

"What if he means harm to you?"

"Convince him over to our side," Simon said. "You can be quite charming when you control that temper of yours. If Lachlann is not the king's man, then he is our man. As it should be."

"And if the weaponsmith is with us, we will soon be an army," Iain Og said.

*   *   *

Lachlann poked through the scrap iron piled beneath a canvas in a back corner of the spacious smithy. He had discovered several thick rods of cast iron and two fat ingots, their crude quality suited only to making pothooks and heavy chains. He shifted part of a broken plough, its iron reusable, to one side.

Against the wall he found a bundle of wrought-iron rods of a finer quality. He remembered leaving those there himself, iron purchased from the ironmonger across the loch, years ago. The canvas had protected it from rust, for the most part, although some spots had developed, but heating would destroy that. Good iron could be made into small knives, axe heads, kitchen utensils, latches, and so on. Lachlann nodded with approval as he searched the pile.

Several worn horseshoes were stacked haphazardly on the floor, and more dangled from nails embedded in the wall. The iron shoes could be reshaped to fit other horses, or the iron could be heated and remade into a variety of items.

Only the best iron could be made into steel to form weapons and sword blades. He frowned, rubbing his jaw as he considered what lay at his feet. Good weaponsmithing required quality materials. Wrought iron, refined by an ironmonger, could be made into steel, but cast iron was too full of impurities to be used.

Lack of materials could be corrected, he thought, but lack of ability could not. His long-held dream of swordsmithing might have come to an end; he was not yet sure. Though he had skill and talent, the smithing of steel depended on eyesight. Nuances of color in heated metal told the smith a great deal. If his vision was faulty, the weapons he crafted could be flawed. If a faulty weapon broke, it could bring about the death of its owner.

He rubbed his fingers over his eyelids. Ever since his injury, colors were sometimes dim, shadows deeper, and erratic flashes of light erupted without notice. Someday, he knew, the weakness in his eye might worsen into blindness; at best, it would never improve. He could never be the swordsmith that he had once dreamed of becoming.

His experiences as a smith in Perth had proved to him that he was still a capable blacksmith for horseshoes, nails, pothooks, door latches, and the like. Cherry red was a color even he could see easily. Working the black metal was little challenge for him now, and he enjoyed the work well enough.

Working the white metal—steel—was different. The sheer magic of mastering the light-bearing metal had fascinated him as a boy, and still held him in its thrall.

Ancient tradition gave blacksmiths the privileges and the mystery of magicians. The ability and the courage to bend hot metal to their will made smiths essential and well respected in their communities. They kept their secrets carefully guarded. And now Lachlann feared that he would never be able to fully use the knowledge and traditions he had learned from Finlay.

Hearing men's voices in the yard, he looked up from his musing, and strode across the smithy to open the door.

Several men, armored and bearing swords and weapons, filled the yard between the smithy and the stable. Lachlann frowned and walked outside.

He glanced toward the house. Last evening, Eva had returned from her wanderings so late that Lachlann had helped himself to food from Mairi's cupboards earlier, and set up a simple pallet for himself in a corner of the smithy. Hearing the dogs barking quite late, he went to the door to see light in the windows of the house. This morning, he had arisen just after dawn, but again Eva was gone. Now, at midmorning, she had not yet come back.

He strode forward as two men walked toward him, an old Highlander in a plaid, his white hair bright in the sun, and a brawny blond soldier in a steel cuirass, tunic, trews, and boots. The old man raised a hand in salute.

Lachlann lifted a hand, too, grinning. "*Failte,* Alpin MacDewar, and how are you?" he called in Gaelic.

"*Failte, gobha*—greetings, smith! Welcome back! It is good to see you again, looking hearty and all in one piece, and not so bad for three years of warring!" Alpin grinned, showing crooked teeth and the same gruff charm that Lachlann remembered. Smiling, he clasped the gnarled old hand, amazed, as he had always been, by the sheer strength in Alpin's knotty grip.

"*Gobha,* this is Sir John Robson, the king's man," Alpin said in Gaelic. "He speaks the southern tongue, so I hope you have not forgotten it, after all the French in your head now. *Gobha* means 'smith,' " he told Robson in English, loudly, as if the man were partly deaf.

Lachlann held out his hand to Robson. "I am Lachlann MacKerron," he said in Scots English. "Balnagovan is my property by tenant's agreement, although I have been gone a long while."

"John Robson, captain of the king's garrison at Innisfarna Castle," the man answered. "Alpin told me you were newly arrived from France."

"And I said you are a fine craftsman, and a man local to this village," Alpin added in Gaelic. "He is a good *gobha,*" he added loudly in English for Robson's benefit.

"We are pleased to have a smith so close," Robson said. "There is a fellow in Glen Brae, but he isna so competent."

"That fellow likes drink and dislikes hard work," Alpin muttered in Gaelic to Lachlann.

"We need a good deal of smithing from time to time," Robson continued. "Just now, some of the horses need shoeing, and our harnesses and gear need repair. Are you trained as an armorer or a weaponsmith?"

"Name the task, and I will see what I can do."

"He is doing it all," Alpin added proudly. "Steel and iron, he is doing it all."

"A weaponsmith? Indeed, how useful," Robson said.

"I have done some of that in the past," Lachlann said. "But materials for good weaponry are not easy to come by." He frowned at Alpin, hoping to curtail any further boasts.

"For now, two of the mounts in there need shoeing—the bay mare and a brown garron," Robson said.

"I will check the others," Lachlann offered.

"Good. I noticed some rust on the harness fastenings too. If you could tend to that soon, I would be glad to pay you for your trouble. Some of the men have weapons in need of repair. I will have those collected and brought to you."

Lachlann nodded. "That I can take care of, as well. What is your business this day, armed and saddled and ready for war?" He gazed past Robson at the men who guided horses out of the stable.

"Their business is trouble," Alpin rumbled in Gaelic.

"We ride out on patrol looking for rebels by king's order."

"Ah," Lachlann said, "so you know where they lurk?"

"Nae yet, though 'twill change if they continue to raid the lands in this glen. We keep the king's peace in the region. A messenger arrived the other day with news," Robson went on. "The king sent a man to Argyll to speak with the MacArthur rebels. Would you know aught about that?"

"I am that man," Lachlann said.

"Ah, I knew it," Alpin commented in his native language. Lachlaan slid him a glance.

"Then you know these rogues yourself," Robson said.

"I do, and 'tis why I am instructed to speak to them myself, and deliver the king's message to their leader. But I confess I canna do so until I know where they are."

"Luck to you, then. Not even the rebel leader's sister, Lady Eva, knows where they hide. Nae doubt you met the lady who stays in the house over there."

"I have spoken with her. I know her from years past."

Robson lowered his brows. "And where are you staying, sir?"

"In the smithy. Eva MacArthur owns the house, and has been sharing it with my mother—surely you are aware of that, sir."

"Aye. But be careful. Lady Eva's betrothed is a powerful man, a Campbell. When he returns, he willna take a kind view of a man sharing this property with his beloved."

"His beloved," Lachlann said curtly, "is safe here, if you imply otherwise." He narrowed his eyes.

"The *gobha* loves her like a brother," Alpin said. "Is it not so?"

Lachlann glanced at him. "How else would it be?"

"Very well," Robson said. "You can help me, then, by watching out for her. I am appointed to protect her, but it is difficult when she willna stay at Innisfarna."

"I heard she didna feel she could stay there."

"Some rogues in my garrison lacked manners, but they have been disciplined for it. She could come back to the castle, but she is a stubborn young woman and willna return."

"You canna expect her to accept protection from men who hunt after her kinsmen."

"For certain, she is not liking that," Alpin muttered in English. Robson glanced at him, but seemed unbothered by Alpin's comments. Lachlann could tell that the man knew Alpin well.

"More than MacArthurs raid in Argyll, but they are the most troublesome of the rebels," Robson said. "We ride sentinel often to prevent more cattle being stolen and barns burned. Their raids grow more frequent. If we ever meet the rebels, it will go ill for them. You are a king's man, sir. If you would like to arm yourself, mount up, and ride with us, we would welcome a man who knows the region."

Lachlann frowned, glancing at Alpin, who raised his white brows high, but for once said nothing. "I might do so soon."

"You do have a message to deliver to the rebels. You will want to be with us when we find them," Robson said.

"I prefer to meet them alone, without a host of king's men."

"Understood, though I urge you to be cautious. Report to me when the king's message is delivered, if you will." One of the men in the stable yard called out, and Robson waved. "Good day, smith."

Lachlann nodded, arms folded, while Robson strode away and mounted the dark destrier saddled and waiting for him. The king's men, more than a dozen in all, turned as a group and pounded out of the stable yard and across the meadow.

He looked at Alpin. "Where is Eva?" he asked abruptly.

"How do I know? I am not her keeper. She might be with Margaret," Alpin said. "Good to see you, smith, and we will talk again soon. When your foster mother comes back to Glen Brae, I will fetch you for a boat ride. I must go now, and ferry those three over the water," he said, pointing at two knights and a small blond boy, a page by the look of him, who stood in the stable yard. He strolled away, and the boy ran toward him.

Lachlann turned and went back inside the smithy, wondering indeed if Eva was with her cousin—or with her brother and the rebels. He was still frowning to himself as he took up a heather broom to sweep the dust from the smithy floor.

Chapter 10

"Keep your balance when you swing," Alpin said. He came toward Eva as she shifted in her stance, and used his toe to adjust the angle of her foot. "Sword leg forward, girl. Remember that. Try again." He resumed a guarding stance and raised his sword, facing her in the dawn light. The air was so chilled that morning that his breath frosted and the tip of his nose was pink.

Movement kept her warm as she lunged and parried. Alpin knocked her blade aside easily. "Sword leg forward," he reminded her.

"Sometimes it feels awkward with my right leg forward." She stopped, flexing her hand on the handle of the wooden sword. "I am not as good at this as you want me to be," she added, feeling discouraged.

"Well, you are a girl. It is not so easy for you."

She scowled. "Shall I call you an old man?" she snapped.

He grinned. "I knew that would stir you up like a boiling kettle. You are good, Eva, graceful and fast, but you are too reluctant to hurt your opponent. Hit me like you mean it. Put your temper into it. Do not hold back. I can defend myself, so do not worry about hitting me. Come on."

Eva rounded on him, raising her sword. Alpin blocked her downward stroke, but she scooped under it and tapped his lower leg. He grunted approval and struck again. She caught his wooden blade with a hard thunk. Mirroring his position, she circled with him, crossed blades, and repeated the sequence.

Finally Alpin lowered his sword and bowed. "Ah, much better. You have fine dancing feet, and this old man cannot keep up. But you move too tightly. Loosen your hold and your stance. Your strikes will be faster and more accurate."

She nodded and bounced, adjusting her stance.

"And keep that left leg back—you place it forward when you are not thinking. Move the right forward for better protection."

She gave him a wry glance. "I have nothing protruding there to protect, as men do." She gestured at her crotch.

He laughed outright. "True! But guard your chest, eh?"

Rotating the smooth pommel in the palm of her hand, she swung the wooden sword in an arc and settled her hand around the hilt again. Spinning on her feet, she came toward Alpin from a different angle, lifting the sword to bring it down.

"Put more strength in the stroke," he advised. "Try again."

She repeated the drill several times, until her breath burned in her lungs. And still she tried again, adding her own flair for quick footwork and rapid shifts in position. The muffled wooden blades clacked in the quiet, and the morning light increased to a silvery glow.

Pausing to catch her breath, she listened while Alpin explained a fine point of quick-changing her grip on the hilt. A movement in the bushes, and the surprising sheen of thick new gold among the russet autumn leaves, caught her attention.

"Alpin," she whispered. The tree leaves rustled. "Someone is watching us! This has happened before!"

"*Ach*, it is the lad in the tree again. Come down, boy."

"What boy?" she asked in astonishment.

"The little page from the castle. He has been running around these woods for weeks, but I finally met him, and now we are friends. And I tell you, that boy needs a friend or two," he added in a whisper. "Come out, it is all right!"

The leaves shifted and parted, and a small, lithe form dropped to the ground. A child came forward, dressed in a shabby plaid and shirt far too big for his slight frame. He paused in the shadow of the trees, dawn mist drifting around him, birds twittering overhead. His face was narrow and pale, his eyes large and blue, his hair a thick mop of burnished gold.

"This is Eva," Alpin said in a mild tone. He beckoned the boy forward. "She is a good friend of mine, and so she will be a friend to you, too." The old man smiled.

The boy kept one hand over his mouth, his eyes wide and timid as he watched Alpin, then Eva. He did not move, but stood tense and ready to flee. He reminded her of someone, but she could not think who just then. Small, perhaps nine years old, and tentative, he lacked the bold manner of most boys of similar age. He reminded her of a delicate golden fawn, lost from its mother and about to bolt.

"Good day," she said gently. "I am Eva. Who are you?"

He kept his hand over his mouth. "Nyahn," he said. The sound was nasal, full of air and effort. "Nyahn-yahn."

Puzzled, she blinked at him, then looked at Alpin. "This is Ninian," Alpin said in translation.

"Ninian?" She looked at the boy in astonishment. "Ninian, the son of Colin Campbell?"

He nodded, golden hair flopping in his eyes. Alpin nodded, too; the boy's identity was clearly no surprise to him.

"I met him only recently myself," Alpin said. "I saw him around the island for weeks, hiding in the trees. Ninian climbs like a wild cat, he does." Ninian nodded.

"You are a page at the castle?" Eva asked. The boy nodded again, and kept his hand over his mouth, as if he was extremely shy.

"He wanders the island, and Robson lets him have a lit-

tle freedom—a good man, John Robson, and ineffectual
enough to keep your kinsmen safe in the hills, eh?" Alpin
added. "Ninian was a help to me in the rose garden this
week. I gave him a little knife to cut down the old blooms,
and he did it very well. Come here," Alpin said, beckoning.
"The soldiers will not see you on this side of the island. And
Eva will not tell anyone that you escaped your duties in the
castle again."

Eva smiled and waved him toward her, as Alpin did.
Noticing that the boy looked at her wooden sword with real
interest, she lifted it. "Would you like to hold this, Ninian?"

He came forward, fist still folded over his mouth, and
took the hilt in his other hand. His fingers, though smudged
and dirty, were elegantly shaped.

"It is all right to show Eva," Alpin said. "She will not
mind. And you need two hands to hold that great sword."

Ninian slid a cautious glance from Alpin to Eva. Then he
took his hand from his face.

Eva hid her startled reaction. His upper lip bore an angu-
lar scar where a cleft had been sewn together, and his teeth
were small and crooked. She had heard of such deformities,
which Mairi had mentioned seeing in some of the births she
had attended. Some of the children had split lips, and some
also had gaps in the roofs of their mouths; Eva knew that
many babies with this affliction did not survive for long,
since they had difficulty feeding and so did not thrive.

This boy appeared to be strong and healthy. The split in
his lip had been closed, but his speech indicated that his
palate was cleft, and that could not be repaired. Clearly he
had been carefully nursed in the early years of his life, and
he had mastered language—such personal challenges
needed effort, determination, and intelligence. He was certainly no oaf or idiot, although Colin had described him that
way to Eva years ago, when Ninian must still have been
quite small.

Remembering Colin's unkind remarks about his son, she frowned. Had she known then about Ninian, she would not have tolerated such lack of compassion in the father.

Ninian watched her, jaw set stubbornly, cheeks pink. She realized he expected her to act repulsed by him. Calmly she reached out to adjust the wrap of his fingers on the hilt.

"Hold it like this," she said. "Use two hands if it feels more comfortable to you. How is that?" She smiled at him.

He nodded and seemed to relax as he tested his grip on the hilt. Alpin corrected his stance, and praised him with such warmth that Eva smiled to herself. By habit, Alpin was miserly with praise, but he was always generous when it mattered.

Despite the scarred lip, Ninian's features had an elegant, feline grace, and his mop of golden hair was wild and beautiful. She could see the father in his coloring and the proportion of his features, though his delicacy must have come from his mother, whomever she had been. Ninian was small and thin, but his arms and legs were muscled and well made, and he was coordinated and quick. He understood what Alpin and Eva showed him, and soon had a nearly perfect stance and grip.

"You will be a fine knight one day." Eva tilted her head. "Ninian, I know your father."

"Colhn Camhbuh," he said with effort. He peered thoughtfully at her. "Will you be . . . my mother?" The words were breathy and forced: *hmoh hmah-harrh*. But Eva understood and smiled. Ninian looked at her with hopeful blue eyes, as if he regarded an angel.

"Your father is my betrothed husband, so I may be your stepmother one day." Despite a binding agreement, she found it hard to admit she would wed Colin—but his young son looked at her with real hope and pleasure. She sighed.

"Will you live with me and my father?" he asked, and Eva understood him this time with better ease.

"I do not yet know what will happen," she answered as honestly as she could. "Colin told me about you. He said his son was grown and did not need a mother. I assumed you were older—even a young man."

Ninian held up a hand, spreading his fingers twice.

"You are ten?" she asked, surprised, thinking him younger.

"And I do not need a mother," he said. Each word was distorted with nasal effort and too much air, his nostrils flaring, for he made some sounds through his nose.

Now she understood him clearly, as if a fog had lifted. She had only needed time to adjust to his mode of articulation.

"Of course you do not need a mother for most things, at your age. You are on your own now, a page for the knights. I am sure you do well at that, for you are a quick-witted boy." He smiled sweetly at the compliment.

Eva felt a surge of anger for Colin's loathesome attitude toward his son. Ninian was clearly intelligent, with the tender sensitivity of any boy his age. "Even older boys need a mother now and then, or a friend who is like a mother," she said, "when they are sick, or hungry, or if they want to hear a story."

He nodded. "I like stories."

"I do too. I would love to tell some to you. Perhaps Alpin can bring you to my house. I live near the smithy."

He looked intrigued. "Near the stable?" he asked. "I have been there with the soldiers, but I did not see you." Eva tipped her head, trying to understand what he said, for he spoke more rapidly now. He repeated it patiently.

"I usually go elsewhere when the soldiers come," she said. "But if you come in the evening with Alpin, I will give you supper and tell you a story. You can see the horses in the stable, and you can play with the dog that you gave to me."

His eyes grew wide. "I remember her. I asked my father to bring her to you. He told you so?"

"He did, Ninian. That was very kind of you, and I never had a chance to thank you. She is a wonderful little dog, though a pup no longer. Come see her. I call her Grainne."

Ninian beamed, joy at the invitation glowing in his eyes. Eva smiled and touched his golden hair, thick and soft under her hand. Her gaze met Alpin's. The old man frowned thoughtfully.

She felt something well up in her, a desperate desire to give this wild, lonely little boy the loyalty and affection for which he seemed so thirsty. She smiled at him again. He grinned, quickly covering his mouth to hide it from her.

Tears stung her eyes and her breathing constricted, as if the uncomfortable knot that tied her to Colin had tightened. The boy, at least, would make the burden and the caging a little easier to bear.

Several days after his arrival, Lachlann stood back one afternoon, satisfied that the smithy was in order. He had wiped the grime from the surfaces, cleaned rust from the tools, oiled the leather casing of the bellows, and checked its wooden plates and workings. Chisel edges were sharpened, hammer handles repaired, pairs of tongs tightened and lubricated, the anvil scrubbed clean, the water tubs filled, the floor swept. After brushing the soot residue from the forge and cleaning the flue, he had collected kindling and charcoal. But he had not set the fire bed alight.

Wiping his forearm over his brow, noting a smear of grime transferred from his face, he turned to look at the immaculate, organized smithy. Later, the place would slide toward the orderly jumble that he preferred when working. The smithy had not been left in chaos, but no one had worked in here for years; dust and grime had collected, and time and climate had affected the tools. Cleaning the smithy to this extent was a necessary ritual for him, a step toward the resuming of his work.

He had taken toll of his tools, supplies, and the scrap iron pile. He knew what materials were available and what must be purchased or bargained.

For now, he would start with minor tasks in the house and the stable, along with the repairs that Robson had requested. Later he would decide if he was ready to attempt steel.

He glanced at one wall, where the top of the thick stone met the rafters under the thatch. Jehanne's sword was tucked there for now. He knew he was not ready for that task yet—if ever.

His throat felt dry, and his stomach growled. He remembered that he had eaten only once that day, fairly early, and he decided to go to the house in the hopes of finding some cheese or oatcakes stored in the wall cupboard.

Eva was gone once again, as seemed to be her habit—up and out so early that he barely glimpsed her before she had disappeared over the meadow or down the hill toward the loch. Once he had seen her in the boat with Alpin, crossing the water. He had walked down to the beach hoping for a chance to greet the old man, but by the time he got there, they were out of sight. And he had hardly spoken to her since the night he had arrived.

Likely she noticed that he was busy in the smithy and thought it best to leave him to it. Very likely, he thought sourly, that he was far too attracted to her to approach her without good reason. A little distancing was a good thing now, he told himself, remembering the overwhelming urge he had felt to kiss her—and more—the first night he had arrived. The fact that he yearned for her bothered him.

Outside, Grainne and Solas began to bark with increasing fervor, and Lachlann went to the door and peered out. Eva crossed the meadow just when he had been thinking of her. He smiled ruefully at that, aware that he had some bond to her that could not easily be broken.

She carried a plaid bundled into a huge sack, bursting

full. Her dark braid trailed over one shoulder, and she moved with sure grace, head high, shoulders straight, body slim as a wand.

The bundle looked cumbersome, but he knew better than to offer to carry the pack. Independence meant much to Eva MacArthur; he remembered her protests each time he and her brothers had made allowances for her female nature.

Preceded by Solas and Grainne, she went to the house and opened the door, shooing the dogs inside. When she left the door ajar, Lachlann saw it as a gesture of welcome, although she had not looked his way while crossing the meadow.

His stomach rumbled again. Hoping that she planned to start supper, and eager against his will to be with her, he headed across the meadow toward the house.

Chapter 11

Knocking, he entered to find Eva seated on the floor in the midst of a deep, colorful mound of fragrant heather. That lovely, unexpected sight quickened his heartbeat, as did her warm and winsome smile as he stepped inside. He returned it easily.

Solas and Grainne rushed toward him, panting and wagging their tails. He patted Solas, then turned to Grainne. "Little *cràineag,* did you find the fox you went after earlier today?" Grainne hopped on her hind legs in evident delight.

"Lachlann," Eva said, still smiling. "Look!"

"Ah, do you want a pat on the head, too?" He was not sure what lightened his humor. Perhaps it was the playfulness of the dogs. Perhaps it was the refreshing sight of Eva, after a day without her, after years without her.

"*Tcha,*" she said, then gestured. "Look what I brought you!"

"Ah, heather." He crossed his arms and surveyed the colorful chaos on the floor. "I missed it in France, but you did not need to bring it down from the hills. I would have walked out to see it sooner or later."

She laughed, then shrieked as Grainne dove into the mass of greenery and delicate blooms. The little dog growled and waggled her upended tail as she burrowed into the flowers, scattering them everywhere. Eva and Lachlann both swooped down for her. They collided, her head bumping his shoulder.

Sinking to one knee in the heather, he curled the terrier under his arm.

Eva sat up and laughed, which soon descended into giggles.

"What?" Lachlann asked. Then he noticed Grainne, tucked in his arm and bedecked in heather blooms. Sprays stuck out of the wiry tufts of her coat, and purple bells draped over her snout. The dog blinked, wide-eyed, and cocked her head.

Lachlann grinned as he brushed the flowers away, then smiled at Eva. "Why did you collect all this heather? Other than to fiercely tempt our little hedgehog," he added.

She laughed again. He wished the sound would never stop; it rang like silver bells in his heart. "I was glad to find so many stems in bloom this late in the season," she said. "*Ach*, you are covered with them, too."

As she spoke, she brushed at the heather clinging to his forearms, and swept her hand over his plaid, where tiny flower petals scattered over the material. Her hand skimmed his thighs casually, efficiently.

He grew very still, aware that his body responded to her innocent touch. Her hand stayed, and she blushed, pink spilling into her cheeks. He turned her hand and filled the cup of her palm with the sprigs that had pooled in his lap. His eyes met hers.

A bloom dangled above her ear, and he plucked it loose and slid it into the plaitwork of her braid. "There," he murmured. "That looks nice."

She smiled, quick and shy, and brushed flowery debris from Grainne's coat as Lachlann held the dog. Solas came up to them and nosed against Lachlann's shoulder in a plea for affection.

"Ho, are you jealous, my girl?" He roughed his fingers over her head. "Fret not, I still love you. Oh, and you, too," he added, when Grainne yelped. He glanced at Eva, acutely aware of what he had said—and left unsaid. Showing love to the dogs came easily to him, though he often shielded his feelings from others, especially Eva.

"Did you collect the heather to celebrate my homecoming?" he asked, pushing Solas away gently, though he still held Grainne to keep her out of the pile of heather.

"Of course not." She smiled a little. "It is for your bed."

"Ah. The one you are sleeping in?" He lifted a brow.

Color filled her cheeks; he liked it well. "This will make a good bed in the smithy," she explained earnestly. "I must sort through it, but first I had best take time to cook a meal for us—if you will stay."

"Certainly," he said, glad she had asked. Grainne squirmed and tried to jump back into the heather, and he set her down, firmly guiding her away from it. "What will you do with all these flowers?" he asked, looking up.

"They will be useful. If you are going to sit there, Lachlann MacKerron, you can be useful too—"

"Sit here? I am keeping this silly beast from destroying your harvest," he muttered.

"—you could sort the bare stems from the flowering bits." She got to her feet. "The tougher stems can be dried and used to weave mats and baskets. I can use some of the bells in infusions, and brew the rest in ale. Heather makes a good tonic for coughs and sniffles, too. With the cold weather coming, we may have need of that. Mairi always makes heather syrups and infusions."

Lachlann nodded. "I remember. It has many uses indeed, and Muime knew them all. I have tasted and smelled heather all my life, as have you—and it seemed common to me once. But now it is wonderful to see it again, to smell its fragrance in the house." He inhaled appreciatively.

He began to sort the stems, although he had to push Grainne away repeatedly. She had a fascination for heather and no sense of the destruction she caused. Solas seemed uninterested in her antics, and lounged calmly by the fireside.

Eva went to the hearth and prodded the peat fire to greater heat, then swung the kettle over the fire on its long chain. She filled it with water from the bucket by the fireplace.

Lachlann watched her move between hearth, cupboard, and table, preparing the meal. Deftly she chopped carrots and onions and tossed them into the steaming kettle with barley. Sprinkling salt into the kettle, she turned to make oatcakes, crumbling oats with butter and salt. Her fingers were strong and nimble as she formed cakes and slid them onto a flat griddle.

"Muime taught you well," he commented. "I apologize for thinking you would be the spoiled wife of a wealthy laird, with servants to do the work for you. Though that will come soon enough," he added in a darker tone than he intended.

Eva frowned and did not reply. She slapped the rest of the cakes onto the sizzling griddle. The tension around her mouth revealed her irritation. "I saw Simon the other day," she finally said. "I told him that you want to see him."

"Where did you find him?"

"I cannot tell you that." She stirred the kettle, then stepped away to take bowls and cups from a shelf and put them on the table. "I am not certain of your mission."

"I intend to make a bid for peace."

"What good will that do? My brother does not want peace, he wants his clan's rights back and his brother free. Has your time in the king's army changed you so much that you cannot sympathize with us, or understand our cause?" She picked up a jug and poured ale into two cups.

He stood up and came toward her, leaning his hands on the table. "Whatever else you think of me, I am no traitor. I am no different from the man I was when I left here."

She faced him across the table, her gray-green eyes

sparking like lightning through storm clouds. "You are changed," she said.

"I am no traitor," he repeated. "Your rebels can trust me."

"Can I believe that?"

"Believe what you will."

She frowned and turned, filling the bowls from the kettle and setting them on the table. With tongs, she picked up the hot oatcakes and slid them onto a wooden platter. Lachlann took that from her while she fetched a pot of butter from the cupboard.

"The food grows cold," she said abruptly. "Sit and eat."

He motioned for her to sit first. She did, and murmured a blessing over the food, which he completed. Then he slipped his wooden spoon into the hot broth, thick with vegetables, and began to eat in silence.

Solas and Grainne hovered nearby with expressions of unabashed hope. Lachlann broke off pieces of oatcake and tossed them to the floor. The dogs nuzzled them, and Lachlann glanced over to see Eva watching him. She looked away, cheeks flaming.

He reached out to spread butter onto a hot oatcake. On impulse, sensing that an offer of peace was needed, he prepared another for her and passed it across the table. She took it tentatively, then broke off a piece and tossed it to Grainne.

"You have no appetite," he observed. She shrugged. "I would think you would be famished. You spent the day walking the hills, pulling heather plants, and seeking rebels in their den . . . in the hills, was it?" He bit deeply into his own cake and dipped his spoon into the savory soup.

She scowled. "I will not tell you where the rebels are, if that is what you are fishing for. Simon will find you when he is ready to listen to the king's message. And I cannot eat when I am upset." She pushed her bowl away.

"Upset about what?" he asked, dipping a bit of oatcake into his nearly emptied bowl.

"Nothing." She stood, cleared both bowls away—brisking his out from under his spoon—and dumped their contents into a wooden dish on the floor. The dogs padded over to it eagerly.

"Ho, I am still eating," he protested.

"How can you eat in the middle of a dispute?" She wiped the bowls vigorously with sand and ash, scooped from the hearth.

"I lack a delicate stomach. And I did not know we were in dispute." He stood and rounded the table, and Eva sidled away. Grabbing another bowl from the shelf, he ladled more broth and vegetables from the kettle and ate quickly, standing by the hearth. Eva wiped the bowls with a damp cloth and set them back on the shelf in tense silence.

She had ever been a volatile and fascinating creature, he remembered, stubborn and high-spirited, with enough temper and moodiness to confound the male children around her. Yet he knew she had a warm heart, integrity, and courage. If she was angered, he trusted she had good reason to be. And she was clearly angry with him; puzzled by that, he wondered what he had done.

He watched her while he ate. She seemed tense as a bowstring. Perhaps she was actually frightened on behalf of her kinsmen, since she had raised the issue of his loyalty. Certainly he was faithful to his old friends, and he thought she should know that without question. But he had secret matters to protect as well.

When he finished, he set the bowl aside and looked at Eva, standing beside him by the hearth. "Tell me this," he said. "Are you upset with me because I bear a message for Simon from King James?" She did not answer, watching the blue peat flames. "The king would have conveyed his warning with troops. I offered to bring the word more peaceably, but I must know where Simon is."

"If I told you, then you might tell the king where the

rebels hide, and he would send fire and sword after them. We know about his plans to quell the MacArthur rebellion."

"How did you learn that?" he asked sharply.

"Alpin said a messenger came to Innisfarna with news of the king's plans."

"I met John Robson the other day," he said. "Nothing was mentioned about that. If it was a royal messenger, I would have been told. Robson knows my business here."

She scowled deeply, slim dark brows dipping above troubled eyes. "The message came from Colin. He is back from France, and will be here soon . . . very soon, they say."

He felt his heart fall hard to his feet. "Ah," he said. "Does that bother you? I would think you would be eager for your betrothed to return." Bitterness shaded his voice, though he wanted to remain neutral.

She shrugged. "I made a promise to Colin and to my father. Despite what has happened to my kin, I must honor it."

"You are an honorable woman," he murmured, "and Colin Campbell is a fortunate man." But he frowned.

Eva looked up at him, and his gaze sank to her lush, rosy mouth. Had the mood been otherwise—had life been otherwise—he might have kissed her. Despite the barriers between them, the temptation rushed hot through him.

Her eyes snapped like steel. "Tell me one thing."

"Say it." He narrowed his eyes, waiting.

"Will you prove your loyalty to the MacArthurs?"

Suddenly he was the one who felt betrayed. Her mistrust cut like a knife, and the news about Colin's imminent arrival gave the blade a twist. He leaned down.

"Listen to me," he said, low and lethal. "I am a MacKerron smith. My kin have served the MacArthurs and the area of Loch Fhionn for generations. Not one of you should question my loyalty. Least of all you," he snapped. "You knew me well enough once to guess what sort of man I am now."

Her gaze faltered, flickered away. "We agreed to forget what happened between us on Beltane night."

"Did I mention that?" he growled.

The color deepened in her cheeks. Without answer, she walked to the wall cupboard to put the wrapped oatcakes inside.

He sighed, regretting his burst of rancor. Fire existed between them, searing hot; he knew the signs well enough. He understood fire of any sort, and he felt the burn now, saw its spark in her. Although their passion could not be allowed to erupt again, that sort of heat had a demanding nature. It expressed itself in continual flares in both of them, like stars sizzling at night.

That turbulence he regretted, for he cherished her friendship. Sighing, he stepped closer. She turned and bumped into him, and he steadied her with a hand on her shoulder. She tensed, as if ready to spring away.

"Were we not friends once, Eva MacArthur?" he murmured.

"We were. But you have changed." Her gaze was solemn. "You are more . . . guarded. You have secrets. I feel it strongly."

He flexed his fingers on her shoulder, determined to keep those secrets from her. Yet the clarity in her eyes pierced him, heart and soul. Her intuitive, forthright nature could discern what he wanted to conceal.

"I am older and wiser," he said. "I have seen things and learned things . . . that I wish I did not know." He lowered his hands and stepped back. "That is what you feel from me. Only that has changed me."

She studied him. "What happened in France, Lachlann?"

Jaw tightening, he glanced away. "No more than happened to any man." Seeing her concerned frown, sensing that she wanted to question him further, he rushed on. "As for this dispute, here and now, I do not like my loyalty questioned."

"If you could prove your support of my kinsmen, would you?"

He cocked his head. "And yet you will not give this up."

"My kinsmen want you to make weapons for them," she said bluntly. "They want your loyalty tested and measured. Simon must be sure of you before he will meet with you."

He scowled, but appreciated her honesty. "I presume these weapons would be used for something other than hunting."

She stared at him without reply, an answer in itself.

Lachlann let out a harsh breath. "You are betrothed to a Campbell. Would you ask me to arm your kinsmen against Campbells, and against the king?"

Furrowing her smooth brow, she shook her head. "Colin's influence may gain them a pardon one day. But they must be able to defend themselves now. And their rebellion is a righteous one. Surely you see that."

"I do. It does not mean I will help them with rebellion."

"Why not?"

"Why should I agree to join this cause before I even speak with Simon? It is insurrection and treason to make weapons expressly for rebels to use against the crown. And there is the expense and the work itself to consider—not to mention the risk to their lives, for love of God," he added fiercely.

"We are not asking you to supply boys with sharp things," she snapped.

"Eva, I cannot do this." He could not tell her why.

"Then Simon will not meet with you."

Something cracked in him, prodded by her anger, by her hurtful mistrust of him, by the continual sizzling tension between them. He took her by the arms, more strongly than he meant to do. A myriad of intense feelings—fear, anger, passion, and an undeniable hurt—thundered through him. Eva gasped and gripped his muscular upper arms, even as he grasped her.

"If you doubt my loyalty, test it yourself," he growled. "There is one way to know."

Almost before he knew what he did, he was kissing her, fierce and hard. His lips moved over hers, and a hunger exploded in him. Eva responded with a faint half cry, sinking into his grip. She lifted her hands against his chest, and moaned softly.

The kiss became another, and yet another, like a bright, hot chain forged between them. She returned each one, and he felt her need meet his, flame to flame, real and hungry.

Lost, utterly lost, and he knew it. Blood and sinew, breath and soul, filled to bursting. Dreams, years of them, flooded him. In urging her to test him, he now tested himself against what he had denied his heart for so long.

Stop, he urged himself. *Before it is too late.* Breathless, he pulled back, hands still wrapped around her arms. Eva leaned her palms against his chest as if only that held her upright. Her breasts heaved, and her lips were blushed deep rose.

"Now," he said severely, "ask your woman's heart if I am a trustworthy man." He released her and went to the door. Yanking it open, he strode outside, grateful for the cool buffet of the wind in his face.

Chapter 12

"Iought to make his bed from twigs and bracken," Eva muttered as she flung bits of heather into two large mounds. Choosing sprigs for Lachlann's bed while she recalled his astonishing kisses, her cheeks burned. The sun sank low, and Lachlann had not returned to the house, and still she sat, tossing heather and muttering like a madwoman.

Another soul-melting thrill went through her as she remembered a ribbon of kisses, one weaving into another. She could not forget the strong band of his arms, the heat of his mouth, as much as she tried to resist each stirring memory. Frowning, she told herself to stomp down to the smithy and tell him that she would not tolerate such advances.

In truth, she desperately wanted to kiss him again. Yet no matter how his embrace had warmed and weakened her, or brought to life her most cherished dreams, any risk to her marriage was a risk to her kinsmen. She would be a fool to allow Lachlann to be anything more than a friend.

Yet she did want to allow him more, and fiercely so. She moaned and flung more sprigs into the pile, realizing that their once reliable friendship, now laced with passion, would never be the same. That prideful, stirring kiss was not the mark of brotherly emotion.

That, she decided, was what she must tell him: to befriend her or leave her be. Snatching up a plaid, she spread it on the floor, dumped the heather foliage in it, and tied the corners together. Then she hefted the bundle over her shoulder and opened the door. Solas and Grainne ran outside with her, and she slammed the oaken planking hard before heading over the meadow.

Lachlann shifted through the scrap iron pile, assessing what was there, but he could not keep his mind on his task. He tried to move the canted plough that took up most of the corner, but it would not budge. He kicked it, and it fell over with a clang. A further shove released a little of his anger and frustration.

What he most wanted in life were impossibilities now: to work steel, though he no longer could; to defend a girl destined to become an icon; and to love Eva with his heart and soul—but that was not to be, either.

Yet he had taken her into his arms and kissed her as if she was his alone. His body hardened at the vivid memory, and he longed to follow the natural course of his desire. All his will had been brought to bear when he had let go of her.

Coming back to Balnagovan was more than foolish, he told himself; it could prove ruinous, even disastrous, for both of them, and for others. He shoved his fingers through his hair in exasperation, then went to the door, yanking it open. The crisp air cleared the turmoil in his mind and lured him outside. He looked in the direction of the house, through the amber glow of the sinking sun.

Eva crossed the meadow, the plaid bundle over her shoulder. She strode toward the smithy, annoyance clear in every step, her expression dark and determined.

He was familiar with Eva's flash-fire temper, although womanhood had softened it. Well warned, he leaned against the door frame and folded his arms to wait.

She stomped through the yard, swung the plaid off her back, and shoved it at him with such force that he stepped backward through the door. Holding the bundle, she backed him up further.

"Here is your bed," she snapped, pushing past him. She carried the pack to an empty corner, where she dumped it with a flourish. The knots slid open and heather tumbled out. "Make it yourself, and may you never have a moment's peace in it! That is better than you deserve!" She whirled.

"Eva—" He reached for her arm, but she jerked away.

"Do not think you can grab me again!"

"Eva, I ask your pardon."

"For what? What you did just now, or earlier?"

"For the kiss. It was . . . unseemly of me."

"*Ach,*" she said, sounding more anguished than angered. "You come back to Balnagovan and kiss me as if you had never left, and then you expect me to dismiss it. Perhaps you can do that, but I cannot. It meant something to me, then and now," she added intensely, "even if it meant nothing to you."

"What did it mean to you?" he murmured. "Then, and now?"

She glanced away. "I am a woman now, not a silly girl who does not know her own feelings. The last few years have been difficult, and I have been . . . lonely. And I try . . . so . . . hard"—she gasped, and he saw that she fought tears—"to do what I believe is right, even when I do not want to do it. And then you come back here, and—oh!" She tossed her hands high in frustration and sent him a little glare. "I am not saying what I want to say."

A brief smile twitched at his lips. He should not enjoy her flustered state, but he did. She was so passionate. So genuine. "What is it you want to say?"

"I do not know," she said, and folded her arms, frowning still.

Something sparked in him then: hope. He had not felt it in a long while, but he was sure of it. He narrowed his eyes, and the little lights, like fireflies or faeries, danced again in his vision. Intent on her, he scarcely noticed them.

One kiss, and the dice had rolled another way. Hope flickered, and brightened further when he saw how genuinely angry she was with him. He knew the temper, and knew the girl. She was stirred, deep within. Her emotions were like water, full of depth; she had returned that kiss with equal fervor.

Perhaps her feelings for him went beyond friendship after all, as he had once thought, on a beach at Beltane. Perhaps years spent dreaming of her could come to fruition somehow, if she truly did not want that betrothal. He hardly dared to think about it, but he saw the potential as clear as a rainbow.

Her chin quivered. Seeing that, he wanted to draw her into his arms again. *Wait*, he told himself. If what he hoped was true, if her feelings for him matched or even touched upon his own, the power of it would not be denied.

"I ask your pardon. I was angry, and thought to prove my point—that I can be trusted, even with you in my arms."

"That kiss proved nothing." She lifted her chin.

"You are betrothed already. It was unseemly of me. We were never intended for each other." He made himself say that, though he believed the opposite was indeed true. But if Eva wanted Colin, and preferred the marriage, he had to know.

"N-never intended for each other," she echoed, looking away, a tiny fold between her brows.

"The daughter of a clan chief, and a blacksmith's son—your father would never have tolerated that. He chose the marriage he thought best for you, and of course you must honor that."

"I—I must. And I want what is best for my clan. But I never wanted—I do not—" She gestured vaguely, gasped. He wondered if it was Campbell she did not want, or the blacksmith's son. He gave her time to say, but she only bit at her lip and looked truly distressed.

He tilted his head. "Well, then. You have my apology. It will not happen again."

She glanced at him from beneath dark, doubtful brows. "The kiss, or the apology?" she asked, her voice unexpectedly meek.

He twitched his lips in a quick smile. "Which would you like me to repeat? The apology—or the kiss?"

Eva blinked, and paused. Instead of answering, she went to the far corner, kneeling in the heather she had dumped there. As she began to neaten up the tangle, he walked toward her. She glanced over her shoulder.

"I am sorry about the mess." She sounded mollified. "I lost my temper."

"I know all about your temper. No matter. I will toss a plaid over this, and it will be a fine bed."

"Let me fix it for you, as I meant to do." She spread the plaid and folded one end to reserve for a cover. Setting the heather in careful rows on the plaid, she arranged the fanned sprigs in a neat, springy weaving.

Lachlann dropped to one knee to help her. They proceeded in silence, enveloped by the fresh fragrance. Finally Eva pulled the rest of the plaid over the bed and made it snug.

"I will bring the wolf-hide coverlet from the house for you," she said. "The nights grow colder now."

"You have need of it on your own bed."

"The house has thick stone walls, which hold the heat of the hearth all night. That bed is never cold, even at dawn."

"I know," he said quietly. "I slept there all my life."

She blushed and smoothed the plaid again. Her arm brushed his knee, and her scent, when she reached past him, was a warm and womanly complement to the sweetness of the heather.

Desire rushed through him, and he imagined tumbling into that heathery bed with her. He had dreamed about that more than once. In France, he had survived on dreams that were astonishingly close to what had occurred since his return: Eva in his house, Eva at his hearth, Eva in his arms . . . Eva with him in a bed of deep, intoxicating heather.

His body sparked like tinder under a flint. But he would not let that natural, powerful reaction sweep him out of control. He had too much to consider, and cautious steps to take.

Hope had bloomed, and it needed nurturing.

"Eva—" He reached out to touch her shoulder, but she bent forward to tuck the blanket around the mattress. Her neatly curved waist and hips swayed with sensual grace.

"There," she said, sitting back on her heels. "It is done."

He surveyed the bed. "That plaid belonged to Finlay," he said. "He wore it for feasts and weddings and funerals."

"Oh! I did not know. I will fetch another. Mairi keeps a store of plaids in the house for blankets and curtains."

"It is a comfort, not a distress. Leave it."

She looked up, her face near. He leaned closer, thinking about kissing her again—with tenderness this time, not in anger and hurt, as before. Her gaze slid to his mouth, and he was sure she shared the thought and the desire. Awareness of that intimacy stretched taut between them. Inclined toward her, he felt the spinning inside of him that only she could cause.

She closed her eyes, tilted her head. The curve of her neck was long, slender, and smooth. He rested his fingers lightly upon her jaw, slipped his hand into the cool silk of her hair.

"I am sorry," he murmured, "for what I did at the house."

"Sorry?" she echoed. "I am not."

His heart slammed. "God, Eva," he whispered, leaning

toward her. "What is this between us?" He should not have acknowledged it so directly, but the words were out, husky and sincere.

In the exquisite gray-green depth of her gaze he saw the softness of true caring, along with sparks that hinted at anger, hurt, and caution—mirroring what he felt himself.

She was part of him, and he knew it; he wondered if she felt it too. She was not promised to him, though in a good and perfect world, she would have been. What existed between them felt strong and pure, as if angels had promised them to each other before they were born. But men had broken the bargain. He wondered if he could right it again.

Foolishness, he told himself. Just the yearnings of a lonely man, deep in love for a long time and never free to express it.

He leaned forward and kissed her, slow and deliberate this time. The choice lay in the balance now, and he waited for her measure.

She returned the kiss in full, slanting her mouth under his, so willing that he nearly lost his breath, his reason, his hard-won control. So sweetly that he almost took her down into the heather, then and there.

Only their mouths met, but that simple union held a completeness unlike any he had ever felt. Heat bloomed in the layer of space between their bodies and their still hands.

Then she pulled back and tucked her head on his shoulder. A sigh slipped from her like a sadness released; he heard, on her in-breath, the sadness recaptured. He stroked his hand over the cool, tousled silk of her hair.

"What is this between us?" Eva asked, as if he had just voiced the question. "I do not know. But I think it has been there a long while." She lifted her head.

He touched his brow to hers. "What do you want to do?"

She sighed, then sighed again, and got to her feet

abruptly. "Nothing," she said. "What is there to do? It stays as it is."

She crossed the room on sure, final feet, leaving him kneeling alone beside the luxury of the heather bed, its fullness and fragrance perfect and undisturbed.

Chapter 13

Rain drizzled on the thatched roof as Eva added oats to a kettle of simmering water and left them to cook. By the time she had fed the chickens and raked fresh hay into the byre for Mairi's cow, a downpour had begun. Water sheeted down with such force that she took her time milking the cow under the shelter of the byre's thatched roof. Finally she ran, bucket in hand, around the house toward the door. Her gown was soaked, her bare feet chilled and coated with muck, and the milk somewhat watery.

She heard a shout and paused to look toward the smithy through the slanting, gray rain. Hoping that Lachlann called to her, she was disappointed to see the smithy door closed, though light flickered behind the window shutters. She wondered when she would see him again.

He had been occupied in the smithy for several days, cleaning and shifting things about, and making repairs to the roof. The sight of him standing on the slate roof one sunny afternoon, shirtless and plaided, had nearly taken her breath away. He had waved to her, smiling, and she had returned it, quick and hopeful. Later he had gone inside the smithy, but that bright moment, and his smile, lingered with her.

He had worked in the stable, too, repairing the doors and replacing the straw, and doing the heavy chores that she did not like to do. Their brief conversations centered on what needed attention in the stable and the smithy. Although she helped when she could, Lachlann seemed to prefer working alone, and she left him to it. He rode his garron daily, and she knew he went into the hills. She wondered if he looked for Simon.

Of course, she thought to herself, Simon would not be found until he wanted to be found. Her brother and kinsmen were clever at hiding to survive.

The shout sounded again, and she looked toward the loch. Heavy rain would keep Alpin and the garrison soldiers at Innisfarna, although Eva had seen them often recently, when the soldiers rode out on patrol. As usual, she had avoided them. She had practiced with Alpin, and visited Margaret and Angus to offer her help and to tell them of the blacksmith's return. Another day, she had collected late apples and found a sheltered place to practice swordplay with a sturdy stick.

The days passed quickly, filled with the peacefulness of simple tasks and few visitors. Keenly aware that Lachlann was around, Eva saw little of him. Even when she invited him to the house for meals, their discussions stayed upon small topics.

Neither of them mentioned rebels, or weapons, or king's messages. No one talked about dreams, or kisses, or yearning, though Eva's thoughts tumbled, and her heart felt entangled. She was grateful for the respite that gave her a chance to sort through her feelings—if only she could have done so.

In such rain, she doubted Lachlann would venture out of the smithy if he had work there. He had a fair supply of provisions now, and had set up comfortable quarters at one side of the spacious room. Thus he came to the house less often, and she found herself missing him greatly.

She looked toward the smithy, lost in her thoughts and still hoping the door would open, while the rain streamed down, curling her hair into tendrils, soaking her simple woolen gown. Solas and Grainne sat by the hearth, watching her through the open door with cocked heads, as if they thought she was a fool to stand there when she could come inside and be warm and dry.

Hearing the shout again, she looked at the meadow. A man and a woman walked toward the house, leading a garron pony between them. The woman held a plaid over her blond head, and the man held a plaid over the pony's back, which was hung with two panniers. Inside the baskets, two small covered heads bobbed. The woman waved then, and Eva waved back, laughing.

"Margaret!" she called, putting her hands to her mouth. "Angus!" The couple must have started out from their house, a league or so away over the hills, before the rain had grown so heavy. Now they ran, heads ducked under the plaids, while they protected their children from getting wet.

Eva set the bucket of milk inside and ran toward the smithy, heels sinking in mud once she reached the yard. She pounded on the door, and Lachlann soon opened it.

"Eva, what is it?" he asked with concern. She grinned and slicked back her wet hair. Lachlann chuckled, shook his head. "*Ochan,* girl, you look like a selkie come out of the loch. Come in and get warm." He stood back to allow her entrance.

She laughed and took his arm, loving the feel of his hard strength, warm and dry. "Come out into the rain with me!" she insisted, pulling. He looked at her as if she had gone mad. "Come up to the house! Margaret and Angus are here!" She pointed to the stable, where the couple now led their garron.

He nodded, then went inside the smithy, returning with a length of plaid, which he tented over both his head and hers. "Run, girl," he told her, and she put an arm about his waist and launched with him into the cool, dashing rain, feet slapping in the mud.

By the time they reached the house, they were soaked and laughing. Waiting on the doorstep for Angus and Margaret to come out of the stable, Eva looked up at Lachlann, who still held the plaid over their heads, shielding both of them from the rain.

Smiling, he combed her wet hair back from her brow. "Look at you, selkie girl," he said in a teasing tone.

"And you, selkie man," she returned, and slicked her fingers through the dark, damp waves that fell over his brow.

Under the dripping shelter of the plaid, his smile faded, his eyes deepened to a compelling blue. Desire simmered there, and emanated from his hand upon her head. She sensed it as clearly as if he had touched her in a more provocative way. Her hand stilled on his firm cheek, the whiskers pricking her palm, and a little throbbing thrill ran through her.

"Lachlann MacKerron!" Margaret called. He looked around, and the moment vanished, though the warmth between them lingered. Eva dropped her hand and turned with Lachlann.

"Do you remember me?" Margaret said, laughing as she approached.

"Margaret MacArthur, how could I forget you?" he replied in the light tone he had always used with Eva's cousin. Settling the plaid over Eva's shoulders, he guided her through the doorway and out of the rain. Then he turned to greet Margaret with a kiss for her cheek and a handshake for her husband.

"This day needs a good hot brose," Eva said. She went to the hearth to stir the contents of a small kettle on a low grate over the embers. With a poker, she coaxed the peat fire to a brisk glow, so that it snapped and smoked. "Margaret and I started making this while you and Angus were down in the smithy," she told Lachlann over her shoulder.

He sat on a stool beside the hearth, running fingers briskly through his still-damp hair; he and Angus had just run back from the smithy, with rain soaking them thoroughly again. He stretched his damp, booted feet out to the heat of the hearth, and glanced at Angus and Margaret.

The couple sat on a bench at the table, speaking quietly together as they tended to the feeding of their two small children—a girl who spooned oats clumsily into her mouth, refusing her father's help, and an infant who nursed discreetly at his mother's ample breast, beneath the drape of her *arisaid*. Angus bent his head, sandy and reddish, close to Margaret's smooth golden-blond head, his wide, brawny shoulder pressed to hers.

Lachlann patted Solas, who lay beside him. "Brose sounds fine just now," he told Eva. "Although the Eva MacArthur I once knew could not have made a good brose."

"She has changed," she replied in a clipped tone that made him glance at her quickly.

"And she will be a wife soon," Margaret added.

"And a fine one," Angus added. "She keeps a good house here while Mairi is away."

Eva sat on a stool opposite Lachlann, extending her bare legs and feet toward the warmth of the glowing peat bricks. With a subtle glance, Lachlann admired the fine shape of her ankles and feet, as elegantly aligned as the rest of her.

He slid his gaze slowly upward with delight: long legs and lean hips, flat abdomen, firmly curved breasts and square shoulders, a graceful throat, and the pale curve of her face, bright in firelight. She was soothing to the eyes, he thought, even when sparks shifted unpredictably in his vision.

Eva leaned forward to stir the kettle. "It is done, and will warm us nicely," she said, and stood to fetch some cups.

I am not cold, he wanted to say, *not while I am looking at you.* And not while he sat here with her like a couple long married, content and at peace in each other's company, as his foster parents had been, as Angus and Margaret so clearly were.

Ladling a thin, steaming mix of oats and water into four cups, Eva poured in fresh cream, added honey and *uisge beatha,* and stirred the blend before handing the cups around. Thanking her, Lachlann inhaled the good scent, vivid with *uisge beatha.*

"*Slàinte,*" Eva said, *health,* and smiled at Lachlann and the others, lifting her cup.

Lachlann returned the toast to all and sipped. The warmth radiated through him, pervading and comforting. The rain sheared on the thatch, the wind howled, and he glanced up at the raftered ceiling. "There was plenty of rain in France, but no brose to warm a man," he remarked, and sipped again.

"What was there to warm a man?" Eva asked, laughing.

He tipped his head, and wished her damp hair did not curl so sweetly around her face, wished her cheeks did not blush so easily, because he could not look away from her.

"Not much," he finally answered. "Sunshine in the days and pinewood fires at night. We slept outside more often than not, or we crowded into rooms or tents that held too many men on too few pallets and blankets."

"Sleeping in clusters would warm a man," Margaret said.

"Or give him fleas," Angus drawled.

Laughing with the others, Lachlann sipped again.

"Now that you are back, I am glad I will not have to ride all the way to Glen Brae for nails for my carpentry work, or to have my horse and ox shod," Angus said. He grinned at Lachlann.

"And thank God you came back safe and sound," Margaret said. "You will have more work than you can handle now. That other smith cannot make anything properly. He goes at the smithing like a troll."

Lachlann chuckled. The little girl, called Maeve, clambered down from the bench and toddled toward Eva, who caught her up in her lap. The child, as blond and lovely as her mother, watched in fascination as Eva took a long string from a basket and wove it into a cradle game.

"Lachlann, I will need some ladles and a new poker, and kitchen knives when you have the time," Margaret said. He nodded in agreement. "Oh, we missed you more than you could know!"

He glanced at Eva, unable to stop himself. She watched him soberly over the child's head.

"I hope my wife did not miss you too much, for she liked you well, years back," Angus said. Lachlann smiled and shook his head, while Margaret elbowed her husband. "Which reminds me, I owe you thanks for what you did, years ago." Angus lifted his cup in salute.

"What was that?" Lachlann asked.

"Do you remember that Beltane night before you went to France? Margaret hoped you would walk out with her, but you left her in my care and went walking with Eva. Margaret was not pleased with you for that . . . *oof*," he said on exhale, as Margaret elbowed him sharply. "But by the end of the night, she was pleased with me, I think." Angus winked at his wife.

"Oh, I was—and you were even happier," Margaret murmured, and patted his bearded cheek. Angus laughed outright, in an exuberant, appealing way that made everyone smile.

"You are welcome for the favor," Lachlann said. "You seem well suited to one another."

"A pity you did not find yourself a wife that night, to warm you well," Angus said, though Margaret gasped aloud. "If he had, he might have stayed here, saving us from throwing good coin away with the drunkard," he told his wife defensively.

Again Lachlann glanced at Eva; memories of Beltane were imprinted on his heart. Eva's pink blush told him that she, too, had some fervent recollections.

"That Glen Brae smith is not a MacKerron, that is his trouble," Angus went on. "MacKerrons have smithing in their very blood, from ages past."

Margaret nodded. "MacKerrons are supposed to have dark faery blood, which gives them their skill—and their dark hair and light eyes, or so they say. Eva has dark faery blood in her, too, from Aeife the Radiant One. You know the story, Lachlann."

"It has been a long time since I heard it," he answered.

Margaret shifted her infant, who mewled and stretched in his sleep, to her shoulder and rubbed his back. "Perhaps Eva will tell the story to our little Maeve, who has not yet heard it."

"Maeve is young for a story, but I would like to hear one myself," Angus said. "A tale told by the fireside on a poor night is the best tale of all. Perhaps Eva will oblige us while we finish our brose, before we leave."

"I will, but you are welcome to stay the night, for the rain will not end soon," Eva said. As she spoke, Maeve left her lap to toddle toward Solas and show the dog her string game. Lachlann reached out a hand to prevent the child from stumbling too close to the hearth, and she offered the string to him. He smiled, and she plunked down on his lap, surprising him.

"We would be glad to stay," Angus said. "Maeve, come here."

"She is fine," Lachlann said, patting the child's soft curls. She relaxed against his chest. "Perhaps Eva will tell us all a story now."

Eva nodded, and paused for a moment. "Be still and silent, and I will tell you a tale worth the telling," she began.

Lachlann leaned back against the warm stones of the

hearth wall, with the little girl cozy in his lap. Spoken in Eva's hushed, mellow voice, the familiar tale held new fascination for him.

". . . And when Aeife took up the sword," Eva said, drawing near the close of the story, "it was feather-light and supple in her hand, with a blade like the sun and a hilt of gold, and a pommel like a clear jewel with a thousand colors in it."

Lachlann frowned. Long ago, he had imagined crafting such a sword, exquisite and unique, replete with magic. But dreams were only dreams, he reminded himself. They rarely came true.

As Eva finished the story, he blinked, coming out of his own thoughts. Margaret wiped a tear away and Angus sniffled. Lachlann looked down at the child, now sleeping against his chest. Gently, he lifted her up and handed her to Angus.

Lachlann smiled at the storyteller, and her eyes sparkled as she looked at him. "And so the tradition continues along Aeife's line," he said, "to our own Eva, the radiant one. Thank you for a fine tale," he murmured. "Well worth the telling."

Embers burned like rubies in the forge, mirrored crimson in the broken sword. Lachlann turned the hilt slowly in his hands. Unable to sleep despite the comfort of his heather bed and the soothing sound of the rain, he had risen before dawn to take Jehanne's sword from its hiding place. Now he studied it, the steel cool in his hands, the heat of the fire warming his skin.

The memory of Jehanne's small, gaunt face, vivid with suffering, was still hurtful, but he would always be thankful for the great privilege of riding with her. He blew out a breath, and sadness seemed to dissolve a little, as if the burden had lessened. Coming home—and, above all, being with

Eva—had begun to heal him. He felt it as clearly as a shower of clean rain.

He closed his eyes, and the accursed stars that so often floated across his field of sight flared. Certainly healing might never occur, no matter how winsome or welcome the remedy. He swore low and fierce, like a dragon's out-breath, and laid the sword on the forge. Firelight poured over the steel like blood.

Jehanne had told him that he would know what to do with her sword one day. Yet still he did not. He had never been plagued by indecision or inaction, yet he had not fulfilled his promise to repair her sword. He did not know if he could.

After Eva had told the story of Aeife and the Sword of Light, Lachlann had gone back to the smithy to lie awake, thinking about Aeife, about Jehanne, about Eva, and about the swords for those maidens, one blade actual and hidden, the other a legend.

He imagined Eva, sword in hand like Aeife and Jehanne, strong and beautiful, determined to defend her island and fulfill tradition. He sighed, considering the broken blade in his hand.

Three sword maidens in his life, three different and dazzling threads: one existed in an ancient tale, and one now had the brightness of legend upon her. And the third he loved to the depth of his being. Of the three, Eva was the one who was inextricably part of him. Living without her would tear at him forever.

He whirled the pommel in his palm, and slid the sparkling blade back into its swath of cloth. With a sudden sense of conviction, he knew he must take action. He needed resolution, not legends. He needed Eva, and somehow he must win her.

Chapter 14

Eva sat straighter in the boat, gazing past Alpin to look at her island, green and steadfast upon the surface of the water, the stone castle rising from a ring of trees and rock. Alpin skimmed the boat past the island through the cool, whipping wind.

"Innisfarna is still a beautiful place," Lachlann said, gazing at the island from his seat on a cross bench behind Alpin. Eva glanced toward him. "It has not changed," he added.

"Innisfarna will never change," she said fiercely. "It must remain protected, and as it is, forever."

"How long since you were there?" he asked.

"Too long," she said, glancing at Alpin. She visited the island often, but kept that to herself.

"She will return in triumph one day," Alpin said, looking over his shoulder at Lachlann. "When she fights for her isle."

"Alpin," Eva warned.

"When she fights for it?" Lachlann repeated.

"Green Colin wants it, but we will not let him have it," he said, and grunted in agreement with himself as he pulled on the oars. "When the time comes to defend, Eva will be ready."

Eva sent him a little glare, but Alpin ignored her.

Lachlann drew his brows together, but said nothing more. The boat glided past Innisfarna quickly on a wind-driven current. A rocky finger of land soon obscured all but the treetops and the battlement of the castle. Lachlann turned to gaze at the shoreline as they skimmed northward on the loch.

She watched him curiously. He seemed relaxed, but she saw a subtle tightening around his eyes and mouth. She wondered if he was eager or worried about seeing Mairi.

Alpin had come early that morning to tell them that Mairi MacKerron had returned to Glen Brae and waited to see her foster son. Lachlann had wanted to travel immediately on horseback, but Alpin insisted on taking him with Eva in the boat.

"There is Glen Brae." Alpin pointed across the water toward the rounded hills that rose along the north side of the loch. "The castle is there, on that hill." He indicated a tower of yellow stone, resting upon the cleared slope of a forested hill.

"I have not been to this end of the loch for several years," Lachlann said. "Finlay and I sometimes made the journey on garron ponies to purchase iron and charcoal, but the distance is over thirty miles and took so long to manage that we generally bought our charcoal closer to home. Glen Brae Castle is held by Stewarts, as I recall," he added.

"Sir Patrick Stewart has it now," Eva said. "He is a distant cousin to the king. Mairi's niece married him."

"The girl with all the little ones?" he asked, smiling, and she nodded. The smoky odor that had tinted the wind was gone now, replaced by the clean scent of the water. She lifted her face to the wind, and Alpin pulled the oars, sending the long, low craft into the spray.

Lachlann sat half-turned, breezes fingering his thick, dark hair, his profile strong in the sunlight, his blue eyes bright and narrowed. Her heart flipped crazily each time she looked at him, and the steaming passion of his kisses whirled inside of her again. She looked away, pulling her *arisaid* close around her, but she felt a wave of desire so fresh that her cheeks grew hot.

Several nights ago, if she had stayed in the smithy, and if she had answered his query differently—honestly—instead of walking away to shut herself in the house, something more might have happened between them. Dreams might have come true.

She sighed, and noticed Lachlann's steady gaze fixed upon her. Certainly he, too, felt the passion that sparked between them. How long she could deny that power, she did not know. It flared within her whenever he was near.

Eva watched the water foam and rush past the side of the boat until Alpin pulled in to the shore and tied the craft to a wooden jetty. They stepped out and followed a path that led up a long hill toward the castle, the climb so steep that Eva felt the burn of it in her legs, though she was accustomed to much walking and running over the hills of Glen Fhionn.

The iron gates were open, and Eva, Lachlann, and Alpin were welcomed inside by the sentry, who knew the ferryman. Alpin's request to see Mairi MacKerron produced a broad smile, and they were waved into the bailey yard. A servant girl led them up a flight of stone steps to a second-level entry.

They walked along corridors inside a castle that was as large and grand as the properties her father had held before the dispossession of her clan. Eva looked about with enough interest to slow her step, and she lagged behind when the servant brought them to a wide, arched doorway and knocked.

The girl opened the door and spoke, then waved them inside when a woman called out in welcome. Lachlann entered first.

"Oh, Lachlann!" Mairi's deep, warm voice rang out, and she rose from her seat to rush toward him. Eva smiled through tears as she watched Mairi wrap her foster son in a long embrace. They were not mother and son in the flesh, yet they were similar in their tall, strong builds and dark heads. Mairi's eyes were a warm, serene brown, and her hair, beneath a bleached linen kerchief, was liberally streaked with gray.

He smiled at her. "When I came back to Balnagovan, you were not there to welcome me," he teased. "I was surprised to find Eva instead—and glad that you had taught her to cook." He grinned. "She made me feel at home again. She even brews a heather ale as fine as your own, and keeps your house and animals well."

Mairi laughed. "I am glad to hear it. Three years and more you were gone, my boy," she added crisply. "Did you expect me to sit and wait for you? I have plenty to do, though I took time to pray for you each day. Ah, Eva, come here," she said, reaching for her. "It is good to see you."

Eva stepped into the firm, warm embrace she had come to love. "Mairi!"

"I am glad you were there when Lachlann came home," Mairi whispered. "You were always dear to him, and I think it meant much to him to find you there." Eva felt her throat tighten while Mairi released her and turned. "Alpin MacDewar, do not think to get a hug or kiss from me, you old goat."

"*Och*, I washed for nothing," Alpin groused.

Eva laughed then, accustomed to the prickly banter between the two old friends. She saw a real flush creep into Alpin's weathered face, and Mairi's brown eyes sparkled.

Lachlann put an arm around his foster mother's shoulders and led her to a backed bench piled with cushions, beside a huge stone fireplace. Several children sat in the vast chamber, beside the hearth and on stools and on the floor. "Introduce us to your brood, Muime," Lachlann said, smiling down at a pair of small girls who openly gaped at him, their handsewn dolls clutched tightly in their arms.

"The four nearest the hearth are the children of my niece Katrine and her husband, Patrick Stewart," Mairi said. "The other four—the small girls, and the two boys by the window—are their Stewart cousins. They are all in my charge for now. Lachlann, sit. Eva, Alpin, you as well. The serving girl will bring refreshments—for you, too," she added to the children.

Clearing a seat for Eva, Mairi pushed aside a board game set up on another bench. A stone playing piece clattered to the floor, and a toddling boy emerged from somewhere to pick up the stone and taste it. Eva plucked it out of his hand and Mairi scooped him expertly beneath her arm.

"Little Patrick is a curious soul," Mairi said. "Elspeth and Robbie, please move your game over there. The adults want to talk." The boy and girl gathered their board game and took the pieces over to a window seat to sit with their cousins.

Mairi settled on the cushioned bench holding Patrick in her lap. A low cradle sat on the floor, and she began to rock it with one foot. Inside the shadowed interior, Eva noticed a mound of silken coverings, two tiny pink fists, and a peaceful, tiny face. "So this is Katrine's newest one," she said.

"Her name is Aileen," Mairi said, looking at Lachlann. Eva noticed a quick frown cross his brow.

"My birth mother's name," he said quietly, as he sat beside Mairi. "No wonder you have not yet returned to Balnagovan, for you are surely busy here. How long do you expect to stay here? Until these little creatures grow tall?" He smiled at Patrick, who watched him with wide brown eyes.

"Katrine and her husband, Patrick, are looking for two young nurses for this brood," Mairi said. "I will stay until they find them. Now, tell me what you have been doing,

Lachlann. I see a new scar on your chin—how did this happen?" She took his nicked jaw in a brisk, motherly fashion.

"An English arrow clipped me at Orléans," he answered.

"Orléans! Where the French girl won the day? I heard you rode with her! That made me so proud." Mairi beamed at him.

"We Scots stayed beside her throughout the battle," he said. "She wiped the blood from my face with her own sleeve when I was hit." Eva looked at him in surprise, for he had said little about his adventures in France.

"I heard she was a courageous, remarkable girl. Did you know her well?" Mairi asked.

"Jehanne was my commander, and I admired her. She was captured, tried for heresy, and executed. What more is there to say?" He spoke mildly, but Eva heard the current of tension in his voice. He turned his attention to Patrick, waggling his fingers and smiling as the child tried to snatch his hand.

"Were you with her when she died?" Mairi asked.

He shook his head, and Eva felt a sense of relief. She was glad he had not witnessed that tragedy, though she found herself wondering what he knew of the Maid of Orléans. "I was not in Rouen then. I was on my way home to Scotland to recover from some wounds I had taken."

"Were you badly hurt?" Mairi asked in concern.

He shrugged. "A cut in the side, and a blow to the head. They are healed now, though my vision is not as sharp as it once was."

"Tell us what happened." She touched his arm, and he shook his head. Watching, Eva felt her heart constrict for him in echo of his pain. He did not look at her.

Patrick giggled, eager to renew the finger game. Lachlann wiggled his hand, and the child lunged, arms extended, toward him. Chuckling, Lachlann lifted the dark-haired, blue-eyed toddler onto his lap. Eva sat silently with the others, acutely aware that Lachlann deliberately hid something about his past.

Mairi smiled, watching him play with Patrick. "That child could be your own, you two look so much alike," she said. "Well, you are cousins, after all."

"What?" Lachlann looked at her over the child's head.

Eva, startled, stared at both of them. "Cousins?"

"His father—who is not here just now, or I would introduce you to him—is your first cousin. Your mothers were sisters. Lachlann, I thought Finlay explained that to you before he died."

Lachlann shook his head. "Finlay told me something about my parents, but not that detail. What else should I know?" he asked in a wary tone.

Eva glanced at Alpin, who looked troubled. All she had ever heard of Lachlann's parents was that they were related to Finlay and had died when Lachlann was a baby. Now she realized that Lachlann himself had been told little more than that.

Mairi sighed. "Finlay wanted the truth kept from you when you were younger. He intended to tell you when the time was right, but he kept putting off that day. Then he died so quickly from what seemed a simple illness . . ." She drew a breath, and Lachlann took her hand. "I knew he spoke to you privately as he slipped away, but I was so heartbroken that I could not bear to hear his last words . . . not then. By the time I found the strength to ask, you were about to depart for France. I waited until you returned. Lachlann, I am sorry."

"I understand. Tell me what you know." He glanced at Eva and Alpin. "I trust you two," he told them, and Eva felt a warm thrill at his words. He glanced at her directly. "Perhaps you need to hear this, too."

*   *   *

The little one in Lachlann's lap squirmed and began to fret. He handed him to Mairi, who soothed him until the child relaxed against her. At the same time, she continued to rock Aileen's cradle with her foot.

"I remember the night you were brought to Balnagovan, to Finlay and me, the night your parents died," she said. "You were just past a year old, the same age as this little fellow."

"Who brought me to you?" Lachlann asked.

"The charcoal burner and his wife," she said. "The old one who lives in the forest above Strathlan. I think he lives there still. Alpin?" she asked, turning.

He nodded. "He does, though he and his wife are quite mad. The man makes good charcoal, but his odd manner keeps many customers away."

"I remember him. Finlay sometimes bought charcoal from him." Lachlann looked at Mairi. "Go on."

"The charcoal burner knows something of what happened the night your parents died. Finlay said the old fellow was the only one who knew the truth but he has never spoken of it that I know. Lachlann, your father was a MacKerron, and a very skilled bladesmith. That much you knew."

Lachlann nodded. "Tomas MacKerron was his cousin. They learned their art from the same man, Finlay's father. And now I learn that I am related to this child through my mother." He glanced at Patrick, asleep on Mairi's wide bosom. "I want to hear the whole of it."

"His grandmother and your mother were sisters, daughters of a Stewart who was a kinsman of the king. Patrick's little sister, here, was named for your mother, Aileen."

He frowned. "I was never told that my mother was a Stewart of Glen Brae."

"Of Strathlan. Do not hold it against us, Lachlann," Mairi said. "Finlay insisted upon the secrecy. I did not agree, but honored his wishes."

He nodded, trying to understand. "Stewart of Strathlan?" he asked, astonished.

"But Colin Campbell holds Strathlan," Eva said. Lachlann glanced at her. She sat forward, her cheeks flushed from the heat of the hearth. The sight of her fresh, dark beauty stirred him, a respite in the midst of his current confusion.

He was glad that Eva would learn about his parents here with him, and she would learn of his obligation for vengeance, too. There were apparently details he had not yet heard, but he knew that Colin had some part in the death of his parents. Finlay had revealed that much to him, although Lachlann had not yet found the right moment to explain it to Eva. But the time had come for truth.

"When Aileen and I were girls," Mairi said, "Strathlan was part of Aileen Stewart's dowry. But she did not want to marry the man her father chose for her. One night she secretly wed her true love—Tomas MacKerron, the local blacksmith. Her father was furious, and disowned her."

"Finlay did not tell me that part," Lachlann murmured. "He said that my father had been a cousin and a fine bladesmith, and my mother a beauty from a fine family. And that they had been murdered."

"Murdered?" Eva gasped.

"Finlay always believed so, with reason," Mairi said. "What else did he tell you?" she asked Lachlann.

"Something about a tradition among the MacKerrons . . ." He stopped, shook his head. "The making of a faery blade."

"Faery blade?" Eva asked quickly.

"There is a tradition that the MacKerrons know how to forge faery steel," Alpin said. "I thought it was just a tale."

Lachlann shrugged. "There are methods in the making of steel, said to have been taught to a MacKerron by the faeries ages ago. Nonsense, of course, but it makes for a good tale."

"It is not nonsense," Mairi said. "Some say that Tomas MacKerron crafted the finest blades because he used those secrets. And Finlay revealed them to you."

"He told me some of it," Lachlann said. "I think he left much unsaid. He was weak, and I did not press him to talk."

Mairi nodded, hesitated. "Lachlann, your parents were happy. They had a good marriage and they both loved their little son." She touched his hand. "But Tomas made an enemy of the man who had first been betrothed to Aileen Stewart. The man sued for her dowry and won it in the courts. Tomas and Aileen had nothing, after that, but what living he made at his craft. But they were content. I want you to know that."

"Who was her betrothed?" Eva asked.

"Murdoch Campbell. Colin's father. That is why Colin owns Strathlan now—he inherited it from his father."

Eva gasped. "Oh! It should have come to Lachlann!"

"It could not, for Aileen's father disowned her. She brought nothing to her husband . . . except her love, which was all he ever wanted of her."

"So Murdoch won Strathlan?" Alpin asked.

Mairi nodded. "He sued for it three years before Aileen and Tomas died in a fire at Tomas's smithy."

"Tell me what you know of that night," Lachlann said. He remembered what Finlay had told him as he lay dying, and it still chilled his blood: in halting words, Finlay had named Colin Campbell as his father's murderer and had urged Lachlann to pursue vengeance. At the time, Lachlann had scarcely heard of Colin, had seen him only once or twice. Yet within weeks of Finlay's death, Colin had been named again, as Eva's favored suitor in marriage. He scowled to himself, wondering if he would ever be free of this enemy—a man he hardly knew.

"The fire started one night while Tomas was working

late, as was his habit. You and Finlay often did that, too," Mairi said.

He nodded. "Color changes are essential to the making of steel," he explained, "but the colors are subtle, and are best seen at night."

"Your mother was with Tomas," Mairi said. "She was lovely, dark and slender. You have her bright blue eyes, Lachlann. How she adored you."

He smiled, but he felt a deep, lonely pang, wishing he had known her.

"She sometimes helped Tomas at the forging," Mairi went on. "That night, you were asleep in the house near the smithy. By the time others saw the blaze and arrived to help, Tomas and Aileen were both gone. The charcoal burner rescued you, Lachlann, and brought you the whole length of the loch to Balnagovan."

Lachlann listened, rubbing his fingers over his eyes wearily, sadly. He had mourned Finlay as the only father he had ever known, unable to fully mourn his own parents.

"I had no babes of my own," Mairi said. Lachlann recognized the grief of that in her voice. She should have had several children, he thought. She surely had the heart for it, but heaven had had other plans. "And I loved you like my own," Mairi murmured.

"I know," he said gently. "I always knew that."

"Who . . . who killed Lachlann's parents?" Eva asked quietly.

Lachlann glanced at her. "Finlay told me that Colin Campbell caused the blaze, and their deaths."

"Colin!" Eva gasped, and looked at him, her eyes wide with dismay. He frowned slightly.

"Finlay had heard so from the charcoal burner who had been at the burning smithy," Mairi said. "Colin—who was a young man then—came to our house asking after the babe, for he had heard that we fostered Tomas's son. He expressed his sorrow over the tragedy and offered coin for the child's care, which Finlay refused. My husband swore it was murder, but Colin denied any knowledge of it—he said he was just visiting out of mercy, and took offense. The Campbells were powerful, and the MacKerrons were few, merely a sept of Clan Arthur. Finlay could not pursue it."

"You did what you could," Alpin said. "You raised Tomas and Aileen's son to be a fine man, and a fine smith."

Mairi smiled wanly. "We did. Lachlann, we never told you all of this because we did not want to poison your mind with hatred. Finlay meant to tell you the truth, but he did not have time, at the end, to say all that he knew."

"He urged me to seek revenge against Colin," Lachlann said.

"He believed it was warranted," Mairi said.

"Then ever since Finlay's death," Eva said, looking at Lachlann, "you have had reason to hate Colin."

"Indeed," Lachlann answered quietly, his gaze meeting hers, "I have reason."

"I understand a need to avenge your parents' awful deaths," Eva said. "But you cannot know for certain that Colin caused it."

Lachlann sighed. "I see that now."

"Ask the charcoal burner," Alpin said. "He is mad as a hare, but he may remember the truth."

Lachlann frowned. "I will do that. Muime, does Colin know me? I remember him only as one of the men who sometimes ferried over to Innisfarna to see the Mac-Arthur."

"I doubt he gave much thought to us after that, living at the far end of the loch. He took Alpin's ferry sometimes, but scarcely spoke to Finlay beyond paying to stable his horse with us. I knew he had important dealings with the MacArthur."

"And now I am betrothed to him," Eva said.

Mairi nodded. "The world is indeed full of ironies."

"Where was my parents' home?" Lachlann asked.

"On a hill overlooking a little loch above Strathlan, northwest of Loch Fhionn," Mairi replied. "The buildings are gone now, but their graves are in the churchyard near there. Lachlann, please forgive us for keeping the truth from you for so long. Finlay did not like to speak about this." Mairi sighed. "As you grew into a man, kind and strong, he did not want to fill your young heart with hatred. He loved you, Lachlann. That is why he waited."

He nodded, and felt tears sting his eyes, and could not speak. He took Mairi's hand, pressing her fingers in silence.

His gaze met Eva's, and the compassion in her eyes soothed him. But he glanced away with a thoughtful sigh.

Water lapped at the sides of the boat as Alpin rowed them home. The lantern glowed on its hook, thrust up in the center of the boat, spilling gold over their heads and shoulders. Eva sat beside Lachlann on the cross bench, for the other bench was piled with the bundles Mairi had sent with them—food and casks of ale and *uisge beatha* of her own making.

Cloaked in darkness, Eva felt safe and comfortable beside Lachlann, his arm pressing hers, his solid body blocking the wind. She looked up at him, and saw him squint at the lantern and at the water, closing one eye for a moment. He glanced at her and smiled a little.

"Does your eye bother you?" she asked. "There is no scarring there. I did not realize you had injured it."

"The trouble is inside the eye, not outside," he said. "I took a blow to the head on the left side."

"Were you fighting beside the Maid at the time?"

He shrugged. "In a way."

"Does it hurt still?"

He shook his head. "Sometimes I see lights and colors that are not truly there." Cocking his head, he looked down at her. "Right now, I see sparkles and starlight all about your head. You look like an angel with a halo and a crown of stars." He gave her a crooked grin. "How well it suits you—unless one knows your devilish temperament, as I do."

Eva grimaced at him, and he laughed. "And if you are not wearing a halo and stars now," he went on, "then my eye is troubling me." He turned somber and looked away.

Hearing the bitterness in his voice, she understood it, for she knew far more than she had before. "How were you injured?" she asked. She was curious about Jehanne, whom he rarely mentioned, and she wanted to hear about Lachlann himself.

"I was struck," he said, "when I tried to save Jehanne and failed. She was taken at the gates of a city, though we tried our best to prevent her capture. Perhaps I am doomed to see angels, and halos, and stars now, so that I will never forget the one who saw angels herself—the one we lost."

Tears filled Eva's eyes as she sensed the agony beneath his words. She sighed, and wondered about the nature of his feelings for the French girl. Wondered if he had lost his heart to Jehanne in France. Suddenly she felt hurt and forlorn. But there was little point in that, she thought, for she herself was promised.

Promised, and confused. Passion sizzled between them, and her feelings for Lachlann grew stronger every day. No matter whom they loved, or what path they took in their lives, Lachlann was, and always would be, her friend. That bond would always exist, although she wanted much more than that.

After a moment, under cover of the plaids, his and hers, pooled between them, Eva reached for his hand. He grasped her fingers in his, and she turned her hand palm to palm with his.

If I can have nothing else of you, she wanted to tell him, *at least let there always be friendship between us.* She only sighed, guarding her thoughts, but she kept her hand curled warm in his.

Chapter 15

S tanding at the forge, Lachlann rubbed flint and wood together to start the fire. He could have borrowed an ember
from the house's hearth, but Finlay had taught him that a
cold forge must be started with a new spark instead of an old
one to ensure good fortune. Certainly he needed that, now
that he was about to resume smithing at Balnagovan.

He shimmied the stick and flint until a thread of smoke
spiraled outward. When a spark and a tiny flame blos-
somed, he set the burning wood on the forge bed and tucked
kindling around it. The fire grew bolder, and he nurtured its
edges with a small hand broom made of dampened twigs.

"Good morning," Eva said.

He looked over his shoulder. She stood in the doorway,
which he had left open to admit sunlight and fresh air.
When she smiled, he felt warmed—not from the newborn
fire but from that whimsical, adorable, familiar smile.

"And to you," he answered, and turned to tend the
flames. With her candid gaze upon him, he suddenly felt
awkward, as if once again he was a lanky, smitten youth
acting busy in her presence. And she was still the radiant
one she had always been to him, fresh and wild and intoxicating.

She approached. "What will you make?" she asked.
"Weapons?"

He sent her a stern little glare to cover up the softening

in his heart. "I will not make weapons for your rebels, if that is what you are thinking."

"I know." She looked up at him. The fire's glow revealed her cream-and-roses skin, sheened her rich hair, and highlighted her silvery, stormy eyes. A balm to the gaze, she was, he thought, clear and perfect. He noticed that the troublesome, erratic sparkles in his vision were not there now.

"There are some tasks at the house," she said. "The chain that holds the kettle over the hearth is rusting, and the handle of the griddle is cracked, and the latch on the byre is loose."

"I can fix those." He prodded the fire.

Eva glanced up as if tallying a list. "Oh, and every hook in the house is in use. Would you make new hooks for baskets and clusters of herbs and onions? And would you sharpen the kitchen knives, and make a new little knife for cutting vegetables? The rings on the bed curtains are flaking with rust, and may need to be replaced, as well."

He laughed outright. "Is that all?"

"One other thing," she said softly. "I have a brooch, a silver pin with a broken clasp. It needs—"

"I know what it needs," he murmured. "I remember." He did not look at her, though he remembered the night, years ago, when the brooch had come loose; moments later he had kissed her. The magic of that night would never leave him.

"Well," she said. "We have been without a good smith for a long time, and I know Mairi would like those things tended to."

"It will all be done. Is there anything else?"

She shrugged. "Not unless you want to make weapons."

Sliding her a glance, he huffed a flat laugh. She blushed and looked away. He regretted the laughter, for he needed to remain firm on that topic. But his mood had lightened when she had walked into the smithy. She had always affected him like that, even now—especially now—when sadness and regret clouded his emotions.

The little spark of hope he felt earlier was still there, stronger now, nourished by a few dizzying kisses, by delightful companionship, by their visit with Mairi, and by Eva's gesture, last night, when she had sought and held his hand. He had trusted Eva and Alpin with the truth about his past, and even though it involved Colin, he knew his secrets were safe.

The dogs barked outside, and Eva turned to peer through the doorway. "Go on outside," Lachlann said. "While the fire heats, I had planned to go up to the house to remove the latches."

She nodded and walked out, and Lachlann gathered the tools he would need to work on the door fastenings—file, chisel, peen hammer, some nails—before going outside as well.

He followed Eva slowly across the meadow, admiring her sure stride, the fluid grace of her hips. That lovely sight caused his body to harden pleasantly, but he frowned and looked away.

He entered the house, ducking his head to clear the lintel, and set to work on the latches, while Eva watched. After filing the cold iron of the hasp, he paused to examine it.

"This needs heating and reshaping," he said, and took up a chisel to pry the riveted end loose with a few sharp tugs. He held the hasp in his palm to show her. "The iron under the rivet has split, do you see? The iron fibers are showing—when that happens during forging, it is a poor job indeed. Now the piece must be remade to sit straight upon the door. If the iron proves too fibrous, it must be discarded." He gathered up the iron pieces and his tools.

She went outside with him. "May I watch you work?"

He shrugged, though he would welcome her presence, and led the way back to the smithy.

Inside, the forge fire burned nicely, its bed limited to a small squarish area, all that he would need for most tasks. Suspended above the left side of the forge was the long horn handle that worked the great bellows behind the chimney. Lachlann pulled downward on the handle to ease out some air to feed the fire. While the heat increased, he looked at the iron latches, thinking about how to repair and improve them.

"You always enjoyed this part of the smithing, I think," Eva said softly beside him.

Lachlann looked up in surprise. He had been so absorbed that he had forgotten she was there for a moment. "What part?"

"Puzzling out the task," she explained. "I remember watching you and Finlay MacKerron. I used to marvel at how well you both knew the craft, and how clever and strong you were to make metal into something as useful as a pothook, or as beautiful as a sword."

He jiggled the hasp and latch. "It just needs some training and cleverness," he said. "And it does not require much strength." He turned to the fire, brushing its edges with the dampened twig broom. Eva was right, he thought. He had always found much satisfaction in the mental tasks of smithing as well as the demanding physical aspects. He could twist a design effortlessly inside his head until he saw it completed and perfect. Then he could duplicate, in hot metal, the image he saw in his head. What she found marvelous seemed only natural and ordinary to him, but he was glad of her interest.

"Is the fire hot enough now?" she asked.

"Nearly so." He pulled the bellows handle again. The flames in the bed filled an area about a handspan square, and blazed brightly and merrily. Though he would do only simple tasks today, he felt excitement and anticipation build in him.

The snap and smoke and bright heart of the fire had always held allure for him. Since childhood, he had respected fire, understood its moods, its gifts, its dangers, and he had always savored the challenge of working with it. For a moment he wondered why he had hesitated to begin smithing again.

Then he remembered. Once again his vision turned to shards of light, independent of the glowing forge. He closed his eyes, now wary of the work. Then he turned his concentration to his task, reminding himself that he was a smith, trained and born to it. Like the fire in the forge, hope and passion had begun to flare in him again, sparked in many ways by Eva. She was a continuing thread of fire in his life and his heart, delicate and powerful.

Picking up a pair of tongs, he pinched the hasp and placed it in the fire. The black iron reddened and began to glow. When it was yellow-red, he pulled it out and rested it on the anvil face. Snatching up a small hammer, he gave the softened metal a few taps, changing its shape as if it were malleable clay.

"It is like magic, what you do," Eva breathed, watching. "You touch iron to fire, and it turns to solid flame."

A sudden hot spiral of lust ran through him at the image her words created in his mind. He glanced at her, nodded.

"Tam Lin," she said, smiling. He cocked his head in wordless question while he worked. "Have you never heard the story? Tam Lin was stolen away by the faery queen, and his lover vowed to save him. He came to her in a dream and told her what to do. 'I will grow in your arms, love, like iron in strong fire,'" Eva sang, her voice low and true. "'But hold me fast, let me not go . . .'" She stopped.

"Go on," he said, and tapped the metal again, so that sparks flew out. "I have heard it, but forgotten."

"'I am your heart's desire,'" she finished in quiet melody.

Lachlann hit the metal too hard. He looked at her and

saw her blushing. "Ah," he murmured. "I do remember that." *Heart's desire indeed,* he thought. Blood simmering, he remained outwardly calm and focused his attention on the work.

Foolish, he thought, smacking hammer to hot iron, to crave another man's bride, his enemy's betrothed. *Foolish,* he repeated on the next strike, to love her so fiercely, yet always hold back. The final slam sent sparks out and dented the metal deeply.

The piece would need reheating and rehaping now. He turned back to the fire, aware that Eva was watching. How much longer could he endure being near her every day, loving her with every fiber of his being, and yet acting cool toward her—but for the dangerous moments when he lost his hold over desire and longing? How long before he kissed her again and could not stop there?

And what would she do if that happened? His body pulsed as he stabbed the iron into the hot core of the fire, brushing the crumbling ash at its edges.

He had to know what she wanted, and he had to find some peace and resolution to the matter, for her sake as well as his own. Strong as steel he might be, but his own core was molten, and would not be contained for long.

He frowned and made himself focus on the iron, which glowed brightly now. He whipped the piece out of the fire to rest it on the anvil. Then he struck it, turning it with the tongs, teasing it with the hammer until the metal bent to his will and approached the image in his mind.

Repeating the steps until the shape of the hasp was precise, he doused the hot iron in a tub of water beside the anvil, then laid it, dripping and still sizzling, on the anvil.

"There is your new lock," he said.

Eva nodded. "In the old tales, the blacksmiths were said to be magicians. Now I see why. That transformation does truly seem like magic. You make it look easy."

"Sometimes it is. Sometimes not." He spoke curtly.

"I am curious to try it." She glanced up at him.

He lifted a brow, but he knew she could do it. Wordlessly, he reached for a pair of leather gloves and a set of tongs. "Pick up that iron rod and put it into the fire. Go on," he encouraged when she hesitated.

She used the pincers awkwardly at first, picking up a short iron rod from the anvil, nearly dropping it. She slid one end into the crackling bed of fire, wincing at the searing heat.

"Careful," he cautioned. "Let it sit there. Now give the fire some air—just enough. Pull on the handle . . . a little more muscle in it now. I know you are strong enough for it."

She yanked downward on the horn handle, then released it. The fire expanded like a living thing.

Lachlann stilled her hand on the bellows handle after she pulled it. "Enough. When the iron turns cherry red, it can be worked. 'Cherry red to pigeon blue, the steel is strong, the temper is true,' " he recited. "Finlay taught me that when I was young. Colors are important in smithing. They tell the smith what to do and when to do it."

"The red is turning more golden now," she observed.

"Take it out. Work fast, for it loses heat quickly."

When she transferred the iron rod to the anvil, Lachlann rested his hand over her gloved one on the tongs, helping her grip the red-hot iron. With a small hammer, he rapped at the metal until it bent, and he demonstrated changing the angle on the strike. Then he handed Eva the hammer.

She gave the hot iron metal a timid little knock. Lachlann helped her turn the rod as she hit it. When her strikes grew bolder, he let go. He smiled to himself as he watched, pleased that she had not retreated from the challenge or the danger.

Then she tapped it so vigorously that a small shower of

sparks flew out. She shrieked and stepped back, into him, her foot tromping on his.

"Easy," he cautioned. Eva stood within the bowl of his arms, and he kept her there, helping her hold tongs and hammer. Heat filled the space between their bodies. He guided her through more strikes, explaining with gestures and few words.

"It stopped glowing," she said, sounding disappointed.

"Just give it another heating."

With greater confidence, she went through the steps again, heating, tapping, heating again. When next she struck the hot iron, it looped for her, luminous and crooked. Eva laughed in delight, and Lachlann smiled.

"What are you making?" he asked her.

"I had not thought about it! Can I make a hook from this?"

"You can make whatever you want. It follows your will. Be firm, be alert and relaxed, and know your purpose. That, my girl, is the secret of the blacksmith's magic." He winked.

She smiled, even glowed. "Will. That is the secret?"

He nodded. "Fire, iron, and tools can be used by anyone. It is the will, the intent, the imagination that makes the difference." He smiled, realizing that he liked teaching her. The errant thought that he would like to teach her something about desire and loving slipped through his mind.

Eva gave him a measuring glance, and he wondered if she read his wayward thoughts. She turned to heat the iron piece again, and laid it out to strike it. Sparks flew, and tiny stars landed on his forearm.

Lachlann winced and shook off the burning, then dipped his forearm quickly in a bucket of cold water beside the anvil.

"Oh!" Eva said, pausing. "I am sorry!"

"Do not stop," he said. "And watch where you wave

your tools when you apologize. Keep going. Heat it and work it."

At last she bent the iron into a passable hook, then doused it in water and held it up, smiling proudly. Lachlann congratulated her, then took out another rod he had already heated and showed Eva how to strike the piece to flatten it into a leaf-shaped pointed blade.

"Simple knives are made this way," he explained.

"Ah," she said. "Then I could make weapons myself."

"Arm your kinsmen with little iron kitchen knives? *Ochan,* that will further your rebellion," he drawled.

She wrinkled her nose. "Show me more. I like this."

"You like it too much." He took the tongs, the half-beaten iron, and the hammer from her. "You would play here all day, and then when would I get my work done, hmm?"

"I will not bother you for long today," she said. "I promised to meet Alpin. But I can help you in here again, if you want. I could help you every day, and be your assistant."

While he tapped heated iron into another hook, he frowned, considering what she said. He preferred working alone, but he could not resist the prospect of more time with Eva—even though he should resist that. "Some of the smithing would go faster with two sets of hands," he ventured. "Nails and horseshoes and that sort of thing."

"Hooks and chains," she agreed. "I could do those."

"You always were a fiery girl," he murmured, and she smiled, cheeks and eyes bright. He grinned, shrugged as if in surrender. "Well, if you want to be my apprentice, you will have to pay close attention. There is much to learn." He slid the rod into the fire for another heating.

She nodded eagerly. "I can learn this. In the past, I think sometimes you and Finlay did not want me around."

"Smiths do not like distractions while they work. We

might get burned watching a girl instead of the hot iron," he said wryly, removing the rod from the forge bed.

"Was I a distraction, back then?"

He hesitated. "Sometimes."

"Am I now?"

"Definitely. Now be quiet. Smiths like silence." He tapped the glowing rod, and sparks burst forth. "Do not stand so close," he told her. "Sparks fly like shooting stars when you are around. I think you make them all by yourself."

She laughed and shuffled back. "Why are you using that sort of hammer? What are you doing now?"

"Hush, you," he said. Eva nodded mutely. He worked swiftly and surely to create more hooks, giving them a practical, elegant S shape. The work lacked challenge, but producing any handsome, useful item brought him satisfaction and pleasure.

Being with Eva gave him a great deal of pleasure, too. He glanced at her again. She was most definitely a distraction, with her hair wisping in dark curls, and a rosy sheen on her face. The smithy had grown hot, and sweat dripped down his back, beaded on his brow. He wiped his forearm over his face.

For a moment, a shadow drifted over his vision. Blinking, he narrowed his eyes to correct the flaw, and wondered if he would ever be able to do more than bend hot iron into simple shapes.

In Perth, he had smithed only black iron, had not worked steel. At Balnagovan, memories and dreams and expectations existed. A faery sword awaited him, and Jehanne's own sword was hidden away. He could not escape broken dreams here.

Glancing at Eva as his vision cleared, he savored the sight of her, like a balm for his weary eyes. To him, she had always seemed to glow, fiery and enduring. He smiled rue-fully to himself, glad she was here, feeling good in her pres-ence, healing a little. And he wondered if he would ever be able to express his gratitude or his love to her.

He looked down, made another fold in the willing iron, and told himself to think only of his task. The forge burned merry and the iron was hot, demanding quick work and quicker thought. The smithing had begun.

Chapter 16

Waking from the strange peace of a wonderful dream, Eva stirred and opened her eyes. The warmth and joy of the dream lingered: Lachlann stood at a blazing forge, his body bronzed and hard-hewn in the amber light. Eva watched while he shaped a shining sword; somehow she knew it was a faery blade. He handed it to her, smiling, and then he kissed her, deep and thorough and tender, until her body melted inside and she clung to him, yearning for more as he touched her fervently with hot, gentle hands.

Outside, the wind howled and the rafters creaked. The stones that held the thatching, slung on ropes, thunked against the exterior walls. Eva turned restlessly in the shelter of Lachlann's bed and thought of him sleeping in the smithy on his bed of heather. After that passionate dream, she ached inside, a hollow of loneliness. Rising from the bed, she dressed in a plain woolen gown, pulled on her *arisaid,* and drew on her shoes. Going to the door, she opened it on a windy, dove gray morning.

Light showed already in the smithy windows, and the hammer rang like a muffled bell. Perhaps, she thought, that deep, driving sound had stirred her dream of him.

After she had tended to the necessary chores and had made some fresh, hot oatcakes, she wrapped a few in a cloth and crossed the meadow. A brisk wind whipped at her hair and her *arisaid,* and as she came closer to the smithy, the steady clang of the hammer continued. She knocked firmly on the door and opened it, stepping into the dim interior.

Lachlann stood at the forge, wearing a plaid and a linen shirt, his dark hair gleaming in the firelight. He nodded to her and turned back to his work.

She closed the door and found a dim interior, for the windows were shuttered against the cold air. The lingering smell of charcoal and metal was strong, and flames burned brightly on the forge bed. Eva moved toward it, lured by that cheery warmth.

"Have you come to help out this morning?" Lachlann asked, smiling briefly. "After I finish a few things here, I will shoe the horses."

"I would not be much help with the horses," she said, for she had seen that process often and did not relish standing behind a horse and coaxing it to put up its hoof for her to pound nails into it. "I brought you something to eat," she said, leaving the oatcakes on a table that held tools. He nodded. "And I came to ask if you would repair this for me." She unpinned the silver brooch at her shoulder. "I know you are not a silversmith—"

"But I did promise to fix this," he said, his glance meeting hers briefly. He took the circlet from her and wiggled the clasp and the broken loop. Then he set a thin poker in the fire until it reddened, and carefully touched the red-hot point to the broken piece, using small tongs to meld the softened silver. After dipping the silver into the water, he laid it on the anvil.

"Careful now," Lachlann said, as Eva reached for the brooch. She winced when she touched the hot metal and snatched her fingers back.

"The first lesson any smith learns," Lachlann said, "is that metal that looks cool can still be very hot even after it has been doused in water. Always test a piece before you touch it."

Eva nodded, and tapped the brooch with a tentative fingertip. Lachlann picked it up. Moving closer, he fastened the brooch in her plaid, his knuckles brushing her collarbone. He stood so close that she felt his warmth, and felt something spin deep inside of her.

"There," he murmured. "I am sorry it took so long to fulfill the promise." His thumb smoothed over the silver circlet, and his fingers brushed her shoulder, rousing shivers in her. "Before I ever went to France, I expected you to bring the brooch to me for repair," he said. "I waited for you, but you never came. And I did not see you when I went to Innisfarna to deliver the weapons I owed your father."

She felt pulled into his brilliant blue gaze. "You waited for me to come to the smithy?"

He smiled a little. "I would have fixed the brooch for you, had you come then."

"Oh," she said. "I—I did not think you wanted to see me after . . ."

"Of course I did," he murmured, then stepped back and turned toward the forge. "I have work to do. When these tasks are done, today or tomorrow, I am going to Glen Brae."

"Alpin will row you over to see Mairi whenever you like."

"This time I will ride. I want to find the charcoal burner," he said, his back to her. "I need to buy some quality goods for the forge, and I have some questions to ask the man." As he spoke, he slid an iron rod into the fire and pulled on a pair of leather gloves.

Eva felt a pang of sympathy, knowing he meant to ask about the deaths of the parents he had never known. "I will go with you if you like."

He paused. "I must do this alone, Eva."

She nodded, and stepped closer. "Can I help you now?"

"You can watch the iron," he said, and handed her the

tongs and a twig brush. While she prodded the ashes, he collected other tools and laid them on the anvil. He slipped a chisel vertically into a hole in the anvil face, so that the point protruded upward.

"The rod is starting to glow," she said, and Lachlann reached past her to pluck the iron out with tongs and set it over the chisel edge. Swift strikes with the hammer divided the luminous rod into sections. Deft and quick, he shaped each piece with tongs and hammer to form links.

"This will be your new pot chain," he said, and welded the links onto a partial chain that he had already begun.

Intrigued by his sureness and speed, Eva watched, listening to the hard rhythm of the hammer. Soon she realized that the smithy had become very warm, with the door and windows shut against the chill. Sweat beaded on Lachlann's brow, and he wiped it with his forearm as he built the sturdy black chain.

He slid more rods into the fire, then paused to slide his plaid off his left shoulder and tug off his shirt, tossing it onto a nearby workbench. He glanced at Eva.

"This place can get hot as summer, even on the coldest days," he said, wiping his damp brow again.

She blinked, nodded, as he resumed work. The muscles of his chest and arms rippled, rounded and defined, beneath smooth, gleaming skin. Her breath quickened as she remembered the unforgettable vision of Lachlann forging a faery blade, his body hewn and bronzed, his eyes like piercing blue flames. Now he was simply an earthly man doing ordinary labor, yet he was utterly compelling to watch.

Desire raced hot and fast through her as she remembered the feel of those broad arms, the delicious touch of his mouth upon hers. Aware that she wanted him keenly, body and soul, she wrapped her *arisaid* more tightly around her as if to smother her feelings.

The hammer chimed and thunked on the anvil, the

rhythm driving down into her body. Eva stepped back, breathing quickly, and when sparks showered outward, she turned away. Lifting his discarded shirt, she folded its inviting scent against her, then hung it on a pegged rack beside sets of tongs. Strolling around the smithy, she trailed her hand over the tools, over the table surfaces. She glanced at Lachlann, who seemed completely absorbed in his work.

In the far corner of the room she saw the heather bed, and imagined Lachlann asleep there. She wondered if he ever dreamed of her, as she did of him, and she sighed.

In a corner, she saw several pieces of iron—horseshoes, rods, and a broken plough. Crossing the room, she picked up one of the horseshoes curiously. "What will you do with all this iron?" she asked.

"Melt it down to make things," he answered succinctly, and smiled at her, quick and wry. "Eva, fetch me one of the vials of oil from that chest by the wall if you will. This chain will need some polishing."

She went to the wooden chest, opened it and found a vial, then closed the lid. Something glittered overhead, and she glanced up. On the ledge formed at the top of the thick stone wall, below the rafters, she saw a long wrapped bundle of linen.

Through its open folds, she saw the yellow gleam of gold or brass. Reaching up, she meant to close the cloth, thinking that Lachlann would want this fine object better protected from the slightly smoky air. The package tumbled from the ledge, and she caught it as the cloth parted further.

Eva gasped, for she held a sword hilt of wrapped leather, with a disc pommel of shining brass and a gracefully curved cross guard of steel, trimmed in brass. The blade was broken at a sharp angle a little below the cross guard; the upper, pointed end of the blade lay stacked beneath the lower blade. Engraved lilies, chased in gold, glittered on both bright remnants.

"Give that to me," Lachlann said gruffly. She turned to see him standing behind her. So absorbed in discovering the sword, she had not heard him approach.

"This is beautiful," she said. "A common, lightweight thrusting sword, but with exceptional crafting. Is it one of the pieces you made before you left Balnagovan?" She continued to look at it. "How unfortunate that it cracked! There must have been a weak spot in the blade. Surely not a MacKerron blade, then," she said with a smile.

He looked grim. "A friend in France owned it, and I brought it back. I promised to repair it. Give it to me." He held out his hand firmly, beckoned.

Puzzled by his tone and attitude, she frowned, but handed it back to him. He began to wrap it carefully.

"I did not think you would wield such a sword yourself. Likely you prefer something more substantial for your grip and your strength, perhaps a two-handed double-edged longsword," she said.

He lifted a brow. "How do you know so much about swords?"

Eva started to answer, then remembered that Lachlann did not know about her sword lessons with Alpin. He was already sour on the topic of weapons for her kinsmen, so she could hardly tell him that, nor could she mention that she needed a good sword herself, something as light and fine as the one he held.

"I know some," she admitted, shrugging. "Enough to see that this one is a beautiful blade, even if it is not your own make. You and Finlay did not use that style of pommel, with a sunken center, and most of your cross pieces were sloped but straight, ending in tiny quatrefoils." Eva opened the linen carefully to point at the blade decoration. "And this one has flowers engraved along the fuller. You and Finlay always cut tiny hearts just under the guard. A heart, as a pun on MacKerron and *mo càran*," she added.

"Mo càran," he murmured, looking at her. "My beloved."

A shiver rippled through her as she returned his gaze, but she could not reply. For an instant, she felt her longing overflow. She glanced away, as he did.

He touched the bare blade gently, and pulled back the cloth to reveal the full sword in two pieces. "The lilies are called fleurs-de-lis in French," he said. "They are a symbol of the French royal house."

"Did a French royal own this sword?" she asked in awe. She traced a finger over the delicate lilies along the fuller, the channel in the center of the blade that lightened the weight of the steel for added flexibility and control.

"Not a royal," he said. "An angel held this one."

She stilled her fingers on the smooth steel to look at him, puzzled. Then, realizing what he meant, she gasped. "Lachlann, is this the Maid's own sword? The legendary blade of Saint Catherine?"

He frowned. "How did you hear about that?"

"My cousins told me about it," she said. "Parlan and William told me something of Jehanne the Maid, and they mentioned that she carried a sword with golden flowers along the blade, of shining brass and steel. The sword was a special one, blessed and magical—given to the Maid by Saint Catherine herself."

"Not magical, but extraordinary in its way." His blue eyes darkened, and Eva saw sadness reflected there. "Jehanne learned of the sword in a dream and sent men to a deserted chapel to find it. It was there, beneath the floorstones. I examined the weapon myself when they brought it to her. She asked me to make a scabbard of leather for it—of plain leather, to suit a soldier," he went on in a husky tone. "She wanted a sturdy sheath, not the jeweled thing the king had given her. It was her way."

She nodded her understanding. "My cousins said the sword broke, and then vanished when her campaign failed."

"She broke it in a temper," Lachlann said. "She struck it downward while arguing a plan of strategy with some of us—it hit a rock and cracked. She had a fierce temper," he added, smiling a little, wan and quick. He lifted the hilt out of the cloth. The light from the forge glinted red on the mirror-bright blade as he turned it.

"Promise me," he said, "that you will never tell anyone that you have seen this."

"I will never tell," she whispered, watching him.

"Her enemies are still about," he said. "The English—the Goddams, she called them, for the swearing they did—would do anything to have this, if they knew it still existed. They fear it has some magic. Whatever it had . . . is gone now."

Seeing the heartbreak in his expression as he looked at Jehanne's sword, she caught her breath. "Then you must keep it well hidden and protect it."

He nodded. "They asked her about the sword at her trial. She refused to reveal its whereabouts to her judges, though she knew that I had it at the time."

"She did not want to endanger you." Somehow she felt that was true. Her awe and admiration for the Maid had always been great, but now it deepened with gratitude, for Jehanne had protected Lachlann. "Were you there, where she . . ."

"In Rouen, where she was tried and executed?" His tone turned bitter. "I was there. I attended her trial sessions. I visited her in her prison cell." The darkness lingered in his eyes, and a muscle jumped in his jaw. "But I was not there when she died."

Now she was sure that he had loved the girl and mourned her deeply. She felt compassion for his grief, but felt, too, a thread of disappointment for herself, which she knew she must ignore. "But you were true and loyal," she said. "She must have been glad you were there."

Something flickered over his face. "I hope so. This sword . . . is all that is left of her. When it broke, she asked me to repair it, and insisted that I keep it. I promised to fix it. Someday, she said, I would know what to do with it. But . . . I do not know what to do with it, except keep it tucked away." He glanced at her. "No one but you would have found it. And I do not mind you knowing about this."

She smiled a little. "Lachlann, you have the skill and the talent to restore this to its original beauty. But perhaps you do not want to change it, and lose that last piece of her."

"That may be." He frowned, traced his hand over the sword, then held it out to her. "Hold it, if you like."

Eva took the hilt and lifted the sword, jagged edge upright, the dark interior of the steel gaping like a great wound. The leather hilt fit her hand perfectly; if the sword had been whole, it would have suited her in length and balance. The light sparked on the polished steel, and Eva could easily imagine a shining, complete blade.

A strange, sure sense of its mystery, its power, shivered through her, as if the sword was indeed magical. The thought of its noble and courageous owner made her feel humble. Light sparkled over the quillons and broken blade, and she remembered another sword, the one in Innisfarna's legend.

"This makes me think of the Sword of Light," she murmured. "I can feel Jehanne, somehow, in this sword—I can feel her pride, her strength, the air of blessedness that must have surrounded her."

"You sound as if you knew her." Lachlann watched her. "You remind me of her."

She glanced at him. "How could I be anything like her?"

"You are similar in appearance—she was dark-haired too, and like you in size and shape, though she was somewhat sturdier in build. And her eyes were gray and full of spark and spirit, as yours are. It is your boldness, your spirit that is most like her." He smiled. "That, and your stubborn temper."

Eva smiled, too, glad to see his humor returning. "She dressed like a man, I heard."

"She did that to protect her virtue among the soldiers. Though none of the men who rode and fought with her would ever have harmed her. She was safe with us—or so we thought, until she was captured."

"Was she lovely?" she asked. She handed him back the sword, and he laid it inside the cloth, swathing it carefully.

"She had a beautiful shape, and her face was serene and pure. But it was her courage and her faith that gave her true beauty. She was like a warrior angel."

Sensing his devotion to the girl, Eva felt it like a blow inside. She knew his heart hurt from the tragedy, and she wished she could do something to help him recover. She sighed. "I wish I had known her."

"She needed a friend like you, I think," he said. Then he glanced toward the door, frowning. "What is going on out there?"

Outside, Eva heard the two dogs barking in a frenzy, and she knew that they had seen something they did not like. She went to the door. Lachlann put the sword back in its niche on the top of the wall and followed her.

Eva stepped into the yard and shielded her eyes with her hand. Grainne and Solas cut across the meadow over the lochside slope between the smithy and the stable, barking furiously. She lifted the hem of her skirt and ran after them.

Two boats glided near the beach, and she saw the glint of armor through the morning mist. She turned to see Lachlann.

"Alpin is coming over the water," she called. "He has some of the king's men with him!"

Chapter 17

As the two boats beached on the shore below the smithy property, Eva recognized Alpin rowing the first, with three of the king's men and Ninian inside. The second boat held more soldiers, rowed by one of them.

"The soldiers cross the loch nearly every day to look after their horses, and they often ride out after my brother and the other rebels." She glanced at Lachlann. "Some of the soldiers have been discourteous to me, and so I avoid them if I can."

He nodded his understanding. When the men began to climb the hill, he stepped in front of her, his wide shoulders and plaid-draped back forming a shield.

Her reaction to that, from another man, would have been to step forward to show she could defend herself. Yet she accepted it easily from him, glad of his gesture of support.

John Robson was a large man, brawny and blond, with a relaxed confidence that Eva found reassuring. She watched him walk nearer. "I have no quarrel with Robson," she said, "though I do not like having the garrison on the island."

"He seems trustworthy . . . for a king's man," he said wryly.

She shot him a little glare at the inference to her initial mistrust of him upon his return to Balnagovan. "I do not hold a good opinion of all of his men. A few showed me such scant respect at Innisfarna that I felt it wisest to leave. That is when I came to stay with Mairi MacKerron."

"Barricading yourself behind locks and latches."

"Exactly so. And to be truthful, I am glad you came back to Balnagovan. I feel safer here."

"Now that I am here, or now that the locks are repaired?" he drawled. "Greetings, John Robson," he called in English, as the men attained the crest of the long hill.

"MacKerron! How are you, sir?"

"Well, and yourself? Another patrol, is it?"

"Aye. Good morn to you, Lady Eva," Robson said, nodding.

"Sir John, greetings," she murmured in English, using the schooled accent of the native Gael: precise, formal, and melodious. Lachlann, she noticed, had mastered the rolling rhythms of Lowland Scots, though he next addressed Alpin in Gaelic, murmuring low and clasping his hand.

"And the boy?" Lachlann asked then, peering at Ninian, who stood partly behind Alpin, his shoulders hunched, head ducked.

"This is Ninian Campbell. He is a page at Innisfarna," Eva said, beckoning the boy forward. He cupped his hand over his lower face to hide his scarred lip, as he often did with strangers. "And this is Lachlann the smith," she told the boy.

"*Failte,*" Lachlann said in greeting. Ninian looked at him with wide blue eyes, as if he had never seen a man quite so tall or so banded with muscle. In the cool morning air, while the other men wore armor and cloaks, Lachlann, by contrast, still wore only the belted plaid, without a shirt. His bare torso and long dark hair gave him a savage appearance, Eva thought, and a wild, elemental sort of beauty. But she knew that he was more civilized and intelligent than most of the men now facing him.

Ninian glanced nervously at Eva, and she smiled. "The

smith is a friend," she said in Gaelic. "You need not be anxious."

Nodding, Ninian took his hand away from his face.

"I am pleased to meet you, Ninian," Lachlann said calmly, taking the boy's slender hand in his huge grasp. He showed no reaction to the child's scarred mouth. Eva smiled, for she had been certain of Lachlann's kind acceptance. Alpin nodded in gruff approval, patting the boy's shoulder.

"We have found some tasks for him," Robson told Eva. "Colin Campbell sent orders that he was to be kept busy, though we have several pages and squires already. The boys tease him, and he scraps with them—a tough fellow, this one—but he keeps to himself. And he is a good worker, when he can be found at all," he added wryly, glancing at Alpin, who looked blatantly innocent.

"There are plenty of chores in the stable and the smithy," Lachlann said. "The boy could do some work here."

Robson nodded. "That would be fine."

Lachlann looked down at Ninian. "You look like a strong fellow who could easily fetch water for the smithy and the stable. And I think you could groom the horses and lead them out to the meadow sometimes too. For now, since the soldiers are taking the horses out, perhaps you could fill the water troughs and put fresh oats in the stalls. There is a huge sack of oats in the stable, but I know you can move it."

Ninian nodded eagerly. Eva smiled. "When you are done with that, come to the house. Grainne would love to see you again," she said. The boy covered a grin with his hand, and ran toward the stable, plaid hem flying about his knees.

Lachlann tilted his head in curiosity and looked at Eva. "Colin sent him to Innisfarna? Is the boy his Campbell cousin?"

Eva hesitated. "He is Colin's son."

"Ah," he murmured. "You will be his stepmother."

"So it seems," she replied. She did not want to think about that. More and more she hated the prospect of her coming marriage, although it would benefit her kinsmen, and Ninian too.

Robson turned from discussion with Alpin, who waved to Eva and Lachlann, then walked back down to the beach. "Have you had a chance to shoe the horses yet?" Robson asked Lachlann.

"Not yet, as the house and stable were in dire need of repairs. And I want to fetch wrought iron from the ironmonger in Glen Brae, and charcoal as well, from a charcoal burner there."

Robson nodded. "Fetch whatever you need for making good steel as well. We need weapons repaired, and new blades."

"I will see what is available," Lachlann said smoothly.

Eva gaped at him, wishing she could point out that he had flatly refused to make weapons for her kinsmen. He slid her a sharp glance, and she saw his awareness of that.

"You are dressed for war," Lachlann said then. "Is this more than a routine patrol?"

"Not as yet, though the crown may order that soon." Robson looked at Eva. "For now, we seek to keep the king's peace. Our obvious presence should help discourage the raiding."

Lachlann's deliberate glance at Eva told her that he did not think so. "I have not yet seen the rebels myself, to deliver the king's message," he told Robson. "Although I would wager they are well aware of the crown's disapproval without the benefit of written messages."

"No doubt. But the king's message must be delivered into their hands. My offer to you still stands. Ride with us."

"You invited the smith to ride patrol with you?" Eva asked, surprised.

"Certainly. He is a king's man himself. And he knows

these hills, and the rebels as well," Robson answered. "Tell me, MacKerron, when you were in France, did you see much of the fray there?"

"I was at Chinon Castle, guarding the dauphin before he was crowned king. For a while I rode with the Maid of Lorraine, as part of her Scots guard. We accompanied her to Orléans, and we were with her at Paris, Lagny, Compiègne, and elsewhere."

"By the saints! What an adventure that must have been!"

"Indeed," Lachlann murmured.

One of Robson's men, listening with avid interest, watched Lachlann. "Did you see the French lassie's end?" he asked. "Were you there for the burning, sir?"

"Nay," Lachlann answered curtly. Eva saw a small muscle pulse in his jaw. Now that she better understood the depth of his feelings for Jehanne, she felt a rush of sympathy.

"No doubt the smith respects the girl's memory and does not wish to discuss her," she told the soldier.

"Well, she had the sympathy of many, including the Scots," Robson said. "A pity naught could be done to help her."

"Aye," Lachlann barked. "I believe your mounts are ready, sir," he said, gesturing toward the stables as a few of the men brought the saddled horses outside. Robson strode toward the horses, while Eva and Lachlann walked on either side of him.

"Lady Eva," Robson told her. "I am glad for this chance to speak with you. Generally when we come here, you are nowhere to be found. I wanted to tell you that I recently had a message from Sir Colin. He assures me that he intends to claim his bride soon." He smiled.

Eva raised her chin. "He sent no message to me. I have had no word from him in nearly a year."

"You will see him within the month, I expect. I plan to return a message to him at Edinburgh. Would you like to send a reply in the packet?"

"I will wait until he arrives, if it will be that soon," she answered. Her stomach tumbled with dread, but she could not think about Colin's arrival, here and now, with Lachlann standing so close to her. Robson nodded farewell to both of them before to catching the reins of his horse and mounting up with the rest of his men.

Lachlann looked at her. "You saw Simon recently."

"And will I tell the king's men that?" she retorted. "I do not know where he is from day to day."

"Surely you can get a message to your brother."

Of course she could do just that, but she was not going to reveal that to anyone, including Lachlann. She thought he could be trusted not to betray her kinsmen, but she had to be cautious. "Are you asking me to tell you where he is? Simon knows what the king wants. He will find you when he wants to speak with you."

"I will not be content with that for much longer."

At that moment, the eight king's men rode out of the stable yard, raising dust and noise. Eva stepped back, watching them go, and she was satisfied to see they rode south, for she knew that Simon still hid north of the loch.

Ninian came to the doorway of the stable, a bucket in one hand, a rake in the other, to watch them depart also, then disappeared inside to resume his chores. Eva smiled at him, and turned to Lachlann.

"You want to know where Simon is, but you are on good terms with the king's men, so how can I share whatever I know with you?" she asked. "I heard what you told Robson. You will make weapons for the king's men so they can better hunt and harm my kinsmen, but you refuse to do blade-smithing for the MacArthurs." As she walked toward the house, he strode beside her.

He frowned. "I promised Robson only horseshoes and

mended tackle. We made no agreement for weapons, if you listened well. Nor will I make that agreement with you." Stopping with her on the doorstep, he reached past her to open the latch. It yielded smoothly, newly repaired and oiled. "Although there is one matter that you and I must agree upon. May I come in and discuss it with you?"

Puzzled, she entered and stepped back to allow him inside. Closing the door after him, she looked up. "What is that?"

"The rental fee for Balnagovan," he said, to Eva's surprise. "I have been thinking about this since I came back. You know this is neither my house, my smithy, nor my land."

"I hold Balnagovan of the crown, as the hereditary Maiden of Innisfarna," she said. With the crackling fire on the hearth, the room felt warm after the crisp air. She unfastened the brooch—the clasp now opened easily—and removed her *arisaid,* then smoothed the single braid that fell over her shoulder. "But your family has always held this place. Finlay's kin," she added, remembering what Mairi had revealed about his parentage.

"A fee is owed you to secure any property within the boundaries of Innisfarna—the isle, and the land along the south side of the loch. The smithy"—he gestured beyond the closed door—"the village, the meadow, the close hills, and the lochside are all part of your demesne. I would guess you have little or no income for the tenancy of these lands currently."

"None since the dispossession of the MacArthurs, true. But I have what I need, thanks to Mairi's generosity." Her heart thumped as she had a new thought. "Since you want to arrange a fee, does that mean you will stay?"

"I will stay until Colin Campbell returns, which is not long from now, apparently." He folded his arms, leaning his weight on his left leg as he stood by the door. Tall and wide-shouldered, chiseled and commanding, he dominated the close interior. But she saw a gentler aspect in his blue eyes, in the curve of his upper lip, the fullness of the lower. She loved that contrast and that balance in his features and his character between power and kindness.

"Will you go back to Perth to smith there?" she asked, feeling the misery of losing him before he had even gone.

He shrugged. Eva glanced away, flustered beneath his steady gaze. She did not want to think about Colin's imminent arrival. Turning, she went toward the table. "Would you . . . can I get you some heather ale?" she asked, reaching for a cup from the shelf, then turning to the clay jug already on the table.

He shook his head, and she set the cup down. "I am not thinking of myself, but my foster mother," he said. "I want to ensure Mairi's tenure here with a rental agreement. I insist," he added, when she began to protest. "The fee, or some sort of barter, is customary. Ask what you want, and I will pay it."

Her heart pounded even harder. She walked toward him, clasping her hands while he stood with his arms folded tight, aware that she and Lachlann locked themselves one against the other. "I will barter your promise to stay," she said.

A frown skimmed his brow. "Eva, I cannot promise that."

"MacKerrons have always smithed for us. That, too, is custom at Balnagovan."

"I made you some hooks," he replied, a twinkle in his eye.

"I mean bladesmithing," she said stubbornly.

"Eva—" He shook his head and huffed out a frustrated laugh. "Let us not go into that again. Just set a fee."

"Finlay smithed for us in return for the use of the land and the buildings, and we also provided him with foods, candles, and other necessities, I think. He did a great deal of work for my parents, and later my father. To be truthful, I would not know what amount to ask."

"Then we shall agree on a yearly amount, in coin or work completed. If our agreement is not met before I leave, I will send the rest—coin or iron work—from Perth." His frown deepened; she wanted to reach up and smooth the creases away.

"Mairi has been generous to me. I cannot accept anything for her tenure here. I would rather grant the right freely."

He shook his head. "Some fee must be exchanged between us. When Colin Campbell returns, he will inquire about Innisfarna's tenants. If I am no longer at Balnagovan, I do not want Mairi evicted. I know you would not do that," he added, lifting a hand briefly in response to her quick and vehement protest, "but I do not trust Campbell."

Eva sighed, knowing he had reason to be wary of Colin. "I will accept only a token, then. Robson can record in the accounts that Balnagovan's fee was paid directly to me. Colin has no right to question affairs at Innisfarna, but if he does, that will suffice."

"What token would you take from a blacksmith for a year's rental? A pot chain, or a bundle of hooks?" He smiled. "A clasp of the hand in good faith, until something more can be bartered?" He unlocked his arms and offered her his hand.

She reached out, and his fingers closed over hers, firm and warm. He took her hand and bowed over it as if he were greeting her in some royal court. He tugged, and she stepped closer, their movements dancelike and slow.

"Perhaps more than a hand clasp is needed," he said. "A token of honor, something more binding and sacred."

"What is more binding?" Her breath quickened, for suddenly she knew. The anticipation made her light-headed yet bold, as if she hovered on the brink of the unknown, about to step over a cliff, to fall or to soar.

"A kiss of peace," he murmured, "might do." He inclined toward her, his face close to hers, and she tilted her head back.

"Might do," she echoed, and her eyes closed as his mouth touched hers, warm and gentle, his unshaven beard rasping over her chin. She sighed as their lips drew apart.

"Is that enough for a year's rent?" he asked, low and soft.

"Oh," she breathed, heart thundering, "I doubt it."

He sighed out, and his lips covered hers once more. Her knees turned fluid, and he caught her with a hand under her elbow. She clutched at his bare, powerful arm, and as his mouth slanted over hers, she felt soft lightning stream through her.

Lachlann drew back. "Is it paid now?" he murmured.

She shrugged in silence, not wanting this to end. Every curve and cleft in her body pulsed. She could not think clearly, could only feel, as she leaned into his strength.

"Perhaps," he said, "you could raise the rental fee."

"I could," she breathed.

He bent closer, and his hand slid down to rest at the curve of her lower back, pulling her hard against him. She went helplessly into the next kiss like a leaf in a whirlpool, spinning, sinking. She looped her arms around his neck and pressed against him, and felt the hardening, heated contours of his body meet her curves. Gasping softly, she welcomed another kiss, felt the intoxication begin, felt herself slip over the edge of the brink she had earlier risked.

Thundery inside, weakening, she surrendered when she knew she should pull back. Opening her lips, feeling the touch of his tongue, gentle but fiery, she moaned. The brace of his arms hardened around her, and she arched closer.

He murmured into her mouth—her name, she thought, repeated, or was it a prayer he whispered—and his lips traced over her cheek, his breath soft in her hair, like ecstasy at her ear. Her knees simply gave way for an instant, and she tightened an arm around his neck, flattened a palm on his chest, where the contour was hard and firm, and his heart pounded like a drum.

He buttressed her waist with one large hand and slipped the other along her arm, his fingers finding, soothing over her breast. She gasped soft and sudden as his touch skimmed the ready nipple, pearled and tingling. The burn ran all through her, like a small thread of fire, newly begun.

One token, she thought hazily, one chaste and honorable kiss had ignited this. She did not think she could stop now; she did not want to pull back, carried onward by intense feelings, by demands that were new to her, yet that she understood somehow. Deep within, she knew what her body desired, and what she most wanted—to fly into the sun, not to sink back again into shadow.

Warm and fine, his hands moved over her, solace and comfort, pleasure and gift, rounding over her breast, slipping over her abdomen and skimming lower. She fluttered within, she ached, she rocked toward him and moaned. His mouth sought hers again, discovered her deeply.

Framing her face, he kissed her again, and then drew back. She moaned in denial, her hands fervent on his chest, at his waist, sliding over his muscled arms as he shifted away from her.

He looked down at her, his gaze as bright as the blue flame in the hearth. "Listen to me, Eva girl," he said, sounding as breathless as she, his voice a raw husk.

She nodded mutely, catching her breath, gazing into his eyes, scarcely able to think for the blood pounding in her.

"This has been brewing between us for a while," he said. "But you are promised, and according to that arrangement, I am not the one for you. I would never dishonor you," he went on. "But by God, it is not easy to be so near you each day. Now tell me this, and tell me honestly."

She nodded again. All she wanted was to feel his kiss, feel his strength wrap around her and fill her. She strove to listen, her hands on his arms. His body felt like sun-warmed, sculpted stone, and his fingertips were gentle upon her face.

"Will you break your betrothal to Colin?" he asked quietly.

Her heart leaped, and she felt the dual tug of sadness and joy. "If I said I would not, what would you do?"

He let go of her and stepped backward swiftly, hands up, palms out. She watched him, hungry, desperate, aching.

"And if I said I would, what would you do then?"

He reached out to trace his fingers along her cheek, brushed his thumb over her lips, so much cherishing in the gesture that she knew what he told her. He withdrew his hand slowly.

She closed her eyes in anguish, wanting to melt into his arms and tell him that she wanted him more than anything she had ever wanted, ever would want in her life. "Lachlann," she said breathlessly, "what is this between us? Is it lust that pulls so upon me when you are near? Just . . . a hunger of the body, a need, like fire needs fuel?"

"What do you think?" he murmured.

She thought she teetered on that cliff edge again. And she felt certain that she saw, in the sincere clarity of his blue eyes, what she so yearned for from him—and could not claim.

"I think I feel much more than lust," she said carefully.

"But you are not sure?" His voice was deep and soft.

"I might be sure," she said crisply, "if you did not spin me so, and stoke me so each time you touch me, and if I could think clearly when you are near."

He pursed his mouth, and she thought he was going to laugh. But that cleared, and he frowned. "I will not take another man's promised bride—even if that man is my enemy. But if the woman herself makes the decision, well, that would change it."

Her heart, her soul, whirled inside of her. She lifted a hand to her brow. She remembered Mairi's story of Aileen Stewart, who had run off with her beloved blacksmith,

Tomas MacKerron, and she fully understood how that had happened, if the father had been anything like the son.

But she was securely manacled by Colin, by Innisfarna and her kinsmen's needs, even by Ninian. She clenched her hands, hung her head, and suppressed a sob.

He watched her candidly, patiently, a little frown between his brows. As if a strong thread stretched between him and her, she felt the tug. She rocked on the brink of the choice. Moving toward Lachlann would fulfill her heart, satisfy her dreams. But a move toward Colin would save her kinsmen and her clan.

She shook her head. "I . . . made a solemn promise to Colin."

"Then that is what you must do," he murmured. "And what I must do is leave here. I thought I was made of rock . . . but not where you are concerned." She realized that what he mentioned went far beyond friendship, something deep, tender, and straight out of her dreams. Her heart pounded as she stared at him.

She wanted to reach out to him, but she felt ensnared in obligations. "If I . . . if I were to refuse Colin? What would you do then?" She was trapped by Colin, but she had to know the answer.

He gave her a quick, crooked smile and lifted her chin with his knuckle. "Come find me if you decide that, and then you will know," he said. He turned, opened the door, and slipped outside.

Eva leaned her palms against the closed door, rested her forehead on its grainy coolness, and moaned as she exhaled.

Chapter 18

Lachlann beat out a fast rhythm, his hammer striking molten iron. Sparks sprayed over his leather gauntlets and apron, and a few stung his forearms, but he shook them off, hardly feeling the burn. Welding shut a link in the chain, he began another, bending the amber-bright metal with a fierce turn of the tongs, threading the new loop into the last link, closing the open ends with a slam of the hammer, spitting sparks.

While he worked, he remembered the sight of Eva with Jehanne's sword in her hands. And he felt again the warmth and deliciousness of Eva in his arms. She had uncommon grace and certain magic, and each day he felt more compelled to be with her. He knew now that he could not stay at Balnagovan if he could not have her.

Turning to heat another piece of iron, watching it transform to solid light, he was aware of the burn within him, body and soul, for Eva. Her nature was like his own, fiery and strong. What existed between them was full of sparks, blaze, and enduring warmth—or could be, if given freedom and nurtured.

Pounding out another link in the chain, he realized that he was glad she had discovered Jehanne's sword, for only she could understand what the sword meant to him. He had loved Jehanne chastely, with the respect of a brother and comrade, or as a man might love an angel walking upon the earth.

His feelings for Eva were deep and fervent, ever increasing, part of the intricate layers of his soul. He sensed her compassion, part of what he loved most about her. But she did not know the darkest part of the tale: that he had failed the angel who had been entrusted into his care.

Slamming the hammer with force and fury, he built the chain, cleaving hot iron, molding it to his will. His memory conjured another heavy black chain, manacled to a slight, stubborn, remarkable girl. He could do nothing for Jehanne now but honor her request and remake her sword.

To finally heal himself, he knew that he must somehow claim his long-cherished dreams. Swordsmithing might prove impossible for him; and his yearning for Eva was a precious dream that seemed so close suddenly, yet still so far beyond his reach.

Soon the chain was complete, its length dunked in water to cool it, the links oiled to a black sheen. Dripping with sweat, Lachlann wiped his smudged arm over his brow and took up the twig brush to scatter the embers and let them burn down.

Opening the smithy door, he savored the cold nip of the wind on his slick skin. Thirsting, he dipped a ladle into a tub of water beside the doorstep, and swallowed. The sky had already darkened to twilight, the day passing faster than he had been aware while he worked at forge and anvil.

He looked across the meadow at the house. The windows were shuttered against the wind, and pale smoke drifted from the chimney. He glanced down when his toe struck a cloth bundle on the stone step. Inside the packet were oatcakes, a thick slab of cheese, and a cooked apple, still warm and savory with spices. A covered jug sat on the step, too, its belly frosted.

Nodding silent thanks toward the house, he took the food and went back inside.

The following morning, after a brave dip in the cold

water of the loch to refresh himself and cleanse away the grime of his work, he smithed iron throughout the day, then deep into the night. He repaired the harnesses from the stables, forged a fire grate for the house's hearth, and created sturdy ladles and small, sharp iron knives for both Eva and Margaret.

Eva did not come to the smithy that day, although he hoped she would. When he went to the house later to set the new fire grate into place, she was not there. He ate alone, murmuring to the adoring dogs, and fed Grainne two oatcakes, for she was greedy. He wished Eva had been there to scold him for it.

Returning to the smithy, he shut himself up with his work, with heat, sweat, and the incessant ringing of the hammer. The steady sound and the constant demands on his attention helped to block his troubling thoughts and emotions, and the intense heat and hard work helped drive out his frustrations.

Exhaustion dragged at him as he worked deep into the night. Hammering, he felt strangely as if he beat upon some inner level, transforming his own will, remaking his own future.

If only it were so simple, he told himself, and he worked like a demon at the forge, hot and fast and half wild with the urge to do as much as he could, no matter the late hour. His vision blurred, and the odd lights spun when he blinked— but it was glowing red iron that he forged, simple and straightforward in its color changes, not fine steel, and so he continued.

When the knock came at the door, it was so quiet at first that he scarcely heard it. It sounded again, and he went to the door, hoping to find Eva.

She was there, her eyes wide, her face pale, and she was not alone. A young Highlander stood with her, in a dirty plaid, hair braided and unkempt, his handsome face remarkably similar to Eva's despite the scruff of whiskers. His eyes were weary and shadowed with care for a man so young. Lachlann stared at them for a moment, then stood back to let them into the warm smithy.

"Simon," he said. "Welcome."

"Lachlann," Simon said, grasping his hand. "It has been a long while. I trust you are well."

"Well enough," Lachlann said, and glanced at Eva, who stood a little apart, as if she were only the escort and not a principal—although Lachlann was sure she was as invested in the MacArthur rebellion as her kinsmen were. "I am glad you decided to see me after all. I have a message for you."

"A letter from the king, but we know what he wants. He means to threaten us with fire and sword."

Lachlann sighed and rubbed at his neck, where the muscles stung with fatigue. "You know what Colin's messenger told Robson, but you need to read the official word."

"What do the details matter? Even if deathly threats are sent out, we cannot run like cowards. We are fighting for our lands, our name—our very existence." Even in the muted red light of the smithy, Lachlann could see that a few years, and a good measure of strife and responsibility, had matured Eva's younger brother into a hard-edged man. This was not the impulsive youth he remembered.

"Simon, I know you questioned my loyalty when you heard my mission. But you have known me a long while. I have changed no more than you have." He felt Eva's steady gaze upon him, but did not look at her. "I understand your cause, but I hope you will see the wisdom of obeying the laws of the land."

"The laws of the land took our father, our properties, and disbanded us for no good reason—except that our father was one of the chiefs who disagreed with the king's plan."

"No matter the past, you must cease your raids now."

"You did not need to search us out to tell us that. The patrols in the hills make that clear." Simon smiled, bitter and tight. "I came here hoping to appeal to old friendship, to persuade you to join us."

"Simon, listen to him," Eva said quietly. "Let him tell you the king's message." Her brother frowned, but nodded.

Lachlann sighed, began. "Not only will the king send fire and sword, but if you do not stop your attempts to regain your lands, Donal will be executed."

"Jesu," Simon said. "Would the king do such a thing, after taking our father?"

"He would, if given cause," Lachlann replied.

"I hoped Colin would—" Eva stepped forward. "Lachlann, is there mention of a pardon in the king's missive?"

"Not to my knowledge, but I have not read the letter myself. It is still sealed. But I know that if MacArthur raids continue past the delivery of this message, Donal's death is guaranteed—that could stay in force regardless of a pardon. Once you are informed, Simon, you become responsible for the outcome, according to the writ. Look at it for yourself."

Crossing the room to fetch his cloak, Lachlann withdrew a folded, ribboned packet from a pocket in the satin lining and returned to hand it to Simon, who tore it open.

Simon scanned the page. "It is true."

"When I heard in Perth about your raids, I offered to carry a message to you, and the king's advisors thought it a good idea. I hoped to negotiate with you, and gain you some time. The king was ready to send troops out then, but he agreed to wait."

"This is a clear threat," Simon said. "Once fire and sword are initiated, King James will not give up until every MacArthur outlaw is caught and hung."

Eva gasped. "But Colin petitioned for a pardon!"

"Apparently without success," Lachlann said brusquely.

"If more troops arrive here, and MacArthurs still run raids, you will all be captured sooner or later."

"We need weapons, not warnings," Simon said. "And we need more men with us. You are a fine soldier, one of the king's best. My cousins said you were in the elite guard in France. You were always one of us before, and you have the skill to arm us. We must know if you are with us now."

"You have my sympathy, but I will not lend you my skill. I lack the materials to arm you, even if I agreed to it. Steel needs charcoal and good wrought iron, and those are expensive."

"We can get whatever you need. We have our means," Simon said. "Campbells and Stewarts have cattle, and so we have our means. We make good coin selling their livestock in the Border markets." Simon smiled tightly, without humor but with pride. Lachlann saw Eva scowl, and noted the difference of opinion between the siblings on that matter—and, he surmised, other matters as well. The tension between Eva and Simon seemed clear.

"That sort of cleverness will win you a noose," Lachlann said. "I have conveyed the warning. There is little I can do if you will not heed it."

"There is something you can do. We need swords, dirks, and axe heads," Simon said stubbornly.

"I will not supply a rebellion." Could not, Lachlann thought. His abilities were compromised, but Simon and Eva—he could see the hope in her eyes as she listened—both had faith in his bladesmithing skills.

"We need weapons for survival as well as rebellion," Simon said fiercely. "Our possessions were forfeited when we were put out of our homes after my father's death. We have scarcely anything now but what we steal from the Campbells and Stewarts who hold our lands."

"And so you should be careful, for Colin said he would

seek to gain our clan a pardon," Eva said. "Surely there is some reference to that in the king's letter." She reached out a hand.

"Colin's name is there, I saw it," Simon said. "You read far better than I. Here." He handed her the page. "She thinks to save us all," he muttered to Lachlann, as Eva perused the parchment. "I have cautioned her not to risk herself for us."

"And if Campbell does not meet his promise?" Lachlann asked quickly. "If he can—or will—do nothing?"

"Then I would be glad to be quit of the betrothal," Eva answered fiercely, glancing up from reading, her gaze meeting Lachlann's steadily for a moment, her eyes keen with determination. He nodded and felt hope glimmer again.

"Then your marriage hangs upon a thread," he said.

"I wish it would snap," Simon commented. "But Eva intends to save Donal and the rest of us—as if we cannot save ourselves, and she must lay herself upon the heading block for us." Hurt and obstinacy flashed in his blue-green eyes.

Aware of the loyalty and love among the three MacArthur siblings, Lachlann felt the discord between these two now. Their distress was heightened by the uncertain fate of their elder brother, yet both were proud and stubborn.

Eva read on, her brow furrowed, lips moving slightly, her concentration total. "Here," she murmured. " 'Regarding the matter and request of Colin Campbell. . .' " Her voice faded.

"Simon, I do not begrudge your anger," Lachlann said.

"It is righteous anger," Simon said adamantly.

"It is. But I warn you to act with caution."

"Campbells sit on our lands, feeding on cattle that were once ours, riding horses that once belonged to us. Their coffers grow fat while we suffer. We take only what we need."

Lachlann shook his head. "Raiding or fighting now, after you have received the king's orders, is plain treason. Add fuel to this fire, and the blaze will only grow hotter."

"Then use that blaze to forge our weapons."

In that moment, Lachlann saw the flash of inner fire in the young man, a mark of the strength of a true leader. Sighing, he rubbed his fingers over his face. Suddenly he felt old—soured, weary, far wiser than he should be. "Simon, I have seen war. I have seen its devastation, its darkness and lack of soul. You do not want to continue this. Believe me."

"We will ask you again to help us," Simon countered. "And again, until we hear the answer we want. Is that not so, Eva?"

She did not answer. Gripping the page in both hands, her knuckles turning white, she turned a pale face to them. *"Ach Dhia!"* she said. "What has he done! The fool!"

"Who? What is it?" Lachlann asked sharply.

"Colin—oh, God—it says here that he has . . . married me by proxy, while he was in France!" She raised huge, shocked eyes to look at Lachlann, then at her brother.

"What?" Simon asked. "Where does it say that?"

"Let me see," Lachlann said, taking the page from her to scan it quickly himself.

"Colin could not do such a thing," Simon said. "He would need your consent, Eva. You must have read it wrong. It is in English, after all," he added.

"She did not misinterpret," Lachlann said grimly. "It is here. Colin Campbell now has the rights to the property held by his wife, through a marriage sanctioned by proxy while Colin was attending to his duties in France—and here, the clerk writes that Campbell's request for a pardon for the MacArthurs is under consideration. Until the matter is decided, the MacArthur rebels are to obey the king's orders."

He looked up. His fingers shook as he handed the page to Simon. "It is true." He looked at Eva. "Colin has married you in the eyes of the Church."

She stared at him and did not speak. Though only an arm's length separated them, he felt as if the world had shifted, and she had slid far away, hopelessly out of his reach. He could hardly speak himself, and returned her shocked gaze in silence.

"It cannot be legal," Simon said, reading the letter again, tracing a finger over the cramped words in black ink. "Eva did not give her consent to a proxy marriage. It is not binding."

"It may be, if Colin had the king's consent," Lachlann said. "Or perhaps he sent a letter requesting her consent, but she never got the letter. That is very possible with such turmoil in France. Some of my messages never reached their destinations. If Colin sent word and did not receive a reply, Eva's silence could be interpreted as consent."

"We will find a way to dissolve the marriage," Simon said.

"You knew," Eva said, still watching Lachlann. "The king knew about it. Surely it was mentioned to you!"

"Eva, I swear I never heard about this," he said quietly.

"But you carried the message," she said. "You must have known. Did it suit your purposes to keep it to yourself?" He saw the heartbreak in her eyes and felt the hurtful stab of her distrust. His own anger and hurt welled up in him.

"This is what you wanted all along," he said curtly. "You insisted on marrying him. Now it is done."

She glared at him, but he saw the sheen of tears with her anger. Regretting his outburst, he murmured her name and stretched out his hand. Eva whirled and fled, slamming the smithy door behind her.

"No matter what it takes," Lachlann said in a low rumble, "we will find some way to dissolve that marriage."

"Think fast, smith," Simon said. "My new brother-in-law will be back soon. And I very much doubt he will tolerate a few rebels for kinsmen—or a handsome smith on his wife's property. There will be no pardons or mercy for any of us." He walked to the door, yanked it open, and slammed out after his sister.

Chapter 19

"You must go back, Eva, dear," Margaret said gently. "It is not like you to hide from your troubles." She shifted the babe upon her shoulder, patting his little back in gentle circles. "Maeve," she added sternly, when her daughter began to clamber up onto an empty stool, rocking it precariously.

Eva picked up the little girl and sat with her, combing her fingers through the tousled blond curls. "I will go back soon," she said. "I just needed to get away and think." Nor could she stay in close proximity to Lachlann, knowing that she had been wed by Colin's betrayal. The irresistible attraction between them must end if she was wife to another. She closed her eyes in anguish.

Until she had left Balnagovan, she had not completely realized how desperately she needed to be with the blacksmith, and how essential it was to end her forced arrangement with Colin. Yet somehow her kinsmen's welfare must be protected.

"Margaret, I thank you for your hospitality," she continued. "Talking with you and Angus and walking the hills to think and be by myself have truly helped me these last few days. But I still do not know what to do." She sighed, looking down, aware of the heavy burden that sat upon her shoulders.

"You should have refused Colin from the beginning,"

Margaret said. "All of us would have understood if you had. I know he promised what you wanted most to hear—that your kinsmen would be safe. But he has not obtained a pardon yet, and if he does not hold up his part of the bargain— why should you honor yours?"

"He married me, and that is much harder to break than a betrothal, even in proxy, without my consent," Eva said. "There is no pardon yet that we know about, but his petition may yet be approved. The king's letter mentioned that it is still under review, so I still have some hope." She sighed.

"You do not sound hopeful," Margaret observed. "I have never seen you so unhappy." She studied her with concern.

"If the king pardons your clansmen, and releases your brother, then have the marriage annulled," Angus suggested. He looked up from his seat by the hearth, where he finished, in the firelight, a small wooden pull-cart for his daughter. He spun the sturdy wheels and began to adjust the axle. "That will not be so difficult, as long as you stay away from the man when he comes back here." He grinned. "Let that brawny blacksmith protect you and keep Colin away until the marriage is ended. Annulling will take a few months. Lachlann can fend him off."

"Angus, that is a poor solution," Margaret said.

"I wish it were so simple," Eva added.

Angus glanced up, cocking a sandy brow. "What other hold does Green Colin have over you? This pardon never seemed enough to me—you are too bold a girl to agree to such a thing. I think the man has threatened you somehow. Is it true?"

Eva glanced away, then nodded. "He threatened that Donal would be executed and Simon hunted down unless I married him," she admitted. "I knew he would see it done. I had no choice."

"Aha," Angus said, while Margaret gasped. "I thought there was more to it. Well, go to the king yourself and report

Colin's wicked threat. Make your own appeal, and expose the cur to all."

Margaret shook her head. "Not with her kinsmen forfeited and outlawed, and the king responsible for her own father's death. Eva is safer to stay here and fight her own battles!"

"A pity she did not pledge with someone else, years ago," Angus said, musing as he sanded the side of the little cart.

"Then the betrothal and the marriage would be invalid." Eva looked up. "What did you say?"

He shrugged. "I was thinking about that Beltane night that Margaret and I met, and made our pledges to each other. You were with Lachlann that night, I remember. A pity you two are just friends. My family wanted me to betroth with another girl, and I was glad for a reason not to do so. And glad Margaret came into my life when she did," he said, smiling at his wife. "If that had happened for you, Eva, you would surely have a reason to set Colin on his ear when he returns."

Eva blinked at him, her thoughts sparking. "If we had— Oh!" she said, sitting straighter. "I must go home!"

"It is dark and windy," Margaret said. "Wait until morn. Whatever it is, it will keep." She tipped her head and peered at Eva. "I suspect it has kept for a long while, has it not?" she murmured. "You never said a word, not even to me."

Eva felt a hot blush creep into her cheeks. "I . . . I thought it was . . . only a wonderful memory to hold in my heart."

"But the last few weeks have shown you that it is much more," Margaret observed. Eva nodded, aware that her cheeks must look filled with flame. "I thought it might be so, when I saw you with him that night at the smith's house."

"What?" Angus asked, looking up, curious but distracted.

"Oh," Margaret said, smiling a little. "Our Eva is even more like her dear blacksmith than I thought—she keeps a secret well." She leaned forward to touch Eva's shoulder.

"Go back to Balnagovan in the morning. You can set this right somehow."

"Perhaps I can," Eva said. She drew a deep breath, and felt the reawakening of true hope. She laughed a little, and sobbed out with it, nodding. "And so I will!"

The midmorning sun was a bright coin in the sky as Eva crossed the wide meadow toward the smithy property. She heard the dull ring of the smith's hammer. Thinking of her conversation with Margaret and Angus, she smiled a little, filled with a faint sense of hope.

But she knew that her troubles were far from over. Even if her early, impulsive pledge with Lachlann was enough to invalidate her forced marriage with Colin, she still worried about her kinsmen's safety. The extent of Colin's greed and vindictiveness might be very great indeed.

If need be, she decided, she could face him herself to save Innisfarna, as Alpin wanted her to do. But to help her kinsmen, she might well have to appeal to the king himself, although she had no desire to face the monarch who had dealt so cruelly with her innocent father and the other Highland chiefs.

As she neared the smithy, she realized that the steady clang of metal on metal came from outside the building. Lachlann stood with his back wedged against the rump of a huge white destrier, his legs apart as he bent over to pull the great hoof between his knees. A small anvil and a portable forge—hot coals glowing in an iron bucket—sat near him on the ground. Ninian held the horse's reins, murmuring to the animal, stroking the long, wide nose gently.

Watching them, her heart infused with love, pride, and a sense of sadness. Ninian looked small and earnest beside the great horse, while Lachlann looked powerful and capable. The camaraderie between the boy and the man was evident even from a distance, as they worked together to soothe the horse, nodding to one another.

Though she wanted to be free of Colin in order to be with Lachlann, she regretted any hurt to Ninian. She did not want to desert the boy to his father's care—which seemed to be little care at all. Others had responded to Ninian's genial but shy nature, and he now had firm friends in Robson, Alpin, Lachlann, and Eva. She did not doubt that all of them, together and independently, would watch over the boy, with or without her marriage to his father.

In the past weeks, as Ninian helped more often in the smithy and stable, Eva had seen him gain confidence around Lachlann, who showed him quiet respect and patience, and expected and got good work from him. She smiled fondly as she approached and saw the boy watching Lachlann carefully, listening to his advice.

"Hold her, now," Lachlann said. "Show her how calm you are, and she will be calm, too. That is the way. Good lad." He turned, and with a set of tongs, plucked a hot horseshoe from the bucket of coals. Judging the shoe against the horse's hoof, he set the iron on the anvil and tapped it to correct the shape.

Heating it and dousing it to cool, he lifted the hoof again. Smoke wafted outward as the still-hot shoe met the tough, insensitive part of the hoof. Lachlann hammered it into place, bent the iron nails over the edge of the hoof, set the animal's foot down, and began to work on the other hind foot.

All the while, he spoke in a soothing murmur. Between Lachlann's deep, calming tones and Ninian's gentle pats, the horse tolerated the process. Eva waited patiently nearby, watching them.

Lachlann finished and glanced up. "Ah, you are back," he said. Ninian peered around the horse and smiled openly at her.

"Margaret thanks you for the pothooks and ladles," she said, coming closer. "And Angus would like to know when his nails will be done. He has a good deal of work to do now, for the priest has asked him to repair the church rafters."

"He will have the nails in a few days." Lachlann straightened and wiped his brow with a smudged arm, then patted the horse and murmured praise. "Ninian, that is the last horse, my friend. You have worked hard this day, and I thank you. Take her back to the stable now, if you will." The boy took the bridle rope and led the horse away, and Lachlann turned to Eva. "He has been a great help this morning. He has an easy way with the horses, and they seem to like him."

"You are finished?" Eva asked. "I thought shoeing horses would take most of a day."

"We started very early. Alpin brought the boy over at dawn to see if you had returned yet. Ninian has been tending to the chores in the house and in the stable too while you were gone."

She nodded, and he sent her a quizzical glance. She knew he wondered why she had gone to Margaret's for several days, but he did not ask. "And I am glad for the extra time, since I want to ride to Glen Brae to find the charcoal burner," he said. He stooped to pick up the iron bucket with its smoking embers. Ninian came running back from the stable and gathered up Lachlann's tools, and the smith nodded approval. "Good lad. Now while I get cleaned up, will you saddle the garron? She will have rested from her ordeal by now." Ninian ran off eagerly.

"Your garron did not like being shod?" Eva asked.

"Garrons are so tough-footed that they do not need shoes, as the destriers do on this rough ground, but I added nails to her hooves to give her better footing on the hills in the winter. She did not like the procedure, but Ninian calmed her nicely. The child has a gift."

"Thank you for being so kind to him."

"Did you think I would be anything less to him? He is a good-hearted little fellow."

"He is," she agreed. "But since he is Colin's son, you might not like him so well."

"I am not so hard-hearted as that, Eva." He watched her.

"I know," she murmured.

He frowned, and seemed as if he would speak, but instead he moved toward the smithy door. "I will be back this evening," he said over his shoulder. "If the soldiers come to the stable, keep Ninian with you, and shut yourself in the house."

"I can take care of myself," she called.

He glanced at her over his shoulder. "I am sure of that. But you have new-made locks. Use them."

"Ninian, not so fast," Eva laughed later, as she followed the boy up the long, steep bank from the lochside to the stable yard. Her muscles ached in a satisfying way after a demanding practice session with Alpin on Innisfarna. As she climbed the slope, her gown swung against her bare shins; she had changed out of the belted plaid and shirt before leaving the island.

After Lachlann had left for Glen Brae, Alpin had ferried over to fetch Ninian, and she had crossed back to the island with them to practice some sword work. Later she helped Ninian trim the vines in Alpin's garden, while the old man grumbled about the effort involved in raising a few flowers.

Taking time to explain privately to Alpin what Colin had done, she did not tell him of her deepening love for Lachlann. She listened to his gruff insights as he encouraged her to refuse the marriage, but she did not mention Green Colin's threats.

As she climbed the hill after Ninian, the dogs barked with excitement, and Eva laughed at their delight when the boy began to run around the meadow with them. Aware that he was hungry, she went into the house to cook eggs and porridge, which she knew he could easily eat; some foods were a challenge for him to chew and swallow, so she prepared his meals carefully.

Stirring the kettle, she turned with a smile when Ninian burst through the door. At the alarm on his face, she straightened and swung the pot off the fire on its new chain. The boy pointed outside, his chest heaving, face pale, mouth working to produce intelligible sounds. Hearing the clatter of horses' hooves in the yard, she realized that the patrol had returned, but that would not normally disturb him. The dogs, too, were barking ferociously.

"What is it?" She came toward him. "What is wrong?"

"Tchoh'n—tchoh'n!" He was excited, even frantic, eyes wide, his words more distorted than usual.

"Slow down and tell me," she said, coming closer.

"Tch . . . oll-hun. Da!" he exclaimed in frustration. "Here!"

Then she understood, and her heart dropped like a stone. "Colin? Your father is here?"

He nodded and pointed. Through the open door, she glimpsed men and horses and heard voices. Before she could reach the door, a man stepped inside. Ninian skittered out of his way.

In breastplate and cloak, Colin seemed larger and heavier than she remembered, but she had not forgotten his thick, ruddy features, or the glower that composed them now.

"Boy, I asked you a question! I expect an answer from you, despite that affliction of yours. Where is the smith, and the lady who resides here as well? Boy—" He stopped, seeing Eva.

Eva watched him, standing very still. Ninian came toward her, and she rested a reassuring hand on his shoulder.

"Eva!" Colin moved toward her. "I have been eager to

see you." He smiled and held out his hands. "Or should I say, wife. It is good to be here at last."

"Colin," she said calmly, though her heart slammed and her fingers trembled on Ninian's shoulder. She did not give Colin her hand in greeting. When he leaned forward to kiss her, she turned her head so that his lips met her cheek. He pulled back.

"You did get word of our marriage?" he asked. "I sent a letter to inform you that it was done. The king thought it best in order to hasten the petitions I have pending. It was not difficult to arrange a proxy ceremony."

"I got the word," she said stiffly, "but not from you. I learned about it from . . . a message the king sent here."

He nodded. "So long as you know. We have much to celebrate, then." His narrowed gaze skimmed her from head to foot. "I hardly knew you, hiding in this dark little hut. You look like a fishwife in that old gown and plaid. That will change now that you are the wife of a man of position."

She lifted her chin and did not reply.

He stepped away to shut the door behind him, closing off the sounds from the yard of the men dismounting, talking, leading their horses to the stable. An oppressive silence filled the room. Eva had never perceived the little house as dim, cramped, or smoky; it had always seemed intimate, familiar, and welcoming. But Colin brought shadows and tension inside with him.

He came toward her. "I hoped to find you well, but by the saints, I did not expect to find you in such poor circumstances."

"I like it here, where I am safe, and welcomed by friends."

"I saw Robson at Strathlan earlier today. He told me you fled Innisfarna—sheer temper, I told him. Still the she-wolf, eh?" Taking her hand in his rough one, he kissed it, his lips cold and dry. "I see you found the boy."

"Ninian." She pressed his shoulder in encouragement. "Greet your father."

Ninian spoke with halting nasal distortion, but Eva understood him. "God be with you, Father," he managed to say.

Colin frowned at him, then looked at Eva. "Taught it to speak, did you?" She sucked in her breath, shocked by his heartlessness.

"Ninian speaks quite well," she said. "You must have forgotten that in your absence."

"I did not forget that I sent him to Robson so that he would learn some simple skills. I did not want him to bother you." He frowned at his son. "He looks bigger."

"Of course," she snapped. "He is a growing child. And Robson says he does his tasks well, and he has been a good companion for me here. Ninian has a gift for working with the horses, too. You would be proud to see that. When you teach him to ride, he will outdo any rider you have ever seen." She could feel Ninian's shoulders straightening beneath her hand.

"When I teach him to ride?" Colin laughed.

Covering a flare of temper, Eva patted Ninian's shoulder. "Go to the stable and see if the soldiers need any assistance, if you please." Smiling, she gave him a little push. He skirted past Colin and fled outside.

Eva glared at Colin. "How can you treat your own son as if he is worthless—scarcely human!"

"I see you went softhearted over him. Have mercy, little wildcat. I am not without sympathy. I do my duty as a father, though heaven fastened him upon me like a trial."

"He is a blessing to you, if you would but see it."

He sent her a perplexed look and strode to a bench to sit down. "Get me some ale. I am thirsty after a long ride," he said. "I doubt you have good wine here, though I sent some to Innisfarna for my use later. What became of it?"

"I have no idea," she said stiffly. She poured some heather ale and smacked the cup down on the table in front of him. "I am not an innkeeper," she said. "Though you are welcome to the hospitality. I can offer you porridge if you are hungry." He waved in refusal. With regret, she realized that Ninian, hungry as he was, had not yet eaten; she would make certain he did so after Colin left.

Dear God, she thought, let him depart soon. She needed time to accept that he was here at last—and that all her dreams, however precious and impossible, had ended now. Whatever hope she harbored wavered in his intense and demanding presence.

But she must cling to hope and the strength of her decision. Marriage with Colin would be unendurable, no matter the benefits for her kin. He had demonstrated already how arrogant, unsavory, even cruel he could be. And she could not imagine life without Lachlann now.

For one fervent, guilt-edged moment, she wished Colin would tell her that he could do nothing for her kinsmen. Only then would she feel free to refuse him entirely. She frowned and arranged her thoughts as if she prepared weapons for battle, then opened her mouth to speak.

"So you took the boy under your wing," Colin said abruptly, wiping his mouth after swallowing ale.

She nodded. "He is a good lad. Colin—"

"He should have died at birth, puling and ugly thing that he was, choking on his food."

"Dear God," she said. "He is but a child!"

"His mother died after he was born, and left him with me. A penance for my sins. She was my leman, and not my first wife, who died childless." He looked at her over his cup boldly, daring her to protest against his penchant for mistresses.

"I see," she said flatly. "Who raised him?"

"My mother took over his care and coddled him too

much. But she brought him healthy to boyhood," he admitted in a grudging tone. "Not easy to do with a changeling."

"Changeling?"

"My mother never believed it, but I am convinced he can only be a changeling child. My own son must have been taken out of the birth chamber and this one left behind. He should have been left on a hill for the faeries to take back. He is a wild creature, most of an idiot, lazy and foolish as faeries are. He scarcely ages, and he will never be a tall man—but hill faeries do not breed strong and beautiful," he added, glancing at her. "Not like your kind."

"My kind?" she asked in astonishment.

"Dark faeries—the tall, warlike ones of old, the ones in your heritage," he said. "Aeife's line. I like to think, my dear," he went on, "that you are very much like her."

She stared at him, her heart suddenly pounding in realization: for all his shrewdness and practical coldness, Colin believed in faeries. She narrowed her eyes, wondering at that oddity in such a hardened, worldly man. Colin seemed fascinated by the ancient line of her descent.

"Ninian is a sprite of some sort. Stares at me like a dimwit and cannot speak. Never will, with that curse upon him."

"My own faery blood is nothing but a legend," she said. "I am sure I am nothing like Aeife the Radiant One. And I do not know how you can speak so ill of your own son," she added.

"Huh. I half expect him to go up the chimney in smoke one of these days. But I have a duty to him, so I sent him to Innisfarna to be a page. It is Christian charity."

"Give him the charity of your heart. He is neither idiot nor changeling, but a little boy. He needs the respect and love of his father, like any son."

Colin scowled. "He has charmed you, I see. So it was with my mother, who spoiled him when she was alive—showed him more mother's love than I ever got, I will tell you! My father never allowed me to be coddled in his household. Ninian needs simple tasks and a strict hand. It is the only way with such a one as that," he muttered, and gulped ale. "Unwise to succor a faery breed. Should have got rid of it."

Feeling a wave of fury, Eva fisted her hands. "Colin, please! Can you not act the proper father to him, and show him some amount of tolerance—even simple kindness?"

He waggled his brows. "Taking your husband to task, are you? We can play that game. But I was hoping for a happy welcome. You are a sour girl."

"You do not merit a happy welcome," she snapped. "I do not consider myself your wife. You did not have my consent for the marriage."

"Listen to me. You were made mine by a formal ceremony in France, under sanction of the Church. I could take you now, there in that bed, and seal the marriage in the eyes of God and man." He gestured with a thumb toward the curtained bed. "I ought to get a true son upon you now, so we need have no more talk of Ninian being my son."

Eva flared her nostrils, fighting repulsion. "You hear me. I fended for myself while you were away. My home was taken over by soldiers and I had to find safe shelter elsewhere. And you threatened my family. After that, I would never fall willingly into bed with you—or into a marriage with you."

"You gave me your promise." He stepped forward to look down at her, his face reddening. "Your temper has not changed, has it? Still fire and spit, and still appealing." He smiled. "No one forced you to leave Innisfarna to stay in this hut—that was your own spoiled nature. But you can leave with me and come to Strathlan to live in far better luxury."

"I will go nowhere with you," she said stiffly. "You married me without consent, and you promised to help my brothers and my kinsmen, and have not done so. What news do you bring of their appeal?"

"I had written permission from your guardian—from Donal, in exchange for my influence in his case."

"Written? Have you seen him? Is he well?"

"I obtained his signature of consent while I was in France. I sent you word of it," he barked.

"I never got it. How is Donal? Will he be freed?"

"Thin, weak, and made docile by his situation."

"Donal would never be docile," she said, raising her chin. "Nor would any of my MacArthur kinsmen."

"Or you," Colin said.

She folded her hands, her heart pounding. "I have waited a long time to hear good news on behalf of my kinsmen. Have you any to report?"

"I have met my promise, as I said I would," he said abruptly, and stuck two fingers inside the arm opening of his cuirass, bringing out two creased and much-folded parchments. "This is an order signed by the king, and another document that will interest you. According to this, Donal will be released and pardoned, and your kinsmen as well, with conditions. So you see, I have done what you wanted of me."

She stared at him, stunned, feeling a burst of relief and a dark tug of sadness. "Let me read it," she said, and reached for the page, scanning it quickly before he snatched it from her.

"The order is provisional," he said.

"Why so? Give it to me. I can read—English, Latin, whatever it is." She stretched, but he held it above her head.

"Conditional," he said, "upon the granting of Innisfarna to me. This other page is the deed to the island, copied out of the property rolls kept in Edinburgh. The place became mine upon our marriage, provisional upon your signature in agreement, which I will send back to the clerk of the crown.

Then," he said, "your kinsmen will be pardoned, according to the king's conditions."

"Conditions?" She stared at him, her blood running cold. "What if I should refuse to sign that page?" she asked softly.

"Refuse?" He snorted in disbelief. "My good influence will be withdrawn and turned against your clan. Donal will die—the king grows short in patience with this matter—and your kinsmen will be hunted down until they are all dead, too." He shrugged. "Of course, it is your choice. Do you have ink and pen in this hovel or shall we see to the signing at Strathlan, in the comfort of our home, dear wife?"

Hand flattened over her heart, Eva stared at him, unable to answer, whether to agree or to protest.

Chapter 20

Following his nose, and the thin veil of gray smoke that hung over the middle of the forest, Lachlann found the charcoal burner by midday. He cautiously guided the garron and the packhorse, whose lead he held, through a pine forest over a path carpeted with russet pine needles. The tangy smell of sap was so pleasant that he pulled in a deep breath.

Then the odor of char grew stronger, and between the trees, he saw a clearing and the conical shape of three charcoal-burning mounds, as large as small houses, from which smoke drifted.

As he emerged from the trees he saw a man and a woman in the clearing. Both were small and shriveled and gray, as if the constant overhanging smoke had withered them. They watched him silently as he dismounted and tied the horses to a tree.

"I told you he would come, and here he is," the woman said, nudging the man forward.

"You are a MacKerron," the man said. "I know the look of your kin. You have been here before, but not for a long while. And your father was here, too, long ago. I am Leod."

Lachlann took the little man's grimy hand. "Leod, greetings. I remember you. Years ago, I would come here with Finlay MacKerron to buy charcoal. He always said that yours was the best quality and made the best steel."

"The best, of course," the woman said, scurrying closer.

"No one can make good steel without our charcoal. We cut the trees and burn the wood in secret ways," she confided. "You are not Finlay's son. The other one was your father. Look at him, Leod, he is the one." She jabbed him with her elbow.

"I know who he is, Nessa," Leod said, sounding irritated.

"And you have the look of his mother, too," Nessa whispered loudly. "Blue eyes, blue eyes, cousin to a king," she sang, and smiled up at Lachlann, so short and hunched over that she scarcely came to his waist.

"What?" Lachlann asked, a little startled by her behavior.

"Your mother," she said. "She had the same bluebell eyes as you have, and she was a cousin to the king. Not that her Stewart blood saved her, or avenged her. But there are kings and faeries in you. Good blood in you." She kept smiling at him.

"You knew my mother?"

"She was a kind beauty, and her love a fine dark man—oh, so handsome, that one! And you have both of them in you."

"Tell me what you know of them."

"Is it charcoal you want?" Leod asked. "Or is it truth?"

"Both," Lachlann said. "I came here to ask you what happened to my parents. Mairi said you might know. And I will buy charcoal—the best you have, for the best steel."

"Ah, he will be making faery steel soon," Nessa said, nodding sagely. Leod scowled at her.

"Go tend the fires, Nessa, or we will have nothing but ash and soot. This man wants the best charcoal we can sell him. Go." He turned back to Lachlann. "We cut the wood and burn it carefully, tending it for weeks at a time to make our charcoal pieces. Those huts there are still burning inside, but I have some of our best new-made charcoal for you."

Lachlann watched as Nessa went toward one of the huts, using a long stick to poke at the embers buried beneath the pile that stood higher than her head. "I can give you as much charcoal as your packhorse can carry and as much as you can barter me for smithing work, or food, or even coin. How much do you want?" Leod asked. "And how much truth do you want?" he added.

Lachlann blinked. "Three sacks for now, and I will pay in smith work or coin, either one. As for the rest . . . tell me as much truth about my parents as you know."

Leod nodded, rubbing his whiskered jaw. "You do have the look of Tomas MacKerron, that dark faery blood—black and tall he was, like you, with eyes like silver. He was a good smith for the finest faery blades."

Lachlann looked at him cautiously. "Finlay told me of a tradition for that sort of thing among MacKerron smiths."

"More than tradition. You wanted the truth. Tomas MacKerron made faery blades, and he was killed for them."

"If you knew this, why did you never seek me out?"

"Finlay knew. And it was your place to seek me out, and so you have," Leod said. "I will tell you now, but I would not carry tales then. There are those who would not like it. I stay out of business that is not my own. I am but a charcoal burner."

"Leod, if you know who killed my father, and why, tell me."

"Nessa and I were there that night, bringing a load of charcoal to Tomas," he said. "He lived just over the hill— that way. You can see the ruin of the smithy and the house, near the great charred oak on the north hill."

"What happened?" Lachlann asked.

Nessa came back, lugging a huge sack of charcoal nearly as large as she was. She dragged it past her husband, who only watched her. Lachlann stepped toward her to help her lift it, but before he could get to her side, she had hefted it onto the packhorse. Smacking dust from her hands, she marched back.

"Well," she said. "Tell him, you old fool. I would have told you myself, young man, but the faeries would not let me."

"They—what?"

"Them, there," she said, pointing. "The little ones watching you. They would not let me tell you. Said it was yours to learn, and when you were ready, you would come to us."

Lachlann looked where she indicated, but saw only a pine forest. Nessa apparently saw more, for she waved and giggled. "There they are," she said. "They are glad you finally came. It is about time, they say. Listen. 'Time, time,' they are singing . . . 'time the smith made his faery sword.'"

He stared at her, then turned back to Leod. The old man smiled as if there was nothing odd in his wife's chatter. "What . . . ah, what happened that night, Leod?"

"It was the old one," Leod said. "Old Murdoch Campbell."

"Colin's father?" Lachlann asked quickly, recognizing the old laird's name.

Leod nodded. "He came to the smithy where your father was working after dark. 'Come out, *gobha*,' Murdoch said, and he held a sword upright." Leod deepened his voice and reached up with his arm, acting out what he had seen. " 'Ho, *gobha,* this is not the sword I ordered from you. Come out, smith, and give me the faery blade I paid for!' And Tomas the *gobha* came out, wiping his hands on his apron, with his pretty wife at his side."

Nessa hurried forward. "And then the smith spoke again," she said, as if eager to take part. " 'I made you a good battle sword, Murdoch. Now go away. You are drunk again,' your father said to him," she recounted, lowering her voice to a masculine pitch.

" 'But I want a faery blade. Give it to me, or you shall have this one between your ribs!' " Leod said, swaggering

and waving his arm like a mummer at a fair as he played
Murdoch Campbell.

" 'Go away, Murdoch Campbell, and leave my husband
alone. You always talk of faery blades when the drink is
upon you!' " Nessa said. "And then your mother shooed him
with her hands." She gestured and minced. "She was graceful as a faery girl."

Lachlann stared, both entranced and horrified by their
strangely comedic behavior.

"Did Murdoch kill my father?" Lachlann ground out.

"Staggered near off his horse, he did, drunk as that man
was." Leod spoke, while Nessa mimed a stumble. "He always talked of faery blades when the *uisge beatha* was upon
him. He even came to me. He wanted a faery sword, you
see, for he had dark ambition in his hard old soul. He knew
he could win that island in the great loch if he had such a
weapon." Beyond them, Nessa waved her arm high as if she
held a sword.

"He what? Do you mean Innisfarna?" Lachlann asked.

"That old fool wanted Innisfarna," Nessa said. "Murdoch
tried to wed the girl who owned it, but she married the handsome chief of the MacArthurs and gave him three lovely
babes." She smiled. "Murdoch always craved that island, for
he thought if he held that, he would hold Scotland in his
power, beyond the king's control. The faeries told me he
could not have it. Not for him, that place. Not for him." She
peered closely at him.

Lachlann stared at her as if he had been struck. "So," he
said, half to himself. "His son Colin wants Innisfarna too."

"That may be, I do not know," Leod said. "But I remember that Murdoch demanded the faery blade from your father, and Tomas said he could not help him. Quiet of voice
and strong of spirit was that young man. 'Leave us be, Murdoch!' Tomas said, and he sent his wife inside and faced the
old man alone."

" 'Aileen, my love, go inside with you!' " Nessa said.

Leod turned. "Go get the blade," he told Nessa. She turned and hastened into a little hut set apart from the charcoal-burning piles, which Lachlann presumed was their home.

"What happened then?" Lachlann asked.

"Murdoch sat upon the horse and threatened, but your father was not afraid of him. Old Murdoch swung the sword, drunk as he was, and caught Tomas in the chest." He shook his head sadly.

Lachlann was grateful that the old man did not act that out for him. He was not so sure Nessa would have held back from it, however. "He killed Tomas then and there. And he told his son to set the smithy on fire," Leod went on.

"His son?" Lachlann asked. "Colin was there?"

Leod nodded. "Murdoch told his son to do it, but he begged his father to leave. The old man was so drunk he set the place alight himself, using the torch that he carried in the dark, and he and his son rode off."

"You saw this?"

"I did not," Leod said. "Nessa saw it, and came running for me. By the time we got back, the smith was dead, the smithy and the house were on fire, and his beautiful wife, oh, she was gone too, taken by grief and by the smoke. I ran into the house and grabbed up the babe—you, Lachlann MacKerron—and I took you to Finlay and Mairi at the other end of the loch. A long journey and, oh, such a sad night." He shook his head.

"Leod, I owe you thanks for trying to help my parents. And I owe you my own life."

"You do," the old man agreed easily.

Lachlann shoved his hand roughly through his hair. "Why was this withheld from me? Was nothing done about their deaths?"

"Murdoch died not long after that—fell from his horse,

they say, drunk again. With your father's murderer dead, who else was there to blame? Though Finlay judged Colin harshly in his own mind for it, I think. The son tried to stop the father, though he did run like a coward with him."

Lachlann pressed his fingertips against his eyelids. "Was the sheriff told of all this?"

"Finlay told him. It was not pursued. Smithies catch fire easily. Tomas's body was burned, and no one saw the wound. Only Nessa." Leod shrugged. "And no one believed Nessa but me, and Finlay! Some think my wife is a little mad," he whispered.

She came back, dragging a long leather sheath along the ground. "The faeries want you to have this," she said, and handed it to Lachlann.

He drew out a beautiful sword, shining and perfect, with a hilt of polished bone and a cross guard ending in quatre-foils. The lower part of the blade below the cross piece was etched with a tiny emblem. Lachlann peered closer.

"A heart," he said. "For MacKerron, as Finlay and I always used . . . but this one has a small 'T' in the center of the heart."

"Tomas MacKerron," Leod said. "He made this blade."

Lachlann hefted it in his hand, raised the tip, which caught the sunlight. "Is this the blade that Murdoch—?"

"Not that. This one your father made for himself. I took it out of his house when I rescued you. I knew one day you might want it, and I kept it for you. This is a faery blade."

Lachlann looked askance at him. "How do you know?"

"Feel the power in it," Leod said.

Lachlann turned his wrist slowly, arcing the blade to the ground, back up again. The sword sliced through the air with a whistle finer, sweeter than any he had ever heard. A delicate shiver began in his arm and spread throughout his body, and suddenly the blade felt feather-weighted and full of sunlight.

"It is beautiful, whatever it is," Lachlann said.

"Tomas knew the secret, and he had the knack," Leod said. "Finlay knew the method, but he could not make a true faery blade. He was a fine craftsman, but your father was an artist of the sword, had the making of them in his heart, see. You are Tomas's son, and you have the knack. I see the spark in you."

Lachlann stared warily at him.

"You know the secret already," Leod said. "But to make the blade sing, you must have the knack. What did Finlay tell you?"

"Air, earth, fire, and water must mingle in a faery blade," Lachlann answered. "That much I understand—those materials are part of all blademaking. He also said that it required the pouring on of light and a magical blessing. He told me more, but he was weak and could not tell me all of it. Not that I could use it, even if I understood."

"Oh, you can. You have the spark," Nessa said. "Ask Leod."

"I know the blessing," Leod said. "Air, earth, fire, water, and the rest."

Lachlann looked at him in surprise. "You?"

"I taught it to your father," the old man said. He held out his right hand, which was bent and disfigured, the fingers fused together by the scars of old, devastating burns. "A smith I was, once, and cousin to your father and Finlay. Leod MacKerron, I am called. I will teach you the charm of the MacKerron smiths."

With his father's sword and sheath secured to his saddle, and his head and heart full of what he had just learned, Lachlann rode back to Balnagovan, leading the packhorse loaded with sacks of charcoal. Although deep in thought as he crossed the long meadow, he heard the commotion in the smithy yard before he saw it.

Several soldiers were in the stretch of land between the smithy and the stable. Some of them were clustered in a circle, laughing heartily. In their midst, two men competed to lift an old anvil that sat near the smithy doorstep. Lachlann dismounted in the yard and stood watching, shaking his head, half laughing as John Robson came toward him.

"I have been scraping mud from my boots on that anvil for as long as I can remember," he told Robson. "And these fools are trying to lift it. Have they nothing better to do?"

"They are waiting," Robson said.

"For Alpin and the boat? Or for the horses to be saddled? Where is Ninian?" He looked around.

"Hiding in the stable," Robson said. "His father is back."

Lachlann felt the shock of that news in his bones. "Colin Campbell? Where is he now?"

"Inside," Robson said, "with Eva."

He was halfway across the yard before Robson finished speaking.

"When will King James release Donal and pardon the others?" Eva asked Colin.

He held up a condescending hand. "When Innisfarna is proven to be mine, then Donal will be free. I will travel to the royal court to remind the king of his promise. Your kinsmen will benefit within the king's conditions."

"What conditions?" Eva asked again, for Colin had not yet answered that query directly.

"Exile," he said. "The MacArthur men must leave Scotland and go elsewhere—France, Ireland, or Denmark will take them in. They can never come back."

She stared at him in shock. "Never? That would kill them! Their souls are here in these hills."

He shrugged. "It is their bodies you asked me to save. Let a priest tend to their souls. This is the only bargain I could arrange for your kin."

"One that takes Innisfarna from me and leaves my clansmen without rights or homes."

"It leaves them alive," he enunciated, leaning toward her.

"You wanted that. I will let you visit them wherever they go. The French favor the Scots, but the Irish are savage—your kinsmen might be more content among them." He came toward her, hands out. She stepped back, and he pulled her away from the hearth. "You will burn yourself. Come here." He kissed her, his mouth moist and ale-rich.

She pushed him away. "Why are you so set upon marrying me? You do not care about my kin, and you could find a wife with a dowry and a powerful family. Tell me why you want me."

"You are lovely, and I am fond of you. And your father was an old friend."

Regarding him suspiciously, she suddenly realized the truth. It rang in the silence between them. "You argue for my clan's pardon, and accept an impoverished bride, only to own Innisfarna. But why should the island matter so much to you?"

"It is not the island, but my devotion to you," he insisted.

"My kinsmen will never accept exile. They will refuse this bargain—and I will refuse to hand the isle into your keeping."

"Then you should all think of Donal. It is an awful fate, to be beheaded. You do not want to condemn him to that—"

"Stop!" She backed away, suppressing a sob.

He came toward her with heavy steps. "And your kinsmen will be hunted down like wolves and slaughtered," he hissed.

As he advanced, she heard a knock on the door and saw the latch move. Expecting Ninian or Robson, she glanced up to see Lachlann loom in the doorway. She felt immediate relief.

"Who the hell are you, walking into a private house?" Colin demanded.

"I am the smith, and this is my house. Eva MacArthur is a guest here," he said, gazing at her as he spoke. "Eva, do you need me?" he murmured.

"I do," she said. "Stay, please."

He walked inside, and the air seemed charged with lightning. She felt the power of it in keen waves.

"Smith, eh?" Colin asked. "I have some tasks for a good smith. Are you skilled in making weapons?"

"Of course," Lachlann said. "I am a MacKerron."

"I should have realized," Colin said, narrowing his eyes. "I knew the MacKerron smith at this end of the loch, but I heard he died. He fostered a son . . . I had forgotten. He trained you in the craft, then."

"He did," Lachlann said calmly. "I am the son of Tomas MacKerron, who smithed near Strathlan . . . when he was alive."

Hearing the low and dangerous tone in his voice, Eva looked at him sharply, noting the pulsing in his jaw, the fisting of his hands. She could see that he restrained himself, keeping under tight control.

"Ah," Colin said. "That was a tragedy."

"You ought to know," Lachlann said.

Colin paused, then slowly smiled. "How fortunate that a MacKerron smith is at work on Loch Fhionn again. If you have your father's talent, perhaps you will do some work for me."

"My work comes at a high price," Lachlann said.

"Well worth it, I am sure."

Eva watched them, sensing at any moment that one or the other might strike, though both stood still.

"I need a sword," Colin said. "A special one. But I must be sure that you have the talent to make it."

"Oh," Lachlann said in that same lethal tone, "you can be sure. But do not be so certain I will make one for you."

"When coin is offered, a craftsman agrees to the work." Colin shrugged. "It is a simple arrangement. There are other matters on my mind now, but when next I return here, I will tell you the sort of sword I want. It will commemorate my marriage to Eva."

Lachlann looked at Eva. She felt herself go pale, as if all her strength drained from her, and she could not shift her gaze from the deep hold of his.

"And it will mark the granting of Innisfarna to me," Colin went on. "A fine sword is fitting for that event, do you not agree, my lady wife?" He moved toward Eva, putting an arm around her. "Congratulate us," he told Lachlann. "We have been recently married."

"So I heard." Lachann did not take his gaze from Eva.

"My wife will live at Strathlan, so you will have your house back again, smith. And there will be better peace in the area. Those MacArthur rebels will come out of the hills in droves once they learn that they have been pardoned."

"Pardoned?" Lachlann narrowed his eyes.

"Colin arranged for my brother's release," Eva said. "He has secured a conditional pardon for my kinsmen."

"Ah." She heard a razor edge in Lachlann's voice. "And of course you must honor your pledge. What are the conditions?" He stared at her, his blue eyes gone hard and cold.

"Exile," she said. "My kinsmen must leave Scotland."

"But they will live," Colin said.

Watching Lachlann, she felt a dynamic tautness stretch between them. Yet his returned gaze was flat and shuttered.

"And all you had to do was marry him," Lachlann remarked. "What a pleasant bargain." He walked out of the house, and the slam of the door ruffled her hair and gown like the breeze from a bellows.

Chapter 21

"**L**ady Eva, I am glad you are here." Robson turned toward her in the yard as she came out of the house, having heard men and horses outside the stable. Solas and Grainne had barked with such ardor that she opened the door to send them outside, and followed them into the midst of the commotion in the yard.

Lachlann's voice, deep and sure among the others, had drawn her there. In the three days since Colin's return, she had scarcely seen him; Alpin told her he had gone to see Mairi and the charcoal burner at the other end of the loch. He returned so late on the third night that she already slept, although the ringing of the hammer woke her briefly, long before dawn.

Distraught herself, she sensed his anger, too, and she regretted finding no moment to speak with him about what had given her a little hope. Now he turned to look at her, his eyes piercing blue even across the yard.

She called to the dogs, and Lachlann, who stood with Robson, ordered them back to the house with an efficient command. To her surprise, they obeyed, even little Grainne, who cocked her head at the tall man and then went scurrying after Solas.

"You are going out on another patrol," she observed as Robson turned to greet her. Men led horses out of the stable, with weapons lashed to the saddles. She frowned. "So soon

after the last one? Has something happened?" With a growing sense of alarm, she glanced at Lachlann, who watched
her steadily.

"A messenger came from Sir Colin at Strathlan," Robson
said. "The MacArthurs stole eight cows from his lands last
night, and he wants the rebels caught."

"He just arranged their pardon!" she exclaimed. She
looked around. "Where is Colin? I would speak with him!"

"He is not here. He sent word that he has gone to Perth
for a few days. His message said that the men should be
taken and held, and he will attend to the matter when he returns."

"Their pardon is not in place yet," Lachlann added curtly.
"Cattle thieving is a crime, not a prank. Sir Colin is not the
sort to overlook that—not even to indulge his bride." His
gaze and his manner were distinctly cool.

She lifted her chin at that, though she could not deny it.

"Lady Eva, if we do find them, it may go ill for them,"
Robson said. "I am sorry to tell you so."

"Fire and sword?" Eva asked in alarm.

"Not this time, but we must escalate our search. Mac-
Kerron, whenever you are ready." He nodded briskly and
walked away.

"Ready?" Eva whirled. "You mean to go out on patrol
after my brother and his men?"

"I do. But I know what I am doing."

"How can you follow orders to harm my kinsmen?"

"Harm them? I mean to find them," he said calmly. "You
will not tell me where they are hiding."

"I agreed to that to protect them!"

"I am trying to protect them as well," he said between his
teeth. "Better I find them than some of these men. Robson
does not care for this task, but he will do his duty. If you
know where Simon is, for love of God, tell me."

"I am never sure where he is from one day to the next."

"Then I must find him myself, before these men do, with or without your help. I have to get my gear." He strode back to the smithy, banging the door behind him.

Panic rising, Eva hurried toward Robson, wending her way through the throng of men and horses. "John Robson," she called. "Some of these men are my own kinsmen."

He turned. "I understand that, but they are acting outside the law. We have little choice, pardon or none. Sir Colin is concerned about his property and that of his neighbors, who have all suffered damage because of your rebellious kinsmen. The MacArthurs risk losing whatever pardon and good graces they might gain through your marriage."

Eva saw Lachlann striding back toward the stable. He had donned his mirror-bright steel cuirass and was buckling the waist as he walked. His dark hair hung down to frame his jaw, and a long midnight blue cloak swept over his shoulders.

She caught her breath for an instant, remembering the sight of him at her door in the moonlight, looking like a faery rider. But there was nothing magical about him now as he prepared to ride after her brother and her kinsmen. She scowled.

"Your garron has been saddled, MacKerron," Robson said.

"Where do you plan to patrol tonight?" Eva asked.

"The raids have been in the northwest lately, so we will ride in that direction," Robson said. "The weather is clear, and the nights grow dark earlier, so the raids have increased."

"The wind is brisk from the north," Lachlann said. "Raiders might venture south rather than into the face of such a wind."

"A good point, but first we will ride into the hills. They were sighted there most recently." Robson walked away to speak with his men, and Lachlann turned to Eva.

"Go inside and lock your door."

"Why are you going with them, after my brother?"

"Your brother, and my friend," he said quietly. "I told you I intend to find them. But I want you to lock yourself inside."

She lifted her chin. "Do not worry about me, smith."

"Eva," he said, a little wearily, "I think I will always worry about you."

Touched by his remark, she hesitated, then made a quick decision. "You know the waterfall that cuts through the gorge up high, that we call the Mare's White Tail."

He nodded. "I remember. There are caves near it."

"If Robson and the men ride that way . . . men might be hiding in those caves. Send Robson another way. Please, Lachlann."

He regarded her for a moment. "Go inside," he repeated brusquely and strode toward the stable, his cloak billowing behind him.

Lachlann expected her to keep to the house, but a fair warning, swiftly delivered, might save lives tonight. Even if Lachlann found her brother on his own, he might be followed.

She watched in the gathering twilight as the men rode away, Lachlann mounted beside Robson, who gestured toward the great ring of hills that rose behind the smithy lands.

Simon and his men were hiding in those very hills. That, if nothing else, decided her.

Hastily she changed out of her gown and chemise into the belted plaid, trews, and shirt that she used for sword practices, and tucked her braid inside the shirt. Then she took from beneath the mattress the old steel sword and leather scabbard that Alpin had lent her for her defense if she should ever need it. Although she hoped never to have to fight a man, despite her training, tonight she would be glad of its protection.

Looping the scabbard to her belt, she left the dogs resting by the hearth and slipped outside. The sky deepened to indigo, and the sunset was a bright band of color behind the dark hills.

Steadying the scabbard with one hand, she ran at a fast pace until she attained the first hill. She skimmed its base to reach the hill behind it and began to climb. The rugged slope was wooded and slippery with leaves. Although the incline could be treacherous, especially as the light faded, she knew a hidden path and proceeded carefully.

On another face of the hill, an easier path allowed access for horses, but this rough route was shortest. Eva could hear the thunder of hoofbeats in the hills, and knew that Robson and his men came near the area where Simon and his men were hiding.

Pausing on a shale outcrop, she looked around at the layered shapes and slopes of rock, hill, and forest. The great loch spread below, mirroring the rich colors of the sunset. Narrowing her eyes, she glimpsed horsemen riding along the floor of the glen, armor glinting like stars. They must have spread out, she realized, into the hills and along the glen.

Farther up the slope, she saw the plume of a slender waterfall spilling out of the dark, rocky scree above the wooded lower part of the hill. Simon had set up a temporary camp in one of the well-concealed caves up there.

Climbing higher, so that her breath burned in her chest, she ran between clumps of pale birches and taller trees, her footsteps crushing fallen leaves, so that she could not move silently. She kept the high mass of rock in sight, with the milky tail of water splicing its face.

Then she heard shouts and crashing footsteps, and saw

the gleam of steel between the trees. She ducked behind a pine and saw three soldiers walking nearby.

Slipping along to hide behind another tree trunk, she watched the men, who did not see her. To reach the caves, she had to cross an open area. When the men turned away, she dashed out of the shadows and ran diagonally across the wooded slope.

"Halt!" a male voice called. "Hold, boy!"

She stepped into the shelter of some pines and waited breathlessly. Then, brushing boughs away, she moved forward and stopped. The men were nearby, close and without warning. They must have doubled back to meet her route. They shouted and advanced, swords drawn.

Eva's blood ran cold. Dropping her left foot back in a wary stance, she drew her sword almost without thinking, her knees flexible, her weight balanced on the balls of her feet. She lifted the sword in her right hand, raising her left in a guarding position as she moved sideways.

The men moved with her, three parts of the circle she completed. Two of them were tall and large men, swords and armor gleaming, and the third was quick, armed with an axe. She hardly looked at the shadowed faces beneath their helmets, intent on the slithering light along the blade edges that tilted toward her.

"Hold, boy," one of them said.

She stepped to the side again, and they went with her. If she ran, she would be caught, for the men were long-legged and fit. Better, she knew, to defend herself facing them directly, ready and trained for the encounter.

She had never thought to draw a sword and face an armed man in earnest, let alone three at once. Now the moment had come with heart-stopping suddenness.

"Hold," one of the men said again. "Who are you?"

"What are you doing here?" another asked, and poised his sword at an angle that would cut at her lower legs if she attempted to flee. The third soldier lunged forward, axe raised.

Bending her knees, she canted her sword tip upward. The man with the axe came toward her, and she swept her blade down to push aside the long handle of the axe. Then she skittered backward, flexing her fingers on her sword hilt, balancing her left hand out to the side. None of the men had shields, and though she sometimes trained with one, she lacked one as well. What she most needed, and did not have, was protective gear; she would have to rely on skill and deftness alone.

A taller man stepped toward her, turning his edge deftly to catch her blade with a clanking sound. As he deflected the tip and pushed her blade aside, she almost lost her grip. Her practices with Alpin had been controlled, every move studied and repeated. Now she needed strength, swiftness, and clear thought. But her heart raced, and her thoughts went strangely blank.

Those endlessly repeated drills served her well, for stances and blade handling were ingrained in her. She lifted to strike, moving in a circular pattern, and the tall man rounded with her. To either side, she saw the others advancing.

Quick and clever, she moved out of range before they could lash out at her or her blade. The second man jabbed at her, his style coarse and blunt compared to the swift ease of the tallest knight. Her diagonal lunge took her out of the path of his downstrike. Letting her blade swing behind her shoulder, she defended her back and moved away again. Turning, blade weaving and wary, free hand extended for balance, she faced them.

The man with the axe lunged close, and his short, deadly edge clipped her blade. She felt the vibration of the blow in her shoulder and back as she stepped sideways. Then the tallest knight swung at her, but the arc of his strike was slow, firm, and relaxed, not a blow meant to harm. She blocked it easily.

"Good," he said as if in approval. Surprised, she countered as he swung from overhead, slow and controlled. "Good," he said again. He turned to the other two. "I can take this one easily," he said. "He is but a lad. It is pointless for us to use three men to fight this one boy. Go ahead, and I will catch up to you." While he spoke, he kept his sword angled and ready to meet Eva in flesh or steel if she tried to move.

The two soldiers hurried off, and the tall knight turned toward her, sword raised. Eva had paused, staring at him.

"I do not wish to harm you, boy. Stop now, and we will talk." He spoke in Gaelic, which none of Robson's men spoke well. Unable to see him clearly in the darkness, she knew that brown velvet voice, felt its thrum inside her.

Lachlann lifted his sword and swept the blade toward her.

Stunned, thrown off momentarily, she stepped through another rote movement of strike and counterstrike, and followed him in a slow dance of swords.

The boy moved like a wildcat, intent and lithe. Lachlann circled warily, with no intent to harm. He assumed that the fellow was a young MacArthur, given the furtive behavior suited to a rebel, and the glimpse he had seen of dark hair and a finely shaped face. Some MacArthur males had almost pretty features, a cause for some teasing in better times.

Which lad this was, he did not know. The Glen Fhionn MacArthurs all looked alike, he thought testily. This one had the same features as most of them, including Eva—

Damn. He stared through the shadows, halting his step. What the devil was Eva doing dressed as a boy, and where had she learned to handle a sword? Frowning, he realized that Alpin must have taught her.

He had sent the guards away so that he could convince

the boy that he was no threat. Now, as Eva backed toward a cluster of pine trees, he decided to play along to discover her game. He advanced as she retreated, holding his sword at a controlled but threatening angle.

"Hold, boy," he said. "Set down your weapon."

Eva stared at him, her oval face pale, eyes wide, dark hair tumbling half out of a thick braid. Lachlann lowered the tip of his sword slightly, and she turned to flee.

He launched after her. Eva's exit was blocked by a tangle of fragrant, piney boughs, and she turned and used her blade to push Lachlann's sword down, so that she could run past him.

He deflected and defended the strike, and they circled into the clearing. She was obviously well trained. Her rapid strikes, deft footwork, and quick reasoning astonished him, as did her thoughtful, strategic movements. Lachlann countered with relative ease, his height, reach, and strength an advantage.

She knew how to defend, how to feint and parry; she faked and blocked, and improvised well. Even when she stumbled, she recovered rapidly to strike Lachlann's steel-protected shoulder.

Swiftly, Lachlann undercut her blade with his and stepped in close, foot to foot, knee to knee, blades pushing against each other, faces in shadow. Breaths heaved in tandem and their gazes locked. The tension between them felt taut, hot, and keen, less that of foes than lovers. Lachlann felt desire heat within him for her, even as he poured strength into resisting her force.

Devastated days ago by the news of her marriage, he had kept his distance from her, hoping to collect his thoughts and let his feelings cool. His anger had calmed, but his love and passion for her would never fade. Now, facing her in so intimate and demanding a manner, he felt his heart burgeon again. Dear God, he thought, how he loved her! He had never doubted the quality of her courage and her fiery, stubborn nature, and he was proud of what he saw in her tonight.

In that still, tense moment, he looked into her fearless glance and knew she recognized him. She did not acknowledge it; neither did he.

Poised in resistance with her, he thought suddenly of the story of Aeife and her prince. They stood for three days and nights, one against the other, hands locked over the Sword of Light; then they fell together from exhaustion, each catching the other. Now he understood such passion, strength, and devotion.

He knew he could disarm Eva easily with a fast snatch at her sword hilt. Instead, he pushed away and let her keep the weapon.

"I am tired of cat-and-mouse," he said. "You have been schooled in swording. Now show me what you can do. I will not let you go, so we may as well both enjoy this."

She adopted a ready stance as a gesture of agreement. Lachlann deliberately slowed his movements and began a drill, and Eva engaged him expertly. He murmured praise, then led her into another pattern, familiar from his own boyhood practice.

Now the contest seemed worthwhile to him, a match of skill and knowledge. He had no interest in defeating Eva to prove his own greater skill. Intrigued by her ability, he found their encounter compelling, a strangely sensual dance of power.

Breathing rhythmically, moving forward as he moved back, then coming together with him and parting, she accepted his slow thrusts and countered him gracefully. He led her through one drill after another. Altercation became lesson; foes had become as equal and careful as lovers.

As a bladesmith, Lachlann knew swords intimately; he knew swordplay, as art and study, better than most knights. Years ago, he had read manuals on the subject in Latin and

English, two borrowed, another acquired at a market in Glasgow. He had pored over every word and every drawing with painstaking care, learning to read and learning about swords. On the fields of France, he had used more of that knowledge than he had ever wanted to use.

Now he called it up in his mind and in the memory of his body, like a scholar reeling out his lessons one by one—only he was the master now.

He initiated a series of lunges and countermoves, and Eva responded, well rehearsed and practiced. Some were traditional, others she improvised with near brilliance, catching Lachlann narrowly more than once. Lachlann increased speed and force, careful to strike only her blade.

As much as he enjoyed this and wanted it to continue, he realized the contest must end before the sound of clashing swords brought the king's men toward them once again.

One powerful swipe from beneath, accurately timed, sent Eva's sword spinning out of her hand. Lachlann felt the jolt in his own arm. The sword landed in a bed of leaves, and she grabbed at her forearm, curling inward as if in pain.

"Are you hurt?" Lachlann asked with quick concern.

"I am fine," came her muttered, recalcitrant reply.

Lachlann lifted his blade tip to point. "Well done. Sit over there." He indicated the base of a wide tree. She sat, legs folded neatly, and cradled her wrist.

Lachlann sheathed his sword and snatched up the fallen weapon. His knowledgeable smith's eye took in the older style, the nicked and well-worn blade.

"Whose weapon is this?" he asked. She did not reply. He stood before her and drove the swords into the earth, folding his hands over both pommels at once. She rose to her feet and stepped into a shaft of moonlight to walk past him. He grabbed her arm. "Stay here," he said. "Eva."

She pulled, made a little frustrated sound. "Let me go!"

"Where are you going? And what the devil are you doing

here?" He turned her, but she looped out of his grasp. "I told you to stay at Balnagovan," he growled.

"Are you my keeper?" She glared up at him.

"I did not think you needed one. I thought you were sensible, but I should have known better. Why the disguise? And where did you learn swordplay? We took you for a man at first, for love of God! One of us might have killed you!"

"I learned how to protect myself while you were in France. Give me that," she said, snatching at the hilt of her sword. "It belongs to Alpin."

"It is mine now," he said. "As victor."

"I let you win," she muttered. "I gave you that last shot."

"Did you?" he said easily. He handed the sword to her, hilt first. "Return this to Alpin, or I will."

"He gave it to me for my own defense." She slid it into the scabbard that hung from her belt. The sheath and sword were too long for her height, angling past her knee.

"When you were young, you followed your brothers and me in most things. But you never wanted to fight with stick swords, as I recall. You did not like to hurt anyone, or to be hurt."

"I have enjoyed the sword lessons, but I never intended to use the skills to fight in earnest."

"How long have you been training with Alpin?" He pulled his sword out of the ground and slid it into his scabbard, hearing the whistle of good steel.

She rubbed her wrist. "Almost two years."

"Well, he is the best teacher you could have for this. He taught me when I was younger, and your brothers too. But why you would choose to do this, even for self-defense, I cannot—" He paused. "Ah, the legend. Aeife's legend. The maiden with the sword. Do you think you must reclaim Innisfarna this way?"

She stilled her hands and regarded him silently.

"Do you not trust your beloved husband to keep your isle safe?" he asked, low and bitter.

"Would you?" she snapped.

"Then why accept the marriage? You can refuse it." He wished she would do that, and soon—or he would take care of Colin Campbell himself. His patience ran thin on that topic.

"Not as easily as you think. We cannot talk about this here." She stepped away. "I must find my brother and warn him."

He grabbed her arm, fearing she would bolt. Robson's men must not find her dressed as a boy, armed and skilled like a soldier—and clearly in league with the rebels. He had to keep her with him, even if she did not want that. "I told you I would find Simon. You should not be out here."

"I did not come out only to annoy you," she snapped, shaking off his grip. Then she winced and rubbed at her wrist again.

"Let me look at that." He took her forearm and skimmed his fingers along its slender length to the elbow, probing gently, turning her slim wrist in his hand. She seemed small and vulnerable in his large hands, but he knew her formidable temperament, had seen her fight with courage and skill. Her fragility was deceptive, her strength and resolve genuine.

"It is not swollen, but it is bruised, and it must be sore. A cold cloth and some of Mairi's willow ointment will help. I struck the sword too hard from your hand. Though if I had not, you might have taken me down," he remarked wryly.

"I may do that yet," she retorted.

She had done it long ago, he thought, plucked his heart from him neat as an apple from a tree. "Come," he said, taking her upper arm. "We are going back to Balnagovan."

"I came out here to find Simon!"

"He is no fool. With all the noise of sword fights and

king's horses out here, he is not about to make himself seen, if he is nearby. I want you safe, and Simon wants that too, I am sure. Come." He walked her firmly toward the downward path.

"I can watch out for myself."

"That is what worries me. Go easy in the dark."

"I know the way," she said, as they edged their way down the hill. "Oh—listen!" She stopped and turned. He heard the creak of steel and leather, and the crunching of feet through the leaves on the hillside. "They are back!" she cried softly.

"Down!" Lachlann hissed, taking her arm. Before she could protest, he slid her sword out of its scabbard and pushed her to her knees and lower, shoving her into a high drift of dry leaves.

Drawing his own sword, he slid it to the ground with hers, and dropped down beside her, swirling his dark cloak over both of them, shimmying into the cover of leaves with her.

"What are you doing—"

"Shh," he whispered, touching his finger to her lips.

Holding her snug, her hair soft against his jaw, he peered over a fold of the cloak. Between the trees a little distance down the hill, he saw the two soldiers who had earlier accompanied him. He ducked inside the cloak's cover and lay with Eva, their forms blending with the leafy rumple of the hillside.

Chapter 22

The incline seemed to tilt beneath her when Lachlann took her down to the ground, swirling his cloak over both of them. Eva clutched at him, fearing they might roll down the hill.

"Be still," he whispered, his embrace tightening. "Wait."

Wrapped in his arms, his breath warm upon her cheek, she lay motionless. His steel breastplate was hard and cold against her chest, and his beard was like sand against her brow. "Why should you hide from them?" she whispered.

"I do not want them to find you," he murmured.

"I would have run—"

"Hush." His finger pressed her lips.

A moment later the ground shook as men walked close by, footsteps crunching through the leaves, their voices clear.

"MacKerron!" As the name echoed, Lachlann's arms tightened around her. "He was here not long ago, and his horse is still tethered down the slope. He must have chased that rebel elsewhere," one of the men said. "No one appears to have been injured here. I will wager MacKerron could not take that quick little fellow and ended up running after him."

Cocooned with Lachlann inside the cloak, Eva felt the ripple of his soft chuckle. She knocked him on the shoulder.

The other soldier laughed. "I swear I heard the sound of

weapons hitting after we left him. But there is no one about."

" 'Tis rutting season. You might have heard two stags clashing horns over some fine doe." More footsteps crushed the leaves. "What a place this is, steep and rugged. Come ahead. The others are waiting down the hill. We canna wait for the smith. He knows that Robson wants us to meet him down in the glen after we search the hill." They walked away, making no attempt to muffle the crashing sound of their departure.

Silence descended over the hillside again. Eva rested her head on his shoulder and felt his hand soothe over her hair. She sighed, glad for such peacefulness, however fleeting.

"Best to wait until we know they are gone," he whispered.

She nodded, willing to linger in his arms inside their dark haven. A turn of her head brought her lips against his chin.

"Be still, you." His tender whisper stirred a sensual force within her. The air between them seemed laden, pulsing. Her body pulsed, too, as her mouth nearly touched his.

She felt an overwhelming urge to throw her arms around him, to feel his passion again. Wanting him to hold her, to love her and never let her go, she closed her eyes and pressed closer to him. "Lachlann," she whispered, wanting to tell him her thoughts about Colin, about pledges.

"Hush." He shifted his head, and his mouth swept over hers, certain and hungry. When he gently tilted her chin and deepened the kiss, she dissolved in his arms. Tender, magical, she did not want the moment to end. A kind of wildness filled her, tinged with desperation. She wanted him fiercely, and felt his desire manifest, firm and urgent, against her hip.

"Dhia," he breathed in her ear. His fingers traced downward, over her shoulder, lingering upon her breast. She gasped as his thumb brushed her stiffening nipple, the feeling deep, startling, irresistible. His palm stilled over her

beating heart and his mouth sought hers again, gave and slaked. She arched against him as his mouth traced over her cheek.

"This is madness," he whispered. "I cannot be near you without . . ." His lips took hers again, and her body responded with a burst of passion, deep and low. "Eva, tell me you do not want that marriage." His voice spiraled into her like a flame. "Tell me so," he said, kissing her.

"Ach Dhia," she moaned, "I do not want it—"

"Good," he murmured, his mouth fitting over hers again. Her lips opened for him as his tongue touched, swept over hers, while she wrapped her arms around him, sighed, began to tremble.

"Lachlann—" she whispered.

"Shhh." He turned his head, his hand stilling at her waist. She froze, aware of the crunch of footsteps through leaves. The silence crackled with another's presence.

"If you continue like that, my friend," Simon drawled, "you will be the one marrying my sister before the night is out, regardless of who else might claim her."

Suppressing an oath, Lachlann flipped back a corner of the cloak. "Simon," he murmured calmly, disguising his astonishment.

Eva's brother leaned easily against a tree that sprouted upright out of the steep hillside. He folded his arms and stared down at them. "Lachlann. Eva, come out, girl."

Eva sat up. "Simon, you cannot stay out here in the open. The king's men are searching for you."

"Looks like one of them found me," he said. "Lachlann, your friends went down the hill calling for you."

Lachlann stood and assisted Eva to her feet, then turned. "We must talk," he said.

"Not here. Follow me." Simon headed up the slope, with Eva and Lachlann close behind him.

Lachlann had climbed this way before, but not for years. Moonlight and the milky froth of the burn marked the way in the darkness as they climbed along a rocky gorge, moving carefully over the slick stones.

He knew exactly where they headed. Above the gorge and to the left of the waterfall, he remembered an excellent cave, large and dry, tucked in the rocky wall that soared above the hillside. Only the locals would know this place; rebels would be safe here.

Eva moved ahead with Simon, while Lachlann followed at a slower pace, encumbered by armor and more cautious by nature than the MacArthur siblings. His polished cuirass shone silvery, and he pulled the cloak around his shoulders to hide the glint.

At the peak of the slope, where the burn poured into the gorge, Eva and Simon crossed the stream, stepping from stone to stone, and walked toward the soaring black rock face.

The cave entrance was as he remembered, a narrow cleft hidden by scree and bracken, further disguised by a dark blanket slung on a rope. They entered a tunnel-like passageway that opened into a spacious natural chamber. Golden firelight flickered on rough walls, and familiar faces turned toward him.

Lachlann paused inside the opening. Parlan and William came forward, grinning. He had not seen Margaret's twin brothers since they had been with him in France, and he returned their hearty embraces with a smile. Then he turned to see three young men, brown-haired, lean, handsome, and lightly bearded. He recognized Margaret's youngest brothers, Fergus, Andra, and Micheil, who stood with an older man he had never seen.

"You have grown, you rascals," he said, grinning as he grasped the boys' hands in turn. "Tall as me now, you are," he said to Andra, the youngest. "Still playing pranks?"

Andra laughed. "Whenever I can."

"Lachlann, this is our father's cousin, Iain Og MacArthur," Fergus said, indicating the older man beside him. Iain nodded his iron gray head in gruff greeting.

Simon gestured for Lachlann and Eva to follow him to the deepest part of the cave, while the others resumed their seats around a small campfire. Game roasted on a spit, and Fergus tested the meat with a short dagger. Lachlann noticed that the smoke spiraled upward and disappeared, drawn by a good draft.

In a shadowed corner, where the ceiling dipped down and the smoky air was fragrant with charred cooking, Eva and Simon took seats on a split log. Lachlann sat on the earthen floor next to Eva and propped a knee up, resting his back against the wall.

Simon leaned forward, forearms on his knees, and listened while Eva explained that Colin had returned with the deed to Innisfarna in his pocket, as they had all expected—and the offer of a pardon for the MacArthurs, including Donal, if they accepted exile.

"Soon you will be free, and Donal released," she said.

"Exile?" Simon asked, rubbing his chin thoughtfully. "Freedom for all of us? And at what price?"

"Eva's marriage," Lachlann said stiffly. "And her isle."

Simon shook his head. "We cannot do that."

"But they hunt for you even now," Eva said. "If you are caught this time, this will be your only chance. Colin is furious."

"That cattle raid was ill timed," Lachlann added.

"The cattle we borrowed will net us a nice profit," Simon said. "We will be able to pay you to smith weapons for us."

Lachlann frowned. "That will do you no good. And Colin is not as tolerant as Robson. I guarantee it."

"You will be free men soon—do not take such risks!" Eva pleaded.

"I dislike Colin's arrangements for us," her brother answered. "Donal would not like them either, if he were here."

"Simon, we do not have a choice," Eva said.

"We do," he insisted. "There must be some other way. Lachlann, we need weapons from you. We will be fighting our way out of this, I think."

"Simon, please," Eva said. "Colin has offered the means to save all of you. Listen to me." She grabbed his arm. "I will do whatever I must to keep you safe, do you not know that?"

"Just because you are older," he said, "you do not have to shepherd me still." He sounded weary but affectionate.

"Our father is gone—and Donal in prison, and all our people sent away from their homes. Simon, I cannot lose you too."

"We will think of some way to free you from this marriage," he said stubbornly.

"I thought there was a way," she said, looking at her brother with pain and earnestness in her eyes. "I hoped so. But now I see that it would save only me, and not you. I cannot ask that sacrifice from you."

"And I cannot ask you to sacrifice yourself for us," he said. "So we disagree once again."

Eva sighed and lowered her head, covering her brow with her hand for a moment. "Simon, I beg you. No more fighting, no more raids. Accept the king's pardon. Exile is often remanded. After a while we will petition again, and the king will let you come back to Scotland."

Simon narrowed his eyes, shook his head.

"I want you to live," Eva said in a raw whisper. "It does not matter to me where you are, so long as you are alive."

Lachlann frowned, watching her. Not for the first time, he admired her tenacity, her dedication, her fire. And he understood clearly then why she believed she must remain married to a man she loathed; she loved her brother and her kinsmen that much. When Eva loved someone, she gave her whole soul and self into the bargain. He closed his eyes, sighed.

Fergus came forward. "We could gather men and weapons, and win Eva's isle for our stronghold. Then we could bargain with the crown on our own, without Green Colin's interference."

Micheil joined his brother, the two young men standing tall and strong together, and within moments the others gathered with them. "We do not want Eva to give in to Colin," he said.

Iain Og stood. "We will fight. Eva should fight, too."

"If you will not make weapons for us, smith," Micheil said, "then make a sword for Eva. You are a MacKerron, after all. You have the knowledge of making a faery blade, and she needs one now, to do what she must do."

Eva looked at Lachlann. "Faery blade?"

"You know it is just a tale," he answered, frowning.

"So is Aeife's legend, but we would be foolish to ignore it," Fergus said. "Magic exists."

"It does, in some ways," Lachlann murmured, gazing steadily at Eva. "But it is ridiculous to ask me to smith a blade for her, magical or otherwise. It will solve nothing."

"Innisfarna must be won back with a sword of faery make, or there will be disaster for all of Scotland," Andra said. Micheil and Fergus nodded. "We must take back Innisfarna, and Eva must be the one to lead us."

"I will not assist such a scheme," Lachlann said. "Simon, are you in agreement with them?"

Simon shook his head. "I have no use for faery blades or superstitious schemes. Nor do I think my sister should give up her happiness for mine. Let me fight my own battles, Eva."

She stood. "I must honor my clan, and I must honor the legend of Innisfarna. I want all of you to be safe, and free!"

"No matter the cost to you?" Lachlann asked. She met his gaze silently.

"Eva, we will take our chances," Simon said.

She shook her head. "You do not understand."

"Eva," Lachlann said, "if we discuss it, we can find some way to solve it for all of us."

"Discuss it! You do not understand—I thought there was a way, but—" She whirled, smothering a sob. Lachlann reached for her, but she paced away. He closed his hand on empty space.

"What do we not understand?" he asked. Her kinsmen still watched them, heads turning as they looked from one to the other.

"I have made a horrible mistake," she said, making a circuit of the long, narrow cave. "I made a bargain with the devil. There is no way out for me. I thought there might be, but if I free myself from Colin, all the MacArthurs are condemned. I cannot trade my happiness for your deaths!"

Simon stood. "Eva, what are you talking about?"

Lachlann strode toward her and took her arm. "What is it?" he growled. "You are keeping something from us. Is it Colin? Why does he have so strong a hold over you?"

She looked up at him, and tears welled in her eyes. "Colin made me agree to betroth to him." She fought a wrenching sob. "He said he would have Donal beheaded. He swore to hunt Simon and the others down and see them all slain. Do you not see?"

Lachlann swore, shoved his fingers through his hair. "I see," he said. "Now I see. He forced you into it."

She nodded fiercely. "He promised to gain a pardon for them if I became his wife, and gave him Innisfarna. I agreed to the marriage. Now it does not matter what I truly want, or what I regret, or what I wish could change—" she gasped out, staring at Lachlann. "If I do not honor the proxy wedding, he will convince the king to declare death for the

MacArthurs!" She stepped away from him again and resumed her agitated pacing.

"Jesu," Lachlann rumbled under his breath. "Eva, how long have you lived with this threat?"

"As long as you were gone," she snapped out. "And longer."

"You kept that from us all this time?" Simon demanded.

She nodded again, walking, turning. "I could not tell you. He threatened—" She sobbed out loud and dashed a hand at her eyes as tears seeped down.

"Colin is a cruel, arrogant—" Simon swore and punched a fist into the palm of his hand. "I would kill him if he were here, for what he has done to her," he muttered.

"That," Iain Og said, "is the best solution."

Eva came back to them now. "I hoped to gain time for Donal. I even thought I could refuse to marry Colin after the pardon was gained. But he fixed the marriage before he even returned from France!" She put a fist to her mouth and spun away.

"Eva," Lachlann said, following her. She shook her head and moved away from him again, crying openly now. Watching her, his heart turned with sadness, with love.

"He was never to be trusted, Eva," Simon said.

"I did not trust him," she said. "But I believed him. Now it is too late. He did not gain a pardon—he arranged exile for all of you!" She sobbed again, covering her eyes with a hand.

"We will have the marriage annulled," Simon said.

"Do that, and Colin will see all of you dead! And Donal will never come home to us! I made a terrible error when I agreed—oh, God. Simon, I am sorry. Lachlann—oh—" Crying, she whirled and ran out of the cave. The dark cloth at the entrance flapped behind her.

Lachlann strode after her, but Simon grabbed his shoulder. "Leave her alone for a little while. You will find her at

Balnagovan soon enough. Meanwhile, we must solve this trouble. I am not eager to be exiled or beheaded, but neither will I let my sister give herself up to Green Colin Campbell."

"Just take that ripe bastard off the face of the earth," Iain Og said. "If none of you will do it, I will do it myself."

Simon turned to Lachlann. "We need your help," he said quietly. "Talk to her, and convince her to refuse him. And help us find the way."

"Annulment or death," Lachlann said. "Take your pick."

"Annulment takes too long," William said. "A blade is faster." He folded his arms and looked at his twin.

Parlan pursed his mouth. "I think she should have married the blacksmith long ago. Then this never would have come about."

Lachlann frowned at him, and saw Simon's speculative glance. "As soon as we have an annulment, the girl must be married quick to protect her," Simon said. "What say you, smith? Will you sacrifice your freedom to our cause, and wed my sister?"

"Quick as you could say it, I would do it," he replied. "But it will not be easy to convince Eva of any plan but her own."

"See to it. She has always listened to you."

Lachlann gave him a sour, skeptical glance. "Are we speaking of the same girl?" He gathered his sword and Eva's, shoved the curtain aside, and strode out of the cave.

Chapter 23

Nearing the smithy lands, Eva heard the thunder of hooves behind her and glanced over her shoulder to see Lachlann riding across the meadow. At first she ran faster, her lungs bursting. Then, recognizing inevitability, she stopped and waited, dashing a hand over her eyes and sniffling.

As he came close he reached down and pulled her up by the arm—his grip had iron—to seat her on his thighs. "No need to run from me. I am not the one you are upset with."

"How do you know?" she demanded, her shoulder pressed against his cold, hard breastplate.

"Because I know you, my girl. It is yourself you are most upset with just now. But you have done nothing wrong. You made no mistakes." He wrapped an unrelenting arm around her and urged the garron to a canter.

He was wrong, she wanted to tell him; she had made one mistake after another in letting Colin overwhelm her as he had done. And she was upset with herself—and Lachlann too.

She wished he would vehemently disagree with the marriage and snatch her away from the situation. She was weary of struggling on her own against Colin for so long. Revealing the hold Colin had over her had brought relief as well as anguish.

She wanted Lachlann to realize what she knew—that their spontaneous pledge of devotion, years ago, could invalidate her marriage now. But he remained cool and reserved, holding his thoughts close, as was his habit.

Strong emotions rolled like waves through her, impulsively and fully expressed. Admiring Lachlann's reserve, she understood it as a part of his depth, but she craved to know that he, too, felt angry and hurt over this, as she did. The love between them could flourish, but not if she was another man's wife, and not if her kin would suffer for her freedom.

Even though it might be too late, she wanted to know that Lachlann loved her as she loved him. Or had she mistaken lust and friendship for a soul-deep bond?

She sniffled as she rode in his arms. No matter what Lachlann felt or thought, she could rely on him to be a rock in the storm, and she needed that now, very much.

The dogs barked inside the house as Lachlann halted the horse in the yard. Silently, he dismounted and lifted his hands to help her, but she slid to the ground unaided.

"Go inside," he said. "When I come back from the stable, we will discuss this."

"Discussion is not what I want," she said.

"Do you want sympathy? Mine will do you no good. I cannot fix this for you as easily as those damned locks!"

"I do not want that either," she said through her teeth. "I just want to know that you do not like this marriage!"

"That should be obvious to you. I need not say so. I am not a man to sing my woes for all to hear."

"I know—but I hoped you would tell me your feelings."

"Why?" he growled. "What difference would that make, since you are so set on your course?"

"I thought this might at least distress you!"

"Distress me? Jesu, Eva." He gave a curt, humorless laugh. "That is hardly the word I would use."

"What, then?" She glared up at him, fists at her waist, leaning toward him in the intensity of her anger. "Angry? Displeased? Disappointed? Sympathetic?" She craned her neck to look up at him. He loomed tall and large in the darkness, in the drizzling rain that dampened her shirt and her hair, and pattered on his armor and cloak. He stared at her, profoundly silent.

"Eva, go inside," he finally said.

She grasped his arm, feeling banded muscle stone-hard beneath his quilted tunic. "Or are you perhaps sorry for my troubles, but glad to be quit of me now that I am wed? I talk too much and argue too much. And now I am keeping you out in the rain when you want to go elsewhere."

"That," he said, "sounds close enough. But none of that will quite do to describe my feelings."

She tapped her finger on his breastplate. "What, then, my friend?" she demanded. "Tell me what you feel."

He captured her finger in his hand. "Devastated," he growled. "Arrowshot, my friend. Laid flat on battlefield with my heart torn from my chest." He lifted his other hand to brush back a strand of her damp hair, while she stared at him, stunned. "But I shall live, and I shall endure it." He smiled, rueful and bitter.

Her breath caught in her throat, and she could hardly speak. "Lachlann—oh—"

"Go inside," he said gruffly, and released her finger.

Devastated herself, she felt as if her own heart had been pulled out of her and lay beating in his hand, for now she saw fully what she had only glimpsed before: Lachlann loved her. "Oh, I am sorry—"

"Go." Hand to her shoulder, he turned her and opened the door, guiding her firmly over the threshold. The dogs tumbled forward to greet them, tails wagging. Solas ran past Eva into the rain, and Lachlann put her back inside. "Go, Solas, and take your mistress with you."

Eva stood in the doorway, silent, unsure what to do. He had made it clear that he wanted to leave her, and now she knew why. The realization cut into her like a blade.

He loved her, and she had not known it. She had given her promise to his enemy, and all the while Lachlann had loved her. In her concern for her clan and kin, she had relied on his friendship, thinking that was all she would ever truly have of him. And she had hurt him unintentionally.

He stepped back, and she could not speak for the tightness in her throat, could hardly see for the tears in her eyes, mingling with the rain.

"Lachlann," she whispered, and her voice broke. She wanted to tell him again that she was sorry, wanted to explain. But the force of the revelation stunned her, and regret weakened her. He had set her firmly aside once again, as he had done before.

"Go inside, you." He spoke with such tenderness that her heart wrenched; he sounded as if he were sending her away forever. "It is a wet night. And I must get the garron into her stall."

He led the horse away. The rain was a faint drumming on his steel cuirass, a soft thudding on the ground. As he walked the animal toward the stable, his armor glinted and he disappeared in the rainy shadows.

After he settled the garron, removed his armor and quilted tunic, and hung them in the stable, he meant to hurry through the rain to the smithy. But his feet took him toward the house while the ground turned soft beneath his boots.

Eva no longer stood in the doorway, but he could not forget the sight of her, silent and dismal, while myriad tiny lights sparkled around her head, added by his injured eye. He had felt his heart break when he turned away from her, though somehow it still thumped hard and sure in his chest.

But he had been swamped by feelings that were deep and strong and overwhelming. He needed to step back, to find a few moments of the seclusion that was so essential to his well-being. What he most needed was to find the strength to express those feelings as she urged him to do, and defeat the long-held sense that she would never be his.

Light flared behind the window shutters, the door was closed, smoke spiraled out of the chimney. Standing in the rain, he felt such longing. That cozy house was the only place he wanted to be. She was there. The rain soaked his shirt and trews, dripped through his hair.

Weeks ago, he had wondered if his return to Balnagovan would prove to be a mistake. Now he knew that destiny had brought him here to resolve the past, to heal, to find his way once again. Anywhere he turned on that path—past, present, or future—and anywhere he looked, Eva was there. She had been with him in boyhood, as companion, confidante, adored; she had been tucked in his heart and in his dreams in France; and she was here now. And he loved her still.

She was a ribbon of fire woven through his life, and no matter where he went, or what he did, he would never stop loving her. That fiery strand of emotion would warm his soul forever.

Rain drenched him as he walked forward. Not so long ago, on another rainy day, Eva had come to the smithy, smiling, bright and enchanting, soaked to the skin. He remembered her laughter, and the feeling returned for a moment—simple, blessed joy.

He wanted that again, not the misery that filled him now. He did not want to lose her, and he could no longer deny the love that glowed and seared within him like a bloom of iron in the fire. What Eva added to his life warmed, inspired, and challenged him. With her, he felt truly alive, deeply aware, charged with a lightning sense of purpose and passion.

He could not live without her.

He strode toward the door and knocked quickly before his natural reserve could stop him. A moment later, Eva stood there with the red firelight behind her. Her plaid and hair were still damp from the rain. He saw the traces of tears on her cheeks and hopefulness in her eyes as she looked up at him.

"I have always loved you," he said.

"Wh—what?" she whispered. He pushed the door wider, stepping inside. Closing the door, he leaned his palm there, arm raised over her head, so that she could go nowhere, so that he could at last tell her what must be said.

"I have loved you since I was a boy," he murmured.

Eva nodded, lip quivering, eyes wide and glossy with tears.

"Though I went away, I never stopped thinking of you, not for one day, not for one night. I tried to stop loving you, Eva MacArthur, when you were promised to another, and I knew you would never be my own. But you are part of me, like heat fills the sun, like water fills that great loch out there. I love you still, my friend, and I cannot stop."

A tear flowed down her cheek. He brushed it away. "You wanted to know how I feel," he murmured. "Is it clear now?"

She uttered a sound, part sob and part joy, and nodded again. Lifting a hand, she traced her fingers over the scar on his jaw, touched his lips. He kissed her fingertips. "Lachlann, I love you," she whispered.

"Is it so?" he asked, dipping his head, while she nuzzled his nose, while his heart thundered and his body pulsed.

"It has always been so," she whispered against his mouth. "You have been in my dreams . . . you still are . . ."

"Not now," he murmured. "Now I am here." He pulled her hard against him, and touched his lips to hers, gently at first, seeking, then with deep hunger. She circled her arms around his neck, took his kiss into her, and drew back to look at him.

"What of Colin?" she asked in a rush.

"You are not his. You are mine." He kissed her again, lingering and slow.

"I have always been yours," she said. "I said so on that beach, so long ago."

"Beltane," he murmured. "I remember. You asked if a kiss could be a pledge, and I said it could, if hearts were true."

"My heart was true that night, and still is," she said. "If we made any pledge of intention then, my betrothal—"

"Was never valid," he finished, touching his lips to hers. Kissing her, taking her breath deep into him, he pulled back. "I gave you my pledge that night, and it has always been yours."

"Oh, Lachlann, I wanted to wait for you. I tried."

"I know," he said, and wrapped her in his embrace. "You did what you had to do. I understand. Tell Colin that you had made another pledge before betrothing with him, so that the marriage cannot stand." He traced his lips along her cheek, so soft, to her ear. "You have always been mine," he whispered. "We will make it so."

She nodded, pressing her brow against his cheek. "What of my kinsmen?" she asked. "What shall we do?"

"We will find a way." He kissed her hard enough to leave her breathless, head tilted, eyes closed. "Hush, now, and let me love you," he murmured. "Leave the rest for later." He kissed the delicate lobe of her ear and felt her sag against the door, heard her gasp, felt that same rush within himself. Her hands skimmed his chest, rounded over his arms, settled upon his back.

Covering her mouth with his, gathering her into his arms, he felt an inner craving. He sensed in her hands and her fervent kisses that she, too, felt the power between them like fire.

She pressed against him, her abdomen flat and small, her body strong and lithe, and his urgent hardness filled, nestled into her giving curves. A thundering insistence shuddered through him, and he kissed her again, holding her against him, stroking her shoulder, her arm, tracing her breast through the damp shirt.

He cupped her, caressed her, and she sighed into his mouth. Now, and every time he touched her, he felt the wonderment of it, the awe of it. He had dreamed of her in France, and thought he must be dreaming again, so sweet was this, so real and perfect. She moaned against his lips, and he kissed her deep, drawing the plaid off her shoulder. Working his fingers at the sturdy belt, he removed it, and the enveloping plaid slid away, leaving her in a thin linen shirt.

With her shoulders against the door, kissing him fervently in return, she pulled at his wet shirt and at the waist of his trews. She laughed a little, softly, as she helped him and he helped her, and he began to chuckle as well, feeling a bubbling of joy. Declaring his love for her at last had levitated soul and spirit in a way he had never experienced before.

Whatever troubles awaited them seemed far outside this enclosure of love. Here and now was all that existed, was fitting and true. He had pledged his heart to her long ago—long before Beltane, he knew.

Feathering his lips along her cheek and her ear, he pulled at her shirt, and she at his. Both tugged in a kind of frenzy, kissing and caressing, so that the final casting aside of the wet clothing and boots was sheer relief. When she stood naked and warm and willing in his arms, and he in hers, his body surged against her with kindled, ready desire.

She was still damp from the rain, her hair curling in tendrils beneath his hands as he framed her face to kiss her, and slid his hands along the length of her, down to her hips and up again, her skin a creamy luxury under his palms. Her kisses were gentle but fervent over his mouth and along his neck, and he sighed out, long and low, gathering her into his embrace. Her hands slid down from his shoulders and braced against his lower back, and he swelled for her, pressed hard against her. She gasped and leaned against him until he thought he might lose breath, reason, control.

Passion raced through him, made him quiver as his fingers covered her breast, the bud firming against his palm. Dipping his mouth to her throat, his fingers teased her nipple, then his lips replaced them to suck gently. She moaned, soft and eager, and her fingers found a whorl along his ear so sensitive that his body spun inside, and his muscles surged, clenched.

He caught her up into his arms then, and she rode lightly as he carried her across the room to his own bed, where she had been sleeping alone for so long. Sliding with her between the closed curtains, he lowered her to the heather-filled mattress and went down on his knees.

The fragrance released in the bed was wild and intoxicating. Years had passed since he had lain here, and now he was with her. Now, at last, he was truly home in body and soul.

She lay back, stretching and seductive, so beautifully curved, warm to the touch, so enticing that he hardened further, felt himself grow firm and hot just looking at her in the shadows. The ruby firelight filtered through the curtain weave, setting her afire like a deep jewel. He leaned forward to kiss her, tracing a pathway along her throat and the valley between her breasts, shifting his mouth upon one nipple, then the other, until she gasped and drew him closer.

Stretching out beside her, letting his hand follow the taut length of her thigh, he kissed her where her heart drummed hardest, at throat and breast. She arched like a bow in his arms as he slipped his fingers over her abdomen, then touched the soft nesting tucked between her legs. She took in a deep breath and moved against him.

He delved within, where she was honey-slick and hot, to touch the rosebud nubbin, drawing from her a cry, a quickening of breath. Rocking, pleading with her body, she rode in his arms, and he knew the instant the flame caught within her. He felt it swirl like wildfire in himself, but he held back, savoring her with lips, hands, fingertips, until she cried out again and pulled him hard against her.

Her hands roamed over his back, his hips, his abdomen, and her fingers found and caressed his hardened length, and lightning shivered through him. He rocked away, too ready, too willing, his body tightening insistently. Instead, he took his time with her, his touch relentless but gentle. He eased her along until she moved like a wave beneath him, her cry as soft as the rain that swept over the roof.

He would have coaxed her again, but the honey and fire that replaced his blood rushed him onward. Her hands found him again, closed over him, hot as embers, himself like iron in them. Warm and lush against him, the softness of her body inflamed him further. When she tucked him into the clefted pulse of her, he gasped at the heat and the richness there, so delicious that he could scarcely think, could hardly restrain himself any longer.

Upon his next breath, he felt himself slip upward inside of her, and he penetrated the thin barrier so quickly that it was done before he realized it, before he could pull back and prepare her with a whisper, with care. She made a little groan of discomfort that was transformed into a sigh of pleasure. Searing inner heat surrounded him, and a subtle, sensual flexing of her hips pulled him deeper into her.

She shuddered beneath him, her body melding with his, her undulating movements creating a power that drew him deeper into the magic with her. Where he ended and she began he did not know. Kissing her mouth, her tongue, he felt the power build in him like flame, rolling through him until he exploded with it, able to control it no longer. Love poured through him, rinsing away years of holding back his feelings for her. All he had ever wanted, all he wanted now, was Eva.

The waves subsided and he came back to awareness,

finding himself separate from her again. He sighed, gathered her close.

"Eva, my own," he whispered into the rich tumble of her hair. He kissed her, the quiet strength of their passion still simmering in his blood. She turned into the shelter of his arms.

"I am your own," she said. "And you are mine. It has always been that way, I think."

Chapter 24

Incessant rain sheeted over the thatch, and Eva added a pine log to the peat fire for brightness as well as warmth. She lit two thick tallow candles and set them on the table while Lachlann finished his meal of cheese and oatcakes. When he divided his last oatcake between the dogs, Eva laughed, standing beside him. Despite the dreary day, a luminous sense of joy filled her.

He drew her to him, and she bent to kiss him, feeling deep gratitude for their night of tender loving and the wonder of waking in his arms. The transformation of their old friendship into something altogether different felt like a kind of miracle. She closed her eyes as he rested his head on her breast, and her heart beat faster beneath her plain gown as his hands slid over her hips, hinting at pleasures yet to come.

Beyond the dreamy enclosure of her newfound joy, her thoughts still spun. Troubles remained that demanded resolution. Soon she would have to face them, though for most of her life she had dreaded the thought of an ultimate contest and a final confrontation. Now she must face Colin to claim not only her island but her self and her freedom.

Despite her training, she did not think of herself as a warrior woman, nor was she as extraordinary as Aeife of the legend. She was an ordinary girl, strong and capable, willful and sometimes bold; and now she knew she was deeply loved.

If she was ever to break free of Colin and reclaim Innisfarna, if she was ever to live a life of peace with Lachlann
and her kin, she would need all that, and more. Somewhere
within herself, she had to find and draw upon a well of
courage.

"Too slow, and off balance." Alpin commented on her
last strike as he circled Eva, eyeing her stance. He had corrected her more than usual while she swung an old steel
sword at the wooden pell, a solid upright post that Alpin had
set up in the alder grove on Innisfarna.

"I am doing the best I can," she countered irritably, and
swung again. The dulled edge of the blade bit into the wood
and stuck. She wrenched it free with an exasperated little
yelp. The sword was cumbersome, and her back and shoulders ached with every movement. When she began practic-
ing, she had discovered herself stiff and sore from the other
night's frantic sword challenge. Lachlann's blows were
heavier than she was used to taking, and her wrists and
shoulders still felt the brunt of it.

A couple of evenings spent in lovemaking had soothed
the aches deliciously while exercising other muscles, but
now she felt the strain. And though she tried to stay intent on
her movements, her mind remained in the smithy, and with
the smith.

The day had dawned cloudy but free of rain, and when
Alpin came over the water, Eva had left without telling
Lachlann. Red light glinted in the smithy windows and the
hammer clanged steadily, and she had not wanted to disturb
him.

Distracted and tired, she lost her footing yet again. Her
next few blows were awkward, the flat of the blade slamming into the pell and vibrating into her arm.

"Awful," Alpin said. "That is a sword, not an axe! What
is wrong with you today, girl?"

She slid him a glance without reply. Although she rarely practiced openly during the day, the sky blew dark with rainclouds and the castle showed little activity. The soldiers, Alpin told her, were resting, as many of them had been out on patrol again until the small hours.

Eva remembered hearing the men ride into the stable yard just before dawn, while she lay in Lachlann's arms, glad of the sense of safety she felt there. But their nights of loving did not change the fact that her decision could bring danger to her kinsmen as well as to Lachlann. That continuing dread made her so anxious that even the headiness of newfound love could not balance her.

With the next overhead strike, she lost not only her footing but her grip on the sword as well, which went skittering across the ground. Alpin threw up his hands in exasperation.

"*Ach,* you are useless," he said bluntly.

"But I am working hard," she protested, flexing her aching shoulders, "and I feel it."

Alpin grunted. "Do that drill again, but think about your overhead blow. Imagine your opponent coming at you."

She huffed as she downstroked, jarring her sore wrist and arm, then repeated the movements despite discomfort and fatigue. Nothing she did seemed to go well, and Alpin continued to mutter at her.

Finally he beckoned her away from the pell to work with him. After donning a quilted jack for protection, she faced him. He lifted his steel sword, and she lunged, countering his strike, but her blade skidded off his. Gasping in frustration, she let temper fuel her effort as she lunged again, hitting his sword on the diagonal, shoving so hard that he fell back a step.

"Ah, there she is!" Alpin said approvingly. He led her through more sequences, blades chiming. Then he paused, lowering his blade as he looked past her. She turned.

Lachlann leaned against a tree, his arms folded, and Nin-

ian peered out from behind him. "So this is where you practice," Lachlann said. "We could have been soldiers. Where
is your caution?"

"*Ach*, I knew you were there, and I let you watch," Alpin
said, though Eva was doubtful of that. Ninian ran forward to
help as Alpin gathered the gear.

Eva wiped her brow, breathing hard, determined to cover
how startled she had been. "No one has ever found us here
before. Ninian makes sure of that. He led you here because
he knew it was safe to show you. What are you doing on the
island?"

Lachlann walked toward her. "A few of the soldiers
rowed across to look after the horses, and said that Robson
wanted to discuss some smithing commissions, so I came
back with them. I hoped to find Alpin to ferry me back. I did
not realize that you were with him, though it does not surprise me, after the other night," he added in a low tone.

"What happened the other night?" Alpin asked. Eva did
not answer, and wrinkled her nose at Lachlann, knowing
Alpin was not as deaf as he sometimes claimed to be.

"I found out that our girl has a bit of the warrior in her,"
Lachlann answered. Alpin grunted as if that was obvious.

Eva bent to pick up the leather scabbard for her sword,
and Lachlann came toward her to take the sword before she
could sheathe it. He fingered the nicks and scratches. "This
is an old blade, and has seen a lot of use. Obviously you
want to keep it blunt for practices. But these scars should be
smoothed out, and the blade polished."

"That is not the sort of swordsmithing I want from you,"
she murmured.

He cocked a brow. "Still after me for weapons?"

"The rebels need them sorely now, if they think to resist
further, or to take Innisfarna."

He frowned. "A few repairs are all the bladesmithing you
will have of me."

She took the sword and jammed it into the scabbard. The movement twisted her wrist, and she winced, rubbing her forearm.

"Does it still hurt?" Lachlann asked. He took the scabbarded sword from her. "I thought it was better."

"I am fine," she said as Alpin approached them.

"What happened the other night?" Alpin asked, looking from one to the other. He pointed to her wrist. "You said nothing of being hurt, only that your muscles ached."

Eva sighed. "A few nights ago, Lachlann and two soldiers saw me out in the hills. They mistook me for a rebel, and we fought with swords."

Alpin looked pleased. "No doubt you bested them! Though sparring Lachlann would be a challenge—I trained him myself."

Eva nodded. "I twisted my arm when Lachlann—"

"She nearly took me down," Lachlann said. "Her skill amazed me. You must be very proud of your pupil."

"I am," Alpin said. "Girl, you should have said so. She will benefit from a hot soak for those muscles," he told Lachlann, who nodded. Ninian came toward them, balancing the wooden practice swords in his arms, while Alpin held the old steel blade he had been using. "You can help her prepare a tub."

"I can," Lachlann agreed, and lifted a brow, glancing down at Eva. She felt herself blush, and saw Alpin's piercing gaze take in both of them. She began to unlace her quilted tunic, and Lachlann helped her remove the heavy garment.

"Look at this old sword, too, smith," Alpin said, holding out his blade. "I would appreciate it if you could repair both weapons. I do not like to take my blades to that smith in Glen Brae. Take them back with you and clean them up, eh?"

"All they need is some grinding and polishing, and a

touch of heat here and there," Lachlann said. "It is easy enough."

"Good." Alpin nodded. "Give that one back to Eva. She needs more practice with steel. The way she fought today, she could not have cut down a straw man."

"The edges were blunted," she said in her defense.

"And you were moving like an old woman," Alpin answered. "You still need practice with downstrokes and stances. I work the girl hard," Alpin told Lachlann. "And she is good, but she could be excellent with more training. The soldiers take up my time rowing them back and forth, and doing chores at the castle like a servant. I have not given her as much time as I wanted." He peered at Lachlann. "You were always a good student of the sword. Perhaps you can work with her yourself."

"I could help her with some moves," Lachlann said.

Eva felt a small thrill go through her. During their sword encounter on the hillside, he had guided her and taught her, and even in those few minutes she had learned and implemented. And his guidance later, in the depths of the heather bed, was natural, tender, and eloquent. Those lessons in particular she was eager to repeat. She felt a hot blush creep up her throat into her cheeks.

"Be sure to work on thrusting," Alpin said then.

Lachlann looked at her, his eyes sparkling, a smile quirking his lips. She pursed her mouth to keep from laughing. "We could do that," Lachlann replied easily.

"Good, good," Alpin said. "Eva, come back to the house with me. Ninian has something for you. Smith, you come, too, and I will take you both over to Balnagovan." He gathered the rest of the gear with Lachlann's help, and led them out of the alder grove, with Ninian trailing behind them.

They crossed the narrow end of the island and headed for Alpin's house, perched on a grassy slope above the loch. The rose garden was bare, the vines sticklike and cut back.

Dry leaves blew in small whirlwinds beneath darkening skies.

Inside the little house, Ninian went to a corner and lifted a cloth sack, which he handed silently to Eva. As she opened it, a wonderful fragrance wafted out.

"Rose petals!" she cried, and sifted her fingers through hundreds of variously hued petals. "Oh, how heavenly!" She inhaled in delight. "You gathered these, and dried them for me?" she asked. Ninian nodded happily.

"When autumn comes and the blooms drop away, I never know what to do with them. Ninian gathered them up and dried them, and said his grandmother used to do that. So did my own wife, as I remember," Alpin added, a smile creasing his cheeks.

"Ninian, thank you," Eva said, and reached out to hug the boy, who blushed furiously and covered his mouth with his hand. "This is a lovely and thoughtful gift. I can use these to freshen the mattresses and pillows, and to make rosewater. The house will smell lovely this winter." Her smile included Lachlann, who watched her with a bemused expression.

She suddenly wondered where she would be that winter: at Innisfarna in her own home, or safe and happy at Balnagovan with the smith; or, God forbid, shut up at Strathlan like a prisoner.

"Take a hot bath with some of those roses, to ease your aches," Alpin said. "Get the smith to help you fill that great tub in his smithy." He grinned, and Eva blinked at him in surprise. "Ninian, you did well, boy. Carry the bag down to the boat for Eva, if you will, and wait for us there. Lachlann will take the swords. We will follow in a moment," he added. "I want a word with Eva about her practice."

"Of course," Lachlann said, and gathered the two scabbarded blades. He put a friendly hand on Ninian's shoulder as they walked away.

Alpin turned to Eva. "What happened the other night?" he asked bluntly.

"Ah, what do you mean?" she asked, and cleared her throat.

"I mean you have his heart, and he has yours. I am not a blind man." When Eva did not answer, he peered closely at her. "When the smith's lad was young, he adored you, girl, though you did not seem to know. It was plain enough to me and my wife."

"You both knew?" she asked in a hushed voice.

"Suspected it, though he is a man who keeps his thoughts private. Sometimes it was keen in his eyes, like a pain, when he looked at you. Likely he kept that hidden from you. And now I see his heart is still in your keeping. I watched you both, and I think something happened recently—beyond sword sparring."

She suddenly wanted to cry, not from sadness, but because Alpin, who was more like a father to her than her own father had been, had touched off some wellspring of emotion. "I do not know what you mean," she said, her chin quivering.

"Do you not? None of your kinsmen want you to stay with Campbell. I am sure Lachlann MacKerron agrees, for reasons of the heart." He leaned close. "Am I right?"

Tears rose then, and she dashed them away, nodding. "I do love him," she whispered. "And now I know he loves me, too."

"And you want to be together," he said. "As it should be. Though I think you have been together already," he added gently, and patted her shoulder. "I was young once, and I remember that sort of fire. Did you think I would lecture you for it? *Ach*, I kept a watch over you when you were younger, Eva girl, but now you are old enough to know what you want. And I like the fellow you love, and so do your kinsmen. Just follow your heart, and all will be well. Do not worry about Green Colin."

She sniffled. "I want to refuse Colin, but I dread the trouble it will cause."

"No matter what it stirs up, we want you to be happy. Your young lads will survive this and regain their rights without the help of that snake."

"What about Ninian? I cannot desert him to Colin's care. He is happy now, thinking he will be my stepson."

"Ninian will always have your friendship. You need not wed his father to give him that. And I will not desert the boy either. But do not let sympathy rule you. Obey your heart, and you will never regret the choices you make."

Impulsively, she hugged him. "We must go, before the soldiers see me here, dressed like this," she said, indicating her plaid and shirt. "Thank you for the roses. I will make you a wonderful pillow stuffed with them."

"That would only make me sneeze," he said gruffly. "If you want to thank me, use that new-sharpened sword to cut down a few soldiers and take this island into your keeping. I have trained a new Aeife, and I think she is ready."

Eva was silent as they headed toward the beach, where Lachlann and Ninian waited beside the boat. She felt a vague, dark sense of dread, not only at the thought of facing Colin, but at the thought of raising her sword to him.

Alpin handed her in, waited for the others, and took up the oars. "Make sure you get that hot bath," he said as he rowed. "My wife always said roses had healing properties. The blacksmith can help you heat the water." He grinned again.

"Alpin," she warned him. He chortled, and Lachlann sent them a perplexed look.

Alpin rowed hard to pull the boat out into the water. "Think of the princess Aeife," he murmured to Eva. "Remember how much she loved Innisfarna, and how she fought for it." She nodded, watching him. "And remember that Aeife had her prince. You need yours, too." He waggled his white brows.

The boat skimmed over the wavelets toward Balnagovan, and Eva thought about the shining sword lost in those depths. She thought about Aeife and her prince, and remembered that, in her daydreams as a girl, he had always resembled Lachlann.

Chapter 25

Lachlann woke beside Eva, who slept like a dove, quiet and still. Rising carefully, he left the house and walked down to the smithy. After starting the fire in the forge, he took Jehanne's sword from its hiding place on the ledge.

Flames licked bright and hot in the forge bed as he unwrapped the sword and turned. He stretched his hand near the blaze, and the heat seared his skin, dared him to draw back. Finally he pulled away.

Fire had destroyed her, yet he knew, in his faith and in his heart, that she was remade now without suffering, finer than she had ever been on the earth. In the profound depth of his soul, he knew she was joyous and fulfilled. Each day, he mourned her less. He was grateful for having known her and he cherished his encounter with her. Because of it, he was a stronger man than he had been.

But his anger at the injustice done to her lingered, and a sense of guilt still darkened his heart. He had a promise to fulfill. Until it was met, he would never feel the burden lift.

He passed his hand through the flames, feeling no burn. But he still could not touch fire to her sword. He snatched up the twig brush to rake the ashes inward and smother the flames.

"Stop," Eva said. He turned. She stood inside the door, just closing it, her plaid draped over her head, her cheeks pink from wind and rain. She came toward him. "Please do not put the fire out, or hide that beautiful sword again. She wanted you to repair it."

He looked at the bright, broken sword now resting on the anvil. "Eva, I cannot."

"Lachlann, why?" she asked, looking up at him. "Why do you always deny your ability to make swords? You are a gifted bladesmith. I do not understand."

He sighed heavily, pushed the broken blade away, and sighed again. "Here is the truth of it, then. I can no longer forge steel."

"I do not understand," she said. "Do you lack materials?"

"It is the eye injury," he said, touching his left brow. "I told you about the changes in my vision, and the odd lights and color shifts that I sometimes see." She nodded. "Without good eyesight, especially for colors, I cannot forge good steel. That is why I work only black iron now. Those simple color changes even I can see."

She slipped her cool fingers into his, and he grasped her hand, feeling compassion flow from her. Her strength shored him up now, while he hurt inside for what he could not do, what he had lost in himself. Her faith in him, her very presence, eased that ache considerably. His time with Jehanne had strengthened and hardened him; but Eva's warmth and love tempered him, made him whole, made him complete again, though he had been shattered.

Realizing that, he lifted their joined hands and touched his lips to her fingers. But he still could not do what she urged.

She looked up, her eyes earnest and steady. "If it is the making of the steel, the watching of it, let me help you," she said. "I can help you."

He shook his head. "You have made a few hooks, Eva, and seen me make a chain and some other things. You do not know what is involved in the making of steel—"

"What I know," she interrupted, stepping so close that

she angled her head and he could feel the warmth of her breasts, "is that you must do this. You are a bladesmith in your heart, Lachlann, more than an ironsmith. You will never be truly happy until you work white metal again. You were born to that. It is part of you—as I am part of you, and you of me, now."

He tilted his head until the shadows shifted and the sparkles appeared around her like faery stars. "I can no longer see the true colors of the steel. My blades would be faulty, and a flawed blade is a hazard to its owner. How can I give such a blade to any of your kinsmen?"

She looked up at him. "Let me be your eyes."

As he watched her, the rain began again, thrumming on the planked roof of the smithy, gusting against the walls. And he thought, suddenly, how Eva was like a flame, strong and true. He closed his eyes, and the tiny stars faded.

"I would be your eyes," she said, while he stood in the darkness of his own making. "I can help you tell the colors, one from the other. Together we can make a new blade."

He pulled her to him then, hardly able to speak for the tightness in his throat. "Be my heart instead," he said, and cupped her face in his hand, kissing her.

Lifting her easily into his arms, feeling her arms circle lightly around his neck, he carried her across the room and laid her down on the wild, soft, deep bed of heather that she had made for him, the bed that he had dreamed of so many times, when he slept lonely in a strange place so far from home. He had ached for her then, but real fervor filled him now.

She drew him down with her, and the gusting rain echoed the cadence of their breathing as he slid her simple gown off, as he slipped his hands into her damp curls, framing her face while he kissed her fiercely. Rain poured down while he poured out his love for her, easing the long years without her, the years before that when she had been so much a part of him, yet so unattainable.

He touched her with awe, with reverence, for she was finely made, crafted like a miracle, smooth and perfect, warm and brilliant in his arms. In the red light of the forge and the slow heat of the room, he brimmed with passion, with the force of his own spirit, irresistibly drawn to her.

Each kiss, each soft cry, the soothe of her fingers along his body, brought sweet, slow, inexorable rushes that heightened his own ardor. In her hands, he became hot iron, and the melding, when it came, felt like a searing explosion of solid light, of flame. The deepening of her own passion beneath him, surrounding him, carried him to a higher, finer peak.

Dear God, how he loved her, he thought later, and he kissed her closed eyes and thanked whatever angels had seen fit to link his soul to hers.

"Tell me," Eva said later, as they lay together in the heather bed, while the crimson glow of the forge bed colored the darkness. "Tell me what happened to her."

After the incandescence of loving, when his hands had been skillful and warm, and love had spiraled through her like a bright, hot light, she lay with him in warmth and peace, and he began to talk about Jehanne at last. Eva knew that the darkness and the love enveloping them allowed him to open that protected part of himself. She listened in silence, her head upon his shoulder while he spoke.

He crafted the tale well, his voice like black velvet, quiet and deep. Eva could imagine the girl, bright with courage, could see in her mind the armies spreading over the fields, beneath blue skies clustered with smoke. She could almost hear the cries of the men, and the girl's melodic voice lifted over all, filled with passion and verve and the true fire of the soul. Feeling Lachlann's pain, his misery, his adoration, his devotion, she brushed away the tears that pooled in her eyes.

He told her of the day Jehanne had been captured, how the portcullis had slammed down at the city gates, separating her from her men. Betrayal and anguish marked that day, and he had taken serious injuries to head and gut as he strove to get to her and failed. His words grew halting as he described that day and the months of recovery afterward. Then he spoke of his frantic journey to Rouen to see her, shut in a tower room made into a prison. She was a waif, only a shadow of herself, by then, but the zeal was still bright in her eyes.

"They said that the ashes and the smoke of her pyre spread over all of France," he told her. "She called for the Lord, and those watching wept, and knew they had burned a saint, not a sinner. I heard later, from men who had been there—Englishmen, those who had condemned her—that a white dove rose into the sky above the smoke of her pyre. And those men wept, too.

"Afterward, there were enough tears in France, they said, to put out that ferocious fire, but it was too late. She was gone, and her like will never be seen again in this world. I believe she was of the angels, and she has gone back to them."

Eva was silent and tearful while she lay in his arms, her hand upon his slow-beating heart. "And you loved her," she said.

"I loved her," he whispered. "In my way."

"I am glad," she said. She kissed him, her lips gentle upon the bristle of his jaw, over the scar that he had taken in defense of the angel.

He turned the blade in his hand once again, considering its features, its damages, as if he had never seen it before. The hilt was good, the attached blade short and angled. Two fleurs-de-lis remained of the original five along the fuller, tarnished glints of gold. A new blade could not be attached. The only way to repair it was to remake the blade entirely.

Frowning, he traced his fingers over the hilt, pommel, and cross guard. This sad, jagged bit of steel and brass was nearly all that was left of Jehanne's extraordinary magic. Her armor was somewhere in English possession; nothing else remained.

It was the last shining thread that connected him to her. Yet she herself had wanted him to take it, change it, remake it.

Releasing a harsh breath, he knew that he was done with doubt, with mourning, with holding himself back. He had always been a man of directness and action, a man who kept his secrets close and relied on his own considerable strength, physical and mental. He must call upon that fortitude now, and let grief and heartaches fall away.

Eva had offered her help, and suddenly he knew he could accept it. He wanted her to be part of the sword's rebirth.

He turned the blade, watched light flow along its surfaces. What he owed Jehanne, he realized then, was not the preservation and concealment of this tragic, broken reflection of her life. What he owed her was a rekindling of its beauty and its power. Jehanne would have wanted that, he was sure.

He could continue to grieve for her, or he could cast that aside, find his courage, and honor her memory with a perfect sword. There had been no way to do that in the field, or in the short time left to her. He must do it now, or he would never lose the haunting sense that he had failed her.

Taking up a small, sharp-edged chisel, he pried loose the top rivet that held the pommel in place. When it came away, he slid the pommel sphere free, then the hollow tube of the hilt—wood wrapped with brass wire and leather—and loosened the cross guard. He slid each piece off the tang, the rough steel extension of the blade hidden inside the hilt pieces. The bare tang, its unpolished steel merged with the angled, shining bit of blade, gave the sword a skeletal pathos.

Cradling the naked sword remnant, turning it, he considered how best to begin.

Chapter 26

"Two thousand nails?" Eva asked, incredulous. "In one day?"

Lachlann chuckled as he worked, and she smiled. He looked beautiful to her, powerful, as the golden-red light of the forge slipped fluidly over his face and bare chest. His compelling strength made her think of his hard-wrought body pressed against hers. Such thoughts had distracted her ever since she had entered the dim, firelit smithy out of a cold rain. Smiling again, she looked into his penetrating blue eyes.

"Easily two thousand," he confirmed. "I have already made hundreds of them since I began this morning. It is a simple process—heating the rods, drawing them out, slicing the hot iron, and so on. You could do it, if you like." He worked without stopping as he spoke, slicing hot iron into pieces as if he were cutting chunks of butter, using hammer and tongs and laying the heated rods over the upended chisel in the anvil.

"I could cut some, but not at that pace." She watched him remove another hot iron rod from the fire and slide still another one into place. He spun toward the anvil, tapping the bright red iron with a hammer, thinning it out and slicing it rapidly on the upended chisel edge. Scraping the nails from the anvil into a bucket of water, he turned back to the forge, tongs in hand, to take up the next rod, fiercely red by now.

"The trick of this task is in the rhythm." Sparks flew as he sliced more nails and used the hammer to sweep them, sizzling and steaming, into the bucket.

"I am happy to watch," she said. She was fascinated by his skill and deftness, but she also loved the luminous colors in the hot iron and bright sparks, crimson, red-gold, pale yellow.

And Lachlann himself was earthy and potent and magnificent. Sinewy muscles flexed beneath gleaming skin, slicked by sweat and firelight, and fine black hair dusted his chest and taut abdomen, arrowing beneath the wrapped plaid about his waist, leading her gaze downward.

Blushing, she melted a little inside as she gazed upon him. Deeply in love with him, she also realized that she loved his body as well, adored its rock-hard, sheened beauty, craved his strong and willing embraces, his tender kisses. Surprised by the boldly sensual delight she took in watching him work, she felt the stirrings of desire again, and smiled to herself.

In the past few days, while rain and dismal weather had cocooned them within the smithy property, Lachlann had helped her to discover a wellspring of desire within herself. When he took her into his arms and his lips and hands touched hers, his body joined to hers, passion quickened through her like spiritual fire, exquisite and transforming.

She could not get enough of him, for she did not know how long she would be with him, or how their troubles would end. The confrontation with Colin was yet to come. Though wed to Colin, she felt no sin in loving Lachlann, for her pledge to the smith years before took precedence in her mind and her heart. Soon, she hoped, there would be an annulment—and a true marriage.

Even a brief thought of Colin introduced a cold, black note into the enduring warmth that filled her. She sighed, wrapping her arms tight around her.

"Feed the fire, Eva," Lachlann murmured without looking up. She drew down the bellows handle, releasing a whiff of air, and watched the flames dance and grow.

Lachlann glanced at her and smiled. Her heart fluttered and her knees went weak. She placed a hand on the anvil to steady herself.

"Not there," he said. She snatched her hand away, and leaned forward to watch him beat out a rhythm on the iron. Golden-red stars flew about. A few vanished, smoking, on her left arm, and she gasped and brushed at her stinging skin.

Lachlann dropped tools and iron to grab her hand and dunk her arm into a bucket of water beside the anvil. He held her arm in the water for a few moments. "Does it still hurt?" he asked.

She shook her head and drew her arm out of the water, but the stinging returned and she winced. Tiny pink burns showed clearly on her skin. "It is not much," she said, though it hurt.

"You are lucky," he said. "When I was a lad, some sparks set my hair afire and Finlay shoved me headfirst into the bosh. Come here." He drew her by the hand toward a table. He took a cloth covering from a pottery bowl, and scooped butter out with two fingers. Slathering the butter over the little burns, he then took out a slice of onion and applied that to her skin.

"This is not my midday meal," he said wryly. "I keep a little butter and onion, or some sort of ointment, here in case of burns. Even I get burned." He grinned at her.

Eva sucked in her breath from pain, and then in amazement, for the sting diminished when she expected it to increase.

"Better?" he asked. She nodded. Lachlann smiled, lifted her arm, and touched his lips to her inner wrist.

"Even better," she breathed, as a dizzy spin began inside

of her, and her knees wobbled. She rested a hand on his bare forearm, sleek and warm and taut under her touch. He kissed her arm again, then her inner elbow. "That—oh, that is better," she gasped. "Oh!" she said, as his lips touched her palm.

"When I was a child and stood too near the forge," he said, "Mairi used to kiss my burns."

"Not like this," she drawled.

He chuckled, low and soft, and trailed his lips over her hand, licking her fingers a little. Eva was sure she would melt like the butter that slicked down her arm. "A kiss takes away pain. It worked quite well when I was small," he said.

"I am not a child."

"I know," he murmured. His other hand snugged in the curve of her waist, his thumb on her abdomen. A throbbing began inside of her. "Is the pain gone?" he asked.

She tipped her head back, her heart thudding hard, her hands now sliding along his sinewed arms to the swell of his chest. "Somewhat," she admitted, while she felt intimate awareness like a strong pulse between them.

"Perhaps we can take away the rest," he murmured, and dipped his head to kiss her. Eva drew in a quick, ecstatic breath and melted into his arms, under the power of his hot, gentle mouth.

"How is it now?" he murmured.

"Oh," she breathed, "it might still need attention." She laughed suddenly as he swept her up into his arms and carried her across the room, kneeling with her on the thick heather bed covered with plaid wool. He shifted down to lie with her, and she threw her arms around his neck, kissing him deeply, taking his tongue into her mouth with delight.

Then she groaned with eager pleasure as he rucked up her skirt and chemise and skimmed his hand, still warm from tending iron, over her legs, and higher. His fingers slipped under her gown and chemise to find her breasts, full and aching for his touch. The gown went even higher, and his breath caressed her skin.

"What about the forge?" she asked, as he rolled over with her, settling into the deep nest of the bed. "What about the fire and the iron?" she breathed. She slid her hands under his plaid, finding him ready for her, heated and fervent. She sighed with utter pleasure.

He kissed her, tracing his lips, moist and ardent, down along her body, until she lay bared and sultry, shivering for him as she drew him toward her, and he covered her with his body.

"I am tending the fire," he whispered, and slipped inside her, hard and exquisite, and then she knew just what he meant.

"So much rain," Eva said, turning away from the window in the smithy the next day, closing the shutter. "I have never seen so much rain. And I love it," she added.

Lachlann looked up from the forge, where he had been carefully stacking charcoal pieces into a pile and setting them alight. "Rain? You always loved sunshine and warmth best," he murmured, and smiled at her. "Sun suits your nature more than rain, mist, and mud."

"I love the rain because it keeps us alone here," she said. "No one has come over the water, no one rides out on patrol, no one comes to the smithy at all. It is just the two of us. I hope the rain continues forever."

"You will sink to your knees in mud if it does," he commented, and pulled the bellows handle, then raked the little fire in the forge bed. He crossed to a sack that leaned in the corner and removed a fist-size chunk of metal, shapeless and greenish. Setting it on the anvil, he took some tongs from a wall rack and the heavy leather gauntlets that he often used.

Eva came closer, curious as Lachlann filled a ladle with water and drizzled some over the fiery pile of charcoal in the forge bed. Steaming, smoking, the charcoal crusted, while its inner core glowed like a cave. "What are you doing?" she asked. "You have already repaired Alpin's swords, grinding and polishing them, and made a thousand nails. What now?"

"And I would have made a lot more nails if not for a certain distraction," he said wryly. "This will be a fine pastime for a rainy day. We are going to forge steel."

"Steel?" She stared at him. "Together?"

"You offered to be my apprentice," he said. "I will be needing that bucket over there, with the white sand in it. And that sack of salt under the table. Get yourself a pair of gloves from the rack too."

Eva did as he told her. "What else?"

"Pour salt into the quenching tub—the large one with the water already in it. Lots of salt, so that the water is clouded and thick with it." As she did that, he heated two iron rods and slipped them, sizzling, into the brine to heat it.

"Are we ready now?" she asked, as he slid a poker into the little cave of fire and pulled the bellows handle, so that the charcoal pile glowed like a living thing. He tended it for a moment without answering, and Eva waited. His patience seemed infinite, his tenor steady and at ease, yet banked with power.

"Now," he finally said, "I will need the sword."

"Her sword?" she asked, breathlessly.

He nodded. "I am ready now."

She went to the ledge at the top of the wall and took down the cloth-wrapped bundle, carrying the broken sword to the anvil, where she laid it down and opened it almost reverently. The hilt, pommel, and cross guard had already been removed and lay in the wrappings. He had been thinking about this for a while, she saw, for he had dismantled the handle. That first step must have required great inner strength from him, she realized.

Lachlann took the two pieces of the bare sword and held

them, firelight shining on the steel. He fitted the cracked edges together into a whole weapon, and she saw the sadness in his eyes. Yet she felt as if the great wound within his soul had finally begun to heal.

"Can you weld the pieces together?" she asked.

He shook his head. "That would create a deep flaw. The blade could crack again. It needs to be made new, but the old sword will be part of the new one."

Drawing a deep breath, he looked down at the bare tang and the short, jagged blade. Eva saw a muscle thump in his cheek, saw him swallow hard.

Then he turned, set the piece in the tongs, and slid the broken end into the fire.

Lachlann watched the remnant of steel take on the first blush of heated color, like blood from within. He turned the piece with the tongs, frowning. Dismantling Jehanne's sword and slipping it into the little inferno he had created was one of the most difficult choices he had ever made.

Now it was done, and he would proceed. "I will need some sand—there is a small ladle in the bucket," he told Eva. "And keep the bellows going steady and easy, if you will. Watch the flames as they are now, and feed out just enough air to keep the fire at this heat."

She fetched the sand, then reached up and took the bellows handle, earnest and silent. He smiled at her, then removed the steel remnant from the charcoal fire cave and poured a little sand over the metal. The sand slithered over the steel and turned to molten glass.

Eva watched avidly, but kept silent. He blessed her for that, knowing it did not come easily to her curious nature; deciding on mercy, he began to explain. "Charcoal burns clean and very hot, and is best for making a clean weld. The sand melts into the steel as glass, and will give it a shining surface when it is polished."

When the glassy coating began to smoke gently, he drew the tanged piece, glowing golden and nearly white-hot, out of the fire and laid it on the anvil. Tapping lightly, he worked the broken blade with the hammer until the hot steel thinned out and grew longer, still glowing. "This will become the core of the new blade," he said. "The new steel will be bonded to this."

"With the sand," Eva murmured, watching.

"You learn quickly," he praised, and turned back to the fire to reheat the piece, easing it into the luminous little cavern until it reddened. " 'Cherry red to pigeon blue, the iron is hot—' "

"'The steel is true,' " Eva finished, remembering the rhyme. She stepped closer, her leather gauntlets pulled high, one hand hovering on the bellows handle. "I will watch the colors for you," she said. "It is very red now, and going more gold."

"I can see that well enough. Later, when the steel is tempered, the colors are far more subtle. Then I will need your eyes." She nodded.

Blinking a little, for there were sparks and dashes of light before his eyes that did not shine in the metal he worked, he heated the piece, hammered it and drew it out longer. Then he repeated the steps until the broken blade was slender and elongated, the tang unaltered. Setting that aside, he took the greenish chunk of metal and introduced it into the fire.

"A steel ingot," he said. "I purchased this from Leod MacKerron, the charcoal burner. Steel is iron heated with charcoal and mixed with sand so that it takes on magnificent luster, strength, and flexibility. This piece is special steel, made not from bog iron or mined iron, but from a sky stone."

"Oh!" she said. "The rocks that sometimes fall out of the sky, glowing red? I have heard of those."

He nodded. "That is the purest iron, and is believed to

carry great magic in it, for the stones are said to be shooting stars fallen to earth." As he spoke, he poured sand over the red-hot ingot. The sand melted instantly, sliding over the steel in a beautiful flux, moving, smoking.

"Is that white sand from our beach?" Eva asked then.

He nodded. "Collected under a new moon."

"I remember once when you gathered it. I was with you."

Glancing at her, he saw the flush in her cheeks and the sparkle in her eyes. "I remember that, too," he murmured. "I loved you then, Eva, but I kept it from you. I scarcely wanted to know it myself. I think it terrified me." He laughed.

"You kept your secret well, smith." She smiled.

"No longer, my friend." He grinned at her. "White sand gathered under a new moon, like this, grants an auspicious beginning." He poured more sand over the lump, and glass particles flew about like stars.

Eva stepped back. When the billet of steel smoked and turned white-hot, he took it out of the fire and began to work it with the hammer, lightly and deftly. The piece took on the rudimentary shape of a blade made of solid light.

Liquid glass flew off the steel, lambent sparks in a fine and brilliant shower. Eva gasped and skipped back. Lachlann felt the burn as a few tiny stars landed on his arms. He shook off the pain and went on hammering.

More heating, more hammering of the blazing, roughened sword. Time passed, sweat dripped from him, but Lachlann hardly noticed. Nor did Eva complain about fatigue, though he could see the strain telling in her. He glanced at her as she fed air into the fiery pit while he turned the steel.

"You have kept the fire well. Now I want you to hammer with me," he said, and laid the piece like live fire on the anvil.

Wordlessly she took up a hammer and followed his silent

lead. After his hammer strike she struck also, and created with him a fast cadence of overlapping blows, a drumming upon the bright surface that flattened the steel further. The rhythm beat down into his bones, into his deep center, pulsed through him like heated, insistent, glorious lovemaking.

Now they no longer needed words, barely needed gestures. Eva sensed what was needed, felt the rhythm as he did, and he blessed her for it. Striking, heating, repeating it, she kept up with him, and between them the blade surged toward being.

He paused to drink from a ladle in a bucket of cool water, and brought one to Eva. Wiping his brow, he watched her long throat as she swallowed thirstily. Perspiration beaded upon her upper lip, her cheeks were high pink, her eyes like vivid jewels.

Silent, she trickled the rest of the water over his head, cool and wet and divine. He did the same to her, and she gasped and licked at it. He kissed her, quick and deep. Then she lifted her hand to the bellows, ready to begin again.

He loved her greatly in that moment, for her loyalty, her willingness, her understanding. He knew he should stop and let her rest, should rest himself, but passion filled him, an urge to keep going. Somehow she knew that, perhaps felt it as well.

The sword was forming, its fluid splendor begun. He could not stop until he had seen it birthed in fire and light.

He laid the larger billet in the fire and took up the reshaped blade and tang, heating both pieces until they bloomed with pale light. Setting them both on the anvil and using tongs with a surgeon's delicacy, he placed the tanged, smaller, older piece on the luminous surface of the new blade. Then he wrapped the larger piece around the remade sword like a piece of dough.

Hammering them together until the glow faded, he

heated them as one piece, pouring sand in a slippery, beautiful stream. Taking up the hammer again, he glanced at Eva. She understood, and took up her own hammer, and the rhythm began.

"So," she said later, when he slid the newly flattened blade into the charcoal cavern. "The old sword—Jehanne's sword—is now the core of the new one."

"Its heart," he said, and then the truth of that, the power of it, nearly sank him to his knees. He paused, hammer in one hand, radiant new sword tonged in the other, and looked at Eva.

"Jehanne's sword is now the soul of the new blade," she whispered. He saw awe and understanding in her eyes. A shiver went through him from crown to heel, and he knew then that all this—all of it, over years, encompassing lives, bringing souls and causes together to draw strength from one another—was meant to be.

One day you will know what to do with this sword, Jehanne had once told him.

Now he knew. He looked at Eva, and he knew.

Chapter 27

Staying by his side through the night as he worked, Eva shared the tasks, though her muscles ached and her limbs trembled with weariness. And yet he drove himself on, and would not rest. She brought him water and insisted that he drink, for he perspired freely; she fetched him food, but he only nibbled lightly, then took up hammer and tongs again. Rain sheeted against the walls of the smithy, but the forge gave warmth, and light, and purpose.

In his capable, driven hands, the lump of steel and the broken blade came together, glowing, and became a new sword. The metal was dark and crude yet, but its graceful shape emerged.

Lachlann brushed his forearm across his brow, rubbed his fingers over his eyes. Eva touched his arm in concern, but he shook his head and kept going, turning from forge to anvil, heating, hammering, shaping the steel. Tending the bellows and pounding the hammer in tandem with him, she felt as if she did little. Lachlann did the work, and Lachlann had the vision.

Later, when the bright heart of the forge pierced the darkness, she faded, losing strength to lift the hammer, or to lift her arm to the bellows handle once again. Yet she forced herself, as Lachlann forced himself, for she would not leave him.

"Eva, come here," he murmured, and set down his tools.

He put his arm around her and guided her to the heather bed, and though she protested, he made her rest. Meaning only to close her eyes, she slept deeply, and when she woke daylight had returned, gray and dismal once again, and the forge was still hot. Lachlann sat beside the anvil on a stool now, bent over the sword, with a file in his hands.

He had not yet rested, she realized, for beside her the bed was undisturbed. The need to finish the sword was yet with him. Still weary to her bones, she rose and went to him.

He smiled at her, his eyes brilliant blue and smudged beneath, his cheeks and chin bristled, his hair tangled. She brushed back the waves from his brow, kissed him, and looked at what he held.

The sword was roughened, dark, without a hilt as yet, but it was whole, and would be magnificent, she knew. He turned it to show her how he had filed the steel to bring out the precise shape and edges of the long, tapered blade.

"When this is done," he said, "it will need more heatings and quenching, then tempering. And then I will need your eyes, my friend, for those colors must be judged true if the sword is to be fine and strong."

She nodded, and he kissed her, and she felt the fatigue running through him like the low vibration of a harp string. Soon she coaxed him back to the heather bed and lay beside him, though the dreary morning light grew stronger. Wrapping her arms around him, she held him until he slept.

Hours of filing, until his arms and neck and back ached with it, yet he would not let himself stop. Days of filing were more usual for a sword like this, but the work skimmed along without regard to day or night, without regard to time. As the cool and drizzling day faded into a colder, rainy evening, the filing was nearly complete.

He set the blade on the anvil and picked up the pommel, hilt, and cross guard that he had earlier removed, and he slid them on, one by one, to make sure they fit. Nearly perfect, he saw, despite changes to the tang from all the heatings. He removed them again and resumed the filing, the sound a soothing, persistent drone.

Glancing up, he saw Eva sweeping the floor of the smithy, a heathery broom in her hands. He was deeply thankful for her devotion, for her help, for her profound, complete understanding, even for the quiet she afforded him. He was glad she made him rest and made him eat; on his own, he might have crafted this blade until he collapsed from sheer stupefying fatigue.

Watching her, he smiled to himself. Eva glanced over her shoulder as if she sensed his regard, his love, and she smiled too. He held up the painstakingly filed blade to show her the result, and she hurried toward him.

"The rain has stopped," Eva said later, turning away from the open door. The fresh, damp, cool night breeze swept into the smithy. Her hair, her gown, her very skin seemed saturated with the smells of charcoal, smoke, and metal. She shoved a hand over her thick, saggy braid, and glanced at Lachlann over her shoulder, where he constructed a long, narrow piling of charcoal, into which, she knew, he would slide the full sword blade.

"Your bath is warmed, my lady." He indicated one of the two great wooden tubs in the smithy, one filled with brine for quenching the steel, the other brimming with water, currently being heated by the addition of red-hot iron rods. The water steamed lightly in the cool air. Earlier, when she complained of the grime and the sweat, he had set about heating the plain water in the dousing tub, which had not yet been used.

Delighted at the thought of feeling clean again, she crossed the room. "Perhaps the smith would like a bath, too."

He shrugged. "I will dip into the loch in the morning."

"There are no rose petals in the loch, and it is cold," she said, slipping her hand into the sack that Ninian had given her, sprinkling some of the dried flowers into the steamy water in the low, wide tub.

Lachlann laughed. "True."

She stripped off her gown and chemise, casting them down beside the clean clothing, linen sheets, and soap she had fetched from the house. Lachlann watched her steadily, his gaze piercing blue even across the room. She stepped into the water and sank down with a sigh, bending her knees to sit curled inside, leaning her shoulders back and closing her eyes, grateful for watery comfort after hours of fierce heat, smoke, and hard work.

He came toward her, sliding to his knees beside the tub. Cupping his hand in the water, scooping up a palmful of blush-colored petals, he dribbled them where her breasts crested the water. "I wish we could both fit in there, my friend," he murmured, leaning toward her.

"So do I, my friend," she said, and slid her hand along his broad neck, pulling him closer, savoring his slow, delicious kiss. His fingers, sensually shaped and darkened from charcoal and iron, traced over her pale breasts. A shiver went through her as his hand sank into the warm water. "Perhaps we could help each other bathe," she said.

"Ah, now, we could do that," he said.

"Now the blade needs heat treating," Lachlann told Eva, indicating the long bed of charcoal that he had formed with a crusted exterior and a red-hot interior. Slowly he slid the long blade into the fiery cavern. "When the steel takes on a red heat, then we quench it in the warm brine."

Eva stood beside him at the forge and watched as the blade began to glow red-gold. He handed her the tongs. "Hold it in the fire," he said, as she took the weight of the tool in her gloved hand. "There is something I must do."

He drew out the short dagger sheathed in his belt and quickly made a thin cut across his forearm. Eva gasped, wincing as she saw that. Taking the tongs to draw the red-hot blade out of the fire, he let a few drops of blood fall upon the searing steel, where it sizzled, then vanished.

"Now I am part of this blade, and it is part of me," he murmured, half to himself. Then he spun around and plunged the blade into the quenching tub. The viscous brine bubbled, steamed, then calmed, while the sword glowed like a lantern under the water.

"The blood," Eva said, looking up at him. "Why did you do that?"

He smiled a little, wiping his arm with a cloth. The cut was long and thin as a hair, barely beading. "An old smithing tradition," he said. "One of the secrets to producing a strong, invincible blade. They say that ages ago, new-made swords were sometimes quenched in the blood of virgins." He lifted a brow. "So you are safe." She made a little face at him.

"Is the blood part of making a faery blade?" she asked.

He frowned slightly and did not answer.

"They say MacKerrons can do that," she ventured, trying to catch his glance. "Can you? Would you tell me if you could?"

"There is work to be done," he reminded her as he pulled the sword from the quench and turned it, eyeing it critically. "A good blade," he said, "but the water, though necessary, makes it brittle. It needs tempering—a softening of its hard nature, until it is both strong and flexible, a merging of opposites—heat and cold, fire and water, hard and soft. Male and female," he added quietly, turning the blade thoughtfully.

He raked the charcoal, adding kindling and a few leaves while Eva fed air from the bellows. When the flames flickered gold and blue, he swung the blade into the fire. "Now," he said, reaching out a hand to pull her close, "be my eyes, love."

She pressed next to him, watching. He held the blade as the flames licked the steel. The metal began to glow.

"It will turn from yellow into brown," he said, "then purple into blue. Watch carefully. A sword pulled out at the yellow point will be too hard, at purple and blue it will be too soft. Just when it changes from brown to purple, that is when it must come out. And I cannot trust my own vision to tell me exactly when that is."

She nodded, watching the steel sway over the flames as a rainbow of color bloomed on its shining surface. Bright golden yellow flowed into the steel and darkened into true brown. Then she saw a tiny burst of purple—

"Now," she said, and Lachlann pulled the sword out and plunged it into the brine, where it sizzled. The glow subsided into a deep shine.

"Is it done?" she asked.

"Not yet," he answered. "There is tempering by fire yet—what the devil is that?"

Startled by a sudden, quiet rapping on the door and the distant barking of the two dogs shut in the house, Eva started forward, but Lachlann drew her behind him and advanced. Grasping the hilt of the dagger in his belt, he pulled the door open cautiously, then stood back. Simon stepped inside quickly, followed by Margaret's five brothers and Iain Og.

"Simon, what is it?" Eva asked as she hurried forward. Beyond the closing door, she glimpsed a black sky laced with mist in the aftermath of the rain, and she heard the clear barking of the dogs, and the fainter thunder of horses' hooves. "What is going on? Are the king's men after you? Why did you come here?"

"They may well be after us for this night's work," he said. "Colin Campbell is after us now. He is back from Perth—we just went past Strathlan."

"Is Colin out there?" Eva asked, as Lachlann shut the door.

"He is coming here, though we did not think he would be after us so soon," Simon said.

"So soon? What have you done?" Lachlann demanded.

"Listen, now," Simon said. "We came here to tell you of our decision, and then we must be off. We thought to stay and celebrate, but there is no time for that now."

"Tell us what is going on," Eva said. Lachlann, ever practical and inclined to few words, began to shepherd the visitors toward the back door of the smithy, and Eva followed.

Simon glanced at his kinsmen. "We are in agreement that Clan Arthur will never accept exile. I will take the responsibility of speaking for Donal. Our chief would never approve of the bargain that Colin made for us."

She touched his arm. "But, Simon, that means—"

"It means you will refuse Colin, and we will take a stand for our rights."

"We will petition the king ourselves," Fergus said, "and seek an audience and a fair hearing at the king's own court."

"I will go with you when you ride to court," Lachlann said, placing a hand on Simon's shoulder. As her brother nodded his gratitude, Eva felt tears sting her eyes. Love and fear, relief and apprehension washed through her all at once.

"Eva, we want that marriage annulled," Simon said, "and no more arguments from you. We have another husband in mind for you." He glanced at Lachlann. Nearby, her kinsmen watched, the twins nodding somberly, the others smiling.

She felt herself tearing up again. "You take a great chance on my behalf."

"As you did for us," Simon said. "It is only fair."

Micheil turned from peering through the window shutters. "They are coming over the meadow."

"Who? What happened?" Eva asked hastily.

"Colin is upset," Andra said. "We, ah, we took his horses."

"You what!" Eva and Lachlann exclaimed together.

"We took six horses from the grazing meadow beside Strathlan, and brought them here," he explained. "We thought to delay Colin from coming here while he found himself a mount. But he had horses and men inside the castle bailey. We did not know he was back from Perth then."

"Dear God, why did you do that?" Eva asked.

"It is All Hallow's night," Fergus said. "Andra and Micheil and I thought it would be a good prank and would keep Colin at home for a few days."

"All Hallow's so soon!" Eva said. "I had forgotten."

"And on All Hallow's Eve," Fergus said, "the faeries do ride. We thought a few faeries ought to ride over to Strathlan."

Lachlann muttered something about fools, shaking his head.

"By the time the rest of us caught up to these three, it was done," Simon said. "So we put the horses in your stable."

"We only borrowed them," Andra said. "When Colin asks, just tell him the horses wandered over here."

"And put themselves in the stalls?" Eva asked, incredulous.

"On All Saints' Eve, anything can happen," Micheil said, and grinned. Eva shook her head, glancing at Lachlann.

"After what has happened lately, that was foolhardy, my friends," Lachlann said grimly. "Out with you now. There is a path behind the smithy that leads down to the lochside." He opened the narrow back entrance. Behind the smithy, the loch spread, shining and black, in the misty darkness.

"We hoped we would have time to celebrate," Fergus said.

"What, All Hallow's? You have done that, it seems," Eva replied sourly.

"Not that, something else very important," Simon said. "We came to ask the blacksmith if he would—"

"Ask him later, whatever it is," Eva said. "You have no time, now that you have crossed Colin. Out with you."

"We only meant to give Green Colin a good startle," Andra said.

"You did that," Lachlann drawled. "And if you want to live to celebrate anything at all, you had best be gone from here." He ushered them, one by one, through the door.

Iain Og turned to Eva. "If Green Colin gives you trouble over the refusal, just take that sword of yours and show him that your pledge is canceled." He winked at her.

"Go!" Lachlann hissed, and Iain lumbered past him into the darkness after the others.

"We will be nearby if you should need us," Simon said, as he stepped outside. "And we will celebrate later, sister." He smiled. Frowning, she hurried him with a little shove.

"Go, and quickly," Lachlann said, and closed the door.

Eva gasped as the rumble of horses increased in the smithy yard. When she heard a man shouting, she recognized the coarse quality of Colin's voice.

"*Gobha!*" he called. "Come out, smith! And bring those rebels with you!"

Chapter 28

"**S**mith, come out, you!" Colin's hoarse cry rang out over the glen, echoing against steep, dark, misted hills. "Lachlann MacKerron! We need to reckon! Bring those rebels with you!"

Lachlann went to the door of the smithy and opened it. The reddish gold light from within the smithy spilled over the doorstep and beyond, revealing four mounted Highlanders behind Colin, who was in the lead on a white horse, wearing armor and the Lowland clothing he favored. Lachlann stepped outside.

"Colin Campbell." As he spoke, he drew the door shut so that Colin would not see Eva, but she pulled it open herself and stood in the doorway behind him.

He wished she had kept out of sight. Her slim, dark loveliness and her bold temper were a volatile mix that could stir Colin to lust and rage. But Lachlann would not order her inside. She had a right to face Colin with her own grudge, as did he.

"Smith, I want something from you," Colin said. "Ah, Eva. Where are your kinsmen? They stole horses from me, and that I will not tolerate."

"They are not here," she said. "But your horses are in the stable. I have no idea how they got there. A harmless All Hallow's Eve prank that anyone could have done. It is not necessary to blame it on my kinsmen."

"Lady, some of your kinsmen were seen."

"It cannot be proved. And your livestock are safe, after a little exercise. Take the horses with you and leave here."

Colin turned to his men. "Go look in the stable. If the rebels are hiding in there with those horses, bring them out to me!" The men rode across the yard, and Colin turned to glare at Lachlann. "Smith, we have business." He lifted his sword, its edge glinting, and swayed in his saddle.

"He is drunk," Eva murmured to Lachlann. "I have seen it before in him, but not like this. He can hardly keep his seat."

"When I learned who you are, smith, I wanted to bring this blade to show it to you," Colin said. "Your father made this sword for my father. It is a good blade. But your father promised mine another sword, and never delivered. I want it now."

"If my father made the sword you hold, then it is the best you can get from a MacKerron smith. You need no other."

"Made it," Colin said, "and died under it." He swayed again, righted himself. "I was there that night. I saw it."

"So I heard," Lachlann replied flatly.

"Tragic night, and it still haunts me," Colin muttered. "And it haunts me more that my father died without holding the sword he craved, the one your father owed to him. I want that from you now, to close an old bargain."

Lachlann looked at the blade, and at Colin. His vision, his very heart, seemed to darken with rage. Drawing a long breath, he turned his head stiffly. "Eva," he said, "on the ledge you will find a two-handed broadsword. Bring it to me."

She spun without a word and went inside.

"Gobha," Colin growled, "we are not done with our business! Do not think to go inside with her, unless you want this wondrous good blade between your ribs!"

Lachlann strode toward him. "No bargain can be made

between us," he said. "Be gone from here, and come back sober. Then we will bargain—or deal otherwise with one another."

"If you do not have the sword I seek, then make one for me." Colin drew a gold coin from his belt pouch and tossed it toward Lachlann. It fell unclaimed at his feet.

Colin turned. "Ah, Eva, back again, and with a fine sword! Is this the one I want?" He leaned down to snatch at the sword, but Eva handed it to Lachlann, who closed his hand around the horn hilt and pointed the blade downward.

"This one is mine," Lachlann said. The power of the blade seemed to travel up into his arm. Rather than keying him to an explosion of strength and rage, his father's sword infused him with a strange calm and patience, like a hand upon his shoulder. Lachlann watched Colin with a lethal glare and did not move.

"MacKerrons are the finest weaponsmiths in Scotland," Colin said. "Finlay made a good blade, but Tomas MacKerron made better—his had faery power. That is what I want. And All Hallow's, when the curtain between our realm and the magical one opens, is an auspicious time for gaining that. I share my father's dream of owning a blade of faery make, but my ambition is greater." He smiled, and his horse shifted under him.

"You are mistaken. No earthly smith can make a faery sword," Lachlann said. "They exist only in tales."

"You are the one making the mistake," Colin said, and leveled his sword at Lachlann. "Give me a faery blade."

"The rarest of that ilk lies at the bottom of Loch Fhionn," Lachlann said. "Go after that one—if you can."

"Get you into that forge, smith, and make me a blade of charmed steel, bright enough to blind a man."

"Such swords are only legend," Eva said. "And you are sodden, and should go home."

"Your island is legend, but I have it now," Colin said.

"My father wanted only the Sword of Light, but I want Innisfarna, and what comes with it—the sword to guard, and Scotland to hold!"

"He is lit like a lantern," Lachlann muttered to Eva. "How he got over here on a horse is an amazement. There will be no reasoning with him. Colin, go home," he said, his voice raised.

"Only the women of Innisfarna can hold that isle and protect the Sword of Light," Eva said. "Enough of this."

"A sword kept by women—I know a better use for a good hard thruster with a woman!" Colin leered at her, then looked at Lachlann. "Have you cuckolded me with my wife, smith? Why is she here with you alone? I do not like that." He waved his sword, swayed, and nearly lost his seat.

Lachlann flexed his hand on the hilt. "Colin, you and I have a quarrel with one another, but it will not be resolved tonight. I will not deal with a drunken man."

"Answer me," Colin said. "Have you cuckolded me?"

Eva stepped forward between Lachlann and Colin's horse and looked up at him. "Colin Campbell," she said, "if you forget this discussion in the morning, I will tell you again, but listen to me now. I do not accept our marriage, by reason of your poor behavior, and my own error. I made a promise to you that I could not keep. Before our betrothal, I had pledged my heart to another man, and that first pledge is the valid one. You threatened me, and I agreed for my kinsmen's sake. Now our marriage must be annulled. I am sorry if that causes you trouble."

Colin blinked down at her. "What?"

"I refuse to be your wife," she repeated simply.

"You *have* betrayed me with the smith!" He aimed his sword tip at Lachlann's chest. Lachlann slapped the flat of the blade away with his hand. Colin teetered in the saddle and shifted the sword to point it at Eva, leaning forward.

Reaching up, Lachlann grabbed Colin's wrist, twisting it

with little effort, and the man fell to the ground, losing his hold on the sword. Eva snatched it up, twirled the hilt expertly into her hand, and adopted a guarding stance. Colin sat up in the mud and stared at her in amazement.

"I must be drunk," he muttered, and stood, stumbling.

Lachlann rotated the pommel of his own blade, arcing the tip upward until it caught Colin at the base of his throat. "I have reached my limit," he growled. "You had a hand in my parents' death, and I owe them vengeance. But you are mean-spirited and sodden, and can barely stand. Get your men and leave this place. You and I will meet again for a fair contest."

"You have no quarrel with me," Colin growled. "I saved your life that night."

Lachlann narrowed his eyes. "What?"

"You must know how your parents died. I know you went to see the charcoal burner and his madwoman. My kinsmen saw you."

"Leod told me what he knew. Go on."

"You were in your mother's arms, and she dropped you when she fell. I took my father away—a drunken old fool, he was that night, or he never would have done what he did. I heard her babe crying, and saw it crawling in the yard. Rode back and put the babe—you—in the house. Knew someone would find you. And they did. The charcoal man took you to Finlay. I saved your life," he repeated. "You have no quarrel with me, smith."

Lachlann stared at Colin, his heart beating slow and hard. He lowered the sword and stood back. "Get you gone from here," he growled. "And do not come back."

Stumbling, tripping, Colin heaved himself onto the horse and gathered the reins. "I will be back for that sword I just paid for." He looked at Eva. "My quarrel with your kinsmen still stands, and our marriage still stands. I am not so drunk that I do not know that. Innisfarna is mine, and you are mine. Remember that when you sleep tonight." He sneered. "And make certain you sleep alone, or I will be killing myself a smith."

He snapped the reins and rode out of the yard, yelling for his Highlanders as he went.

Lachlann took Eva's arm, stepped over the gold coin lying in the mud, and went into the smithy.

"Tempering," Lachlann said later, as he waved the new sword gently above the yellow flames, "must be repeated several times to produce a strong yet flexible blade."

Eva stood beside him, watching the steel, which had yet to turn the straw yellow color that preceded brown. Her thoughts were preoccupied with Colin and the harm he could cause all of them. She looked up at Lachlann, not following what he had said.

He frowned. "You are exhausted. I can finish this."

She shook her head. "I will help. You are nearly done. And then we must both rest."

"Go up to the house," he said quietly, shifting the blade in the flames, "and lock yourself inside."

"Only with you," she answered, and leaned her head wearily against his solid upper arm. "I am not afraid of Colin Campbell. He will have such a headache and bad stomach that he will threaten no one for a while." She tried to laugh, but it flattened. "I am worried about my kinsmen, though. They did not come back—I did not expect them to—but with Colin so set on finding them, I cannot rest well until I know where they are. Something is wrong—I feel it."

Lachlann frowned as he waved the sword blade over the flames. "I will go out soon, and find out what I can."

She nodded. "Oh! It is brown—now, take it out now."

He did, and plunged it into the heated brine, then pulled it out to examine it. "Nearly done," he said. "For the final tempering, it is left inside the charcoal bed while the embers burn down around it."

"And then it is finished?" she asked.

"It must be polished and the hilt pieces added," he said, "and then it is . . . nearly done." He slid the supple blade into the long bed of embers. "Now let me see what I can learn about your brother." He kissed her and left the smithy.

Eva turned to the forge bed and watched the hot red glow seep into Jehanne's restored sword. Flames licked around it, and the heat seared her face and hands. She stepped back from the intense warmth.

"He loved and respected you very much," she said to herself, to the sword, as if the girl who had once wielded it could hear her. "Thank you for sending him home safe to me."

She went to the heather bed in the corner and lay down upon it, suddenly so weary she could hardly keep her eyes open, could hardly pull the plaid around her for comfort. Within moments, sleep took her into its gentle darkness.

When she woke, the forge fire was a tiny red glow. Lachlann was not beside her, and Eva rose, still weary but filled with a heavy dread that would not allow her to sleep. She went to the door and opened it.

The night was black and cool and foggy, peaceful at first, until she heard the murmur of men's voices far below on the lochside. She went outside, walking toward the long bank, and stood listening, wrapping her arms around herself in the chill.

The voices grew more distinct, though still not loud, and she recognized Lachlann's and Alpin's voices with others. She hurried to the crest of the hill as they climbed upward. In the inky, misted darkness, she did not see them until they were a few feet from her.

"Who is there?" she asked. "Has something happened? Oh, Fergus, it is you! And Micheil! I was so worried." She reached out to touch her cousins' shoulders. Their faces, even in the darkness, were pale and grim. Alpin stepped closer, his hand to his head. A dark streak on his face, she realized then, was blood.

"What happened?" she cried.

"Eva," Lachlann said, taking her arm. "Simon was taken a little while ago. Colin has him. Fergus and the others were with him, and Colin's men rode them down. Simon was the only one taken—the others were left here."

"Is he at Strathlan? We will go there." She turned, but Lachlann held her back.

"He is at Innisfarna. Colin took him there not long ago."

Her heart dropped like a stone. "Held in the castle?"

"They took my boat," Alpin said. "I came over the water in the darkness because I thought the lads called to me. But when I got there, it was not the lads, but Colin and his men. Colin was so stupid drunk he could barely stand—and a mean drunk he is, too. Hit me so hard with the flat of his sword I thought I might die, right down there, on that beach." He kept his hand over his head. "I heard Green Colin say they would cage a wolf pup, and see if the she-wolf would come to them," he said. "He expects you to come over to Innisfarna."

"And so we shall," Lachlann said.

Eva took Alpin's arm. "Come up to the house and I will get some of Mairi's ointment, and a cool cloth," she said. "Then you must rest."

"And you must ready yourself, Aeife," Alpin answered. "It is time. Save your brother—and your isle. I have trained you for this. All you need do is face them, as the legend demands, and let us do the rest. Lachlann and the lads will gather a force from all over the hills, from every house and every cave, every man and every woman willing to bear arms for this cause. Together we will take back the island.

But you must be the one to set foot first upon the isle and call for its surrender."

She said nothing as they walked toward the house. She knew, in her heart, that he was right. The time had indeed come.

And she also knew that she must face Colin alone.

Chapter 29

"Lachlann, I must ask you something," Eva murmured.

"Ask." He glanced up from his task, the polishing of the sword with various sands, coarse to fine, rubbed on with tough pieces of leather. Even in the dimness of the smithy, the blue of his eyes had a unique, startling clarity.

The day grayed toward night; Eva had spent most of that time tending to Alpin, a surly patient, and speaking with her cousins, who came and went in their effort to spread the word around the glens and hills that the leader of the rebellion had been taken, and would be rescued somehow, along with the island. She knew the men spoke with Lachlann as well, and she had seen Angus come and go with the others.

But she had seen little of Lachlann until now, and a peaceful hour with him in the smithy seemed like a gift.

She saw that the sword was nearly finished. The hilt pieces were fitted in place, and Lachlann had chased lily designs into the blade, filling them with gold scraped from the old sword. He had repeatedly polished and sharpened the blade. The result, delicate and powerful and shining in his hands, was magnificent.

"Ask," he repeated. "You have been deep in thought. Eva, we will help Simon somehow. What is it?"

She drew a breath. "Would you make a faery sword for me?"

His brows pulled together. "I would do anything for

you," he murmured. "But not that. MacKerron faery blades are a legend, just as Aeife and her Sword of Light are legendary."

She watched the mirrored surface of the blade. "That looks like a Sword of Light to me."

He lifted the blade. "The old ones, when they discovered the trick of turning iron into steel, called the new blades swords of light, for the mirror shine. That is all a sword of light is—a steel sword." The blade seemed to release sunbursts as he turned it in the gloom.

"Do you not see the magic in that blade?" she asked.

He frowned, and she sensed his natural guard sliding into place like a gate. "Whatever makes this sword special does not come from me, but from its first owner."

"You are a MacKerron smith, and you have talent and knowledge. There is something extraordinary about that sword. And your knack is in it. What if faery magic does exist?"

"If you want a sword of light, there is one in the loch. Surely you have some family secret for calling that thing out of the water when you need it."

She felt the sting of his words. "That is not helpful, and you know it. I need a special blade, and you can make one for me."

He narrowed his eyes as he rubbed the leather over the blade. "There is no real magic in my smithing, Eva."

"But Colin believes there is. He might release Simon and give up the isle without protest if he knew I had such a sword."

"He is no fool when he is sober. We will rescue Simon through stealth and force—not through a girl with a sword. Iain Og and the rest of us are planning it now. Have patience."

"I cannot ignore the legend, Lachlann. Do you not believe in faery magic at all?"

"Some," he murmured, watching her. "But not in this."

She frowned. "But you do know the methods."

"There are secrets passed among MacKerron smiths, ways to imbue a blade with uncommon power. Or so they say."

"What methods?" she asked. Then, suddenly, she knew. "Ah. Blood in the steel. White sand gathered under a new moon. Iron from a sky stone . . . Is it so?"

He looked at her evenly, but she saw a glimmer in his eyes. "Charcoal made from trees taken from faery hills," he said. "Fire made from need-fire. Water from a faery source—"

"From Loch Fhionn, which holds the Sword of Light," she said, as excitement bloomed in her. "You used the old methods in making this sword—and never told me!"

"Smiths like their secrets." He turned the blade in his hand. "But you figured out most of it, quick wit that you are. Air, earth, fire, water—all those elements went into this blade, for what it may be worth." He shrugged.

"There is one more element, more powerful than faery lore," she said. "Love forged this blade. You and I together."

He smiled then, crooked and warm, and the light in his eyes revealed his agreement. Her heart surged within her, and she gathered the courage to speak her thoughts. "You could lend that blade to me," she said, "for one day's use."

He began to polish the steel again, and did not answer for a few moments. "I am proud that you are so skilled with swording," he said. "But I cannot put a sword in your hand myself, and watch you go into battle. I have seen that before, and I do not want to see it again."

She understood immediately. "Jehanne was a true sword maiden. I would be too, just for one day, one cause."

"Eva, can you not understand? I cannot lose you." His voice was gruff with intensity.

She moved toward him. "I ask only for a ceremonial

sword. I will not place myself in danger. Colin would not hurt me, but my appearance as Aeife's descendant armed with a sword of light—a faery blade—might convince him to release my brother and give up his cause."

"Listen to me." He took her by the shoulders, his grip vehement. "I will say it again. I will not risk losing you."

She searched his gaze. "I am not like Jehanne."

"More than you know, my friend." He gathered her into his arms. "More than you could know."

"If I share anything with her, it is love for you, my friend," she whispered. "And you are the only one who can help me now. The sword is finished. Lend it to me, if you will."

He sighed into her hair, and she heard his surrender and his agreement. "It is not finished yet," he said. "There is one final step. Gather your plaid and come with me."

In the stillness of the hour before dawn, Lachlann woke and looked around. The hillside where they lay was close to the rocky gorge, and he heard the steady rush of the waterfall. He lay wrapped and comfortable in a thick plaid with Eva, who slept soft and quiet in his arms. Last night, they had climbed the long hillside behind Balnagovan to sleep, fasting and chaste, with the sword sheathed between them.

He woke her with a hand to her shoulder. In silence she sat up beside him, and he kissed her. Then he rose, bringing her to her feet, and took up the sword while she took up the plaid. They walked to the nearby burn and washed their faces, refreshed themselves, and Eva turned.

"Now?" she whispered.

"Nearly," he answered, and took her hand to climb to the top of the peak. Once there, he slid the sword from its leather scabbard and turned toward the east, with Eva by his side.

He held the sword upright, blade tip high, and began to

breathe deeply, as Finlay and Leod had told him, as his father would have taught him had he lived. He breathed in the
cool mountain air, the air of silence and purity and peace,
seven times. Then he turned the hilt of the sword and
breathed into it and over it, filling the sword with his own
life force.

The sun began to crest the mountains far across the loch,
far across the world. He held the sword in front of him, point
upward, hands joined on the hilt, and waited. Eva stood beside him, patient and silent.

Dawn bloomed golden, spinning out the first strand of
light. The sword blade captured it, mirrored it, and sent it
outward in a blaze of gold and bronze and silver, intangible,
ethereal fire.

He turned the blade in a downward arc until the tip
pointed to the earth. The blade caught the light again, flash-
ing like a jewel. His hands trembled, and he felt as if the
light entered him somehow, filled him. He closed his eyes,
and saw the brightness still.

Then he handed the sword to Eva, who took it in her
hands and held it as he had, reverently, still as a statue,
charging self and sword with the power of the light. The sun
soared higher, a red-gold disk above the mountains.

"Now," Lachlann said, "it is finished."

When she offered it to him, he shook his head and took
her hand to walk down the hillside, while she carried the
sword.

Veiled in mist, the morning felt gentle, peaceful, not like
a day for warring—though it might come to that later, Eva
thought. She stood on the shore of the loch, wearing a belted
plaid and shirt, trews and boots, her hair neatly braided. Still
and quiet as the fog itself, she waited for Alpin. She could
hear the *plash* of the oars in the water as he came toward her.

She rested her hand upon the sword sheathed at her side,

feeling its power and its magic like a thrill. Sadness filled her too, a loneliness in her quest, the only sort of courage that she could find in herself, finally, when she knew the time had come. She had slipped out of the bed they shared in the house without waking him, readying herself quiet as a breath, closing the door without a sound. She had her own secret to keep.

Soon the prow of the boat appeared through the mist, and then she saw Alpin, head still bandaged, white hair wild about his head, shoulders bowed.

Somehow she had not realized how old he had become, she suddenly thought, how he had aged in the past few years, with care and strife, and with the burden of his love for the island.

She was going to win Innisfarna today, for him as much as for anyone else. For them all.

Alpin stilled the boat and she stepped inside, wordless. Equally silent, nodding to her, he took up the oars and pulled, and the boat skimmed over the loch toward the island, over the place where the Sword of Light was said to lie scabbarded in the water. Eva stood, her foot upon a cross bench, her hand upon the sword hilt, her face lifted to the wind.

Lachlann slid his sword into the scabbard with a whistling sound, muttering a curse under his breath as he strode toward the lochside. He turned to see Angus hurrying along behind him, followed by Margaret's five brothers with Iain Og and the rest of the MacArthur rebels—a handful of men, but all they could manage on short notice.

"Did you see her?" he asked as Angus caught up to him.

"Nowhere," Angus answered. "She has gone over the water and no doubt about it, just as you thought."

"She went over to save Simon, and her island," Fergus said, his lanky legs bringing him into stride with Lachlann.

"I am sure of it. You said the sword you made was gone, along with her plaid and boots."

"She knew we were gathering men and arms," Lachlann said. "She knew we were making plans to take the island and win back Simon as quickly and safely as we could. Why the devil did she not wait? This is hardly something she should attempt on her own. She could be killed over there."

"Smith," Iain Og said, huffing along behind him. "You know the girl. You could not truly believe she would wait for us!"

"I did not think she would go over so soon, without a word to me or anyone. I thought she knew we needed time to gather our forces and make our plans, and that she would be leading us."

"If Alpin came for her, she would go," Iain Og said. "The old man has been wanting her to do this for years. He has trained his warrior princess. No one believes in that legend more than Alpin MacDewar. He is part of Aeife's line, too."

Lachlann ran over the sand, the others keeping up with him. "Footprints," he said, as he neared the water's edge. "Hers, I am sure—smaller boots than any of ours. She waited here, where Alpin would have come for her. Damn," he swore. "Where is another boat?" He turned, paced down the beach, came back.

"There," Fergus said, pointing toward the water.

"What?" Lachlann looked and saw a boat emerging out of the mist on the loch. One small ferryman was at the oars. "For love of God . . . Ninian!" He splashed into the water, ankle-deep, Angus with him, and stretched out to draw the boat inward. "Ninian!" He lifted the boy out, setting his feet on the sand.

Ninian spoke to him, breathing hard and pointing madly, saying Eva's name again and again. Unsure what the boy said, Lachlann dropped to one knee to look at him on the same level. "Tell me," he said. "What happened? Where is Eva?"

"And how did you get all the way across in Alpin's boat by yourself?" Iain Og asked. "Quite a lad!" He beamed.

"Can he speak?" Andra asked. "I have never heard him talk, though we have seen him about with you and Eva."

"He does well, given the chance," Lachlann said, and kept his hand on Ninian's arm as the child spoke again.

"What is he saying?" Iain asked doubtfully.

Ninian pointed over the water, his words distorted, until Lachlann got the rhythm and the sense of it. "Eva," Ninian was saying. "At the castle, with her sword! She came with Alpin. I took the boat. Come, you must come!" He hauled on Lachlann's arm.

Within moments, Lachlann and a few of the others stepped into the boat, and Iain Og took up the oars. As they skimmed over deep water, Lachlann watched until the castle and the island appeared through the mists. What he saw on the rugged swath of ground that spread between the narrow beach and the massive stone castle made his heart hammer with dread.

A figure stood there alone, slight and straight. In her hand was the glint of bright steel.

"Hurry," he told Iain, and the man pulled with all of his strength.

Chapter 30

S he stood before the castle, her lifted sword gleaming like a white torch. "Green Colin!" she called. "Come out to me!"

Alpin stood nearby, motionless and watchful, his hand on the hilt of his own weapon. Eva's heart beat like a drum. She did not feel like Aeife the Radiant One—but she felt angered, and purposeful. Perhaps that was enough.

Ahead, the castle gate had opened, and Colin stepped out of the shadows to stand in the angled gap, wearing a steel cuirass over his quilted tunic and hose. "Eva," he said. "What is this about? Why are you dressed like that?"

She walked forward and raised the blade tip, which caught a pale light. She saw the surprise register in Colin's face as he looked at it.

"That is a beautiful sword," he said. "Incredible craftsmanship. Where did you get such a weapon?"

"Faery make," she said again. Rotating the round pommel in the palm of her hand, turning her wrist, she brought the point upward again. Colin raised a brow.

"You seem to know what to do with it," he said.

"Of course I do," she said. "I am the descendant of Aeife the Radiant One, the first keeper of this island. You have no claim here, and you must leave this place."

He did not shift his gaze from the mirror-bright blade. "Is that Aeife's own sword? Where did you get it?"

"It is of faery make," she said again. "Its metal came from a fallen star. You can see it is no common weapon." She drew arcs in the air, and the blade seemed to trail a banner of light.

"Give it to me," Colin said. "I paid for that sword."

Eva stilled the weapon. "You have my brother. Release him, and we will talk about bargains."

"He is a horse thief and a rebel."

"Simon did not steal your horses." That, at least, was true; her cousins had taken them. "And he has a king's pardon now. You cannot detain him."

"Our marriage was the condition of the pardon. If you will not honor that, I will not honor the other."

She watched him evenly. His gaze went again to the sword, and she swayed it back and forth slowly. "You want the faery blade, do you not?"

"We can barter, you and I," he said. "You want Simon, and I want the sword, and the right to this island undisputed. I suppose there is no point in saying I want you for my own." He narrowed his eyes. "You gave yourself to the blacksmith and betrayed our vows, and so your isle is now forfeited to me."

"You cannot lay claim to Innisfarna. Leave here."

"I see we will not easily come to an agreement." He stepped back into the shadow of the door and began to close it.

"Green Colin," Alpin said. "She is right. You must give this place back into her keeping."

Colin glanced at him. "Why should I listen to a ferryman?"

"Do you think that holding this island will put all of Scotland in your grasp? It is not so. Only Aeife herself has guardianship of this isle, and the privilege of protecting Scotland. For anyone else, this place invites only disaster."

Colin gave a short laugh. "That is ridiculous."

"Unless she and her kind hold it, there will be ruin for Scotland. A bargain was made long ago between the dark faeries and humankind that the isle would be held in peace by Aeife's own, and the Sword of Light protected. But since you breached that agreement, what has happened? Think of the Highland chiefs, and all the rest. The ruin has begun." Alpin nodded sagely.

"You cannot blame that on me, old man!"

"The faeries are not pleased, Green Colin. Do not risk making an enemy of their kind."

"You are a madman," Colin said. "Eva, shall we bargain?"

"Bring my brother out here," she answered.

"Come inside and see him."

"I am not a fool, Colin."

"Foolish enough to face me alone, with only a lunatic old man for your servant!"

She waved the sword a little. "But I have this."

He watched her for a moment. "Simon will come to the gate, but no farther. Then we bargain." He spoke an order to someone behind him, and moments later Simon appeared in the shadowed vault beyond the door. His hands were tied behind him, and his face was bruised. A few men stood with him; Eva did not recognize any of them.

"Simon!" Eva stepped forward. The sight of him, so battered and weakened, tore at her heart. She glanced past him, expecting to see the familiar faces of the king's men she had seen so often, but these were unfamiliar Highlanders.

"Where is Robson?" she asked. "Where are the king's men?"

"Gone," Colin said. "Innisfarna is mine by deed now. I sent the garrison back to Perth yesterday."

She remembered hearing men at the stable the night before, bringing out horses; she and Lachlann had not gone out, assuming that they were forming another patrol. "Surely they will be back when the king gets word of this."

"That may be. But for now we can solve our troubles in private, you and I." He smiled. "Give me the sword, and your brother is free. You can both leave the island alive."

Eva frowned, glancing first at Simon and then at Alpin, while she kept the sword point ready. Beyond, out on the misty loch, she saw a boat skimming over the water, with several men inside. Within minutes, she knew Lachlann would set foot on the shore.

But she did not have time to wait. Colin stepped back into the shadows of the door, prepared to close it.

"The sword is yours," she said, "if you can win it from me."

He laughed. "Eva, I always admired your spirit. Now you want to fight with swords like your rebel kinsmen. I am not surprised. There was a girl in France like you, brave and foolhardy. She rode and fought and dressed like a man, and tried to accomplish what only men can achieve."

"She achieved much," Eva said. She twirled the sword again, and it sparkled. "Win it from me, if you can."

"That would be too easy, and unchivalrous." Colin shook his head, smiling. "And how am I to know that is a true faery sword, and not just a good weapon?"

"You must take that chance."

"Hand it to me and let me look at it."

"Win it," she said. "This sword needs combat, not surrender. Even I can feel the power in it, and I am just a woman. Think what it would feel like in your hand." She saw his eyes glitter.

Colin stepped out of the doorway, gripping a sword as he walked toward her. She backed along the grassy incline toward a wide, flat area. The Highlanders came to the doorway with Simon to stand and watch. Colin's men looked tough, amused, and disinclined to interfere.

Circling warily, she kept her guard arm up, kept her balance fluid as she moved. Facing her, Colin retained a tight, unaware smile, as if pleased by the prospect of besting her.

He held a longsword with a two-handed hilt, the blade lengthy and wider than her own sword. Her thruster was slender and tapered, its lighter weight and higher balance well suited to her size and strength.

She would need quickness and cleverness to compensate for the greater reach and strength of Colin's longsword. If she was to avoid his lethal blade, she would have to stay close to him, so that he could not extend and give the weapon its best use.

Taking a long step forward, she forced him to follow a tight circle. Colin flexed his hands on his sword's hilt as he moved. She stepped with him, her gaze on his, a wary initial test of wills.

At first, he tried to snatch the sword from her with a few impatient gestures, but she neatly avoided him. Then he swung his sword in an overhead strike. She blocked it efficiently and sidestepped close to him, turning so that she stood behind him.

Clearly astonished, he turned clumsily. Eva saw an opening and swung high, nearing his armored shoulder. He parried and shoved her blade back, but she pivoted swiftly. He pushed forward into nothing.

She waited, bouncing on the balls of her feet, as he made a lumbering recovery. Growling, he sliced toward her. She lunged forward, deflecting his sword by pushing the flat of her blade against his, extending her sword arm swiftly to angle her hilt against his head. The knock was audible. She spun behind him as he put a hand to his brow.

"Where did you learn that trick?" he demanded breathlessly.

"Not from the faeries," she said, shifting the pommel in

her hand, stretching her fingers to release tension in her grip. She circled with him as he rounded heavily, like a bear.

"I do not want to hurt you," he said. "But you had better give me that sword." He struck, and she stepped diagonally, hanging her weapon down to guard her shoulder and back. Again the move took him by surprise, for when he lunged, she simply was not there, and he stumbled on the tufted grass.

He was lethal but predictable, his technique unschooled. Using his sword like an axe, chopping down, sideways, and in arcs, he was most dangerous because of his strength and the size of his weapon. But her training and greater nimbleness gave her a clear advantage. Although she felt as if she moved slowly and deliberately, with time enough to think and observe, she realized that she was moving like lightning. The feeling was heady; her heart raced, her breathing was deep, her thoughts were clear.

"Eva, I want that damned sword," he growled. Anticipating the reach and direction of his next strike, she danced sideways and turned. Again he struck into empty air.

This time he roared. Frustration and effort reddened his face. No doubt, Eva realized, he also battled the aftereffects of excessive drinking. He launched sideways again, his range longer than hers, and the blades clashed. She felt the jarring through her arm into her shoulder.

Stepping close to him, she pivoted around him, back to back, and whirled to face him again. He rounded, looking for her, but she was already waiting for his next strike. She sliced downward to tap him on the shoulder, a clang of metals.

Their circling took them into the widest part of the incline. She glanced then at Alpin, who had kept close. Past him, in the loch, she saw the boat drawing closer to shore.

Colin rounded again, and she with him, so that he came within a few feet of Alpin, who rested his hand warily on his sword. Breathing hard now, Eva lifted her blade and danced sideways expectantly, ready to counter Colin's next move.

The darkening hue of her opponent's face, his increasing fury and clumsy strokes told her that he no longer played a game with her. His anger made him an even greater danger. She came in closer, knowing that the two-handed sword he used needed a wide sweep.

She neatly circled him, her sword weaving slightly as she waited for him to turn. Colin growled low, and when she expected him to strike at her, he suddenly swung another way entirely. Using the long reach of his sword, he swept at Alpin. The old man snatched at his sword and stepped back, and Colin hit his knee with the flat of the sword. Alpin stumbled, and Colin was upon him before he could draw to defend himself.

In an instant, Colin had grabbed Alpin's plaid and hauled him forward. Casting the longsword aside, he drew a short dirk from his belt and caught Alpin under the throat, grabbing the old man's arm and twisting it back in a vicious grip.

"Give me the blade, Eva," Colin growled. "There is no doubt that it is a faery blade, with the skill it gave a mere girl. I want it!" He emphasized his demand by tightening his grip on Alpin, who stood unflinching as stone.

Eva caught her breath, glancing quickly at Simon, who stood in the open doorway. Then she flicked a glance at the loch, past Colin's shoulder, where the boat now met the beach. Lachlann leaped out, splashing through the shallows, her cousins behind him. Hope strengthened her, and she knew she could wait forever. But Alpin had only seconds.

Colin pressed the blade further, and Alpin flinched as Eva saw a trickle of blood below his jaw. With scarcely another thought, she hefted the hilt toward Colin.

He snatched the sword in midair, a neat catch, and shoved the old man away at the same time. Eva moved toward Alpin, but Colin lunged, snatching her up with one arm as if she were a doll. Hooking a powerful arm around her throat, he dragged her up the incline toward the gate, while she half ran with him to keep her feet beneath her.

Huffing hard, he pulled her close to the open doors, and his men stepped back. They no longer looked amused, but startled and uncertain—for they gazed past Colin to see the loch.

"Campbell!"

Hearing Lachlann shout, Eva gasped, pulling at Colin's arm around her neck as he dragged her over the grass.

"Campbell!" Lachlann roared, as he strode near them, his father's sword in hand. "Let her go!"

Colin turned, swinging Eva around with him, her heels skidding on the grass. Her captor held Jehanne's gleaming sword in his other hand.

"I have her, and the faery blade," Colin said, "and I hold this island. Do not think to take them from me, as your father tried to steal from my father." He backed toward the entrance and sidestepped, shoving Simon out of his way and growling an order to his men.

Lachlann saw Simon stumble and fall to one knee, his hands tied behind him, his dark hair wild over his bruised face. Then he staggered to his feet, attempting to trip Colin, who stepped out of range.

The Highlanders ignored Colin's order, arms folded. One of them waved Lachlann on, as if to signal that the conflict and the fight did not belong to them. Lachlann ran past them to reach the gate as Colin drew Eva into the gloom of the entrance tunnel. He knew the others followed to watch, heard someone creak the door wider, saw them gather like shadows behind him, but he did not turn.

Lachlann stepped into the vaulted space, his hands wrapped around the hilt of the longsword. "Let her go, Campbell."

Colin swept the blade in a wide arc, and Lachlann caught
the blow deftly, steel smiting steel, shoving until Colin
stepped back. Lachlann swung again, cutting low to catch
Colin's leg, but the thruster caught Lachlann's longsword,
the echo harsh inside the stone-walled tunnel.

Pushing Eva aside so roughly that she thudded against
the wall, Colin struck again, but Lachlann rounded on him,
sword ready, and deflected hard and fast, meeting the
thruster blade and forcing it back. The force shoved Colin
toward the wall.

Stumbling, Colin raised his arms to swing again, but
swerved suddenly and aimed for Eva, who had little room to
get out of the way. Lachlann pushed the smaller blade away,
but Colin made another attempt to strike at Eva. He missed
her when she moved like a flash out of range.

The power of his thrust drove the sword into the wall.
With a strident grating, the shining steel blade sank into the
mortar between two stones. Colin wrenched at it as Lachlann stepped toward him, sword raised.

As Colin pulled and twisted, the sword snapped audibly,
and the hilt broke off in his hand.

"*Ach Dhia!*" Eva moaned. Lachlann felt the force of the
break as if it tore through him, body and soul.

Colin roared, the sound ferocious inside the vaulted tunnel. He jabbed the angled edge of the hilt piece at Eva, and
Lachlann lunged forward quickly. But Eva raised a foot and
kicked Colin in the knee. Buckling, falling backward, he
braced an arm up on the wall as he fell hard against it.

Lachlann kept a wide stance, and held his sword warily,
judging how to knock the hilt piece out of Colin's hand.
Then the man seemed to seize up and sink to the floor. As he
fell heavily, the broken hilt clattered out of his hand.

Eva sobbed aloud, her hands clasped over her mouth. She
looked at Lachlann, her breath heaving, eyes wide. He stood
over Colin, frowning. He saw the ugly wound under the

armpit, and the broken blade that protruded from it, sunk deep into the rib cage, where the breastplate had not protected him.

"Oh, God," Eva said, dropping down beside Colin. "Did he hit his head? Oh, I did not mean to—"

Lachlann set aside his sword and leaned down, grasping Eva's arm and bringing her to her feet. He could feel her trembling as he gathered her into his arms.

In that moment Simon came into the shadowy tunnel, and Eva turned to him with a cry, throwing her arms around him. As soon as Lachlann freed his hands, Simon embraced his sister and then looked down at Colin.

"You did not kill him, Eva," Simon said. "I was watching. The blade in the wall got him."

"He would have recovered from that kick you gave him, to come at you again," Lachlann said quietly. "It was the faery blade that ended his life."

Still sobbing, she slid her arms around Lachlann's waist. He kissed the top of her head and looked up at Simon. The young man nodded approval, and Lachlann returned a sad smile.

Eva pulled away again and bent to pick up the broken hilt. She rose and handed it to Lachlann with shaking fingers. "Lachlann, I am so sorry—"

Silent, his heart rendered raw within him, he turned the piece in his hands. The break was similar to the original cracking, a few inches down from the cross guard, jagged and lethal.

"Her sword killed him," she said. "She would not have wanted that."

He gathered her close. "Look at this," he murmured, turning the hilt. "This is Jehanne's sword, the hilt piece. This did not kill him—nor did it harm you when he swung at you. The blade that took his life was the part that I crafted—with faery methods."

"The faery blade," Eva whispered. "The blade he wanted for his own."

"I can remake this, stronger and finer," he said. Eva wrapped her arms around him, and he rested his head on hers. "She would have understood the irony of what happened here, I think," he whispered. "She would have liked you, my friend." She lifted her face to his, and he kissed her. "My love."

Epilogue

I was a while at the smith's mystery.
—from an ancient Celtic poem

The fire crackled in the forge bed, and Lachlann turned away from its intense heat toward the anvil to set down the lump of steel that he held in the tongs. Striking the glowing mass lightly, he elongated its rudimentary shape. He worked on this piece at night when the darkness was deepest, and the colors of the steel were the most true—and easier for his faulty vision to discern, although Eva was always willing to help him with that.

He blinked, noticing the small lights dancing in his sight. One day soon he would send a message north to invite Aleck Beaton to Innisfarna. Not only did he want to introduce his friend to Eva, but he was ready to hear Aleck's opinion on his eyesight. His vision problems had not worsened in a long while, and the changes were tolerable. And he had Eva's help with the steel smithing now. If later in life the vision in that eye diminished, he knew he would have a loving family around him.

Setting the steel back in the forge fire, he resolved to hurry. He enjoyed the quiet nighttime hours when he could seclude himself in the smithy for a while. But this particular evening visitors were expected—in fact, he had heard voices and the sound of horses' hooves in the yard not long ago.

Smiling in anticipation, he set the steel aside to lose its heat. He would return later to transform the lump of metal into the blade he pictured in his mind: a small, beautiful thruster sword, a twin to the one he had repaired and hidden away, never to be used again. This second one he meant as a gift for his wife. His betrothed, he corrected himself; the wedding was soon. Very soon, and he had best hurry if he was to attend it.

He noticed the grime and charcoal traces on his hands, and the sweat slicking his bare forearms. As he rinsed his hands in the dousing tub, he heard a light rapping at the door.

Simon stepped inside, greeting Lachlann with a wave. Several others crowded the step behind him. Through the doorway, the night sky sparkled like diamonds on black velvet.

"Are you ready?" Simon asked.

"In a moment," he answered.

"But we are here, smith, and eager to see this wedding," Iain Og said, and shoved open the door. "You will just have to put down your hammer and tongs for a while. Though we will not say what set of hammer and tongs you will be using later." He guffawed, and someone laughed, but Iain Og was rapped on the shoulder for his quip by Mairi MacKerron, who came inside after him. Lachlann went to his foster mother and embraced her, glad to feel her cool, practical kiss on his cheek.

"You have not cleaned up," she said, patting his sweat-dampened shirt. "And it is time for your wedding!"

"I thought all of you would come later," he said.

"It is later," she said. "You were lost in your work."

He chuckled at the truth of that, and stood with her while the others entered the warm, dim smithy. He greeted them, smiling at each familiar face, all of them dear to him, some of them known to him over the span of his lifetime.

The five male MacArthur cousins came inside, followed by their sister, Margaret, and Angus, who each carried a little one. Alpin followed, escorting Ninian with a hand on his shoulder. Then Eva entered.

Lachlann's gaze softened as he watched her. She wore a simple gown of dark red wool, with an *arisaid* of brown and red fastened by the silver circlet he had repaired for her. Her hair, loosened and glossy as midnight, was glorious around her shoulders, and her eyes sparkled as she smiled at him.

He noted, too, the lush rounding of her breasts beneath her gown, and her body, taut where she carried the child that only she and he knew about as yet.

Blacksmiths like their secrets, he thought, smiling.

He reached out to take her hand. "You look like a flame, *mo càran*," he whispered, kissing her cheek. "You look beautiful."

"And you could use a little scrubbing, my handsome, brawny smith." She laughed, resting her hand on his bare arm. "But that can wait. I love you like this, with the traces of your strength and your work upon you," she confided in a whisper. "I have some rose petals for your bath later, if you want."

"It is not flowers I want in the bath," he murmured, and turned with her to face the others. "I have an announcement," he said, raising his voice over the happy chattering.

"We know—you are getting married," Andra said. The others laughed, and Lachlann smiled, waiting for quiet.

"I wanted to tell you—and Eva—that I am leaving for Perth in a few days," he said.

Eva's grip tightened on his arm. "Perth!"

"Only for a little while," he assured her. "I have requested an audience with the king to discuss the MacArthur situation, which is still uncertain following . . . the events of several weeks ago."

"Why would the king listen to a bladesmith," Eva asked, "even if you are a knight, and acted as a messenger for him?"

"He might listen to a king's cousin," he said. "My mother, Aileen Stewart, was second cousin to the royal Stewarts."

Astonished, she looked up at him, then glanced at Mairi, who nodded in confirmation.

"The Stewarts of Glen Brae are closely related to the king," Mairi said. "So Lachlann can claim that kinship as well. I think it is a good idea. The king may remember Aileen Stewart for her beauty and kind heart, and he might be inclined to consider mercy for the MacArthurs."

Lachlann looked down at Eva. "It is worth the chance."

She nodded. "Then I did not need Colin's influence after all to help us. I had you all along."

"You always had me, Eva," he murmured.

She smiled, her hand clasped in his. "Perhaps Donal will be here with us by the new year. Lachlann, I dreamed about him the other night. He was with us at Innisfarna again, and he and Simon were bouncing our children on their knees."

He cocked a brow. "Children?"

"Two little girls," she whispered to him. "Aeife and Jehanne, you called them, in my dream." Her chin quivered a little as she said it, and her eyes shone with tears.

He could not answer for the tightness in his throat.

"Ho, blacksmith," Iain Og said. "Are you ready now?"

Lachlann nodded, and led the way across the room to the anvil. Ninian carefully removed a pair of tongs and a hammer from the anvil surface and set them on the edge of the forge. Then he smiled up at Lachlann openly, without hiding his scarred mouth, with its feline, strangely elegant shape. His blue eyes twinkled.

Lachlann rested a hand on the boy's golden head. "You will be a good smith one day, if you want to be," he said. "And I could use an apprentice. Soon Eva will be too busy to spend much time in here with me," he added. Ninian grinned and nodded, and Eva smiled at them both.

"Tell us, blacksmith," Simon said, when all of them gathered in a partial circle around the anvil. "Have you ever performed a wedding?"

"I have not, but Finlay did so several times. A wedding at the forge is an ancient tradition," he told them. "Back in the time of the mists, before the Christian priests, it is said that smiths were essential members of their villages, gifted with the knowledge of transforming and joining metals. So it was deemed appropriate for smiths to bind couples in marriage. The tradition is hardly used anymore, but it will do well for us." He smiled down at Eva.

"You will want a priest later, but this will do until the priest comes to our glen again," Mairi said, nodding.

Simon took his sister's arm and positioned her in front of the anvil, facing the forge. "We will witness your marriage," he said. "I always thought you two were well suited," he added. "Donal thought so, too."

Eva glanced at him. "Donal? When did he say so?"

"Years ago, when your betrothal with Colin was first discussed, Donal told Father that you would be happier wed to Lachlann the smith's son, who would care for you and treat you well, and whose talents would be an asset to the clan. He said that you could not wed a finer man than the smith's lad."

Tears pooled in her eyes. "I never knew that."

"Donal never told you, for our father was adamant about his choice for you. So you see," Simon said affectionately, kissing her cheek, "you have the approval of your clan chief, too."

She turned, smiling tremulously, to face Lachlann. He stood across the anvil from her in his usual place, with the fire warming his back. "If we pledge our hearts in marriage to one another in the eyes of God, we do not need witnesses or a priest in the land of Scotland. Yet these witnesses are welcome to share this with us, and to take it into their hearts as we take it into ours."

He held out his hands. Eva took his fingers, across the anvil, and he felt her hands tremble slightly.

He looked down at her, with her eyes storm-colored and softened with unshed tears. In the rich light of the forge, she glowed in his eyes.

"I take you for my wife, Eva MacArthur," he murmured. "Over this anvil, with strength of iron and warmth of fire, in the eyes of these witnesses and in the presence of God, I make this marriage with you. This will endure forever," he added, his gaze deep in hers.

"I take you for my husband, Lachlann MacKerron," she murmured, and repeated the words he had said, words that came from his heart, and chimed out now in her mellow, loving voice. "To endure forever."

"Let it be forged between us," he whispered, and bent to kiss her with the anvil between them, and the light and heat of the fire upon them, and the love of the others in a ring around them.

Then, in a blur of laughter and sniffling embraces, he received the congratulations of all those he loved so well. And at last, eager to reach Eva, he stepped around the anvil and gathered her into his arms.

He kissed her, deep and endless, while the cheers rose around them. Drawing back, he brushed at a wayward strand of her hair. "I think this marriage was made between us long before this moment, my friend," he whispered. "We began forging it long ago. But something so good and so strong, and so very valuable takes a long time, and a lot of care."

"Then we will continue to work on it, smith," she answered, smiling up at him, "day and night."

"Ah," he said, wrapping an arm around her, "now that we will do."

Author's Note

This story originated when I learned that Joan of Arc had a company of Scots riding with her, members of an elite group later known as the Royal Scots Guard. During the medieval centuries, Scotsmen were often assigned as complementary guards to foreign monarchs, especially the French, with whom the Scots had an "Auld Alliance" of support. During the Hundred Years' War, thousands of Scots went to France to assist in the struggle against the English; thousands of Scotsmen died there, and many others, especially those of noble rank, were rewarded with land grants, titles, and knighthoods.

In 1429, several Scotsmen assigned to the French monarch, Charles le Dauphin, accompanied Joan of Arc (she signed "Jehanne" herself, and the actual documents use that spelling as well, so I chose that form for the story). For example, documents show that a Sir Hugh Kennedy from Galloway was with her until her capture at Compiègne in 1430, and his loyalty to her is remarked upon.

Joan's sword, called the sword of Saint Catherine of Fierbois, revealed to her in a dream and discovered in a chapel at Fierbois exactly as she indicated, was apparently broken at Lagny. Although the facts are unknown (speculation says she broke it in a fit of temper), a blacksmith examined the sword at the time and declared it impossible to repair. When asked at her trial about the supposedly miraculous sword, she admitted that it had broken but refused to reveal its whereabouts. The sword itself, described by eyewitnesses, has never been found.

Smiths were essential craftsmen in medieval society, and their skills were imbued with mystery. In Scotland, blacksmithing and bladesmithing were well developed, although in the later Middle Ages most steel weapons were imported from Europe. The Scots had a long tradition of excellence in bladesmithing that reached back to the remarkable skills of Celtic and Viking smiths. Rob Miller, a bladesmith from the Isle of Skye, gave me valuable insights into the old traditions and processes of this ancient craft; his work, and some photographs of blade forging, can be seen on his Web site at www.castlekeep.co.uk.

Medieval swordsmanship was an art in development, and illustrated treatises survive that presented techniques and drills in detail. Many dedicated groups pursue the study of historically accurate swordplay, such as the Mid-Atlantic Association for Historical Swordsmanship, and HACA (Historical Armed Combat Association). For medieval reproduction swords and information, visit Albion Armorers at www.albionarmorers.com.

The Sword of Light is a familiar element in ancient Celtic lore, sought by heroes in various tales. Faeries tend to be wary of iron, but they are said to have stolen humans to smith for them—thus the traditions in the story came about.

I hope you enjoyed *The Sword Maiden*. For more information regarding my books, or to contact me, please visit my Web site at www.susanking.net.

LOOKING FOR ANOTHER FAVORITE ROMANCE WRITER?

Turn the page for a special preview of

Crooked Hearts
by Patricia Gaffney

New York Times bestselling author of
The Saving Graces and *Circle of Three*

When Grace Russell meets Reuben Jones
she's dressed as a pious Catholic nun; he's
posing as a blind Spanish aristocrat. But then
the pretty sister lifts her skirts to adjust the
silver derringer strapped to her thigh. . . .
So begins this sexy, rollicking ride through
the sinful streets of 1880s San Francisco,
where two "crooked hearts" discover
that love is the most dangerous—
and delicious—game of all.

A Signet paperback in December 2001

Don't steal; thou'lt never thus compete
Successfully in business. Cheat.

—Ambrose Bierce

Sister Mary Augustine's little silver derringer was cutting into her thigh.

And it was hot, hot, hot in the airless stagecoach, which needed new springs. The cowboy sprawled unconscious on the opposite seat smelled like an old drunk rolled up in an alley. How could the blind man sitting next to him stand the stench? They said blindness sharpened the other four senses; if that was true, the poor man must be half dead from the fumes.

A cold beer and a pillow for her behind, that's what Sister Augustine needed. Stirring furtively on the leather seat, she tried to shift the derringer without fidgeting; it must've slid to the back of her garter, because it felt like she was sitting on it. "Be careful with that thing," Henry had warned her; "don't shoot off anything important." If she could just get her hand under her thigh for two unobserved seconds, she could move the damn gun. The blind man sure wouldn't see her, and neither would the smelly cowboy. She slanted a glance at the fourth passenger, seated next to her. He'd been dozing a few minutes ago.

But now he was lying in wait to catch her eye. "Sister," he greeted her, with a big, friendly smile. "Mighty hot for early June, wouldn't you say?"

After three weeks on the road, Sister Augustine recognized his type, because there was one on every stage, train, or ferry boat she'd taken since leaving Santa Rosa: he was the one who wanted to talk. A whole hour of silence had gone by since the stage had left Monterey, so this one must've decided he'd waited long enough.

"Indeed I would, sir," she answered smartly. "But remember the psalm: 'With the Lord as thy keeper, the sun shall not smite thee by day, nor the moon by night.' " Sometimes, she'd found, you could head a talker off at the pass by going straight at him with the Bible.

"So true. And don't forget Matthew: 'He maketh the sun rise on the evil and the good, and sendeth rain on the just and the unjust.' "

She nodded in devout agreement, stumped.

"George Sweeney's my name," he said, sticking out his hand.

She gave it her nun's shake, limp but fervent, and murmured, "Sister Mary Augustine," while inside she rejoiced. Sweeney—Irish—_Catholic_!

"A real pleasure, Sister. What's your order?" He eyed her plain black habit curiously.

"The Blessed Sisters of Hope. We're a small community; our mother house is in Humboldt County."

"You're a long way from home, then." He leaned toward her and jerked his head sideways at the snoring cowboy. "Is it safe for you to be traveling all by yourself?"

"I don't, normally," she confided. "But my companion, Sister Sebastian, fell ill in Santa Barbara and wasn't able to go on. After we determined that she would recover without assistance, we decided that I should continue our work alone. We believe it's God's will, and we have absolute faith that He'll protect me."

He sat back admiringly. "Well, I don't doubt it for a second." He'd taken off his derby hat in her honor, a generous gesture since it had been hiding his bald spot. He was short and plump, and his little feet in their shiny patent-leather shoes barely touched the floor. She'd pegged him earlier as a traveling salesman because of all the luggage he was carrying, stacked over their heads on top of the Wells Fargo stagecoach. Now, studying him more closely, she decided he looked too flush for a drummer, and too clean. All the better. And praise the Lord, his name was Sweeney, which automatically doubled her estimate of his donation potential.

"What is your work, Sister, if you don't mind my asking?"

Easier and easier. She clasped her hands to her breast with subdued fervor. "I'm on a fund-raising mission for our order, sir. We desperately need money for one of our hospitals in Africa, because it's in danger of having to close—which would be a catastrophe. We've been collecting donations from the dioceses throughout the state for several weeks now. I'll be going home after one last effort in San Francisco. After that, I hope to be sent to Africa myself, where my true skills can be put to better use."

"Your true skills?"

"As a hospice nurse. But, of course, our sacred mandate is to accept God's will without question, and for now it seems His will is for me to toil for the little children in this humble way."

"It's a children's hospital?"

"Orphaned children. With incurable diseases."

Mr. Sweeney's pudgy cheeks pinkened with emotion; she thought there might even be a gleam of moisture in his pale blue eyes. She glanced away, but in her peripheral vision she saw him fumbling for his purse. "I only wish this was more," he whispered discreetly, pressing a bill into her hand.

"Bless you. Oh, bless you, Mr. Sweeney!" she whispered back. A tenner, she noted with satisfaction; exactly what she'd bet herself he would give. God, she was getting good at this. She slid the greenback into her black leather pocket-book to join the other bills and gold pieces she'd collected in the past three weeks: a little over four thousand dollars. Henry wouldn't tell her exactly how much they needed, but she was pretty sure it was more than that. Still, four thousand dollars was a hell of a start.

She glanced hopefully across the aisle at the blind man, wishing he'd feel a similar charitable tug on his own purse strings. She guessed he was awake, but it was hard to tell; his round, cobalt-blue spectacles were opaque and his eyes behind them were invisible. She'd been staring at him off and on for the past hour, feeling guilty about it but unable to stop, because his tragic good looks fascinated her. Had he always been blind, she wondered, or only since some terrible accident? How did he make his living? His black broadcloth suit was very fine, his gray silk necktie sedate and expensive. That was all to the good, but a man's shoes were the surest clue to the health of his finances, and in this case they gave Sister Augustine cause for concern. Run down at the heels and cracked across the insteps, they were the shoes of someone who was either rather poor or rather careless about his appearance, and neither trait seemed to characterize the handsome blind man. Or—distressing thought—they could be the shoes of a man who couldn't *see* his shoes. The idea made her sit back, ashamed of her rude, sneaky staring. The poor man! So young, so vital and strong. So good-looking.

He had beautiful hands, too. She'd noticed them right away, clasped around the carved handle of the walking stick that jutted upright between his knees. Long, clean, sensitive fingers, artistically bony, and short white nails. No rings. A priest's hands, or a sculptor's. She heartily wished one of them would start reaching for his wallet.

Nuns didn't initiate conversations with male strangers, so she was relieved when Mr. Sweeney, who had been darting secret looks at the blind man with almost as much vulgar curiosity as she had, said straight out, "How do you do, sir?" He took care to aim his voice precisely, so there wouldn't be any doubt as to which man he was addressing—not that the reeking cowboy was in any condition to misunderstand.

"How do you do," the blind man replied readily. He had an English accent—the last thing she'd have expected. "It's Mr. Sweeney, isn't it? I'm Edward Cordoba." He held his hand out toward Sweeney, and they shook. "Sister," he murmured, with a small, respectful bow in her direction.

"Mr. Cordoba," she murmured back. He was _Spanish_?

You could count on Sweeney not to beat around the bush. "Do you come from Monterey, sir?" he asked directly.

"A little south of there. My father owns a ranchero in the valley."

Sweeney made a knowing, impressed sound.

"One of the smaller ones," Mr. Cordoba added with a deprecating half-smile. "Only a few hundred thousand acres."

His voice was low-pitched and intimate, like a cello playing a slow waltz. It took her a few seconds to register the last sentence. When she did, she had to remind herself to close her mouth, which had fallen open.

"Cordoba," Mr. Sweeney said slowly. "That's a Spanish name, isn't it? And yet I could swear your accent's British."

Mr. Cordoba smiled. He had extremely white teeth. "You've got a good ear, sir. My mother is English. I studied in that country for a number of years."

"Aha—Oxford?"

"Cambridge."

"Well, well! You're a scholar, then?"

His smile withered. He turned his face toward the window. "I was once."

She and Mr. Sweeney exchanged looks of chagrin. There was an awkward pause.

"What takes you to San Francisco, sir?" Sweeney asked, rallying. "If you don't mind my asking."

"Not at all. I've enrolled in a school there to learn to read Braille."

"Is that so? How does that work, now? I've heard of it, but never really understood how they do it."

"It's a system of raised dots, each representing a letter of the alphabet; one feels them with one's fingertips." He dropped his chin, as if he were contemplating his long, elegant hands. Sister Augustine contemplated them with him. They looked capable of reading raised dots to her.

"Then you haven't been blind for long, I take it?"

She stared at Sweeney, confounded by the bluntness of his prying—although he hadn't asked anything she wasn't dying to know herself.

"Long?" Edward Cordoba repeated, very low. A minute passed; she thought that was all the answer he was going to give, and began trying to decipher it. But then he said, "No, I don't suppose you'd call it long. To me, though, it seems . . . a lifetime."

The painful pause lasted much longer this time. She wanted to comfort him somehow, but she couldn't think how; touching him was out of the question and, under the circumstances, a sympathetic facial expression wouldn't accomplish anything. So she only said quietly, "I'm so terribly sorry, Mr. Cordoba."

He made a graceful gesture with his hands, at once dismissing her concern and thanking her for it. "And now, sir," he said with strained heartiness, "it's your turn—tell us your traveling story. Where are you from and what takes you to San Francisco?"

"Ah!" Clearly Mr. Sweeney had been hoping somebody would ask him that question. "Well, you might say I'm on a mission too, like Sister Mary Augustine, although mine's a much more secular mission. I'm the assistant curator for Chinese antiquities at the Museum of East Asian Art in St. Louis. For the past six weeks, I've been touring your fine state with a small collection of objets d'art." He turned to Sister, politely including her in his answer. "It's a cultural swap, you might say, a reciprocal traveling art exchange between our museum and the Museum of Art in San Francisco."

She murmured politely.

"Do you mean you're traveling with the exhibit now?" Mr. Cordoba asked. "It's actually on board the coach?"

"Yes, indeed. I'm on the last leg of the trip—I'm *not* sorry to say, delightful though it's been—and starting the day after tomorrow, San Francisco will host the final display."

"It must be a very *small* exhibit."

"Select," he corrected dryly. "And if I may say so, very, very special."

"I imagine the pieces must be quite valuable," Sister Augustine mused.

"Priceless. Beyond price."

She touched a thoughtful finger to her chin. "What sort of pieces are they?" she asked, and Mr. Sweeney began to talk about Ming funerary sculpture and Tang jade, screen paintings and water colors and enameled ceramics. "How fascinating," she exclaimed when he finally wound down. "Would you happen to have a catalog?"

"In my trunk, yes. I'll dig one out for you when we stop for the night, shall I?"

"That's very kind of you." She happened to glance over at Mr. Cordoba just then. He had a thoughtful finger on his chin, too.